THE LIFEGUARD

A NOVEL

BY R. W. HOGAN

AUG 23, 2014

TO ████, I HOPE YOU
ENJOY THE READ

Raymond Hog

THE LIFEGUARD

For my mother, Doris – I'm sure she's in Des Moines.

CHAPTER 1

*N*IGHT BETRAYED RITA.

Late Christmas Eve, Rita Wishwood holds tight to the kitchen counter with one hand while the other clutches a multi-colored knit cap. Frozen braids dangle between her fingers, a reminder of terrible loss, terrible loneliness. Nothing matters now. Rita's knees buckle beneath the weight of a dwindling world.

The hollow clacks of winter-dead trees break the solitude governing the town of Solomon. Only echoes of empty moments. Through the window, above the trees, the town's angel statue shimmers, casting shadows against an iron-grey sky. Storm clouds hide the sliver moon, the stars, slamming night shut like a silent gate. Below, a white shroud covers the streets. Rita sees none of it. A sudden charge electrifies the night sending winds cascading through the town.

Rita draws a shallow breath and in a merger of grief and dread, tears continue to fall. Her muscles tense, a rage takes hold as she resolves, What can God do now?

The kitchen clock ticks out the time, 12:01:30 and with one savage swing, she clears the counter's contents. The plastic fruit bowl rockets across the room smashing against the oven door handle tipping out its contents: two apples an orange and one ripe banana. They form a face in shadow across the stove–his face.

Her head reels from the force of the blow, her rattled nerves slow and the atmosphere inside her home gels. The glass shakers strike the refrigerator door exploding in grey and white spice plumes, sprinkling each with crystal glass shards. A salt rain begins to fall. 12:01:31–in that second time stops. Rita's world, her life pauses as she stands locked in place, an unyielding human statue.

Breath-stilled, arched in anger, Rita holds her pose now a fixture carved into the inanimate structure of the house itself. Beyond the windows, snow flecks remain suspended in a perfect portrait of small town life worthy of a Norman Rockwell painting. The air quivers with a second charge, the clock's second hand stirs, attempting an advance but fails to shift past thirty-one. Waves of wind erupt through the empty streets and batter the home, tipping the kitchen clock sideways. The second hand stammers, yet fails to move. Nothing stirs; not time, not space, nor Rita's grief. Silence follows– thirty-one echoes again–

Three weeks before Christmas the recently divorced, Neville Wishwood slept through a winter storm once again revisiting an uncompromising past.

That night the town of Solomon lost power for a short time and as Neville slept his new electric alarm clock, sans battery back-up (the battery back-up would have been another five dollars) blinked out 4:04 a.m. His legs churned beneath the covers, his fingers clawed the top sheet while the light of early day subdued the darkness. The dream once again spilled into his unconscious, taking him back.

Neville returned to the beach, the sunny day that was. The open azure skies, the wooden tower where he stood guard, binoculars in hand. What he sees never changes; a crowd of people gathered near the shore, staring. Their eyes follow the balding fat-man: cheerful, sitting in a red racecar, gunning the throttle. Bare-chested in a bathing suit he spins the giant rear slicks wildly, forcing sand to swell behind the car. In the dream, beside the fat-man, Jennifer Capaldi sits sleek and slim in her black and white side-slashed bathing suit, laughing, urging on the driver to chase the tires faster and faster. She wears black sunglasses. The shade matches her flowing dark hair and as she waves Neville's way, her hair flops and flounces. In his vision, Neville always keeps a keen eye on Jennifer.

The wailing crowd stares past the fat-man, past Jennifer and watches while a young blond girl stands silent atop the ever-increasing mound whipped up by the wheels of the racer. Standing erect, her limp head rests on her chest. Her feet stay locked in place with arms extended out forming a cross-less crucifix. The young girl's body radiates electric white, a human halo set against dulling twilight. The fat-man laughs and Jennifer Capaldi pumps a fist spurring him on. The rear slicks continue their maddening run, swelling the sand pyre, elevating the young girl to glorious heights above the beach, above the gently lapping bay waters. On the beach, the multitude peers up and weeps.

Through the glasses, Neville watches the young girl rising atop the sand mass. The young girl is little Lily Delysle. The child's mother stands before the fat-man's red racer crying, her arms extended wanting only to hold her daughter, touch her daughter, join her daughter. Yet the young girl rises too fast, too far from the beach and all those waiting, wanting her return.

As Lily Delysle ascends the night sky, Neville continues to stare from his wooden tower. He shifts his view. Jennifer Capaldi laughs with the fat-man, watching as the sand advances higher propelling a luminous Lily Delysle to ever-loftier heights. The once brilliant sun slips beyond the horizon; open skies morph grey, on to sullen black and the transient beach mob cowers in the loss of daylight, their faces veiled by the coming of night; their wails, whimpers lost beneath the sound of the revving engine.

Lily Delysle continues into the reaches of black space. Now a lustrous glow in the heavens, her features fade with distance. Roiling bay waves erode the erected sand pyre and it dissipates. The car shuts off, the laughing stops and all eyes lift to witness the final resurrection of little Lily Delysle into the void. As she takes her place among the timeless stars– stars set brilliant against a deepness only dreamscapes conjure– Neville sees the magnificent light that Lily has become, brightest in the sky above and he cries.

He cries and climbs slowly down from his wooden station leaving the binoculars behind. They have deceived him. He cries and stumbles off toward town never looking up, never looking back. Lily is gone and Neville is alone.

The dream always ends the same way; him walking away, hearing the wails of the crowd, and he joins in their sorrow. Through tears he sees only night.

At times, he dreams the bay gulls float above the scene, flapping, cawing, minding the weeping crowds. *Scavengers. Maybe they cry too.* He thinks.

On harder nights, Neville returns to the dream again and again. Those nights he screams one word aloud, *'No… no, no.'*

His denial changes little. The words reverberate unanswered and the dream continues. The past stays alive in his tortured mind. Frequently he awakens and weeps himself. On those nights, with the nightmare fresh, more often than not, he has wished for a life less complicated; to live in a world where Lily still lives, released from this burden of the past. To be whole again.

Tonight the dream did end and with it, he heard the ringing, ringing… ringing, louder with each passing second. Suddenly awake, Neville realized it was the phone.

Still groggy he answered. "Hello."

"Woody, it's almost eight-thirty. You're late!" It was Dell.

Annoyed, he stared into his bright bedroom, to his clock. "I know… the storm knocked out my alarm clock. What are you doing up?"

"I've been up most of the night thinkin' about the squirrel problem."

Here Neville paused and pulled himself from beneath the bed sheets unsure if he wanted to ask—but he did. "What squirrel problem?"

In a hushed voice his friend Dell followed, "Didn't you notice how few squirrels there were in the neighborhood lately?"

"Of course… it's winter! They'll all holed up, like bears."

"Maybe. But maybe there's something else goin' on," Delbert Willows said, Neville's closest friend these last eleven years and his father's upstairs tenant.

Again, Neville hesitated. You see, his friend Dell was indeed…

unusual. Yes, unusual was the best way to describe Dell. Not crazy, not even confused, but certainly he had his own unique take on life. He believed in signs, mystical happenings, the metaphysical; that merely living held meaning, mystery, far deeper than anything outwardly visible to most. Sometimes Dell held onto those aspects of life and found a deeper message, at least for him. And sometimes the world seemed but a torturous maze, lapsing into detours ultimately ending in a baffling abyss, like standing in the middle of Wal-Mart watching people whiz by with full carts and suddenly realizing you came for something yourself, yet wondering what it was.

Since befriending Dell eleven years ago, Neville had learned to expect the occasional blip on Dell's radar. Eleven years had passed following his escape from his small town home in Bishop's Bay, Maine. Escape was the operative word.

"You know what Aunt Claire thinks?" Dell asked.

Frustrated, beginning a frantic race around his bedroom, Neville shot back, "No, but she's not late... I am!"

"She told me squirrels tell us a lot about life."

"That's true and right now they're telling us it's winter. Now get down here and keep an eye on dad."

"Sorry Woody, I guess I just got carried away with this squirrel pelt I found. Thought those new neighbors two doors down– you know that weird lookin' couple with the humpback son? Maybe they were hunting down the street squirrels."

"What squirrel pelt?"

"The one I found on the road, all flat... looks like it's been brushed."

"That's not a pelt Dell, that's a squirrel that's been run over by a car... bones, guts and all. If I were you, I'd ditch that thing before you get some kinda disease from it.

"And those new neighbors? The Kaplans? I met them in the grocery store... that's not their son and he's not hunchbacked. He was a moving guy dragging a trunk on the ice with a strap the day we saw them," Neville said.

A clunk sounded from above. Dell dropped the road-kill-squirrel. "So he's not a hunchback, you say? Maybe that's good."

"No, he's not!"

"Alright… I'll be down in two shakes of a goat's tail!"

"Lamb's tail, Dell, lamb's tail," Neville returned, correcting his friend.

"Lambsdale? Where the hell's Lambsdale? And what's it gotta do with anything?"

"Never mind…"

Neville jumped from bed, scrambled for his clothes lying on the floor by the bed and standing, began slipping on the first sock. As he did, he spotted the second sock and in a panic hopped over to pick it up. Nearing the sock his one foot landed on his pants lying across the polished hardwood floor and it slipped back, launching his body head-long into the dresser's closed top drawer. Hitting face first, he flipped backwards and found himself seated on the hardwood, his forehead leaking blood. The handle's imprint left a checkerboard pattern on his injured head.

"Je-oh-my-friggin'-god that hurt!" he whispered, trying ever so hard not to swear.

Neville sat mystified. How could the day be starting so… painfully? Never one to make decisions easily he weighed his options: dress first or fix the wound? It took a while.

Finally he stood, making his way to the bathroom. He opened the above-the-sink cabinet, and sweeping aside its meager contents, he found his first-aid accoutrements– a half empty box of Flintstones Band-Aids. Dazed, he affixed one to his forehead. Bam-Bam Rubble holding a wooden club arrested his medical emergency for the time.

Neville scurried back inside the bedroom and went about the quick business of dressing. It took only minutes before the front door opened with Dell arriving safely from upstairs. Dressed in dark track pants and a gray cable knit sweater he walked in unannounced, seating himself at the Wishwood kitchen table. Certainly no fashionista, Dell did maintain himself in an extremely sanitary way, a product of his upbringing by his widowed Aunt Claire. Unconventional aptly described Dell's childhood.

Neville swallowed back a mouthful of instant coffee. Dell coiled strands of damp black hair behind his ears and started again, "No breakfast this morning?"

"No time. Wake dad up in about a half hour, and don't give him any of that prune juice today."

Dell spotted Neville's wound. Curious, he stood and approached his friend, closely examining the Band-Aid. "Bam-Bam, huh. What happened to you? Roll outta bed?"

"No, the dresser... it leapt out at me this morning."

"Want something for that?"

"What?"

"Tiger balm... it works for everything. Chill that pain right out," Dell offered as he turned toward the front hall. Dell's first mission of the day had begun—retrieving the tiger balm.

"I think it's gonna be okay," Neville said grabbing his friend's arm, holding him back.

Dell sat down. "What about Dewey, he coming today?"

"Not today, tomorrow. Rita's schedule got screwed up so he's with us tomorrow."

Dewey was Neville's five-year-old son. He shared custody with his ex-wife, Rita whose profession as a dentist allowed a flexible work schedule. On those days, Neville and his friend Dell took over primary care of the youngster.

Dewey remained Neville's unsullied oasis of hope. His young son's innocence reminded him of those childhood characters from the TV sit-coms of the fifties and sixties; how life seemed so simple, uncomplicated. Neville was prone to compare both people and life situations to those moralistic visions of youth, the way he had grown up seeing life through the ever-idealistic prism only television could provide.

Finishing his last gulp, Neville picked up a binder from the hallway table and headed for the door. While he pulled on his cherished maroon and maize University of Minnesota varsity jacket, Dell watched. Calling it his lucky jacket, Neville wore it on special occasions these days.

"Takin' your book to work?"

"Yeah, I want Sam to read it, give me some feedback."

"Doesn't my opinion count for anything? If I say it's good, it's good. My parents wrote a book and, well, I'm their son and all."

"Of course your opinion counts Dell, but literary talent isn't a hereditary trait. I'm glad you liked it but…" Neville shrugged heading out. "Anyway, your father's was a How-To book, non-fiction, not a novel. Sam knows the business and he knows books. He's been writing all his life and says he'll critique it for me. I can't pass that up. And don't forget dad's medication."

"No worries… just another day here at the office for me too, you know."

As Neville rushed out the front door to meet a bright December day, several divergent issues played on his mind. Driving down the street his concerns began a countdown inside his head; right turn, and his mind wandered to an ailing father, Arthur Wishwood, caught in a downward cycle of Alzheimer's; along Spencer Street he began to think of Dewey, and then Rita, the woman he quietly still loved, even after their divorce. On a left turn to Welland, his brain latched onto the two car payments he had missed and a plan to catch up with his Christmas bonus. He banged the dashboard hoping for more heat while a wheezing draft of air barely cleared the windshield. The heater core was toast, but maybe, just maybe, that bonus would cover that too.

Within seconds, his book once again occupied his thoughts. He had worked long days and nights on its conception only to have it relegated to a cheap copycat rendition of a Stephen King novel, Under The Dome, about a town caught beneath an alien dome, similar to Neville's concept in his manuscript, *Seven Days*.

He continued down Welland toward the downtown core, switching over to his job and the disappointments created there. Preoccupied, Neville continued driving into a sun that seemed to rise from the white road. With the glare hitting him, he squinted, shifting side to side. Here, Neville considered his job and how long he was willing to work at a small town newspaper. He added the ghosts from his past to the growing list of distractions: the eternal Lily Delysle and, of course, Jennifer Capaldi. They never left him. They were Neville's hard dreams. At times, he wondered how Lily would be living today. If she would have attended college like he had or married, or if in some parallel universe, she was happy.

At that very second, from the right side parked cars, a blue haze leaped out in front of him. Neville hit the brakes hard. A dull thump sounded and the blue haze disappeared beneath the front end of his car. His panicked brain had seen a set of hands reach up to cover a face. His heart was pounding, his hands shaking as he slipped the gearshift into park. As he hopped from the vehicle, Neville looked behind. Another car stopped and as its window came down, he heard a woman calling out, "My God is he all right?"

Neville took a timid peek out past the fender. There, on a crush of snow, lay a man, a pink halo forming in the hard packed snow beneath his head. A bright red trickle oozed from his mouth and even as he lay unconscious, an innocent smile creased the fallen man's lips.

"Oh my god! Call 911!" he shouted back to the woman. She did.

Neville knelt beside the fallen pedestrian, removed his lucky jacket and placed it beneath the man's head and neck. Sprawled on the pavement the man's left leg twisted out at the knee in an unnatural angle. His eyes quivered beneath shut lids, dancing in tandem as if signaling a message in some ancient code.

"They're on the way," the woman driver said arriving at Neville's side, staring over his shoulder at the fallen man.

"Thanks."

"He stepped right in front of you. I saw it. I couldn't believe it!"

Leaning down, Neville listened for breathing and heard his faint gasps. The man was alive. By now, a small crowd had formed around them, all gawking, whispering, pointing to the bloodied snow, to the man's obviously injured leg and to Neville as the driver. It made for an uncomfortable scene yet Neville stayed planted next to the victim.

The crowd grew, pushing in closer and Neville looked around, calling out, "Give 'im some room… the ambulance is on the way and they'll need room!" His words ended with the wailing sounds of an emergency vehicle piercing the cold Minnesota morning.

The accident had occurred in the beginning blocks of Solomon's downtown district, a tiny thriving community thirty miles north of the state's twin cities, St. Paul-Minneapolis. With a population nearing twenty-three thousand, it seemed as if everyone in town was Christmas shopping early that day as gawkers continue to swell the scene.

Paramedics parked and two young men unloaded a stretcher from the rear, pushing open a route to the front of Neville's car. Acting in tandem they quickly cut away the torn trousers the man wore. Even though they moved him ever so carefully, you still heard a mournful groan from those standing nearby as they straightened out his floppy leg.

"Please, everyone stand back." The paramedic faced Neville and asked, "Do you know him, sir?"

"No… it was my car that hit him. He stepped right in front of me."

"He did. I was right behind this man when it happened," the female driver added.

As they worked on the unconscious victim, police arrived. Still in shock, Neville watched as the medics placed a plastic cast over the man's leg, latched it and lifted him onto the gurney. Once elevated they wrapped white gauze bandages around his bleeding head.

"Okay… okay… let's break it up here! Let the paramedics do their job!" one officer called, politely pushing through the crowd. Neville knelt back down and picked up his lucky varsity jacket. Blood stained the collar.

"Whose car is this?" the second policeman asked as both officers eased people from the scene. Staring unblinking at the injured man Neville suddenly awoke and answered, "Mine officer. It's my car that hit him."

"That man." the woman witness said, pointing to the victim being loaded into the ambulance, "…he stepped out from those parked cars right in front of him. He had no chance to stop in time. I saw it all officer."

Neville's eyes never left the injured pedestrian and as he stared, a sense of recognition came over him yet he was unable to summon a connection. He walked over to the second attendant as police took charge of the accident scene.

"What do you think?"

"He banged his head pretty hard... leg's bad, but he's alive."

"Where you taking him?" Neville asked as he wheeled him toward the ambulance.

"Our Lady of Mercies."

Neville stood his distance staring down at the oddly familiar man. The paramedic closed the ambulance doors and ran around to the driver's side. The lights and sirens fired-up again and the vehicle slowly inched its way from the congested street. Neville watched it disappear around the corner and in a quiet unwitting prayer whispered, "God... hope he's going to be all right."

With the ambulance now gone, Neville moved his car to the side of the road. It took only twenty minutes for him and the woman witness to give their statements and Neville was free to leave. All agreed the accident had little to do with neglect on Neville's part and rather, it seemed likely the fault of a distracted jaywalking pedestrian.

Exiting the police car, Neville turned back inspecting the accident scene. He stopped suddenly and surveyed that section of road. Although the injured pedestrian hit hard and bled profusely, the road showed no signs of it, only virgin snow. Neville continued to stare back as he returned to his parked vehicle. The sight made him question not only his first assessment of the road itself but also his version of events.

Climbing behind the wheel it was now well past ten o'clock and Neville was still late for work. This time he had an excuse.

CHAPTER 2

"UP 'N AT 'em Artie, breakfast's ready!" Dell called from the hallway.

Eventually the bedroom door opened and Neville's father trudged into the kitchen wearing his usual green terrycloth bathrobe and brown leather slippers.

"Where's Angela, Dell?"

"Angela? Your Angie checked out on you and Woody some twenty years ago. Left town with a traveling rug salesman, if I'm not mistaken."

"She did? How come I don't know that?" he asked, trying to reconcile Dell's explanation.

"Well, in the first place you don't remember things like you used to, Artie. We have this conversation two, three times a week. You just forget a lot of what's happened," Dell followed matter-of-factly as he scuttled about the kitchen holding tight to his spatula.

"Have I turned into a retard or something?"

Dell grinned but thought better of a sarcastic response. "No… you just forget people and things pretty easy these days is all. It gets all jumbled up in your brain."

"Well I certainly remember you! You're Dell, from upstairs! How come I remember you?"

"We've just kinda buddied up I guess. Maybe 'cause I make your breakfast every day… I dunno. Anyway, sit down and eat your eggs. Scrambled today. Bacon'll be ready in a minute."

Still confused Arthur sat at the kitchen table. "Are you sure?"

Placing three strips of bacon on the older man's plate, Dell leaned down. "Sure as the sun's shining outside, but it doesn't matter… in ten minutes we'll be on to something else and you'll be okay again."

The elder Wishwood failed to understand any of it, but as Dell explained, his distress would fade, as would his memory of their conversation. In his early sixties, Arthur had come down with Alzheimer's. The beginnings were subtle, a forgetfulness about the little things; mislaid keys, a payment missed on the odd bill; too much salt in the meals he cooked. Over time, sections of his life began disappearing from memory and the simple chores of daily living became increasingly difficult. In his mind, Arthur Wishwood saw only the split ends of his life's journey, with none of it cohesive enough to make much sense. And when it did make sense, it was soon forgotten.

Dell scooped out his share of eggs and several slices of the bacon and joined his charge at the kitchen table. By now, Artie had started eating. Three mouthfuls in he turned to Dell. "They shoulda never traded Bobby Orr!"

"Bobby Orr?" Dell asked.

"Greatest defenseman that ever played the game. They traded him to the Black Hawks. And for what? Nothin' I can figure!"

"Is he still alive?"

"Alive… course he's still alive. Playing for the Chicago Black Hawks is all. Too bad!"

Dell continued to eat, staring back at the elder Wishwood knowing the topic of discussion was at least thirty years old, but he didn't argue any more. He had learned long ago that in a few short minutes they would move on to something else.

Breakfast ended with Dell loading the plates into the dishwasher. He began humming. It was a familiar ditty heard all across America on a nightly basis: the theme from the TV game-show *Jeopardy*. Closing the appliance door his humming grew louder. He stared toward the elder Wishwood and suddenly Artie's eyes widened.

"Is it gin rummy time?"

"You got it, Artie."

Arthur gave Dell a stern look. "You owe me money."

"You don't remember much but that you remember," an exasperated Dell said.

"How much? I don't remember how much?"

Dell pulled a dog-eared spiral notepad from his back pocket and after leafing through the first few pages he answered, "Only four-hundred-and-eighty-six dollars and fifty-three cents. A drop in the bucket!"

"When am I gonna get it?" Arthur asked with furrowed brows.

"Tomorrow. I'll have it tomorrow. But you have to go get dressed. And don't wear that green plaid shirt again today."

While Arthur left to dress, Dell opened a kitchen drawer, pushed aside a few odds and ends and found the cards and the cribbage board, and dropped them on the table. They used a cribbage board to keep score, finding the peg race an easy method to follow. Dell first encountered the game in the rec-hall while attending classes with Neville at the University of Minnesota. His schooling in those years took on more of a leisurely attempt at education while he searched for distraction outside the confines of the classroom. Gin rummy remained one of Dell's many distractions.

In a weird twist of life, Arthur Wishwood retained the memory and guiding principles to the card game taught to him by Dell two years ago. Even with the onslaught of Alzheimer's Arthur maintained a clear preservation of the strategy involved and as an everyday routine, he hammered his caregiver into submission. Perplexed at the outcome, Dell continued on knowing one day his luck had to change. The odds demanded it, or so he thought. Dell had a gambler's heart, so winning was never his true impetus. Playing the game, whatever the game, was the motivation. Always the game.

Returning from his bedroom Arthur displayed the newest additions to his limited wardrobe; a red plaid shirt, a pair of denim slacks and Nike runners. The game was on.

"Alright, let's go! Penny a point?"

"Of course," Dell said, riffling the cards. Neville's father watched intently, his eyes never leaving Dell's hands. Trust was an issue.

Dell finished shuffling, stood and raised one finger announcing,

"One minute Artie, I have to pee." As he left, the elder Wishwood brandished a sour, disappointed look. The bathroom door closed and within seconds, the telephone rang. A smile replaced Arthur's scowl as he scurried out of the kitchen, down the hall like a child chasing the ice cream truck. He picked up the phone sitting on living room sofa side table.

"Hello," came a woman's voice, "...is this the man of the house?"

"Angela, you know you've been out too long. You get home now, this instant!" Arthur said in obvious confusion. Dell heard the phone and his charge's response and hurried to finish his business.

"I'm sorry... is there–" the woman restarted.

"You should be sorry! Come on home now," Arthur interrupted.

The toilet flushed, the bathroom door flew open and Dell made three quick strides to where Arthur stood scolding the woman on the telephone. From behind, Dell wrestled the phone from the surprised senior and silently pointed a finger in the kitchen's direction. Neville's father shuffled back along the hallway, stopped for a second, looked back to Dell, who once again pointed him toward the kitchen. Arthur hung his head and reluctantly returned to the kitchen.

In these last few months, Neville's father had mistakenly understood all phone calls by women to be his long estranged wife, Angela. Funny in a sense for the confusion it created, but ultimately sad as to the depth his diseased mind had retreated.

With his eyes following Arthur's retreat, Dell finally addressed the caller. "Hello."

Silent seconds ticked by. "Is everything okay there?"

"Everything's good. Who am I speaking with?" Dell asked with cool regard.

"I'm Sandra, and I'm with Magazines Direct. We provide the most popular magazines on sale at a discount of up to forty per cent off the newsstand price. For women: *McCall's, Cosmopolitan, Allure, Flare, Good Housekeeping, Vogue,* and on and on. For men: *Sports Illustrated, Golf Digest, The Hockey News, Maxim, Penthouse, Playboy* and many, many more. For all around news, we offer *Time, Newsweek, People, Star Magazine* and many other favorites. Seventy-two different and exciting reading choices all for your reading pleasure, and at a great savings," the telemarketer pitched.

"What about guns? Do you have any gun magazines?" Dell asked.

A second of silence ensued. "Yes, yes we do. *Guns and Ammo, American Sportsman...*"

"I like guns," he whispered into receiver. Of course, Dell really didn't care much for guns. Dell had never held a gun or seen one up close. Sill he continued. "How much are they?"

"For the gun magazines?"

"No, for all seventy-two magazines," Dell shot back.

On the other end, the telemarketer went silent. Finally, she asked, "You want all our magazines?"

Without hesitation, Dell said, "In triplicate."

The telemarketer paused. "Who is this?"

"Arthur Wishwood, and you my dear, who are you again?"

Another longer pause ensued. In an uncompromising voice, she reengaged the conversation. "Sandra," she said again, "...and I think you're just wasting my time here, Mr. Wishwood."

"Precisely my sentiments Sandra." Dell hung up.

He returned to the kitchen, shuffled the deck and dealt out the cards to begin the game. Arthur's rather sullen demeanor was evident in the beginning as he grumbled for the first few minutes of the game about the telephone, his imagined wife's late arrival home, and Dell's interference on both counts. Dell played on unaffected by Arthur's foul mood. It soon transformed into a jovial interaction. The reason for the change was easy to define: his red peg again began to outdistance Dell's blue peg on the board, and like every day since their tournaments began, Dell complained loudly at his undeserved fate.

As their match went on, Artie started, "I had a customer tell me the other day that old fish don't use their gills. He's an angler by trade and he said fish're born with small oxygen sacks and when they get older, they breathe from those sacks they're born with rather than their gills. Kinda strange, eh?"

Dell looked at him knowing. "When'd he tell you that?"

"I dunno... last week some time I think."

Here Artie looked up from the game and stared at Dell for a few seconds, forgetting he had last seen his shop or his customers well over six years ago. "Maybe it was old fishermen used sacks filled with air to find fish to catch."

Arthur stood now, trying to remember how the story went. His empty eyes searched a space beyond Dell and the kitchen walls. "No, I think it was old anglers used inflated sacks of air and swam after the ancient fish in Europe because they didn't have their gills yet. Shit, I dunno... I never liked fishin' anyway."

Dell saw the distress in Arthur's face, leaned in and placed a hand on his shoulder. In a calm voice he said, "It doesn't matter Artie, it's your play."

They refocused and the entire conversation faded into the oblivion of compassionate time. By noon, Dell owed the elder Wishwood another two dollars and thirty-two cents, adding the day's losses to his note-pad grudgingly. Artie paid a price for winning again. Exacting his own small, Pyrrhic victory, Dell burnt Arthur's lunchtime grilled cheese sandwich.

The Solomon Sentinel, the newspaper where Neville worked, took up most of the center-town square's north-east corner. Named St. Gabriel Square, the plaza itself represented their most architecturally attractive quarter of town. All that transpired in the community, either business or social, centered here around this small, tree-filled park. A stage and band shell, cut out from the southeast edge of evergreens, provided a venue for summer concerts. On the park perimeter, past the cobbled two-lane roadway bordering the site, St. Gabriel Square sat surrounded by most of the community's upscale retail shops, restaurants and local businesses all of which faced this resplendent oasis of greenery. On the eastern perimeter the square's largest building, the three-story town library stood between several shops and storefronts each ornamentally diverse, yet all merging in aesthetic exactitude. Randall's bookstore flanked one side and on the other a quaint coffee shop, Bellick's, offering rare teas, espressos and foreign coffees all in an intimate patio setting in spring and summer months. Rita Wishwood's dental clinic nestled in among the row of storefronts on the south side.

Set along the square on both sides of the roadway stood antique black lampposts in imitation of the pillars that marked distances in Roman times. With the advent of the holidays, these pillars stood bedecked in opulent holly wreaths of reds, greens and golds. Built in a baroque turn-of-the-century style, the decorative brick facades sent visitors well back in time offering a sure sense of Victorian elegance to the blood-center of Solomon. The Snake River, half-frozen, stretched in winter-white along behind the newspaper's yellow brick building, seen easily through the gaps between the colored stone structures. Its simplicity made for an irresistible picture-postcard feel in the color scheme; common brick reds and yellows, tree-greens accented by freshly fallen snow-whites. The town's market square exuded a vitality that life not only maintained in this small community, it flourished.

The true focal point of the square though remained its namesake angel, set high upon the forty-foot cenotaph column erected after WWII. Created from glorious white marble, the column overshadowed the band shell along the south walkway. The names of seven valiant Solomon-born soldiers were inscribed: men who had sacrificed all for the cause of freedom. A black marble statue of the angel Gabriel mounted the apex of the cenotaph, winter edged in snow, wings fully unfurled and clutching a stone tablet in one outstretched hand proudly depicting God's heavenly guardian in flight. His opposite hand pointed skyward.

Visually stunning during daytime, the statue's true beauty flourished at night when two spotlights planted at the monument's base shone on the angel itself, throwing arc-light and shadow to spectacular effect into the heavens above. The significance of the angel had always been a special part of town lore; that on this plot of land, St. Gabriel kept watch over all the God-fearing people of Solomon.

It was nearing eleven o'clock when Neville parked behind the Sentinel in a lot skirting the frozen Snake River. From the back end of their lot, a small berm rose up and leveled off to form a short expanse to the river. The prior summer the town had started the construction of a public walkway all along that section of the Snake. The city slated the project's completion for the upcoming spring, so temporary orange safety fencing announced the danger of open ice. Neville stared out past the orange barriers, across the iced plain of the Snake, seeing only a slip of river rippling near its center. His thoughts returned to the accident and the injured man as he watched the ice chunks flop and flow past, joining the rush downstream. Preoccupied, he turned back to the Sentinel and made his way to the second floor office he had worked in these last four years.

The newspaper press-works took up the lower level. His workstation sat on the second floor, along with all the staff cubicles. With only thirteen full-time employees, the Sentinel was a microcosm of big-city dailies, yet they maintained a rural flair. Local flavor and interests supplemented the second and third sections, most days the shortest section. Staying true to their liberal roots the Sentinel passed on the most interesting stories hot off the AP and Reuters wire services. Neville did all the proofreading for the paper and as a bonus he wrote all the sports articles and editorials related to his cherished varsity hockey team, the University of Minnesota Golden Gophers— a job he also held in his college days for the weekly newspaper. Neville, like his father, was a huge hockey fan.

Reaching the second floor offices Neville walked in with purpose, carrying his finished manuscript, but his thoughts stayed stuck on the accident. Here he encountered his nemesis.

"Late again, eh Wishy!" Roland DeWitt waltzed along the line of desks, sashaying as if weights hung from his boney hips. Below his narrow chiseled chin, a red silk bow tie flopped as he made his way towards Neville. The floppy tie was certainly telling but Roland's pencil-thin blonde moustache elicited a darker, more sinister memory. He twitched it reminiscent of the ever-despicable Black Bart of the silent films seen on PBS during late night breaks from writing. Neville envisioned his archrival tying a curly-locked heroine to a set of railway tracks and snickering while watching her lay helpless, waiting for the inevitable train from down the line.

"It's Woody for the nine-thousandth time, and yes I'm late Roland, if it's any of your business."

"Wishy... Woody, what's the difference. It's all the same to me," he said, mocking Neville with not only his words but also his contentious tone. He smiled an inconvenient smile as always.

"What, are we in grade school here, Roland? You're not my boss, so back off."

"You're right. I'm not your boss... yet. Still I think Walter should know." His usual smug look followed as he swaggered down the aisle as if sprouting a full peacock-plume. He disappeared inside editor, Walter Hendry's office.

"He's an asshole," Sam Charters said as Neville stopped near his desk. Sam was the senior news reporter at the Sentinel and held little respect for the effeminate Roland. Two desks up the aisle John Winterburn, the newspaper's other reporter chimed in. "I saw him two nights ago... in Minneapolis. The Aldridge Office Supplies Christmas party and he was with a woman...she looked young, too."

"Roland... can't be! Had to be his sister," Neville added in utter disbelief.

"I saw him too... but did you get a good look at the girl, John?" Sam asked.

"No, not really. Why?"

"You know that Willis kid from the mail room? She looked just like him, except wearing a blonde wig and minus that scrawny moustache of his," Sam said, a huge smile taking over.

"Willis Ogland... the young guy in the mail room? Our Willis Ogland?" Neville asked.

"None other. At least that's what she looked like to me," Sam said.

Just as their conversation slowed the elevator door opened and the young man in question, Willis Ogland, pushed his wire mesh cart onto the second floor. Exhibiting incredulous stares, all three men watched him make his way in their direction. For the record, he was clean-shaven today. They tried valiantly to hold in the hilarity of his timing, but as he closed the gap, Sam and John began to snicker uncontrollably. Eyes averted, both men covered their mouths.

Nearing their desks Willis started. "Hey guys, need anything..." He stopped short, looked gamely at all three men and asked, "What's so funny?"

Holding back a laugh, Neville made a quick recovery. "Just a joke, Willis. I didn't think it was that funny, but..."

The mail-boy, infected by their laughter, began to giggle and it was no ordinary laugh. More the high-pitched squeals a young school-girl might make if the boy sitting next to her slipped a frog down her dress. Sam, John, and Neville could no longer contain themselves. They began to howl, which sent Willis into a higher pitched, penetrating version of his original schoolgirl giggle. It took time for any of them to set eyes back on their young co-worker.

The laughter slowed and Neville remarked, "You shaved Willis."

Willis Ogland hesitated, his impish giggle slowed. "I had a date."

His admission started all three men up once again. Caught up in the moment Willis began shrieking his girlish howls louder fuel-ing their already raging hysteria. Just when it appeared they would never stop, the door to Walter Hendry's office opened. Roland DeWitt emerged, smirking, his hip swaggering more evident than when he had entered.

The laughing stopped immediately and they watched Roland's skinny rear gyrate down the aisle, passing the four men gathered near Sam's desk. He pitched Willis Ogland an intense glare. Reaching his desk by the front windows, Roland sat, staring back with obvious concern. Finally, he slid behind the section partition. Within seconds, Willis took his leave.

The editor's door opened again and Walter Hendry's head poked out, calling heatedly, "Woody! Get your ass in here!"

"Goddamn Roland," John let slip.

After a quick glance to Sam and John, Neville acquiesced. Walter Hendry was a man in his early sixties, much the same as Neville's father: self-made, hard working. He knew the young man's situation as well as anyone and up until today, Walter had treated Neville even-handedly.

Neville joined him. From behind his desk, Walter silently put his hand out, pointing to an empty chair. Walter's head swayed back and forth in deliberate fashion, his eyes directed away from Neville. His hands wrung themselves as if to calm a rage inside. Neville wondered just what was about to befall him.

Walter abruptly stood. "I don't like squealers. And I don't like Roland, but…" Hendry paused, his eyes narrowed. "Your attendance is getting to be a concern, Woody."

Neville's hands fidgeted. "I had an accident. With my car."

Hendry's hands flattened against his desktop. "Yes, there's always a reason, but it's not just missing time, Mr. Wishwood. You seem preoccupied and it shows in your work. Get with it." Hendry paused as he took his seat. "Do you think you can manage to come out your funk?"

"Yes, sir."

"Good." Walter pulled his bulky frame in closer to the desk. "I think Saturday would be ideal to make up for the lost time, don't you?"

"I suppose it's only fair. I'll be here Mr. Hendry."

Walter went about sorting papers on his desk without answering. After realizing Neville was still waiting he announced, "That's all."

What Hendry left unsaid was the crucial point: Roland DeWitt was no ordinary young man. His father was Gregory DeWitt, the elected representative for Minnesota's 6th congressional district and a man of infinite influence in the area. His years of congressional service coupled with his many political and business connections made it easy for his son to maintain the position he held at the Sentinel. Roland's father and owner Carter Ellison were best of friends and had been since college. Carter Ellison was Roland's godfather.

Gregory DeWitt used his influence to help his son advance quickly knowing it would serve him well in later life. Roland's recent promotion to head up the advertising accounts of the Sentinel was a result of that influence. With a business degree from Princeton, Roland seemed well suited for the position even though there was little doubt how it came about. His father imagined passing off his Minnesota district to Roland one day, and Roland knew it.

For everyone involved, Roland was hard to take, even in small doses. No one knew this more than Neville, who had been the target of his constant jabs for the four years they had worked together. Roland used his privileged upbringing to his every advantage and rubbed Neville's nose in it without conscience. Neville rarely allowed Roland's false sense of superiority to affect him.

As Neville lifted himself to leave Hendry paused, his bulbous cheeks puffed out further and he discharged a rasping belch. "I think I need another bromo," he said, pulling the blue bottle from his desk. "That's it. Go on now," he said, mixing the white brew in a conical paper cup. As Neville left he heard Walter mumbling aloud as he faced the back wall gulping back the contents of the cup. Neville joined his two coworkers back by Sam's desk.

"Well, what'd he say?" Sam asked.

Neville smiled. "Nothing really, just I have to come in Saturday to make up the time."

Sam sat on the edge of his desk. "He's changed since Sara died… a little distant, less focused. When he looks at you there's a disconnect, like he's somewhere else."

Walter Hendry's wife had died four months prior from an infection of the heart lining. Walter still struggled in dealing with her sudden passing. Neville reached across the aisle, lifted his manuscript from his desk and handed it to Sam.

"Is this the great work?" Sam asked, a sarcastic twist in his voice.

"It is, but let's not get too carried away just yet. Read it and let me know what you think."

Sam looked at the title page. "*Seven Days…*" he read the sub-title. "*In one week our world will change…* sounds interesting. Now, if I find any mistakes or editing suggestions, can I mark up the manuscript?"

"Sure, it's a working copy," Neville answered.

Neville trusted the older, more experienced news reporter with his work because of who he was, and the handsome resume he had composed over the years. His main body of work began in Boston some twenty years ago, where he was one of The Globe's most prolific investigative reporters, garnering a Pulitzer Prize nomination for his stories pertaining to the 9/11 attacks. His work helped root out the timetable of the Boston-based hijackers prior to their seizure of the jet from Logan Airport.

Shortly after this career achievement, Sam and his wife decided to simplify their lives and move to a smaller, less hectic setting near his wife's aging parents in Solomon. He had no trouble finding employment at the Sentinel. Along with his daily duties, Sam had begun work on his own book–a narrative on the twenty-first century politics and policies that ultimately led to the September 11th attacks.

"Give me a few weeks and I'll get back to you," Sam said, as he leafed through the first few pages. He set the book aside.

"Sounds good."

John piped in. "Hey, what about me? I'd like to read your master-work."

Neville shot him an unsuspecting glance. "Really?"

"Sure, just because we're newsmen doesn't mean all we read is newspapers," he said, "But no editing. I'll leave that to Sam."

"I'll run off another copy," Neville said with an obvious sense of pride. After Dell and Sam, John Winterburn would be his third full-fledged fan.

Neville slid into his chair across the aisle and booted up his computer. Waiting for his desktop to come alive his thoughts returned to the accident and he wondered about the fate of his victim. Neville worried his personal distractions were a determining factor in the accident. Another, new, nagging distraction added to his growing list of nagging distractions.

Down the aisle, behind the blue padded office partition, Roland stood staring out onto the town's central plaza. Coating the expansive windows, a crystal film distorted the scenic view of evergreens, black lamps and the morning bustle of town business below. Roland saw a different version through the opaque glass. He saw the snow-decked evergreens as sailboat masts set across a sun-washed bay. He saw the bright haze of grey from a cloud occluded sky morph into the sun disc descended from the heavens of an equatorial island. And the angel statue, St. Gabriel, at the plaza's far end, he saw as a surfing native islander. What he saw was himself, living his dreams in a foreign land, living a foreign life–a new life. He envisioned his own ambitions come alive.

"You have to be careful. I don't trust any of them," he said to Willis, who sat studying small notes pinned to the back of Roland's cubicle. He seemed disinterested in the conversation.

"Why?"

Roland turned back, his tone more forceful now. "Because they're not like you and I."

"What do you mean, not like us?" Willis asked, turning his attention now to Roland's computer and clicking on the internet.

From behind the partition, Roland could hear his co-workers talking. From where he stood nothing in their conversation was discernible. Willis sat completely oblivious to the goings on.

"They're talking' about us... right now," Roland continued, standing next to his friend, staring past the partition.

Still distracted Willis asked, "What're they saying?"

"They're saying we're different, we're gay."

Confused, Willis now turned to look Roland's way. "But that's what you just said. We're not like them... so they're right, according to you."

Roland smiled a knowing smile and sat next to Willis placing a firm hand on his slim shoulder. "You're so innocent. You don't see it do you?"

Again confused, Willis answered, "I guess I don't." Willis didn't argue. It was not his nature to argue. Raised by loving parents who accepted him as he was, Willis remained undeterred by the societal standards applied by a narrow-minded few. In that way he was very different from Roland, who had experienced the world through bitter eyes. Early on, the DeWitts had judged their son's lifestyle as a choice and had censured him for living it. For them, his predilection represented a serious moral flaw rather than a result of nature.

Roland stood watching his friend as he clicked on a You-Tube video, a cat dunking his head under a running kitchen faucet. Willis watched the video and when it finished found another of a mother cat chasing and retrieving her kittens as they slipped down a child's slide.

Willis had an obvious affinity for cats and with the proliferation of cat videos available on You Tube he was not alone.

The video ended and Willis clicked off the internet now fully amused. He found Roland staring out past the windows, the square plaza, his face aglow with a contemplative all-knowing sneer. Roland looked well beyond the Solomon town-square, those snow-bound evergreens, the crowds of shopping citizens seeing something much more significant to him– his future.

"What's with you?" Willis asked.

Lost in thought, Roland absently replied, "What?"

"The stare. You seem to be on another planet."

Roland turned back to his friend, his lover. "Plans. Just plans, Willis my friend."

As his words settled and Willis wondered, a short musical interlude jingled from Roland's i-Phone. He scrolled his texts, found the newly arrived message and studied it for just a minute. A pronounced grin swept his gaunt face.

Noting his friend's change, Willis asked, "What is it?"

"My way out of this insufferable job and this backward little town."

Plagued with the visceral images of his morning collision Neville's day passed in slow motion. Worries surrounding his victim's health gnawed at his conscience until finally, just past five o'clock, he made a decision. He called Dell.

"Dell, how's dad?"

"He's good. I have him duct-taped to a kitchen chair and I'm force-feeding him broccoli through a funnel. Just like mom did for me."

Dismissing his friend's antics, Neville continued, "Listen, something happened on the way to work this morning…"

Neville explained the details of his morning mishap and his growing concern for the man's wellbeing. He had decided to visit him in the hospital and would be home after.

"How late?" Dell asked.

"Six, six-thirty. No later," Neville said.

"Okay, because Bob De Rossa's picking me up at six-thirty."

"Running Acres?" Neville asked.

"I'm feelin' it today, Woody... and Bob says he's got a live one running tonight." Running Acres was the local horseracing track in Columbus, outside of Minneapolis. In the winter they ran races simulcast from all over the country. During the summer months Bob De Rossa worked in the barns there as a groom for the live racing season. Bob and Dell had recently been involved in a rather delicate escapade in St. Paul, so Neville asked, "What about Bob... he any better?"

Dell's answer was cryptic. "Let's just say he's gettin' there."

Neville somehow knew there was another story behind Dell's evasive reply, but he also knew now was not the time.

CHAPTER 3

THE GRAVITY OF the accident and the injured man's condition struck Neville with full force on his drive to Our Lady of Mercies. Pulling into the parking lot, he nearly sideswiped another car exiting the lot. Once inside, he approached the information desk on the first floor. The desk's attendant was on the phone and he waited, his eyes circling the clean well-lit, pastel green reception area.

"I'm looking for a young man brought here this morning... he was struck by a car."

Without looking up she asked, "Name?"

Neville stammered for a second, "I-I, don't really know his name... but the accident was on Welland, about ten o'clock this morning."

Finally glancing up she said, "Lemme see if we have any new admissions."

She punched in several keys, a new screen popped up and she traced names across the computer monitor. "There's Joseph Tremblay, room three-o-six... forty-four years old."

"Too old," Neville said.

"Stanley Mesner, room five-fourteen... thirty-eight years old."

"Still too old... but closer."

Still searching she came up with one last name, "We've got a John Doe... age undetermined. He's in room two-twenty-one."

"Maybe… I'll try him, thanks." As Neville walked away, the receptionist called him back.

"Sir, it says visitation by family only. If you're not family you can't visit. Not today."

Neville stopped, stunned. He thought for a second. "He's a John Doe, I understand that to mean you don't have a name for him, and if you don't have a name… who's family?"

"Well," she stalled, "… family's family and it usually means he's in bad shape sir, so you can't go up there."

Neville thought for a few seconds, coming up with a viable option. "I'm his brother."

She stared back at Neville, sizing him and his explanation up. "Okay then," and her eyes dropped back to the desk she manned. *People are strange in their own particular ways,* he thought. He set out to find this John Doe.

The second floor was a hive of activity. Nurses, blurs of blue-garbed orderlies and white-coated doctors ran the wide aisles, their faces set serious. Nearing the nurse's station, he saw a sign, ONCOLOGY WARD, which stopped his progress. Regaining his composure, Neville followed the room numbers to 221 and found the door open a crack. He listened first, and hearing nothing pushed open the oversized entryway.

It was a quiet room, dim with only low voltage lights shining out from beneath wall valances above the two beds inside. A thin draw curtain ran between them separating the two patients. To the left an old man lay sleeping, his skinny arms blotched and bruised. A clear I-V line drew from his left arm to a hanging plastic bag and from his right arm an array of wires and tubes connected him to three or four lightly beeping, buzzing monitors.

To the right of the half-drawn curtain a younger man lay sleeping, connected to his own vital-sign monitors. Bandages wrapped his head and he had his left leg locked in a gray plastic cast at the knee. It was him. Neville approached the bed, unzipping his varsity jacket as he came closer.

He stared down at the face of the man he had hit that afternoon and again that feeling came over him, the one that evoked such a real sense of recognition, yet it continued to elude him. Who did this man resemble?

As Neville approached the stranger in bed, the door swung open and a nurse pushed her way in, a small white tray in tow. She was no ordinary nurse as Neville was quick to notice. She slipped in showing the deepest dark auburn hair cradling a flawless face and as she looked up to see Neville, her grey-green eyes sparkled. Her bright jade hip-hugging uniform displayed a slender shapely frame. A cautious smile slipped across her lips. Simply stated, the nurse was a knockout.

"Oh–" she said startled.

Neville in his usual friendly greeting that doubled as his usual pick-up line elicited an interested, "Hello!" It was his most seductive, I'm available and you're certainly my type, '*Hello.*'

His eyes darted to her left hand and seeing no rings, he continued, "I'm here to see him," pointing to her sleeping patient.

"Yes, our John Doe. He came in without identification." Looking past Neville, she gazed with what appeared to be profound affection for her patient.

"What, no wallet, no money?"

"Just this." The nurse slipped closer pulling the white cart and reached over to the bedside table opening its top drawer. She removed a small silver digital camera. "That's it. He's been unconscious since. You wouldn't happen to know his name would you?"

"No, I just dropped in to see how he was doing. The camera, has it got anything that might help identify him?"

"I don't know. Either it's broken or the batteries are dead," she said sliding the drawer shut. "Like I said, he's been unconscious. They operated on his leg earlier, but he still has a few problems."

"My name's Neville by the way, Neville Wishwood. Unfortunately, I'm the guy who hit him… with my car. It was an accident." Inspecting the hospital room, his eyes darting around at the various machines and monitors, he asked, "Why's he in the Oncology Ward?"

Moving in front of Neville, the nurse offered a sensual smile and placed an electronic thermometer into John Doe's ear. "No room at the inn, Mr. Wishwood. This was the only available bed."

"It's Neville and you're?"

"Audrey, Audrey Timmerman. I'm the afternoon shift nurse," she said with yet another seductive glance. Removing the thermometer, Audrey checked the reading and wrote the numbers on a chart. She looked Neville's way, noticing his varsity jacket.

"University of Minnesota grad?"

"Yeah, graduated, what… seven years ago. Did you take nursing at Minnesota?"

"No, Northwestern," she said, her eyes alight with interest. Audrey's lips were full and certainly inviting, especially to a man who had gone dateless for almost a year.

"Good school. So you're here every afternoon?"

"I am. Until eleven."

"So these problems he has… John Doe. Are they serious?"

"Well, not as serious as Mr. Eleazar next to him here, but serious enough." Holding his chart, she lifted the top page and read the notes. "He's had several tests… they show brain activity is normal, so the doctor figures he'll come out of the coma at some point soon, but the leg…" Her finger traced to the bottom of the chart, stopping at the very last comment. "…the operation was successful, except that he's not getting sufficient blood flow below the knee. They're afraid it's going to infect and they'll have to amputate. He's on antibiotics so we're still hopeful."

The nurse replaced John Doe's chart and circled the bed to attend her second patient, Mr. Eleazar. She removed the plastic I-V bag and replaced it with a full bag from the cart.

As she took his temperature, Neville asked, "What about him… Mr. Eleazar?"

"Mr. Eleazar has terminal bone cancer. He's on a morphine drip. It's the oncology ward, Mr. Wishwood. Unfortunately we see a lot of people lose their fight here," she said quietly staring down at her patient, her grey-green eyes carrying the hint of a tear in them.

"Sad."

"Very sad, but…" she stopped, looking up as if to clear her thoughts.

Neville's stare returned to the newly named John Doe. "So no one's come in to identify him?"

"No, you're his only visitor so far. He looks quite serene though doesn't he."

John Doe's face appeared pale yet he maintained a rather congenial countenance, a kindness that sleep imparts. He did look serene almost content, but he knew none of what had transpired. Again, Neville experienced pangs of recognition.

The nurse interrupted. "Mr. Wishwood…"

"Neville, please."

"Neville… I just hope he makes it okay. Look at him lying there, without a worry in the world. He seems so innocent."

Nurse Audrey finished her duties in room 221 and Neville watched her thoughtfully arrange the bed cover over each of her patients. With the white cart between her and Neville, Audrey pumped a dribble of disinfectant on her hands and rubbed it in.

"I have other patients, so I have to go."

"I'll be back, Audrey and hopefully I'll see you again. You've been… quite helpful," he said with a sly grin.

Neville was never very outgoing where women were concerned. Neville's way with the opposite sex was somewhat reticent, a trait inherited from his romantically inept father. Was it nature or nurture? Who really knew? Yet with Neville, women found his personality grew into easy and fulfilling conversation over time.

Dell set up Neville's last date shortly after his divorce. His friend had introduced him to an attractive young woman he worked with at the bakery. A nice woman, still, it ended up just the one date. Neville realized after his night with Dell's friend that he was nowhere near ready to abdicate his love for Rita. That became evident immediately.

In Neville's mind, no one compared to his first and only love Rita, and he knew from his mental checklist he could never be fair to any woman until he settled that part of himself. Even with this past difficulty, Neville believed he was closer than ever to restarting his life.

Audrey smiled back. She was hard to read, still Neville wanted to believe he saw a slight wink from the auburn beauty. For several awkward seconds the two stood flushed and silent near the nameless pedestrian, a scene reminiscent of a tryst at a high school dance rather than two adults conversing in a hospital room.

The young nurse veered her cart toward the door and exited room 221. She offered one quick look back, a good sign. A smitten Neville Wishwood watched her every move until she disappeared through the door. He gave his unconscious stranger one last look and proclaimed, "I'll be back."

Shortly after 6 p.m., Neville arrived home. It was dark as Dell waited anxiously. "Artie's had dinner and he's watching the news in the living room. Still some meatloaf left in the fridge. Enjoy."

Dell slipped on his coat as Neville checked on his father. After making a quick survey of his dad, Neville pulled off his own jacket and joined Dell back in the vestibule.

"So what's with Bob? Is he gonna be okay?" he asked.

A smile fluttered across Dell's face as he slid a stick of gum in his mouth. "Kinda," he said, chewing.

"Kinda. What's kinda mean?"

"The hypnotist said he can't break it. Said Bob's an odd case, first of its kind. So he could only swap out the command."

"Swap out the command? What's that mean?"

Dell tried avoiding Neville's glare. "Well, instead of barking, he does something else now. It'll fade in a few weeks."

Bob De Rossa was a friend to both Neville and Dell from the years all three attended the University of Minnesota. A big man with a sturdy build, Bob was a most affable sot. After college, Bob served two tours of duty in Iraq, but he came back slightly off kilter. Bob's senses seemed hyperactive at times, and he exhibited signs of a growing paranoia. Nervous ticks consumed him; a constant blinking, a rattling of his hand as he walked and as if near deaf, statements directed Bob's way were often answered with an emphatic, "*What!*"

Then there were the clothes. Bob continued to wear his camouflage fatigues... everywhere. God love 'im, Bob had issues.

Neville had heard at least the first part of Bob and Dell's latest foray into the big city only last week. In mid-November, Dell and Bob went into St. Paul and after several drinks ended up at a cabaret where a hypnotist was headlining. At times, drinking liberated Bob from his exacting personal demons and half-drunk that night, he volunteered to assist the Great Reshtroppa, a Jamaican born hypnotist touring the lesser-known nightclubs in the Midwest.

Dell watched Bob stumble on stage and join the Great Reshtroppa and his near naked wire-haired female assistant. The assistant was surely the draw for Bob. Using a revolving gold medallion the Great Reshtroppa put Bob under in seconds. Hypnotized, Bob spoke in a monotone zombie-like voice, rejoining all questions with only monosyllabic replies of "yes" and "no". Playing before a packed house the hypnotist convinced Bob he was obliged to bark like a dog when he heard the command word, *eggnog*. After snapping him back, the Great Reshtroppa engaged Bob in conversation and began inserting the word *eggnog* in every second sentence. And every time the word *eggnog* came up, Bob barked loudly three times.

The act went amazingly well and a stumbling drunk Bob played it up for all it was worth in front of a packed house. The end of the act consisted of the hypnotist releasing Bob from his hypnotic trance and Bob returning to his seat to a near standing ovation. Walking back to their table, Bob had no idea what he had done to earn the applause. Everyone in attendance seemed satisfied. Dell thought it all great fun, laughing loudest at Bob's onstage pranks.

On their way home that night they discovered the odd after-effects. At the wheel, a sober Dell continued to laugh over Bob's onstage antics and somewhat casually said the word *eggnog*. Bob barked three times. Since that night, Bob and Dell had returned to the small cabaret where the Great Reshtroppa performed and explained Bob's plight. Stymied, the hypnotist failed to correct the condition citing Bob's low intellectual aptitude.

As Dell moved toward the front door, Neville stopped him.

"Dell what do you mean… something else?"

"He couldn't go on barking like that, Woody."

"Dell…"

Dell chewed hard on the gum, still avoiding eye contact with Neville. "He said all he could do is change the command, and I suggested something less vocal. It was embarrassing to hear him bark in public like that, so… well, now he pirouettes. Like a ballet dancer."

"What?"

"It's not so bad. He's much quieter now, and how often do you hear someone say *eggnog* anyway?"

Neville worked at holding a stern look as Dell's eyes finally flicked up. A smile involuntarily crept along Neville's lips and he fought it valiantly for at least five seconds, until…

"Whose idea was that?"

Seeing Neville's grin widening, Dell hesitated. "Mine I guess. But you haven't seen him. Actually, he's quite nimble for a big guy. And it's a helluva lot better than barkin' all the time."

"All the time? How often can *eggnog* come up in conversation?" Inside his head Neville held the mental picture of Bob, toes pointed, spinning a pirouette in his camouflage fatigues. It broadened his already beaming grin. Dell's impish glare mirrored back the answer to his question.

"You're the only one aren't you," Neville said.

"Maybe not," Dell said, defiant yet guarded. "… maybe when I'm not around people are sayin' *eggnog* all the time. I can't be there twenty-four, seven. 'Tis the season for *eggnog*, Christmas 'n all."

A shadow passed along the front window curtains casting the silhouette of a car in front of Arthur Wishwood's duplex. A car door slammed. Relieved, Dell opened the front door. "There's Bob… I gotta go."

In the dark, the street appeared deserted. A mechanical echo carried up from the corner, coupled with the blinking of an approaching beacon. Yellow light bounced off the neighboring windows. The sound grew closer, the yellow shine more vivid as a snowplow passed curling snow and grey mush from the roadway. After passing, the sights and sounds of the plow faded in the distance.

From behind the glass storm door, Neville could see Bob striding up the walk, head down, seemingly deep in thought. A strapping human specimen, Bob bounded up the snowbound walkway fully dressed in his customary combat fatigues. As Dell stepped out onto their covered porch Neville joined him, calling out, "Hey Bob, what's up?"

Startled, Bob's head popped up. He bellowed back a surprised, "What!" as if a mortar had exploded somewhere in the front yard. Nearing the lighted porch his hand jangled and his eyes darted in wide arcs across the tundra-white lawn. Bob was on guard for any unseen enemy.

"Bob, it's me, Woody. Just saying hi." With no visible enemies to report, Neville's words brought him back to reality.

"Oh, hi Woody. Thought I heard somethin' else." His eyes keened the dark corners of the lot. After several silent seconds he asked, "Ready, Dell?"

"Let's get going," Dell said. The porch light shone brightly on both men as they turned to leave. "You've got a live one you said."

"Annabel Lee in the sixth. Sure winner," Bob exclaimed in his typical boisterous voice.

"Annabel Lee? That's Edgar Allan Poe," Neville noted.

"No, Jamie Schuster's drivin' her tonight," Bob said bluntly, unaware of the reference. "I never heard of Edgar Poe. He from Michigan?"

"He's a poet Bob. Edgar Allan Poe is a poet," Neville said in a kind but incredulous way.

Bob stared vacantly at his two friends. A crooked smile finally curled his lips and he asked, "Why would a poet be drivin' a horse at Running Acres?"

"He wrote the poem, "*Annabel Lee*", Bob. Edgar Allan Poe? He's kinda famous. Woody just mentioned it as a point of conversation," Dell explained. Any banter with Bob had the propensity to get lost in translation given Bob's somewhat limited attention span and capacity. Three years of university had done little to expand Bob's intellectual horizons and anything he had gained most likely deserted him in Iraq.

As they neared the car Neville heard Dell begin again, "So yah hear this Annabel Lee's gonna be there in the sixth. I hope they gave her enough, *eggnog*, so she'll run like a champ."

Dell over-emphasized the command word *eggnog* as he glanced back to Neville. The wicked smile Dell beamed back was certainly one that would earn him entry through the gates of hell. Camouflage Bob stopped dead, a statue standing fully erect in sand shades. He joined his hands gracefully on each hip, slipped one meaty arm in front of his waist and the other to the back. A tawny right leg daintily toe pointed in mid-air, his left foot lifted to his toes, elevating his massive frame and his clevis-arms swung him clockwise starting the spin while his one airborne leg kicked once to complete the pirouette. Ending two full twirls Bob's feet aligned perfectly on the snow-covered sidewalk and his hands met gracefully above his knit cap.

Now to say Bob's display was a re-imagining of Rudolph Nureyev would be a lie. It was more like watching an oversized armadillo jack-knife off a diving board (a most extraordinary feat by any stretch of the imagination) but Dell was undeniably right about one thing: Camouflage Bob De Rossa did display a savage grace.

In the spray of porch light, Bob's face beamed in proud stoic rapture. Suddenly the trance faded, the glow dulled and his arms dropped to his sides. Immediately he realized what had happened and his fierce eyes caught Dell standing near the car, smiling back, trying desperately to portray a specter of innocence.

"Dell, did you say… that word?"

Dell's smile vanished. Bob was a big man and at times, if his internal wiring were crossed, he could be considered a cruise missile gone rogue.

"Course not Bob. It was just a mistake. You know, two words coming together to make one odd conjugation. Like egg rolls, and, say, possibly, noggin. I said, after the track let's get some egg rolls, if you don't get your noggin kicked by a horse in the barns. Egg rolls. Noggin. That's it."

Without waiting Dell quickly opened the car door and sat. Confused, Bob made his way around the car. Before Bob got in Neville could hear him say, "Don't say that word Dell. Especially when I'm driving."

As the car pulled away into the darkness, Neville saw Dell's face pressed flat against the window, flashing that demonic smile.

With Dell and Bob literally off to the races, Neville took out the leftover meatloaf. He added a few boiled potatoes and sat down for his dinner. After eating, he went down the hall to check on his father. Neville knocked at the bedroom door. "Bruins game tonight, dad."

He waited and with no response, he pushed open his father's bedroom door. There sitting on his bed quickly closing up a small pewter hued chest sat the elder Wishwood, surprised and looking rather annoyed. Bristling at the interruption, Arthur Wishwood dropped to his knees and slipped the tin chest into the open lower drawer of his dresser, closing it as Neville stood watching. He popped up erect and with a child-like innocence asked, "Bruins game? Tonight?"

"Pregame starts in about five minutes," Neville said staring down at the closed drawer.

Neville's father scurried past his son, down the hall and into the living room. Neville was tempted to investigate the box, but even sick this was still his father and decided against intruding on his privacy. Probably some keepsake from his steadily dwindling past, Neville told himself.

Arthur propped himself atop the leather lounger and clicked on the television. After grabbing a beer from the kitchen, Neville joined him and switched the channel to the Bruins game. His father sat passively watching the pre-game show waiting for the puck to drop.

Neville took a swig of beer and sat across from his father on the sofa. "Dad, I've tickets for the Gopher's game next week. We'll all be going," he said, trying to elicit a smile.

Arthur Wishwood sat listless, his eyes directed toward the television, seemingly watching the hockey game. Neville watched him watch the game and thought of the man he once was, the father he had known in years gone by. Time had eroded the man he loved.

"They're playing Wisconsin," Neville added.

On some level, Arthur understood and glanced his son's way.

"That'll be a good game." His father's unexpected awareness took Neville by surprise. These small feats are what kept him hopeful and they sat again in uninterrupted silence as the Bruins game played out. Minutes later Boston scored and a telling smile creased across the elder Wishwood's stoic face. He still had his small pleasures.

"You've got a doctor's appointment tomorrow dad."

Arthur turned toward his son. "Is it that doctor I like? I don't want to see the one I don't like."

Neville smiled. "It's Dr. Ranjit. You always liked him. He's got your results back."

"Okay." His doleful eyes returned to the television. Neville swallowed a short gulp of beer while his father watched the game.

Neville's thoughts returned to Bishop's Bay and those times after his mother left.

A huge Boston Bruins hockey fan, his father had started a seven-year-old Neville in the sport. He remembered those winter weekend trips to the arena in Rainard; the conversations they enjoyed. Sometimes they would laugh off the outcomes of the games, and sometimes a more serious discussion would take place, mostly on how Neville could improve his play.

In his youth Neville developed a frustration with his father's criticisms seeing it through the eyes of what he was: a boy. Now, a father himself, he saw it for what it truly was: a prideful push to challenge a son to be the best he could be. To teach him to conquer doubt, conquer the adolescent fear of failure and excel in spite of his age, in spite of the odds, and in Neville's situation, in spite of a certain lack of hockey skills. Neville realized now, through this fatherly prodding, he did not have to be the most talented hockey player, but his father always expected a hard work ethic. He recalled his father's words in many life circumstances: *Hard work trumps talent every time.*

Remembering the man his father was once he gently said, "Dad…"

Arthur's head turned in Neville's direction. His eyes were empty. Empty of understanding. Empty of emotion. Empty of life. Neville saw it from that one protracted glance.

"I still love you dad."

Arthur smiled back, a hint of perception showing but his eyes quickly returned to the television. Neville finished his beer and later that night helped his father to bed. The one thing Arthur Wishwood did well these days was sleep, and he was soon under the spell of Mother Night. Neville followed his father's leave.

That night when Neville's head hit the pillow and the worries of his busy life dissipated, he drifted off. Tonight the dream that had haunted so many of his nights was held at bay.

CHAPTER 4

*I*MPRISONED IN A *timeless state, Rita holds her static pose. As quickly as they had arrived, the winds ebb, returning the streets of Solomon to relative calm. The second hand sounds, wobbles and shifts back once– thirty. Her dread subsides and as she chokes back sobs, Rita's body arches upright.*

The seconds reverse. Twenty-nine: The salt rain recedes to the point of origin by the refrigerator door; the pepper cloud implodes back to center and those smashed crystal shards realign to capture their spices, forming two solid shakers.

Twenty-eight: Her pain dulls. Rita's arm jerks back; the shakers take flight, returning to the counter as if pulled by invisible strings. The overturned fruit bowl levitates, then speeds to join the shakers

Twenty-seven, twenty-six: The bowl wobbles, tips level and the fruit pieces reset, ordered once more inside the dish. A scream chokes its way back down her throat. Tears ladder up Rita's cheeks and squirm a return, refilling red eyes.

Twenty-five, twenty-four: She rears toward the re-living room spotting the Christmas tree carved in silhouette. Beneath its lowest boughs, colorless grey shapes spill out three deep heightening the pain. Tears continue to retract.

Twenty-three: Her scarf wings a retreat to an open hand and rewinding itself, re-covers her neck–

The alarm clock, now reprogrammed, clattered out a loud rock tune at 6:30 a.m. Neville's eyes popped open. He lay immobile for only seconds and remembering the day prior reached up and touched the scab on his forehead recalling his soul-crushing effort to dress. Avoiding a repeat, he was soon awake and waiting for coffee to perk in the kitchen.

Neville called Dell who joined him in the downstairs kitchen. They fixed their coffees and sat silent at the kitchen table. Dell buried his head behind the front section of the Solomon Sentinel. Already knowing the news Neville returned to his bedroom, gathering up the newly printed copy of his book for John at work. He had run a copy off while the Bruins game was on the night before. Placing the copy by the front door, Neville returned to the kitchen.

"Hey, how'd you make out last night?" Neville asked.

"Three-fifty," Dell said, rustling the paper.

"Win or lose?"

Neville watched the newspaper lower, exposing Dell's ravenous grin. It answered the question without further discussion. "Dinner's on me tonight."

Neville shook his head as he gulped back coffee. "How is it you always win? And Bob? "

"Bob? Bob got change back for the parking. That's the only ticket he cashed all night."

"Poor Bob," Neville said. "I'll be back about ten-thirty. Just make sure Dad's up and ready to go."

Folding up the newspaper Dell asked, "You gonna find out today?"

"I think so. Tests are done, and Dr. Ranjit's got the results."

As Neville downed the last of his coffee, Dell put down the paper and held out both hands. On each, his fingers were crossed. "Here's hoping for the best."

But Neville knew his father would need much more than good luck. He had seen the signs. Arthur Wishwood was slowly deteriorating, becoming increasingly dependent on his caregivers for direction and the performance of even the simplest tasks.

Dell understood and maintained an air of optimistic self-delusion.

Both men wanted the best, but unfortunately, continued to witness the worst. Lost in this chaotic downward spiral, they held virtually no control over what governed Arthur's health and well-being and they felt helpless to change any of it. They were two men held prisoner by time and the fates themselves.

Neville curled an arm inside his coat sleeve, zipped it, clutched his manuscript and headed out. Before the door closed, he called back, "Dewey'll be here after school."

On his morning drive to work, the day's beginnings were dull and grey with wisps of snow sifting through low morning light. Distracted by his father's desperate condition, Neville missed his first turn onto Spencer Street and backtracked. He tried to stay hopeful. From the Sentinel parking lot, out beyond the lines of orange fencing he spied the sinuous Snake River rushing wild and torrential through its interior. Miniature ice flows bobbed with the current and he recalled days passed, when tempted by an escape that way. The way of ice, the easy way of water. But in his heart, Neville could no more end himself than gnaw his foot off at the ankle. These were reckless thoughts spawned by the inner pain from a divorce he neither desired nor endorsed.

He walked away knowing, *It will never get that bad,* and in that moment of pure clarity he thought of Dewey, his son, and his mood switched instantly, igniting a wide proud grin to face an otherwise disheartening day.

Trudging into the Sentinel building, he remembered the childlike smile of the man lying nameless in a hospital bed and wondered who he was. The elevator-door opened on the second floor and it all quickly faded from thought with his first sight of Roland striding purposefully toward Walter Hendry's office near the elevator. As Neville passed, Roland smirked and called, "Mornin' Wishy-boy," in a sharp sarcastic tone.

Neville nodded, returning only an emotionless, "Roland," and kept to himself as he passed. Nearing his desk, he removed his coat and slipped across to John's desk, plopping his novel next to the computer monitor.

John Winterburn looked up from reading a small pad near his keyboard. "This it?"

"That's it. Read it and tell me what you think."

"Now, no essays Woody," he said, touching the binder's plastic cover. "Just an overall honest opinion, no more."

"Okay."

Neville craned to look at John's monitor. "What's that?"

John propped back in his swivel chair and stretched his arms above his head. "Last night the State Police located a car that was carjacked in St. Paul two days ago. They found it in the parking lot across from the bus terminal at St. Gabe's Square. Hendry called me... he'd gotten a tip so I went out and interviewed the officers at the scene. Quite a crowd, mostly police."

Curious, Neville leaned in and began reading the story. Suddenly he stopped and looked down at his co-worker. "There was a body in the trunk?"

John nodded. "Yeah, the woman kidnapped with the car unfortunately. From what I understand, she had several stab wounds. Pretty gruesome."

"Wow, big news here in Solomon."

"That's not all. Six months ago, they found another carjacked vehicle in the same lot. We covered the story, just a small one at the time, but the state police think they might be connected. Possibly the same perps."

"Makes sense... let me know what happens."

"You'll be the first, I'm sure."

Slipping his hands in his pockets Neville turned back toward his desk. Before he wandered away, John whispered, "Woody, sit down for a second."

Slouching into the chair next to John's desk, Neville asked, "What's up?"

John's eyes narrowed as he leaned forward. "Neville I'll be leaving soon."

"I'm sure. Late night with this and all," he said.

"No, no… I mean leaving the Sentinel. I've got a job offer in Phoenix, the Sun-Times. I'll be leaving at the end of January."

"That's great John," Neville whispered back.

"Yeah. It's better money and the weather's a little more to our liking. I loved it here don't get me wrong but– it's time to move on."

"Have you told Hendry yet?"

"Not yet. After New Year's but that's the point. He'll need to replace me Woody." John leaned back cocking his head in Neville's direction. Neville understood immediately.

This was his first real chance to prove himself, not only as a reporter, but as a writer and in a sudden karmic shift, Neville's world began to open up to far-reaching possibilities. His eyes slipped past his Sentinel co-worker and although initially excited, he came to a sudden fateful realization.

"Hendry will never give me that job John. Not now anyway." His eyes lowered understanding how his relationship with Walter had deteriorated since the editor's wife had passed away. Then again, all of Walter's relationships had suffered.

"You never know… he might see your potential again. He did hire you," John said trying to lift his coworker's spirits. He had come to know his young associate quite well over these last few years. John Winterburn knew the struggle Arthur Wishwood engaged in and could only surmise the emotional toll it had taken on his son. They all knew, and not because Neville had ever complained or even spoke of it.

Last year the newly divorced Neville had his best friend accompany him to the Sentinel Christmas party and Dell inadvertently mentioned their home situation while mingling with Neville's colleagues. It was an innocent slip, never meant to elicit any real reaction, just an afterthought in conversation. They watched Neville maintain a stoic façade, never offering up his father's illness as an excuse in any of his dealings at work. Neville's father had always preached perseverance. As his father's son, he forged ahead in silence.

"Woody, don't say anything for now."

Returning to his desk somewhat dazed, he called back, "E-mail me the story and I'll proof it and send it on."

John leaned forward, picking up Neville's manuscript. "I'll start reading it tonight."

The next few hours he went about proofreading not only John's story but also Sam's current political editorial and Walter Hendry's take on the Letters to The Editor. He would leave Roland's advertising power point presentations for the afternoon.

Nearing ten o'clock, he informed Walter of his father's appointment and left. A cold day, the drive to Minneapolis remained clear with only flurries. Arthur sat subdued, unaware of the traffic, the weather or any other diversions.

They waited in the reception area sitting directly across from a younger woman and what Neville presumed was her stricken mother. The older woman gazed wide-eyed out past the reception desk with little emotion. Dr. Ranjit specialized in Alzheimer's diagnosis and treatment.

To Neville's left, the office door opened and a new couple entered: an older man followed by a younger woman guiding him from behind. His steps were short, unsure and he whispered to his caretaker as he shuffled past Neville to sit. As he watched the newest patients, the frosted glass window slid open and the receptionist called, "Mr. Wishwood, Dr. Ranjit will see you now."

Neville shepherded his father, shuffling his own short steps down the hallway to the office door. They sat in blue fabric chairs directly in front of the doctor's grey metal desk. While settling in, Arthur asked in a quiet voice, "Is this the doctor's office?"

"Yes," Neville said, searching the room with eager eyes. Dr. Ranjit's plaques and certifications lined the wall behind his leather office chair and to the left an illumination panel mounted the wall. To the right an oil painting of a red wood barn edged in white and set in a rural landscape stared back. Alone on the wall it seemed misplaced.

Dr. Ranjit pushed in from a side door, carrying a manila folder. "Mr. Wishwood, good to see you again. How are you feeling?" He took his seat behind the metal desk.

Arthur stared unaware.

"Dad, the doctor's asking how you feel," Neville prodded.

"Oh… good."

Dr. Ranjit smiled, slipped his half-glasses down and opened the file. A man in his early forties, the doctor's heritage was East Indian yet he spoke perfect English.

"The results, are they back?" Neville asked.

"Yes… yes they are Mr. Wishwood." The doctor hesitated, shifting pages inside the manila folder. He stopped near the end of a small stack of loose sheets. "I'd like to show you an MRI cross-section of your father's brain from eight months ago first."

Arthur sat staring at the red barn on the wall.

Gone were the days he owned and operated his hardware store. The wife he married popped into his head on occasion, yet she had deserted her family some twenty-two years ago. These facts melted away, vaporized in the disease's advance. With it, less and less of Arthur Wishwood survived. Within the continuum of his collapsing world, few if any thoughts remained of his Vietnam War experience and the fear that followed him and all of his soldier brothers, tramping jungle lowlands in search of an invisible enemy. His lack of memory concealed those gallant efforts, rewarded with both a Purple Heart and Silver Star.

Fear consumed him in a shrewder sense these days. A smaller yet pervasive fear; a fear of everything, a timidity as if seeing the world draped in a murky cloak with all about him new and intimidating and fraught with undefined danger. Today Arthur sat unaware of fear itself and unable to recognize its harsh effect.

Dr. Ranjit pulled a flimsy film from the folder, lowered his head to read the date and stood to attach the film to the light panel. He flicked the light switch on, turned toward Neville and started. "These areas here…" He pointed to several small whitish spots located in all four quadrants of the brain. "They show the early onset of the disease. They're called amyloid plaques, or senile plaques, and they develop in the brain inhibiting the neuronal-receptors. As this plaque spreads it causes a loss of neurons and synapses in the cerebral cortex."

Arthur Wishwood's eyes idly followed the wall decorations around the room, oblivious to the ongoing conversation. Dr. Ranjit reached into the folder and removed a second film, attaching it next to the one already mounted.

"This is from the MRI two weeks ago. As you can see…" He again pointed to the white areas in the cross-section. "…they have spread substantially, mostly in the three quadrants pertaining to short term and long-term memory. Here…" The doctor pointed out the lower left quadrant. "…it's spreading, just not as quickly. Those are the motor skill centers of the brain. He isn't having trouble with balance, or walking, talking yet is he?"

"No, not really," Neville said with a certain resignation in his voice. His father's cross-section showed a marked increase in areas usurped by the white plaque.

"Unfortunately Mr. Wishwood that will happen soon. I'm sorry to break it to you this way but your father's condition is deteriorating very rapidly."

Dr. Ranjit moved back to his desk and sat, closing the folder. He too had a dour look on his face and lowering his glasses, began scribbling on his prescription pad.

With a sudden awakening Neville's father spoke. "Is that me?"

Dr. Ranjit looked up and smiled. "Yes Arthur, they're pictures of your brain."

Staring into the light panel, a grin formed. "Looks like my brain needs a shave, eh."

Both men returned a broad smile of agreement.

"Yes, I guess a shave wouldn't hurt at this point." The doctor's eyes refocused on Neville, handing him the prescription. "I'm changing his prescription. Give him this twice a day– once in the morning and once at night."

"What is it?"

"Donepezil. I'm hoping it slows the advance." The doctor looked down at his patient's closed folder. "There is no cure here, Mr. Wishwood. Your father…" His eyes shifted toward the elder Wishwood, rendering his sad responsibility. "…your father will only get worse. His memory will continue to deteriorate and with it, his vocabulary will eventually disappear leaving him unable to speak. His motor functions will decline to the point where even the simplest of tasks will be impossible for him. At that point you'll have to consider putting him in a long-term care facility, I'm afraid."

"How long?"

"It's hard to say—maybe a year, maybe less. The disease is progressing rapidly."

Neville forced back tears. Dr. Ranjit witnessed this scene several times a month and even with the practice he had garnered over the years, each new diagnosis affected him. With as professional a demeanor he could muster, the doctor waited for Neville to compose himself before ending. "I wish I had better news."

Neville stood, reaching out to shake the doctor's hand. "Thank you."

"Are we done now?" Arthur asked, his eyes flicking back and forth between the two men, like a child waiting to be excused from dinner.

"We're done, Dad," Neville smiled as he led his father back out through the office door.

"He's very nice Woody. I like him," his father whispered.

"I know." He cradled an arm around him and ushered his father through the reception area, staring into the unfortunate eyes of the two waiting patients, looking all too much like carbon copies of his father. They were not alone in their predicament.

His job disappointments withered with news of his father's future. Today both men faced an untamable foe, invincible and unrelenting in its aggression. With this final diagnosis, Arthur's premature end was in sight. Neville's thoughts revisited not only his life but also the life of the man who raised him.

Until his move to Solomon, Arthur Wishwood lived his entire life in Bishop's Bay, Maine. Growing up, he witnessed the town's transition from struggling fishing village to a summer mecca for sun-worshipping vacationers. From his father's Main Street hardware store, Arthur watched the rickety town boat docks torn out, the beaches dredged and re-graded with thousands of tons of pristine white sand all to reshape and beautify the coastal boundary of Bishop's Bay.

Summer cottages sprang up along Oceanfront Road and within a few years, the town became the preferred destination for city-dwelling tourists to escape the heat and congestion of everyday life. They came from Portland, and Boston, as far away as New York City all to experience small town relaxation, sun and fun along the quiet coastal beach of Bishop's Bay.

The small hardware store thrived and when Arthur's father died years later, he took possession. It was here, in Bishop's Bay that Arthur raised Neville after his wife's abandonment and years later the place he too left on a whim. After a weeklong visit to Solomon for Neville's wedding, Arthur realized just how much he missed his only child. Once there, he sensed the same small-town atmosphere he always enjoyed in Bishop's Bay. In his late fifties, Arthur sold his business, sold his home, retired from the working life and travelled to Solomon to join Neville and his new wife, Rita. To augment his retirement, Arthur bought a duplex several blocks from his newly married son and in a quirk of fate, Dell, Neville's best friend, moved in to be Arthur's first and only tenant. Neville's father and Dell hit it off famously, sharing the occasional game of chess, the same taste in movies and of course, the same dry sense of humor.

All went well until Neville's separation. Forced to find a place to live, Neville joined his father in his first floor flat. With three bedrooms, it served as an easy transition for the heartbroken Neville. With shared custody of Dewey, the third bedroom worked as his home away from home, and as a huge bonus Dewey grew so much closer to his Puppa Artie and his Unca Dell.

Shortly after moving in, Neville began to notice the ticks in his father's behavior. It was then that Dell offered to care for the slowly deteriorating Arthur Wishwood, quitting his full time bakery job to stay close to Neville's father.

The first six months Arthur struggled mightily with his degeneration, but after, as more and more of his life disintegrated, Arthur quietly accepted what he didn't know or understand of his past. Today, as Neville looked into his father's eyes he saw the shadow of a once vital human being.

It had become both father and son's sad destiny.

After filling the doctor's prescription Neville dropped his father at home. Returning to work, he spent the afternoon wallowing in a somewhat tainted version of life events. From deep within, he was experiencing the loss of a parent again, and the unsettling emptiness of what he could only describe as abandonment. Yet, Neville knew neither his own full history, nor the history of the father he loved. Still, he revisited the past that day confident in its authenticity.

CHAPTER 5

NEVILLE WISHWOOD'S SEEMINGLY ordinary life began with his father Arthur, long before he was born. At the age of twenty-six Neville's father inherited the small hardware business in Bishop's Bay, Maine. The next five years he worked a demanding schedule to make it successful. One of the many town residents he met during this period was a young woman by the name of Angela Burdick. Her natural beauty enamored Arthur and in line with his show of interest, she reciprocated, viewing his inept advances as the shy flattery of a somewhat unpretentious man. At the age of twenty-one, several years younger than the thirty-one-year-old bachelor, Angela had few real suitors through her teen years.

As fate would have it, she found Arthur Wishwood attractive for his sensitive and caring ways– both traits she had seen little of growing up. Buried beneath the hand-me-down clothes and what little make-up she wore, Arthur recognized the radiance of a freshly mined gem— rough, yet truly remarkable.

During the course of a slow-moving courtship, Arthur finally won Angela Burdick's heart, delighting her parents to no end. In Arthur Wishwood, they saw a man of means, a business owner and someone who, unlike them, maintained a responsible position in the community.

They married and one year later, they celebrated the arrival of baby Neville, naming him for Arthur's paternal great-grandfather, Neville Osborn Wishwood. Neville grew up influenced mainly by the women in his life. Angela attended Neville exclusively through his formative years, doting on him as any loving mother would. Arthur left the child rearing to his wife and continued working long hours to expand his new family's hardware business.

As time passed, Angela's once caring ways slipped to indifference. She questioned the staid life provided by Arthur and her constant duty of caring for their budding son, Neville. Disillusioned, Angela Wishwood felt compelled to fill the void and she began spreading her stunted wings. She sought solace in the occasional drink and her drinking worked to augment her limited awareness of a life outside her marriage. That awareness resulted in a new attitude toward her outward appearance. With the addition of finer clothes, makeup Angela transformed her outward façade and others took notice–mostly men. Angela blossomed into a social creature enjoying the attention of men who had once spurned her. Caught up in the excitement of the chase she experienced the exhilaration missing in her youth, this all-too-human primal hunt. Thus began Angela's liaisons outside the marital home.

Her newfound confidence led Angela away from what she so callously called, 'the awkward husband she married young.' It also impaired her abilities as Neville's primary caretaker and on many nights, Neville stayed with his maternal grandparents while his father worked late at the store.

In the years that followed, attractions outside her marriage grew stronger. Her maternal instincts waned as she favored plunking him down in front their thirty-two-inch Zenith color television with a box of Ritz crackers. Neville ate hundreds of boxes of Ritz crackers before ever stepping into grade school.

It was here, before the all-seeing Zenith, Neville learned of life while he continued to whet his appetite on cheese crackers, diet Coke and the occasional peanut butter sandwich. And Angela continued with her many new friends craving the excitement found beyond the walls of what she termed, a love-starved home. Her romantic forays became increasingly more frequent, and with Arthur engaged in the family hardware business, he suspected none of it at first. As for Angela, her issues became manifest in a self-obsessed life style.

Her most heartfelt conversation with her young son began like this; "More Ritz crackers, Neville?"

"Sure mom."

That described the extent of her motherly instincts.

From that point in their marriage, the Wishwoods mutual discontent escalated. With his timid nature, Neville's father tried to guilt his wayward wife into living a homebound life. He reasoned that Angela's complaints, her absences were just the adverse effect of the responsibility heaped upon her as a mother and a wife.

Neville was seven years old the day he last heard his parents argue. The transcript of their final words remained locked in his brain to this day.

That August afternoon Angela Wishwood sat smoking a cigarette on the sofa while Neville, as always, lay hunched on the living room carpet watching television. An amber glass ashtray sat on the gray glass table next to a short glass tumbler half filled with something clear. She liked gin back then for its pure clean look. Later in life, Angela would switch to vodka for the same reason.

Her agitation was evident even to the young Neville. He watched her reflection in the picture tube, crossing and uncrossing her legs, chain smoking Marlboro Lights and mumbling a litany of complaints he failed to comprehend. He saw a reflected high-heeled foot nodding a rhythm, smoke billowing around them both. Butting out her cigarette, she switched to the other leg over leg position and her other foot began the same rhythmic nodding in reverse, except on this side she tapped an annoying beat along the edge of the family's wooden coffee table. This went on for more than an hour. Half-past six, Arthur came in and she stood in confrontation.

"You're late!" she screamed, butting her latest Marlboro Light in her amber ashtray.

Neville saw his father's face, his slumped shoulders, his head sunken in defeat–a whipped puppy. "I have a business to manage, Angie... sometimes it doesn't run like clockwork."

She stomped out of the room toward the bedroom. Arthur,

his pain reflecting back from the television tube, followed. The door slammed behind them. Neville silently looked on wondering.

Neville heard her muffled words cry out, "I can't stay here, not now... I just can't end my days like this! I can't live like this anymore! I want *my* life back Artie, and I want to be able to live it the way I want to live it, especially now."

"Angela, Neville and I... we love you," he pleaded, "Just stay and we'll make it alright. It'll be better, you'll see."

Then silence. Caught in the quiet, Neville turned down the volume on the living room television to hear any new developments. His mind raced with possibilities. Had Dad hit her? Had she collapsed from sheer mental trauma? Could he be strangling Mom? Is this when Dad completely loses it?

After a long respite, he heard his father's gentle sobbing. The door flew open and out marched his defiant mother, a new cigarette burning between her cherry-red lips. With the television sound off and the argument over, silent seconds filled the home. Sitting erect on the living room carpet, Neville stared wide-eyed in her direction, studying the suitcase weighing down her left side. She slowed and looked to the small son she had raised, his face drawn, his hands desperate to find a place to settle. She lowered the case. The tension eased relaxing the furrows along her forehead.

Angela's hand reached out again butting the Marlboro Light in the amber ashtray and with a sudden realization dropped to her knees. Her hand trembled as it reached for Neville's face. Her touch was warm, a sensation foreign to Neville. His sullen eyes cocked up, he reached out for her and they embraced with an innocence only children can have and give. Neville held his mother for what seemed an eternity and when she pulled away, one single tear fell on Neville's shoulder. It disappeared into the cotton white of his shirt. From the floor, his vacant eyes stared up as she spoke.

"I love you Woody, but it's my time to leave. I hope someday you'll remember me... and forgive me."

With those irrevocable words, Neville's mother stood, wheeled to her suitcase and reclaimed it. She walked toward the door and never looked back.

"Angie... don't go! Not now... not like this, please!" Arthur cried.

She stopped for just a second, never turning. "I have to," she said holding back the emotion. Three quick steps later, she was out the door.

It took Arthur Wishwood several minutes to recover and when he did, he looked Neville's way. He saw a lonely, mistreated young boy and he loved him now more than ever. He joined Neville near the sofa and wrapped an arm around his shoulders. A quiet determination took over.

"We'll be alright Neville. She doesn't know what she's giving up. It's her loss today, not ours."

Yet he cried. They both cried that last day.

As they sat crying Neville wanted to ask, *Where is mom going?* But he did not. He didn't ask because somehow he didn't need to ask. He knew. She was never coming back.

As time passed, Neville managed to relegate this terrible hurt into remission, like a cancer; and just like a cancer, he cut away the part of his heart as it pertained to his mother.

Devastated by abandonment, a gaping hole formed in his life.

Since then there were times a young Neville cried for his mother: where did she go and why? Resolute, Arthur Wishwood never cried again, not after that last day. And he never explained why she left, not to Neville, not anyone. Neville tried on many occasions to ask but he always failed. He feared hurting the father who had stuck by him, raised him and loved him. He never asked and Arthur Wishwood never said.

This all-penetrating wound caused Neville to turn inward and where women were concerned, he maintained a cautious distance so as not to be blindsided again. It seemed a somewhat natural defense in lieu of what had happened early in life.

Neville turned to the thirty-two-inch Zenith trying ever so hard to lose himself inside the plots and premises that aired daily on prime and not-so-prime time TV. His head filled with serial nonsense and his direction seemed set toward a nonsensical life, a life of scripts and

stories; of good turns and fairy-tale endings; a life of wishes and wants—
a writer's life.

Given the circumstances of his parents marital dissolution and
unable to fathom the adult questions at play, Neville's mother morphed
into the villain in his life burdening him with new fears, new questions.
He saw her desertion as a personal rejection and a chase of some per-
verted model of happiness. Or so Neville believed.

To help fill the void, Arthur started Neville in a sport both would
come to love—hockey. That fall Arthur enrolled his son and at seven-
years-old, Neville began playing hockey, the sport that would lead to
a lifelong source of pleasure. It all began in Rainard, a town thirty-
five miles west of Bishop's Bay and the closest ice rink near their small
community.

Neville never came to be the most talented yet he competed with
the utmost enthusiasm. Through the winter weekends, Arthur watched
his son's continued improvement from the cold stands. The sport
bonded the two in a way that was missing before Angela abandoned
them.

This began Neville's self-styled amnesia, and in it, his mother
disappeared.

CHAPTER 6

RITA'S RED SUV pulled into the driveway of the Wishwood duplex. With an insistent hand motion, Rita directed her son, Dewey as she bounced out from behind the driver's door. Petite and well-tailored, she appeared the picture of style and substance. Her red hair swept down from beneath a floppy grey wool beret, her eyes blue and bright, yet her usually soft face held a stern look about it. Dewey slipped out from the passenger side trailing his mother and dragging a rucksack bursting its seams. He was bundled in an oversized red parka, his head topped with a colorful woven cap dangling tendrils of braided wool. From the cap's front, wisps of blond hair protruded.

Stopping near the porch, Rita showed little patience for Dewey, checking her watch as he trailed up behind her. It was her day off, which was today's problem. She was different from Neville in the way she considered all events. Neville, although a dreamer at heart, was more pragmatic, while Rita lived in a scripted world yielding faithfully to lists, to schedules and routines established to barter time and develop a healthy discipline– or so she believed. She idealized the very nature of living and interpreted issues of importance only as black and white. Life could never be grey or ambiguous in Rita's world so her days off were sacred, intimate time for Dewey– personal time for family.

Today she had rescheduled two patients for evening appointments because of a backlog created by her denturist. Their teeth-making machine had broken down (or some lame excuse along those lines) and she was now three days behind. Because of the delay, she reallocated two of her evening appointments to her first day off that weekend. She was not very happy with the imposition.

A restless Rita waited while Dewey climbed the three steps. She quickly followed in behind. Dell swung the door open before she could ring the bell. Standing in his socks, wearing a red polo shirt and black pants he started to sway, strumming his air-guitar, singing,

"Lovely Rita, meter maid

Nothing can come between us,

When it gets dark I tow your heart awayyyy..."

Dell stopped, stood erect, peered down at Dewey and his eyes lit up. "Hey champ what's up? Here with the good guys tonight are we?"

As he bent down to give Dewey a hug, he glanced back up at a silent Rita, "Just kiddin' Rita–we still love you."

"Better not say anything, Unca Dell. Mom's got a mood," he said dropping the sack. He slipped by Dell into the foyer and bent down to remove his boots.

With an unnatural scowl, Rita stared back. "Not today Dell–Dewey's not far off." Rita wheeled the rucksack past Dell as he watched. She *was* indeed in a foul mood.

"I'll pick Dewey up tomorrow after school," she barked, retreating from the porch. Walking away, Dell called, "So, does that mean you're not stayin' for dinner?"

Dell's comment swelled the veins along Rita's temples, compelling her to admonish this insolent friend of Neville's. As she readied for an attack, in those a few short seconds, she cooled. In her walk back to the car, she remembered Dell as the friend he had always been. She remembered how much Dell loved her son, Dewey and how close they had become; how her marriage to Neville had bonded the three in an inexplicable way and since Dewey's birth, their kinship had only grown– even in divorce.

She remembered the day Dewey was born and Neville's first call– to Dell. She remembered their first visitor at the hospital that joyous day. It was Dell. Realizing the abrupt manner she had treated Dell, before reaching the car she stopped dead in her tracks. Her internal review had taken only seconds and in it, she understood her misplaced wrath and felt ashamed. Dell was not the enemy and never was.

Rita stood stuck now, her head low, chin against her chest as she composed herself. She needed to right the wrong. Whirling around, she retraced her steps to the Wishwood front door and rang the bell. Dell appeared and from behind, Dewey's fresh face poked out. "You've reconsidered dinner?" he asked.

She took only seconds and with an awkward grin said, "No, but I..." she hesitated, "I apologize for being so snarky. It's been a screwed up day and I'm running late. Sorry."

"I get it. Don't worry... no offence taken. We're having pizza though, and you're welcome to it."

"Some other time, Dell."

Dewey moved in next to his Uncle Dell and as his mother retreated to the car, he called out, "See yah tomorrow, Mom." Dell's hand settled on his shoulder.

Rita stopped on the snow-covered walk. "How's Artie doing Dell?" She had grown close to Arthur Wishwood over the years, seeing homespun qualities in him lacking in her own father.

Dell stepped onto the porch, closed the glass door, shielding Dewey from Artie's newest forecast. "Not very good..." Dell's eyes shifted sideways. "It's only a matter of time now."

Rita paused. She knew the situation. "I'm so sorry. Tell Woody to call me." She waved and soon was off.

Dell led Dewey into the kitchen. "How'd you like some hot chocolate?"

"Yeah."

Dell was heating the water and readying a packet of the hot chocolate mix when Dewey asked, "Why do you sing that song every time Mom drops me off, Unca Dell?"

"Your father hasn't played the Beatles for you yet? Dewey my boy, *that song* you refer to is by the Beatles–the greatest rock band that ever was. "*Lovely Rita.*" It just works for your mother. It's off their greatest album–*Sergeant Pepper*, and that, my dear boy, is part of any young man's education. Your father has all their albums."

"CDs." Dewey corrected.

"Yes… CDs."

While the water boiled, Dell disappeared into the living room. Within minutes, "*Lovely Rita*" echoed down the hallway. Dell reappeared mouthing the words.

While they listened, Dell poured boiling water into a mug of hot chocolate. "Where's Puppa?" Dewey asked.

"In his room," Dell said, stirring the drink. "Here, try this." He placed the mug on the table near Dewey.

He sipped froth from the edge of the mug and made a sour face. Dewey slid off his chair and with both hands carried the mug across to Dell, placing it onto the counter next to the stove. Staring wide-eyed up at his uncle, he asked, "Can you put an ice cube in it, please?"

Sergeant Pepper played on and while Dell wriggled to the beat, he ruffled Dewey's blond tufts, reached into the freezer and retrieved an ice cube. With delicate precision, he placed the cube in the cup forcing a smile from Dewey. After a short wait, Dewey picked up the mug returned to the table and sat. Satisfied, he swilled back his sweet chocolate drink.

Dell joined his nephew in a mug of hot chocolate and called a local pizzeria for a delivery that night. Finishing his drink, Dewey asked, "Is Puppa okay today?"

Hearing apprehension in his voice, Dell said little to further Dewey's concern for his grandfather. "He's good Dewey, just tired."

Over his short life, Dewey had developed close attachments to both his grandfathers but Neville's Dad remained his favorite, having spent much more time with the elder Wishwood. He had asked his father why Puppa had been acting so oddly these last few months and Neville explained a brief uncomplicated version of his grandfather's medical predicament. After a short silence, Dewey's only response was, *How could we help Puppa through his problem?* Neville was never so proud of his five-year-old son than when he heard that.

Knocking on his grandfather's door, Dewey opened it. He spied Arthur piling his pillows on top of blankets and bed sheets, forming a fabric tower on the night table. Arthur had removed the lamp and positioned it on the windowsill.

"Hi, Puppa. What you doin'?"

Arthur whirled. Startled, the sight of his grandson settled him. He waved him in and whispered, "I'm building something here, come on in Dewey-boy."

Dewey looked perturbed. "Is it a tower, Puppa?"

Pulling away from his manic undertaking, he hesitated unsure of the question. In a sudden swing Arthur answered, "Yes…yes, a tower it is. Wanna help?"

Dewey edged further into the bedroom. "Sure."

"Hand me that cushion on the chair."

Dewey retrieved the cushion near the bureau and handed it off to his grandfather. The phone rang from the living room. The familiar sound stopped Arthur's progress for the moment.

Dell was quick to answer. "Dell's sausage emporium."

"How's everything? Dewey there?" Neville asked.

"Good, he's in with Artie right now."

"Put him on for a second."

Dell called Dewey to the phone.

"Hello," Dewey said.

"Hi sport, how's it going?"

Sergeant Pepper continued to play, "*When I'm Sixty-Four*", while Dell stood listening, suspicious of Arthur's ongoing antics. From down the hall he heard a loud thud.

"Good. Puppa's building a tower, and I just had some hot chocolate."

"A tower, eh, and hot chocolate– sounds exciting."

"Pizza's coming too. Unca Dell already ordered it."

"I'll have some when I get home, but I'll be a little late okay."

"Sure."

"Okay, I love you. Put Uncle Dell back on."

"Love you, too. Here's Unca Dell." Dewey handed Dell the phone and made his way back to his grandfather's room.

"I'll be a little late, Dell. I'm going to the hospital after work."

"To see… what's his name?"

"That's it, what's his name," Neville said.

"And maybe what's her name too? Audrey, that's it–the beguiling Audrey." Dell's smile was hard to contain and even Neville could sense it across miles of phone lines.

"Yes, and probably the lovely Audrey, Dell," Neville answered.

"There'll be pizza when you get home. And Woody–good luck."

Dell hung up and retraced his steps back to the thud. Dewey was helping his grandfather up off the floor after he had slipped from his nightstand tower. Inside Arthur's murky thoughts, mounting the bed linens made perfect sense, gaining him an advantage in a good and important way. But then again, who truly knew what motivation sent him to the top. To Arthur Wishwood, it could have been the Everest of towers, an everlasting pinnacle of achievement.

Dell shepherded both into the kitchen to wait for their pizza. Above the playful banter of all three, Ringo's soulful voice sang, *I'll get by with a little help from my friends,* from Sergeant Pepper.

The pizza arrived and Dell unboxed it, handing out slices on paper plates and filling paper cups with Diet Pepsi, ever aware of the work of washing dishes. As they ate, Dewey watched his grandfather's wily smile, measuring his Puppa's playfulness as he chewed. Dell ate staring at the bill. Arthur watched Dewey watch him and with his cheeks choked with pizza, he opened his mouth displaying the soggy mix. Dewey giggled.

Dell looked up and saw the ugly jumble. In a semi-serious voice called across the table, "Hey, Artie!" waggling a finger in mock admonition. Arthur abruptly closed his mouth, frowned and quickly finished chewing his food looking away from both Dewey and Dell. While Dewey chuckled at his grandfather's antics, a wide, almost proud grin stretched across Dell's face.

"Mom would be mad at me if I did that," Dewey confessed.

"And rightfully so, Dews. It's one of those things you don't do at the dinner table," Dell said, an important tone attached to his words. Within seconds of issuing his affirmation of Rita's dinner protocol, Dell took a gulp of pop, a hefty bite of pizza and with both his charges looking warily his way he opened his mouth and showed his chewed food. Squirming in their chairs, they laughed and giggled, chomping their food openly, offering up the meal for all three to see. After several rounds, Dell sat back and let out a loud burp.

"And don't do that either," he announced with conviction.

Nearing the end of dinner all three laughed and chirped as the thundering piano that begins, "*A Day in The Life*", played.

Neville slipped into room 221 to the low beeping sounds of monitors. Audrey stood padding a cloth across the younger man's forehead. With his bandages from the prior day absent, his thinning brown hair lay matted against his scalp.

Audrey heard the door creak and swiveled around. A smile set off her perfect teeth, brilliant in the room's fluorescent lighting. As she shifted sideways, the matching pastel pants and pink flowered tunic she wore hugged her slim hips, lending a soft feline charm.

"Mr. Wishwood, I'm surprised."

"Woody... and why would you be surprised?" he asked, impressed that this attractive young nurse had remembered his name.

She placed the cloth on the nightstand. "Well, to be honest I thought yesterday's visit was merely obligatory on your part, and people do have busy lives. I just didn't expect a return visit, that's all."

Neville crept closer to the bed, and Audrey. "Busy lives yes, but I *am* interested. How's he doing?"

She turned back to the man lying unconscious on the bed. "Better. Much better. His lower leg is getting blood flow and the brain scan this morning said there was increased activity."

"And you? How are you doing with all of this?"

"It's my job–Woody..." and she emphasized his name, "...but then again, he looks so innocent, so helpless laying here. It's hard not to feel sad for him."

From the next bed, Mr. Eleazar's breathing became louder, shorter, as he huffed and wheezed from a deep sleep. Suddenly the monitors beeped and buzzed. As Neville watched, Audrey walked around the beds and shut down the alarms. His huffing escalated while she stared woefully at her patient, making no move to help.

"Is he okay?" Neville asked.

Audrey looked toward Neville, sadness in her eyes, "No, but he's DNR."

"DNR... what's DNR?"

"Do Not Resuscitate."

Her eyes switched back to Mr. Eleazar. Neville stood back from the bed, his eyes searching for somewhere to go. They rested on the young man and he watched his victim's eyes flutter wildly beneath closed lids. He wanted to alert Audrey, yet she seemed occupied. In those few seconds Mr. Eleazar took a heaping deep breath, his eyes opened revealing glazed grey orbs. Staring steadily skyward, his lips slowly parted and in one gruff perfectly pronounced word he groaned, "Hello."

Before Neville or Audrey could respond, the young amnesiac stirred, his eyes popped open and he announced his own perfect reply, "Hello!"

Both sets of eyes shifted to the waking man while in the next bed Mr. Eleazar sighed with a long wheeze and passed on. His time was over. Audrey slid her hand over Mr. Eleazar's weathered face closing his grey eyes. She pulled a stethoscope from a side pocket and checked for life– he was gone. One man had died and one had returned, all in a matter of seconds.

"I'll be right back," she said, slipping quietly from the room.

The newly wakened young man scanned the small room ending at his lone visitor.

"How you feeling?" Neville asked.

Unsure, a smile appeared on his lips. "Okay... but where am I?"

"Our Lady of Mercies Hospital... you've been unconscious for two days."

His eyes circled the room and noticed Mr. Eleazar in the next bed. "And him–what's the matter with him? Is he sick too?"

Neville hesitated. "Not any more. He just passed away. That's why the nurse left, to get help."

Staring compassionately toward Mr. Eleazar, the younger man followed, "I'm sorry." He looked back to Neville. "Did you know him well?"

"Not at all. I was here visiting you."

He returned a cautious look. "Do I know you?"

"No… I'm the driver that hit you–that's why you're in here. You stepped in front of my car the other day. My name's Neville–Neville Wishwood."

With a bright smile, he raised his hand to shake. "Hello Neville, I'm…" He stopped in mid-sentence contorting his face. "I'm…" Stalled again, he stared off toward the door. "Who *am* I?" he asked exasperated.

"We don't know. You didn't have any identification on you. Maybe you just need a little time," Neville said.

"Maybe… well it's still nice to meet you Mr. Wishwood, whoever I am."

Creeping closer to the bed, Neville shook his hand. "So, can you remember anything? Where you live, where you work–what you do?"

The young man readjusted his legs on the bed and seemed to concentrate on what Neville had just asked. After several seconds, his head swiveled sideways. "I can't remember anything about me, my life or anyone in it. Isn't that funny?"

The hospital room door swung open and in whisked a white coated doctor, a man in his early forties. He stopped suddenly, staring toward the newly awakened patient.

"You're awake. How long have you been up?" he asked as he made his way to Mr. Eleazar. His white coat offset what appeared to be a deep tan as if he had just stepped from the golf course. He looked toward the younger man while plugging a stethoscope into his ears. He listened to Mr. Eleazar's chest for a minute or so and removed his ear-plugs, stuffing the silver scope back into the coat's top pocket.

As the young amnesiac answered, "Couple minutes I guess," the doctor checked his watch and wrote down the time on the old man's chart. Neville nodded agreement.

"He was a trooper… let's hope he didn't suffer," the doctor said, returning his attention to Neville and his newly awakened patient. He shifted toward the re-animated man and Neville stepped behind him, watching over his shoulder. "I'm Dr. Nichols, and you're..." he asked moving closer, lifting his patient's eyelids one at a time and inspecting his pupils.

"I'm... not sure."

"Not sure, or don't know?" Dr. Nichols asked.

"Don't know," he said unsettled.

The doctor turned, looking at Neville. "Do you know him?"

"No doctor. I... I'm the guy who hit him–with my car."

"I see," he said in a way all doctors do.

Dr. Nichols took out his pen and held it upright two feet from his patient's eyes. "Focus both eyes on the pen and follow it as I move it back and forth."

He slowly shifted the pen side to side and surveyed the young man's reaction.

"Good," he finally said and reached to the foot of the bed retrieving the chart hanging from the bed frame. He wrote a few words and replaced the chart.

"Your head, how's it feel?" he asked.

"A little sore... at the back."

"What about your leg?"

The man smiled, lifted his sheet and saw the grey plastic cast. "Seems okay," he said as he swiveled the leg side to side.

"Great. Let's do a word association."

"Okay," he said energized. Neville watched and listened.

"White," the doctor started.

"Black..." he fired back answering as if playing Password.

"Man."

"Woman..."

"Left."

"Right..."

"What about... live," Dr. Nichols asked.

"What about... die. Is that good?" He asked with guileless skepticism.

The doctor returned a satisfied grin. "That works fine, Mr... Mr. Doe I guess. We'll do a few more tests another scan but I think your memory issues are only temporary. You have cognitive responses to all the words, your eyes seem clear. My guess is your memory will return over the next few weeks, probably little by little. I'll see you tomorrow."

"Thank you, Dr. Nichols," the amnesiac said.

The doctor walked past Neville, gave a nod, which Neville returned, and left.

Neville moved back to the side. "Well that seems hopeful."

"It does Mr. Wishwood."

"Call me Woody, please." Neville paused, staring down a little bewildered. "You don't seem too upset about this amnesia thing."

A foppish smile formed on his face. "I guess I just trust what the doctor said. It must be my nature, whoever I am." With a sudden look up he asked, "Say, is there any water in here?"

Looking around the room, Neville felt a surge of new guilt for the man's condition. In walked Audrey, a Styrofoam cup full of ice water in her hand. She placed it on the tray by the young man's bed. "I thought you might be a little thirsty."

"Thank you." He gulped back half the cup. The timing seemed flawless, a mating of wants perfectly met. She circled round the two men back to Mr. Eleazar's bed and pulled the sheet over his head, tucking it in along the edges of his frail body.

"Poor thing," she said looking down patting his chest lightly.

"Yes..." Neville lamented. He turned his attention back to the amnesiac still stymied by his sense of familiarity. "...and you're awake, your leg is improving... maybe I should go–let you rest."

"Will you visit again, Woody?" the man asked, near pleading. But it was Audrey's eyes Neville caught sight of as she made her way back around. Those charismatic ghost eyes showed interest and her pouting smile projected an irresistible lure, tempting him to interpret her wants–or were they his? Riddled with guilt and a haunting desire, Neville made a fateful decision. "I'll see you tomorrow."

Both patient and nurse appeared reassured by his decision. On a cold, crisp winter night, Neville made his way home. The day's flurries left the town layered in a film of white and with traffic light; the streets of Solomon seemed dreamlike, cast in an incorruptible pallor. His head filled with the day's events: the news of a possible promotion, his father's prognosis, the visit to the hospital and the accident victim's unexpected awakening. And of course, Audrey, this alluring beauty Audrey.

He thought of the man, doe-eyed and simple lying helpless in a hospital bed, alone, without family, friends, absent of any living experience to draw on for survival. In his predicament, he saw the parallels to his father and in them felt the same sadness. Yet it remained a strange introduction; the final moments of one man quickly transferring into the beginnings of another—one's last word, the others first. The improbabilities resonated within.

Neville opened his front door and met his excited son as he raced from the kitchen. Dell's musical education continued with the Beatles *White* album. The sounds of "*Ob-La-Di, Ob-La-Da*", echoed in from the living room.

"Dad, come on," Dewey said grabbing a hand, leading him back to the kitchen.

"Whoa, whoa—how's my guy?" he said trying to slow him.

"Good, but Puppa and Unca Dell are showing me how to play jen rummy," he said, dragging his father around the corner into the kitchen. At the table, Dell sat grim faced and intense across from Arthur who appeared quite content, smiling and humming the song to himself. Neville lifted Dewey up into the chair next to Arthur.

"Gin, Dewey, it's called *gin* rummy," he said removing his coat.

Without looking up, Dell announced, "Pizza's in the fridge." There was a cold edge to his words as Neville noticed his father's red peg outdistancing Dell's blue one on the board.

"Hello Woody," Arthur greeted, looking up.

Dewey wriggled in his seat and ended up on his knees pointing to a card in his grandfather's hand. "What about that one?"

Arthur considered his grandson's selection. "Maybe, but we'll play this one for now," he said, laying the six-of-clubs on the discard pile. Dell's eyes shifted first to the six, then back to Arthur. Dewey watched the game in quiet anticipation.

They finished the round, counted points and Dell moved a few notches closer. While Arthur shuffled, Neville ate. With Dewey hanging over the playing table, Dell asked, "Well how's your newest friend?"

Between chews, Neville answered. "He woke up tonight, unfortunately right after his roommate passed away. It was weird–the old man, Mr. Eleazar said one word, *hello*, and died. At that moment, this young guy's eyes popped open and repeated the old man's hello."

"Well, who is he?" Dell asked, waiting for cards. Arthur fumbled the deck and Dewey helped him reassemble the cards.

"He doesn't know. It seems he has temporary amnesia–at least that's what the doctor thinks. And I keep getting this sense I've seen him before."

"I've never met anyone with amnesia," Dell said.

"What's amnesia?" Dewey asked as his grandfather dealt the cards.

Shifting, Neville put an arm around his son. "It's when someone forgets who they are, where they come from–that sort of thing."

As both men checked their cards, Dewey interpreted. "Like Puppa then, like Alzheizer's."

"Something like that," Neville said squeezing Dewey's shoulder.

"Poor man."

"You goin' back Woody?" Dell asked concentrating on the game.

"Tomorrow… why?" Neville asked puzzled by his friend's interest. But then again who fully understood Dell's interests.

"I wanna go–meet this amnesia guy and see for myself."

"See what?"

"Your victim whoever he is and of course you know who," Dell said, now looking up from his cards crafting an odd smile.

"You know who–who's that?" Arthur asked without raising his eyes from his cards, understanding nothing of their conversation.

"A woman dad, just a woman."

As they sat in the kitchen, Neville juggled this mystery man, Nurse Audrey and his sudden attraction to her, and his father's deteriorating mental condition. Although seemingly content, Arthur remained lost in his own world, a world where only the cards made sense. These conversations around him seemed only a buzz in his ear, causing even less impact than the song playing in the background: "*While My Guitar Gently Weeps.*"

He too, had long been a Beatles fan.

—*Twenty-two, twenty-one, twenty: The clock's second hand sweeps back and in hurried stiff steps, Rita marches rearward toward the door. A slam sounds; the door abruptly opens.*

Time now rewinds in quick cadence. Ground snow shoots upward like white tracers re-seeding an unsettled sky. Clouds shift revealing one glimmering white star.

Rita sits shivering inside an idling car, inhaling sobs as time continues to spin back. Holding the knit cap close to her cheek, Rita's words yammer back, ".daed eb t'nac eh… on, on, doG raeD"

Her head drops to the steering wheel, weeping and though told to pray she judges it futile. Yet she mutters back the words of the only prayer she knows, "…nevaeh ni tra ohw rehtaf ruO"

Time sweeps back past the cusp of Christmas day and into the approach once more. A long look down the street reveals the car has returned to all that once was. Memories erased, those hard hours previously lived now need retelling. Futures once set find an escape in this uncanny repeal of life; what was is no longer.

CHAPTER 7

ROLAND UNFURLED THE pastel green duvet on his queen-sized bed, swung his legs over the side and pulled on his underwear. A naked Willis Ogland lay splayed across the bed. Willis reached down, retrieved the covers his lover had just removed and recovered his thin porcelain white body. His child-like build sprouted black hair from his flat chest and pubic area. And he wore the blonde wig. Somehow, this dichotomy seemed absurd.

Willis yanked the yellow-green sheet back up to his shoulders. Covered to the neck, Willis exhibited his more feminine side, especially with the blonde wig. His frail talc-white shoulders jutted up above the sheet that now covered his black man-hair. A wisp of a man, he took on an oddly alluring pose staring back at his lover, Roland.

Roland stood taller, just as thin and white but his frame showed more definition, masculine, and while Roland dressed, Willis continued their conversation started minutes before.

"Your dad isn't all that terrible. Look what he's given you."

Rushing to dress Roland snarled. "Given me? What he's given me Willis is ever living contempt. My father has despised what I am for as long as he's known."

"Give him time…you never know," Willis said.

"Time! I'm twenty-nine years old. When's this magical transformation going to happen?"

Roland continued to dress, slipping on light brown slacks and bending to retrieve his shoes. He sat on a blue velvet chaise and tied the laces.

"What about your job? He got you that job."

As he stood to pull on his shirt Roland barked, "The job... it's what I hate most about the arrogant prick. Now I'm stuck there in that land of simpletons, trying to advance beyond their Cretan ideology, and what do I get? Some pinhead editor friend of my father's telling me, 'Wishy does this, Wishy does that' and 'maybe I oughtta cut him some slack'. Wishy's never going to amount to any more than writing obituaries for the Saturday morning edition. Can't they see that? Don't any of these journalistic wizards get it? He's such a putz. But things are about to change, at least for me."

Willis twisted beneath the chartreuse sheets, wrapping himself tight within the linens. An arm slipped out and Willis propped his head on a hand to face Roland. The blond wig swiveled sideways exposing the darker hair below, shifting his appearance into the world of the weirdly absurd.

"What's that mean Roland? You got yourself another job somewhere?" Willis asked, worried. For all of Roland's faults Willis cared deeply for his older, more ambitious lover and was afraid of him abandoning the Sentinel–abandoning him.

A smile crept across Roland's face. "Not to worry, Willis. I'm not leaving you behind. I have plans. Big plans. And they're already in the works."

"Is that why you have to go out tonight?"

"I have to meet someone in Minneapolis. An old friend and yes that's why I'm going out. I'll be late so go to sleep. We'll talk tomorrow," he said fastening his belt. Roland stepped toward the bed, leaned over and cupped Willis Ogland's face in one hand further tipping the blonde wig.

"Night, Roland."

He switched off the light and whispered, "Go to sleep."

Davis Jefferson waited in a booth by the blacked out front window of

The Trillium Bar, a nondescript watering hole near the University of Minnesota Mall campus. It held little appeal among the students yet it remained convenient and private. Black leather booths lined the front window and one wall. The bar's techno musak gave patrons the sensation of riding in a large elevator.

Here for just the second time, Davis anticipated his meeting with the same man.

His name indicated easy first associations. Originally from Atlanta, his parents were old-time southerners, proud of their rebel heritage--thus the name. His father directed the family business: an import-export consortium regaled for fulfilling the voracious wants of the uber-rich. To that end, Davis's father had become quite successful and indeed used his wealth to further his son's ambitions. One of those exorbitant ambitions was to attend Princeton University.

At Princeton, Davis Jefferson met Roland DeWitt. Although they shared a dorm room for two semesters it became apparent the bond between them ended there. Davis never liked Roland, and Roland expressed the same sentiment. Davis struggled with Roland's openly gay lifestyle and Roland resisted Davis's bigoted, narrow-minded vision of life. The best description of it was they tolerated each other. Like being in a bad marriage both knew that eventually, it would end. And it did, with both young men parting on tense terms.

Roland sought out his former residence mate in spite of what he remembered as an impertinent attitude. Roland needed something, something very special--his one-time roommate's well known acuity in computer sciences. The stars had aligned for Davis Jefferson and in the years following graduation he had elevated his unique talents in the computer-programming field into some notoriety.

Davis Jefferson had a checkered past. His resume showed a sparkling working relationship inside both Microsoft and Apple, on separate contracts of course, followed abruptly by a trail of failed business ventures ending just last year with an arrest for illegally embedding a virus into the software programs of retail megastore, Home Depot.

The virus Davis created had attacked the inventory system, skewing the numbers and prices in their centralized accounting software-- a payback for what he had deemed insufficient compensation for a project he had contracted with the retailer. In the aftermath of his ill-conceived vengeance, Davis served six months house arrest, secured an enormous judgment against him for restitution, and shattered his once stellar reputation. Now he needed money, and quickly.

Roland's timely contact was about to make his money problems disappear.

The bar's motif of black and silver trim created a cold ambience. Sipping his beer Davis felt a new chill and in a glance, he saw the door close. Roland DeWitt stood by it shaking off the snow that had started to fall. There was no wave, or reaction from Roland. Instead, he walked with purpose to the black lacquer bar in the corner. The bartender watched the final minutes of a hockey game on a television set above rows of liquor bottles. Four seats down, the bar's only other patron sat swilling a beer. Both men stared when Roland interrupted their evening entertainment to order his drink.

A peeved Davis drummed his fingers along the tabletop, took another swig of beer and watched from the booth while Roland waited, unwinding his red-striped scarf. Once again, Davis felt the slight of a man he neither liked nor wanted an association with—but his priorities dictated otherwise. Finally, Roland made his way toward the booth. He held the drink with both hands sipping it from a small straw as he sauntered over. An irritated Davis called out, "You're late."

Roland returned a grin as he found a seat opposite his former roommate. "Gave you time to have an extra beer didn't it? I've heard you rednecks like your beer."

Davis wanted to say something nasty. Not say something nasty, *do* something nasty but he held his tongue and hands still.

Roland took another measured sip. "Have you got it?"

Davis fired a restless stare across at Roland. His right hand slipped inside a pocket and retrieved a small memory stick and he held it out. Roland reached to take it but Davis closed his fingers around the device, pulling it back below the table's black top.

"Not so fast, *Rolly,*" Davis said with emphasis knowing he hated his abbreviated name.

Roland put down his drink. "Are we going to play games, or get this show on the road?"

Davis Jefferson's eyes never left Roland. Speaking with that same acerbic edge he asked, "What about the split?"

Roland hesitated, his eyes rolled sideways and with fresh charm said, "I was thinking, maybe seventy-thirty... for me."

Davis choked out a short pretentious laugh. "Fifty-fifty... *Rolly*."

Roland's hands flattened against the table and bracing himself, he leaned forward. "Sixty-forty."

Davis repeated, "Fifty-fifty."

Roland's face contorted and in a whiny voice he complained, "It was my inspiration to set this all up Davy-boy, and through *my* work-place to boot. Without me, there wouldn't be a goose to lay this golden egg. Sixty-forty's the best I can do."

Davis took no time at all. "Fifty-fifty." Unmoved by his college colleague, he stood firm on the deal he felt entitled to. He had performed most of the work and his expertise provided the means to extract the money.

Hesitating, Roland offered a wry smile. His fingers spun the drink glass in a slow circle as Davis stared back. A new plan hatched inside his head and in a sudden reversal, he capitulated. "Okay, fifty-fifty. Show me what you've got."

Sitting erect Davis slipped his hand above-board releasing his iron grip on the data storage device. As he did, Roland reached across. Holding the device, he asked, "What's it do?"

Davis leaned in. "It's a Trojan but with one major difference; it's designed to completely destroy itself at a programmed time. I like to call it a Yo-Yo."

"All I want to know is will it transfer the money?"

"It will..." Davis started, "but it all depends on the type of bank accounts your clients use and the software they purchased for accounts payable. They all pay their invoices through on-line bank withdrawal nowadays but there are several factors influencing how. Some of the larger retail outfits, Wal-Mart, Target, use a Sun Microsystems software that handles accounts payable from a dedicated bank account, then integrates payments made through their company software and reports it all back into their mainframe to track and replenish inventory automatically. Their accounts are dedicated, meaning separate from the incoming cash deposits, and they can have a limited amount of cash in them."

Roland seemed surprised his former roommate had such an easy understanding of business protocol and knowing their intended larceny listened intently while he clarified the issues they faced. After all Roland had earned his business degree at Princeton, knew the ins and outs of accounting procedures from a purely business standpoint, but was ignorant in the ways and means of the actual movement of money–especially in the Internet age.

"Some of your smaller, less sophisticated advertising clients will have only one account for both receipt deposits and expense invoicing. Sadly for them my little Yo-Yo here," he pointed to the memory stick in Roland's hand, "will syphon off all that remains of their funds."

"Did you input the numbered account in the Caymans?" Roland asked.

"I did, and remember I have the number too." Davis plucked his i-Phone from a coat pocket and flashed it at Roland. "The transfers from all your client accounts will be registering here. I'll instantly know how much money the Yo-Yo funnels in, so don't even think about cheating me."

Roland's eyes glimmered with news of a money transfer. A beguiling smile forced its way across his pale face. His pencil-thin mustache curled at the corners. Davis remained impassive, unimpressed with Roland's display of approval. After all these years, there was still little trust between the two men.

"So what do I do with it?"

"Tomorrow you plug it into a USB port on the Sentinel's primary. It'll take about five-six minutes to download and while it does, it'll show the title, Account Reports. If anyone asks you've set up a program to retrieve account information for all the Sentinel's customers."

Smiling at last, Davis Jefferson continued his description. "But what it really does is wait. Any accounts settled through internet banking between the time you download it and Christmas Eve my little Yo-Yo will trace, log as destinations and they become the target accounts. Once the link is established, it just waits for other account information from your Sentinel clients and logs them the same way.

"On December twenty-fourth, at 6:01 p.m. it begins to reach out, or 'Yo-Yo' back to all those logged accounts transferring all monies from them into the numbered Cayman account you provided. It should take less than an hour depending on the number of contacts logged, but just in case, I have it timed to implode at 12:01 a.m., Christmas Day. The Sentinel system will crash but should come back on line with a re-boot.

"And remember Rolly," Davis was emphatic here, holding up his i-Phone once again, "all the numbers will automatically transfer here."

The southerner's sharp stare continued while he reached for his beer and downed the last of it. Both men sat on the edge of their opposing black leather seats. Both men saw fortune in each other's eyes. Both men had plans, elaborate plans.

"I'll be in touch," Davis said as he left. He still did not like his former roommate. Actually, he loathed him but he contained his emotion.

And what of the wily Roland DeWitt?

He had given in to Davis Jefferson's demands and felt the sharp pang of his former Princeton schoolmate's contempt, but he too felt obliged to foster this charade and follow Davis's lead, at least for now. The more important fact remained. Their conspiracy was underway and in time, a new strategy would emerge. Of that, he was supremely confident.

Roland sucked back the last of his drink and left the Trillium Bar excited for the beginnings of this new intrigue. He saw it all ultimately leading to a life without need of a contemptuous father, or an indifferent mother. An imagined life, preordained; of leisure, of pleasure and of course, freedom from want.

Roland had become what he despised most in his parents—a self-proclaimed arbiter of life.

CHAPTER 8

UNHAPPY IN WHAT she believed to be a stagnant marriage, Rita searched her soul and found her husband lacking a certain romantic flare she thought vital to lasting love and marriage. All the books said it, the movies professed it: this undeniable attraction between two people, a magnetism of epic proportions cementing the human condition between man and woman. For her, this timeless equation seemed absent.

Renewed by a dream, she clung to a past filled with memories of one such man. Through the idealized prism of yesteryear she grieved a lost love–Jerome Spikowski, her high school boyfriend. The love she lost before Neville and marriage, before Dewey, before life swept her down a road of disillusionment. Young and vulnerable, the relationship ended. Somewhere lost in this dream, her heart yearned to find such a love again, or so she imagined.

Since their divorce, Rita had dated five men (but only one twice) and found nothing equaling those memories of youth. Yet she remained optimistic, almost intuitive of such an encounter and soon. An anticipated weekend blind date with a workplace friend of her brother-in-law Richard gave her hope. Rita truly believed that fate would provide another chance at love, happiness and the ever-elusive elements of what she considered a fully contented life. Rita chased the will o' the wisp.

As she sat on the edge of the bed, the phone rang. "Hello."

"Hi." Neville sat in his father's dimly lit kitchen.

"Hi Woody, I just wanted to know how Artie's doing. Dell said it's not good."

"No," he said, resigned. "The doctor says it's only a matter of time now. A year, maybe less, but there's no doubt he's getting worse, and fast."

Rita stayed silent for a few seconds. "I'm so sorry. Your dad's been like a father to me, and he's so good with Dewey..." Her words stalled.

"I know–he always said he loved you too, Rita. But it's all disappearing. He still recognizes us, but the attachment keeps getting thinner and thinner."

Composing herself, Rita asked, "What about you? How are you handling it?"

"I'm okay. He's going to need my help, and I'll have to be there. And Dell's been great. Through it all, I sometimes think Dad's grown closer to Dell than anybody else. Maybe that's a good thing."

"I don't know–you and Artie always had that special connection. You're his only son, his only child."

"I guess, anyway I know he's safe with Dell. Same as Dewey–Dell loves 'em both."

"Maybe I'll drop by and say hi in the next few days. Is that okay?" Rita asked.

Neville hesitated, finally offering, "Sure, what about this Friday–you can stay for dinner."

An awkward silence followed. Tension filled the empty space. "This Friday's not good, Woody... I have something going on."

Neville knew what the silence meant. Being divorced, Rita kept company with those of her own choosing. Inevitably, her choices no longer included him and that affected his already desolate mood.

At times Neville dwelled there–dark places filled with uncertainty and longing, tormenting himself with thoughts of Rita with other men, other lovers, living another life without him. Intellectually he understood the separation, emotionally it took a toll, but he persevered with his dream of winning her back. He still loved Rita.

Longing hung in the silence. Finally, Rita started. "Woody you know I'll always love you… for Dewey. You know that, it's just–well let's not get into it again."

Neville hesitated, his one hand picking at the cardboard pizza carton. His voice barely above a whisper he said, "I don't want you to love me just for Dewey."

He left the rest unsaid. Tugging at her phone cord Rita answered in the same small voice. "I can't stop feeling the way I do just because you want me to." Her head dropped as she hesitated. "I'm sorry."

"Guess I already knew that Rita… looks like I'll just have to wait for Huey and Louie," Neville said, referring to his joke to name his three sons, if he had three, after Donald Duck's nephews. Neville switched hands with the phone. "Stop by and say 'Hi' anytime. Dad would love to see you."

"I will. Night Woody."

"Goodnight…"

Dejected, Neville walked back to the living room. On his way to bed, he could see light beneath his father's bedroom door. He stopped and knocked–no answer. Waiting only seconds, he opened the door and witnessed his father sitting on the end of his bed rustling through the same small box. His bottom dresser drawer was open.

Arthur looked up at his son, this time unshaken by the interruption. Looking past Neville, he seemed lost in some calculation. Closing the metal case, he announced, "It's eight."

Puzzled, Neville moved in closer. "What's eight Dad?"

Without a word Arthur stood and gently placed the box back into the lower drawer and slid it closed. Quietly he returned to his spot on the bed. All his movements were deliberate, enacted with reverence, mechanical to the point of ritual. Neville sat next to him.

"What's eight?" Neville asked again.

Beaming back a smile he answered, "Cards. It's eight cards now."

"Of course…"

Neville thought of his father's love of gin rummy and felt relieved to understand the reference. "Get to bed. You need to sleep," he said wrapping an arm around his shoulder.

"Okay."

Under Neville's watch, his father slipped under the covers. He turned out the bedroom light and closed the door. Neville returned to the living room and sat. Through the open drapes, a full array of night stars filled the sky. The snow amplified the streetlights setting Neville in a bright half-haze. In some twisted way, he wanted to feel sorry for himself because of Rita or his father but he could not. Not with what he knew—there was just too little time.

He thought of time and the curative effects of its passage. How it made so many things well. How it ebbed and flowed like ocean tides, steady, unrelenting, transforming all landscapes. How it changed one's perspective inside the living process itself.

Wallowing in this reflective state, his mind skipped to Rita, the woman he loved; how he missed her laugh, her gentle touch, a selfless kiss and the sound of her indulgent voice coddling their son, Dewey. What went wrong? Was it the writing and its solitary function that had separated him from his wife? Was he so busy with his own life that he missed all the signs? Did he take Rita for granted and allow his ambitions to reign over his wife, his child?

Disappointment set in and as it did from above, he heard the sounds of Wagner's Ride of The Valkyries beginning. Dell was watching *Apocalypse Now* again, and had the volume up. Dell loved the sounds of Wagner's strains; the simple start, the rising tempo and its eventual heart-thumping crescendo; the wild trip Captain Willard embarks on down the Yangtze River, all to meet and assassinate the enigmatic Colonel Kurtz; the moral implications involved from their divergent points of view. Dell called the Vietnam-era story a mind bender.

Neville sat in the quiet listening to Wagner's overture from above and remembered telling Dell the book Coppola's movie was based on— Joseph Conrad's *Heart Of Darkness* and the metaphor it played on—the searching of one's soul in desperate times. For director, Francis Ford Coppola that desperation manifested in war, the brutality involved, and the choices left to those who waged it. Winning versus the moral imperative involved. Both Coppola and Conrad's versions used the implications to great effect.

Dell saw it more as a play on the absurdity of war, enjoying the surrealistic misadventures of the boat crew as they travelled down river to drop off Captain Willard. Then again, Dell opted to see the world differently, a byproduct of his unconventional upbringing.

Neville smiled to himself as he thought of yet another facet of Dell's personality, that of a collector. He had amassed the most renowned collection of bobble-heads ever seen in the state of Minnesota. Although impressive, how many people collect bobble-heads anyway?

For Dell, it all started innocently enough with two favorites of his early years, the Lone Ranger and Tonto. In his late teens, he found other collectables such as The Bobble-Head Beatles, scooped from a flea market outside the Minneapolis-St. Paul area. From there his interest grew, expanded to fairs, small curio shops and eventually the internet where he found the main characters from the television shows, *Lost in Space*, including a steel grey Robbie the Robot; Detectives Joe Friday and Frank Smith from *Dragnet*; Zorro and Sargent Garcia, and the crew of the Starship Enterprise from the original *Star Trek* series. Even Lucille Ball and Desi Arnaz made his assembly. At a garage sale, he managed to find three bobble-headed Marx brothers, with the Groucho figure hunched in his famous scurrying pose. The Harpo figure's head had locked up, so Dell, equipped with two years of mechanical engineering at the university, cleverly replaced the broken plastic swivel pins with small metal pins. Harpo's head bobbled with ease after the operation. While at times eccentric, he could fix pretty much anything.

The true pinnacle of Dell's collection though, reigned from its perch atop the highest glass tray of his display cabinet: the characters from *The Wizard of Oz*. Sweeping the internet, he had found reproductions from Frank L. Baum's story: Dorothy clutching a wicker basket with a tiny bobble headed Toto inside it, the Tin Man, the Scarecrow, the Cowardly Lion and the Wizard himself. Triumphantly he found the Wicked Witch on E-Bay along with three Munchkin bobble-heads– the Lollipop Kids, and three Flying Monkeys each with different menacing facial expressions. His only omission from his collection remained the ever-elusive Glinda, the Good Witch. This last week,

Dell just missed winning his absent piece losing at auction by twenty dollars.

Dell took remarkable care of well over two-hundred and fifty bobble-heads, ensuring his prized collection stayed clean, wiping down each piece with a mild soap solution at least once a month.

That was Dell, obsessive, possibly compulsive, always interesting.

There were people who questioned Dell's intelligence when confronted with his hobby, but he took little heed of those who doubted him or his ambitions. Dell was inherently secure in himself. Where Dell's self-awareness was rooted remained a mystery to Neville, but he never doubted his friend's authenticity.

Neville met Delbert Willows over a chessboard in the student lounge their first week of classes at the University of Minnesota eleven years ago. During the chance meeting, Dell challenged Neville to a game and to make it interesting suggested putting up five dollars as a wager. Neville agreed and in the first match, Neville lost his bet to Dell in under an hour. They went on to play a second game and Neville lost again. Gloating, Dell asked for a third match and Neville agreed on condition that they raised the stakes to twenty dollars. Dell accepted.

Playing the white pieces Neville moved a pawn out first. Dell smiled and quickly moved his coinciding pawn out two spaces. He was on the attack. Neville countered moving his right side knight into a position to protect his forward pawn. Dell answered shifting a pawn out to protect his own first move. Next Neville slipped a bishop out to join the knight, looking as if to protect it. Dell studied the board and in a fatal misjudgment slipped his queen into the fray to guard his king. The next four moves went quickly, ending with Dell in checkmate after losing his queen. In nine lightning quick moves, the game was over.

Dell's eyebrows arched. "How'd you do that?"

Neville returned his vacant stare with a grin. "I was president of the chess club in high school. You play a good game just too conservative. You have to be willing to sacrifice pieces to gain an advantage. Sorry 'bout that."

Dell reached into his pocket and paid out the twenty. "You

should be sorry... that's chess hustling. I think they break a man's thumbs for that."

Still smiling, Neville took the money. "I think that's pool. They break your thumbs for hustling pool."

"Yeah, like Fast Eddie Felson. What do we do to chess hustlers?" Dell asked half-serious.

Neville laughed. "I've never thought of myself as a hustler, but I guess I did set you up. Didn't mean it that way. Let me buy you a beer and I'll tell you what went wrong."

The two chess wizards wandered off to the university pub. They talked first of chess and moved on to other more personal matters. Neville spoke of leaving Bishop's Bay and moving west to Minnesota. Speaking openly he laid out his life history; his father, still living back in Bishop's Bay and of his mother's flight those many years ago. He was careful to omit the real reason he had come to Minnesota.

Dell told of his Aunt Claire; how he lived with her while attending college. Dell said little of his parents, their whereabouts or his relationship with them. Both were candid to a point, but from there each held onto something personal, something very personal.

From the beginning of that first semester, Dell and Neville quickly established what would become a lifelong friendship. Neville felt at ease with his quirky new friend, finding common ground in their matching unflappable natures.

Dell remained an enigma, in that he cared little for status, or money or any of the ambitions that drove most young men. Women elicited a rather robust response from the dark haired Dell, but again he never seemed preoccupied in chasing their company. What Dell liked most was to laugh, and when involved in leisure activities they mostly entailed a wager, like their chess match.

When Neville seemed stressed by situations, Dell always found the lighter side, paying little attention to consequences. They shared the same love of old movies and TV shows, finding comfort in simpler times, simpler issues.

Over the course of their budding friendship, Dell spoke of his past on occasion, but there were large chunks of his life that he failed to share. It was meeting Dell's Aunt Claire when that all changed.

After classes one early November day, Dell brought Neville home to see his bobble-head collection and meet his Aunt Claire. Dell spoke fondly of his aunt and from the conversations; Neville understood the close bond they had formed. Still there was little talk of his parents. They remained somewhat of a mystery in Dell's life.

They arrived shortly after four o'clock at her Mountjoy Avenue home in Solomon. She was in the kitchen cooking when they came in the front door. Without turning she called, "Dell?" as she poked a fork at something frying in a pan. On the back burner a large pot bubbled.

Neville followed his friend in as he crept up behind his aunt. "What-cha cookin'?"

She turned, wiped her hands on her apron flashed a great smile and gave Dell a hug. Aunt Claire noticed Neville standing near the open kitchen doorway. A short woman, she was dwarfed by her six-foot nephew. Her hair was black, shorn short with the odd streak of grey tinting her temples. She beamed an infectious grin, transforming her small round face and immediately wiped her hands once more and moved to greet him. Her black eyes came alive, seizing Neville's attention.

"And you? Who might you be young man?"

His eyes glanced to Dell for a second. "I'm Neville Mrs. Brimner—a friend of Dell's," he said caught in her fierce but obliging gaze. For a small woman she held your attention. Dell's widowed Aunt Claire lost her husband years ago in a work related accident. Childless, Dell remained the sole beneficiary of her affection.

"It's Woody, Aunt Claire. No one except the professors call him Neville," Dell added.

She reached out clutching Neville's hand and again he hesitated, shifting his eyes briefly to his friend. Feeling a genuine warmth in her grip, captivated by her penetrating black eyes and sensing the enthusiasm beaming from her bright smile he acknowledged his welcome with his own moderated version of a smile.

Still clenching his hand, holding his apprehensive gaze, Aunt

Claire's eyes gleamed to a new intensity. "You're a Pisces, a water sign," she said with excitement.

Surprised, Neville answered. "I guess. I don't really follow astrology."

"When were you born Neville?" she asked drawing him closer.

"March fourteenth... why?"

"Yes Pisces... very strong. Your inner spirit is quite clear for a man so young. Pisces is the most powerful of the water signs. Undeniably, water will rule your life."

Neville tried easing his hand slowly from Aunt Claire's grasp. He stepped back nearly tumbling over an ottoman. Regaining his balance, he eyed Dell's aunt suspiciously. "How... how can you know any of this? About water, my life?" She had hit a nerve.

"She has a gift," Dell said, moving to the stove. As he surveyed the cooking food, Aunt Claire again wiped her hands on the apron.

"I see things in people. It's what I do, what I've always done," she said. She turned back to Dell and pulled him away from the stove. "Don't touch. It's not ready yet."

"Mmnn, spaghetti and meat balls—my favorite," he said fork in hand scooping one from the pan.

Dell's aunt pushed him toward the dining room. "Go sit. Dinner'll be ready in ten minutes. Neville, you're welcome to stay," she said, her black eyes finding his.

"Thank you, Mrs. Brimner."

"None of this Mrs. Brimner. Aunt Claire—you call me Aunt Claire, and I'll call you Woody," she said wagging a finger in his direction.

"This gift," Neville started. "How can you see into people's lives?" Concern resonated in his voice.

Dell sat at the dining room table. Neville joined him, continuing to keep a watchful eye on Aunt Claire. Returning to her stove she followed, "It's something I was born with. My mother thought Belinda, Dell's mother had it, but she was mistaken. I inherited our mother's gift."

Unaware of their ongoing conversation, Dell reached into the wicker basket on the table, took a piece of bread and buttered it. Neville seemed intrigued by Aunt Claire's gift. "So you can see people's future just by touching them?" he asked.

"Sometimes... sometimes I see the past. And sometimes I see nothing at all. Everyone's different, Woody." She turned smiling at both young men, cracked the spaghetti noodles and dropped them into the bubbling pot. From there she scooped the meatballs from the pan and added them to a second pot simmering red sauce.

"It's not always actual events. It can be qualities a person may possess or things that will affect their lives."

She turned toward Neville. Dell continued to chomp on bread as she approached the table. "With you I see water, lots of water. But then you're a Pisces, it all makes sense."

Neville turned away. "Water, huh..."

"Water will change your life," she said again.

Neville did not smile. Instead, his eyes avoided Aunt Claire. *It already has*, he thought.

Aunt Claire returned to the stove, Dell continued to eat bread and Neville sat revisiting his past and the very reasons he came to Solomon. Aunt Claire had seen a side of Neville no one in Solomon could know and water played a huge role.

Ten minutes later Aunt Claire joined the young men, placing a bright blue plastic bowl of salad on the table followed by a larger earthen bowl brimming with fresh steaming pasta and meatballs. After a long day in school, they dug in.

While Dell heaped spaghetti onto his plate Aunt Claire, always direct, a trait her nephew obviously inherited, asked, "Your parents, where are they Woody?"

Neville stopped mid-bite and swallowed. "My father still lives in Bishop's Bay, Maine. He runs a small hardware store there. My mother..."

Here he paused. "I don't know where she is. She left when I was seven," he said, pushing out a smile.

She reached for the bowl and as she did added, "Well that's her loss, Woody."

Neville peered at his host. "Funny you say that. It's what my dad said when she left."

Between chews, Dell injected a comment. "Yeah women... they should round 'em all up and put 'em in pens."

"Dell, what kind of logic is that!" Aunt Claire scolded, though she was clearly amused.

"Not you Aunt Claire. Just the ones under thirty, they're the real troublemakers. And only let 'em out on Saturday nights. You know... so they can go out and play—with us."

Neville laughed. "And how do you expect to keep them alive, penned up and all?"

"Truck in tons of potatoes and Kraft macaroni and cheese. They're women. They'll get by," he quipped, digging back into the spaghetti.

Dell's thoughts on women lightened the mood and as they ate the conversation steered to school, the approaching winter and Aunt Claire's circumstances living in Solomon.

Dell's aunt began clearing the table. "How long have you lived here Aunt Claire?" Neville asked.

"It's been what, twelve years now hasn't it Dell?"

"Twelve years and counting," he said, wiping his mouth with a napkin.

"I moved out here after Ernest died. We're originally from California." She went about cleaning off the dishes and loading them into the dishwasher.

Hesitating, Neville asked, "Ernest... was that your husband Aunt Claire?"

Her fiery onyx eyes ignited as distant memories resurfaced. She closed the dishwasher door. "Yes... a flyer, my Ernest. The best."

"What did he fly?" Neville asked.

"Not that kind of flyer, Woody. Ernest was a trapeze artist, and fifteen years ago there was no better," she said bubbling with new enthusiasm. "Didn't Dell tell you?"

Confused, Neville glanced to his new friend. "Tell me what?"

"He's descended from a long line of circus people. Dell's mother and I, his father, our parents on both sides and our grandparents all come from circus stock, born and bred."

Dell offered a shrug of his shoulders and a lopsided grin. Dell's heritage looked like one aspect of his life he seemed eager to forget. He did not pursue it, not now. Instead, after a prolonged pause Neville offered an impressive note from his own birthright.

"My great-grandfather was the last American casualty of the First World War. I was named after him," he said, a certain pride in his tone. In the century since the episode transpired the story had morphed into a fable of sorts, at least within the family. Very few knew the real story of Neville Osborn Wishwood.

Camped outside a small town in Northern France, Neville namesake Ossie's infantry regiment, the 101st, had hunkered down waiting for orders. The encampment backed onto a densely wooded plot of land and rain had pelted the site incessantly those last days. Burrowed deep into that dark timbered tangle, spirits were at low ebb. Then news of the Armistice came in. That was the beginning of the celebration.

By dinner, most of the men were well past drunk. Ossie forged ahead drinking his share, his brother's share, his sister's share, his mother's share.

He celebrated into the night with six or seven comrades-in-arms. Ossie soon found a need for their makeshift latrine and staggered off behind the canvas structures, past the cook tents away from the bonfires into black night. Little light shone from the free French skies, but he managed to find the latrine, conduct his business and re-emerge. Here his problems began.

In his drunken state he had lost all sense of direction, and instead of turning left, back to the campfires and his fellow drunken soldiers, he turned right. He zigged when he should have zagged. Disoriented, he made his way toward the woods and a large open pit excavated for human waste. Even with empty lime barrels barricading the latrine pit's border–the very lime used to quell the odor–an inebriated Neville Osborn Wishwood managed to stumble blindly to his fateful end. He drowned in a sea of urine and feces. By some quirk of fate, he had bypassed the barrels guarding the trench and ended face first in a lake of excrement.

His commanding officer summarized the incident in his report as Private First Class Neville Wishwood going over the barrels in a fall. Of course, the official announcement mentioned none of the unfortunate circumstances, stating only, "Died by misadventure". Who could argue? Many have said no man should ever witness the making of laws or sausages. Add to that idiom, the vagaries of combat.

Named in honor of this fallen combatant, Neville thought it a noble gesture. Still, it seemed a mercy that his great-grandfather's true exploits remained mired in lore.

Dell pushed back from the table. "That's kind of a sad legacy. Can't say anything that significant happened in our little family. Except maybe when Uncle Hennie lopped off two fingers with a skill saw helpin' dad with the cabin."

"Speaking of the cabin, what about your father's book, and the fire? I'd call that significant," Aunt Claire offered. She jerked to a stop, somehow caught in the middle of a realization. Her eyes shifted, catching Dell's sharp stare. The conversation ground to a halt. Several uncomfortable seconds passed until Dell broke the silence.

"I guess…"

Aunt Claire backtracked. "Maybe not. It really wasn't that big a deal."

Neville was intrigued. "A book? Your father wrote a book? That's what I want to be, a writer."

With Aunt Claire now in the kitchen, removed from the conversation she started, Dell shrugged it off. "Yeah– a How To book. I'll tell you about it sometime," he said with little zeal. It became clear this was not the topic to pursue, at least not today.

After dinner, the two young men disappeared into Dell's bedroom. Dell showed off his bobble-head collection, explaining the parameters for acceptance as a collectable piece. All figures had certain dimensions to adhere to–bobble heads could not be less than four inches in height, and no greater than five and a half. Five inches remained the optimum height and widely considered the most valuable. Neville was surprised to learn that bobble-heads first appeared in the early nineteen-fifties.

Over the next few weeks Neville, Dell and Aunt Claire formed an odd alliance. Neville joined them on numerous occasions for dinner, conversation and old movies on DVD. Neville first watched *Apocalypse Now* with Dell during that time. As the movie's opening scenes played, Dell disappeared into his bedroom. He quickly returned with a Vietnam era helmet atop his head. It set the tone was how he explained it. Aunt Claire nodded, already well acquainted with her nephew's idiosyncrasies. Their friendship grew and Neville continued to learn more about Dell and his aunt. Within weeks, Aunt Claire, considerate of Neville's plight, offered him a place in her home for the remainder of his college stay in Solomon. This money-saving proposition for Neville also provided income for her. Neville's bonus was Aunt Claire turned out to be a wonderful cook.

After the Christmas break, Neville moved into her spare third bedroom, happy to join his friend and his affable aunt. He found Aunt Claire a woman of effortless charm, respectful of both Neville and her nephew Dell, a substitute mother, friend and confidant who easily shared wisdom as well as worry. Seeing the pleasure she gained from doting on them, Neville often thought what a shame Aunt Claire had never had children of her own. Yet she accepted that fate with utmost grace, never complaining. For Neville, it was a time filled with changes—a new town, new friends and a new direction in life. He savored the chance to begin again.

CHAPTER 9

A FTER HIS RELOCATION, Neville continued to learn about Dell, his past and this vague attitude he maintained toward his parents. Yet Neville witnessed Dell's reverent loyalty to Aunt Claire. This contrast in allegiances puzzled Neville. Curious, he waited for the right time. It came one Saturday while Aunt Claire attended an appointment in Minneapolis. Early that afternoon they settled on the sofa to watch a DVD. Dell sat munching microwave popcorn waiting for the opening credits to roll on another favorite movie, *Forbidden Planet*, a fifties Sci/fi classic. The movie starred a young Leslie Nielsen and Anne Francis with Walter Pigeon playing Dr. Morbius. Loosely based on William Shakespeare's play, The Tempest, it had gained cult status.

Somewhat hesitant, Neville started. "About the fire Aunt Claire mentioned... did your parents die in it?"

Dell stopped chewing. "The fire?" Dell peeled strands of black hair behind his ears, gulping back popcorn. "It wasn't like that. The cabin burned down, and at first we thought they were in it, but..."

"But what?"

A spaceship appeared against a star-filled backdrop, *Forbidden Planet's* beginnings. As the ship approached a shadowy planet, Dell began the story of life with his parents, and with Aunt Claire. To this point, Neville had heard only dribs and drabs of Dell's past and most of that was vague at best.

"They built a log cabin north of here, in the woods. Where we lived there was no school so growing up I stayed with Aunt Claire in Solomon during the week. I was here that Friday morning when we got the call. A neighbor called, said my parent's cabin was on fire. I was sixteen."

"If they're not dead, where are they?"

Dell plucked a few popcorn kernels into his mouth as he stared into the television screen.

"They're in Colorado–skiing. They love to ski."

"What about this circus thing?"

Dell picked up the TV remote and clicked pause. The screen froze. "My mother, father and Aunt Claire were all kids of circus performers. Mom and Aunt Claire were the daughters of the circus Ringmaster and a fortuneteller. My father was the son of midway carnies. They were young, in love I guess, and in training to take up circus jobs, like their parents. Mom was my grandmother's apprentice in the fortunetelling gig and dad was a circus rigger, putting up and tearing down the rides, tents. He also ran the Tilt-a-Whirl. As a kid he ran the bottle-game on the midway– said he hated it with a passion."

"The bottle game?"

"Yeah, you know… a table full of empty pop-bottles and you have to throw those small plastic rings and circle the neck of one to win a stuffed bear, or a panda or snake… or whatever they're givin' away. Actually I'm a natural at it– must be heredity. That's why I've got all those stuffed animals in my room. I never lose."

Here Neville gave him a queer look.

"What'd you think I was some kinda retard, collecting stuffed toys?" Dell said, half-laughing.

"No… well, maybe. But what happened with your parents?"

Dell put the popcorn on the coffee table. "Thirty years ago, when the circus was in Oxnard, California, my parents packed up and ran away. They ended up in what they called an open lifestyle commune just outside of Bakersfield. That's where I was born, in Bakersfield, or just outside. Six-seven months later, they left the commune. They always said I'm the reason they left so they could give me a more normal life, a better life than they had."

"So they… *ran away from the circus, and the commune?*" Neville asked.

"Yeah, pretty cliché, huh? But they wanted to leave the circus life far behind and the commune life even farther behind. When dad heard there was work up in Minnesota logging, they packed up and headed here. That's where he got the idea for the log cabin– working as a logger north of here."

"What about Aunt Claire? How'd she end up here?"

"When mom left, Aunt Claire became the new apprentice fortune teller. By all accounts, she was good at it. In time, Aunt Claire married a flyer from the circus. Mom kept in touch, secretly of course, but when Uncle Ernest died, Aunt Claire decided to join them here in Solomon. She wanted out of the circus life so she took Ernest's life insurance money, moved east and bought this house. Now she uses her gift to make a living here."

"Gift? Gift for what? Telling fortunes?"

"Seems so. I mean she can't predict global catastrophes or anything like that, but she has this uncanny insight on people. I can't explain it. She understands things on a different level."

"So they came here and built that log cabin that burned down," Neville said.

"Sort of. It took a while. I was nine years old when they started building it. By then I had been attending school in Solomon for three years. Every Sunday mom would drive me in from our trailer up north and I would stay the week with Aunt Claire for my schooling. And every Friday after school, Aunt Claire would drive me back.

"Most weekends I helped on the cabin. Just holding stuff so dad could nail it down, or getting tools, dragging things here and there, sweeping up. Dad kept a journal while they were building it. I remember seeing him write in it at night. I never understood that part back then. The cabin ended up taking almost three years to build. Up near Shaner's Mountain, but it wasn't really a mountain. Dad called it Willow Hill.

"After finishing the cabin, Mom and Dad took the notes they'd collected and set out a guide to building this log cabin of theirs. They found an agent and sold the book to a small publisher in the Midwest. It sold over fifty-thousand copies within a year. One reviewer called it the *bible* for anyone considering building a cabin on their own. A few years later my parents were staying in Prescott for the night and the cabin caught fire." Dell's head lowered. "Willard died in the fire."

"Willard?"

A solemn pause followed. Dell lifted his head level. "My German Shepherd– he stayed in a pen alongside the cabin." A definite sadness resonated in his voice. Dell had named his dog after the Martin Sheen character in *Apocalypse Now*.

"Funny, most weeks I took Willard with me but that week he stayed at the cabin. The next day I made a decision to stay in Solomon with Aunt Claire. After the fire they moved to Colorado–for the skiing."

Dell picked up the remote and clicked play. The movie restarted. Dell's melancholy quickly passed and within minutes, he returned to usual sarcastic state. On the TV screen both watched a hulking bubble headed, bubble bodied mass of grey steel lumber onto the screen, greeting a young Leslie Nielsen, who played the spaceship's captain.

"Hey there's Robbie-the-Robot. He's the real star here," Dell quipped, spotting the prop robot. In later years the same robot would co-star on television's *Lost in Space*.

Neville sensed there was more to Dell's story than what he told. It seemed less than it should be, unfinished. As he watched his friend reach for the popcorn again, Neville knew there was more. Yet, instead of asking, he settled back to enjoy their afternoon movie. *Time will tell*, he thought and so he waited. Something in Dell's makeup, perhaps his temperament, allowed him to keep the past where it belonged, in the past.

A few weeks later, with Dell working his part time job at the bakery in St. Gabriel's Square, Neville asked Aunt Claire the details. She was hesitant to explain her nephew's state of mind during that difficult period. Her usual buoyant traits transformed and she sat as if overwhelmed by the question. Or was it the answer?

"My sister... God love her and Maurice, Dell's father..." she started, "...they were a pair." Thoughtlessly twisting the dishtowel, she returned to a time when she was much younger and more impressionable. "I so wanted to be like her. I idolized Belinda." Her eyes suddenly found Neville again and she released the towel. "I told you we grew up in the circus, yes?"

"Yes."

From here, Aunt Claire went on to explain much of the same details Dell had shared. Young and in love they left the circus and after Dell was born Maurice read an article about logging in *National Geographic*, purchased a used travel trailer and moved his young family to Minnesota.

Aunt Claire leaned closer and folded her thin arms on the tabletop. "I replaced Belinda at fortune telling. It seems mother was wrong. I was the one who had inherited the gift."

"And the fire?"

"That's later," she said. "Well after Moe worked in a logging camp for years. Moe was always a worker, so he had no trouble getting a job in logging. It's hard work but so is rigging a circus. Moe had his own gifts, being mechanically inclined just like Dell.

"He set up a campsite with the travel trailer wherever they went logging and Belinda scratched out a home for her little family. From her letters they seemed quite content. Moe made good money and because of their lifestyle, they spent little of it to survive. Dell was getting older, and when he turned six years old, Belinda tried her hand at home schooling. That's where I came in. My sister didn't have the patience or the education to school Dell. Ernest had just died, so I decided to join Belinda, Moe and Dell here in Minnesota."

"Your husband, Ernest.... did he die in a fall?" Neville spoke his words with great care.

"It's strange how he died. A virus they said, from the monkeys caravanned next to our trailer. Try as they might, the doctors in Sonoma couldn't solve it. Ernest died less than three weeks later. It was a crazy time, and to add salt to the wound, the monkeys survived. They put them down for safety reasons. God took Ernest well before his time."

Neville stayed quiet for quite some time as Aunt Claire's eyes searched the room for relief. With her husband's life insurance money, Aunt Claire left the circus and joined her sister, Moe and her nephew, Dell in Minnesota.

"So you have a faith in God, Aunt Claire."

"Faith? I guess you can call it that. What I see is someone, some-*thing* far greater than our human intellect. God's as good a name as any." Her gaze returned to Neville as she forced a smile. "What about you Woody? Do you believe in God?"

"Dad never talked about God or religion growing up. Faith-wise we went to an Episcopal church on Christmas, and most Easter Sundays, that's about the extent of my spiritual experience."

"So you don't believe in a God."

Their conversation had spiraled into a philosophical deliberation. No one had ever questioned Neville on his beliefs. Here, in his first year of college, he faced the fact that he held no opinions on either God or religion.

"It's difficult for me to imagine that some unseen, all-knowing force is driving the universe. They say God performs miracles even today, yet no one I've ever known has seen or heard of one."

"That's what faith is, believing in something sight unseen. So you know small miracles happen every day, Woody. To see them all you need do is open your heart." Aunt Claire's words reverberated inside Neville's brain, challenging him to see the world and its people in a unique way; a way of compassion rather than sight. At that time in his life Aunt Claire's spiritual views allowed Neville to comprehend there were options in considering faith a reality.

"So you see your husband's death as the will of God?" Neville asked.

"We all experience the loss of someone or something we love. Look at Dell: he lost the one thing he loved most in that fire– his dog Willard. And you Woody, your mother left you as a child. Acceptance is our only answer. It's difficult at times, but life is difficult. Who truly knows the will of God, but that one tragic event did bring me here, to Solomon, and into Dell's life. For that, I'm grateful."

Aunt Claire's spiritual appraisal resonated with Neville as he recalled his own hardships. As she explained, there were no choices involved, merely an acceptance of the circumstances dealt. The only justice in life was the knowledge that as human beings we all face similar fates. From her heartfelt account, the practicality she expressed in regards to faith, Aunt Claire imparted a consciousness never before present in Neville, giving him reason to question what he once thought unquestionable: that life might involve a much deeper intimate function than just the endurance of time and the all-out struggle to survive.

Wagner's *Ride of the Valkyries* thundered from above returning Neville to the present. In the semi-dark, he pulled himself up from the chair and drew the curtains shut. In total darkness, he thought back to those first months with Dell, with Aunt Claire and the bonds they formed. Certainly, Rita had become the primary female relationship in his life, but Aunt Claire ran a close second. Then there was Sharon Thurber—and others. He had vanquished any memories of his mother long ago. A ghost, long forgotten.

In a sudden shift, his thoughts interchanged to Audrey, the nurse at Our Lady of Mercies, and the possibilities she presented. Attractive, compassionate, she posed a most pleasant distraction against the angst of a crumbled marriage. Could she replace Rita in his heart? Making his way to bed in twilight Neville considered the future, and what was missing. He thought of the past—his father's and his.

CHAPTER 10

ROLAND GRAPPLED WITH sleep, thinking only of his future, lazing on powder white beaches scenically set beneath sun-stoked cloudless skies. A long night behind him, he arrived at work under black skies transitioning to grey. A misty glow rose to the east. It was early at the Sentinel, an hour earlier than his usual arrival.

He clicked on the second floor lights and the room materialized in detail: the stone flecked floor, the steel frame desks and swivel chairs set between barriers of blue; the still dark monitors, wire paper trays, some filled, some not and along the beige walls, framed stories and photos from the people who came before. A hum sounded from the fluorescent lights signaling his solitary presence. He unbuttoned his coat and removed the memory stick Davis had given him the night before. It was time to implement the second phase of his grand scheme.

Suzanne Hutchins' office cubicle sat next to Walter Hendry's enclosure. They were the only two who had office doors in the entire newspaper complex. His door protected the editor's privacy; hers protected the Sentinel's mainframe. She maintained the company records, invoiced all moneys collected and disbursed, and generally support the computer systems with onsite programming. The mainframe connected all the Sentinel's computers in a closed network, governing not only the office units but also the computers running the first floor presses. In addition to her office functions, Suzanne wrote a weekly tech column for the Sentinel, offering advice on new products, technical advances and their use in the computer field. For his interaction with Suzanne, Roland transferred all his advertising invoices to her and she did the actual billing. Here rested the gist of Roland's problem. To work as anticipated, he needed to download Davis Jefferson's Yo-Yo onto the mainframe, but in his last verbal exchange, (or confrontation) with Suzanne Roland called her, *a humorless bitch.*

In a feeble attempt to be funny, Roland made an offhand remark about Suzanne's weight in front of the entire office staff. No shrinking violet, Suzanne told Roland where to go and how to get there. After that incident, neither had attempted reconciliation. Instead, they chose to ignore each other. Roland knew Suzanne took her responsibilities seriously and needing to continue his plot, he opted for stealth that day in place of an apology.

Roland was second gatekeeper of the mainframe so he had access, a precaution if Suzanne were sick or disabled in any way. Inside the office, her computer screen rippled with geometric waves of color. He unlocked the office door and flicked on the light. Roland slid into the swivel chair, too low for his long legs and he popped up the adjuster. He punched the escape key and the desktop flashed on. An access window appeared and he entered the password, Martha Louise, Suzanne's cat's name. Roland had tricked his coworker into divulging it during a drawn out conversation weeks before.

The screen switched to new wallpaper and all their company programs lined up on the left. With the memory stick in his sweaty palm, he slipped it into a USB port on the tower sitting near his knees and waited for a new window to pop into existence. Save or Download. He clicked Download. After a quick glance behind him, he watched the progress bar turn green–fifty-two percent, sixty-eight percent, eighty-one percent, ninety-four percent, one hundred percent. Complete.

"What are you doing, Rolly?" Suzanne's shrill voice sounded, freezing Roland statue-still. His wonky head felt the penetrating gaze of two angry eyes. Discretely he slipped a hand down by the tower and pulled out the memory stick.

He swiveled the chair sideways. Holding a briefcase and bundled in her winter coat, she was unable to see his actions. Suzanne's steely eyes stared unrelenting, perturbed by his invasion of her private domain.

Fingering keys on the keyboard Roland stalled. "What am I doing? Checking an invoice... I wasn't sure if I sent it off or not." A swallow of saliva slipped down his throat, twitching his ruby-red bowtie.

She stepped into the small office, moving closer. The door slammed behind her. "You could have asked." Her eyes accused and she spoke in a formal cadence. Blindly fumbling with the mouse, he managed to close the progress window. Relief set in.

Roland eyes spun up to his co-worker. "Well, I guess I just didn't want to bother you, my dear Suzanne," he said inserting a certain cocky flair.

Suzanne dropped her briefcase, began pulling off her coat and as Roland stood she said, "Next time ask."

Roland slipped past Suzanne toward the door. "I will..." he said smiling, "You'll have to adjust the chair. It was too low." He looked down as she took the seat and readjusted the chair. "Your stubby little legs *are* short, aren't they?"

Suzanne's eyes narrowed as they followed Roland. He slid out the door and back to his own section of office. Unaware of his real motive, Suzanne checked her terminal inspecting not only the screen but also any exterior signs of abuse. In some sordid way, she was hoping to find a reason to rip into her co-worker. Although suspicious, she settled in for the day.

In the next half hour, Hendry arrived, followed closely by John Winterburn, Sam Charters and of course, Neville. Still well before eight o'clock, Walter Hendry's door flew open. He looked left, toward the windows and Roland's prime piece of office space.

"Roland DeWitt... my office," he called. Still in morning hibernation, the remaining staff perked up and watched Roland scurry down the aisle wagging his limber hips while his shoes squeaked out along the polished stone floor. Roland disappeared behind the fogged glass of Hendry's office door. All exchanged a wondering glance as the next few minutes went by.

Hendry's door opened again. Walter reappeared, lines furrowing his sizable brow. "Neville... come in here please." His eyes remained planted on the floor. Neville looked up, confused but respectful and joined Walter, slipping past him into the office. Hendry closed the door.

"It's Wishy's fault," Roland said as the door clicked shut. "I sent him the ads—that's his job... proof-read."

Standing near the door, Neville's wide-eyed stare followed Hendry as he took a seat behind his desk. "What's going on?"

"Sit down Neville," Hendry said.

"He should've found it," Roland injected.

Walter's lips formed a lop-sided swipe across his face. "Roland... be quiet." Hendry pulled his bulk up to the desk's edge. "I got a phone call this morning from Gamble's Appliance. It seems we printed his advertisement yesterday with the wrong sale price in it."

Walter opened a section of yesterday's newspaper. He pointed to the ad in question and the error, now circled in red. Neville turned the page and looked at the advertisement. It read, *Westinghouse Toaster Oven—Sale priced at $9.95.*

"The sale price is supposed to read, $29.95," Hendry explained.

Neville looked up at Roland, standing in a smug cross-legged pose near Hendry's desk and back to Walter. "If it's a mistake, I'm sorry but I'd never know. Roland doesn't send the copy, so I really only check the ads for spelling and format issues."

Hendry's eyes darted to Roland. In a calm clear voice, Roland answered. "I sent him the advertiser's copy."

"You never send the copy Roland. In the year you've been doing the advertisements you've never sent me the copy. No details whatsoever," Neville said. Hendry's eyes followed the conversation.

"I sent you the copy," Roland repeated in a firm denial. His eyes aimed like little black bullets staring unrelenting at a defenseless Neville.

"You didn't, you never do."

"I did, Wishy."

Walter's hands clenched. "Enough! Neville, you go check your e-mail and Roland you sit down and be quiet." Walter reached into his top drawer and pulled out the blue bottle of Bromo-Seltzer. Neville retreated to his desk to bring up the evidence while Walter mixed a cup of relief. Neville whisked by Sam, who watched intently.

"What's up?"

Without looking up, Neville said, "Just Roland being Roland."

He opened his e-mail saw two memos from Roland DeWitt. The first carried the PDF ads Roland always sent. He highlighted Roland's second e-mail from yesterday. Immediately he noticed an icon in the right hand column he failed to recognize the day before— a paperclip. He double clicked the mouse and opened Roland's inter-office communique. Below the subject window were seven attachments. Neville opened the one titled Gamble and a new window appeared. In it, the advertiser's sale price for the toaster oven showed $29.95.

"That son-of-a-bitch, he sent the advertiser's copy," said a stunned Neville.

Sam looked up from his keyboard. "What?"

"Nothing, nothing..." Neville collected himself and made a slow determined walk back into Walter Hendry's office. Roland swiveled in the chair, his chin lifted as if he were about to receive an award and if a smile could spread past the ears, his did.

Defeated, Neville quickly admitted the error and waited. Hendry swallowed back the remains of his bubbling white mix.

"Back to work Roland," Walter barked without looking.

Roland started his rant. "I told you Wishy was..."

Walter's eyes darted across the desk, catching Roland's in mid-sentence. "Roland!" he menaced. Roland took the hint and left without further discussion.

"I'm sorry Walter. I screwed up. Take it out of my pay if you need to," Neville offered, his eyes averting his boss. Neville sat waiting for the lash. Walter had turned away and refilled his glass with plain water. Taking a swallow, he turned back.

Hendry's voice wavered. "Mr. Wishwood, two days running you've sat before me and all to do with your performance here at the Sentinel. There was a time I thought you a bright, efficient young man. Now, if not for the season, I'd let you go. Any more issues and even that won't be enough to save your job. Do you understand?"

Neville's head dropped. "Yes sir."

"Make sure you write up a correction on the Gamble's ad. I want to see it in the next half-hour."

As Neville left, Hendry leaned back and massaged his belly with both hands. He was still the editor of the Sentinel and ready to make the hard decisions.

Alone at his desk, Roland smiled to himself. He had bested his archrival with a simple but effective ploy.

Back home Dell made arrangements with a neighbor to watch over Arthur while he accompanied Neville to the hospital. Anxious to meet the amnesiac, John Doe, who in some strange way reminded his friend of someone and of course, the woman Neville seemed enamored with, Audrey, Dell waited. It offered new intrigue into what he felt had become a rather mundane existence. But that was Dell, always up for something new, exotic, like a mystery man and a seductress. In his state of distraction, he lost another $2.25 to Artie playing gin.

Shortly after five p.m. Neville arrived home. Waiting for him was Dell.

"You remember Russell Wardle, here," Dell said introducing the gawky teenager. Arthur stood behind them watching.

Wiping his shoes on the foyer rug, Neville looked up. "I do. How's your dad doing–haven't seen him in a while."

"He's good, his hair's growing back and he's walking with a cane now Mr. Wishwood." Russell's voice slipped through a range of octaves and coupled with his acne pocked face, showed signs of his changing physiology. Russell's father had undergone brain surgery two months prior, a result of Russell's mother pounding him with a fireplace poker. The rumor floating around the neighborhood alleged the attack was the outcome of a dispute over the TV remote. A court ordered psychiatric report relegated the entire Wardle clan to eating with plastic cutlery in order to keep sharp objects out of the equation. Mrs. Wardle had a temper.

"Good, say hi to him for me. We won't be long–an hour, an hour and half at most," Neville said, avoiding the obvious difficulties the Wardle family faced.

"Okay."

A fixated Arthur walked up to the young man and asked, "Do you know how to play gin rummy?"

They hurried out holding back their laughter. Nearing the corner, Dell started. "I think Artie's a gin savant. There's something strange going on inside that head of his."

Grinning, Neville asked, "How much do you owe him now?"

"Almost five-hundred. He just can't lose. I haven't won a game since that first week, what... two years ago?"

Neville banged the dashboard hoping for heat. "Try another game."

"No way,' Dell argued, his head nodding back and forth. "I'm no quitter, and I do have *some* pride, Woody. My time will come, and when it does I'm going to post it on the calendar in the kitchen in big block letters, *I beat the gin rummy savant, Artie.*"

They arrived at Our Lady of Mercies hospital and made their way to room 221. Dell had waited anxiously to put a face to Neville's victim. Before walking in, Dell grabbed Neville's arm. "Remind to ask this nurse Audrey for a few pairs latex gloves They buy them by the gross here at the hospital."

"For what?'

"To clean my collection of bobble-heads. The soap gives me a rash," Dell said.

They found John Doe alone on the bed eating dinner. He

looked up and quickly swallowed. "Hello Woody," he said, pushing back the rollaway tray.

"We're interrupting…" Woody said. "We'll come back."

"No, no I'm finished. Come in, please. Who's your friend?"

Dell pushed in past Neville, extending a hand. "Dell, the name's Dell– and Woody was right. You do look familiar, very familiar." Dell stared at the bulbous eyed stranger. "You're Barney Fife if I've ever seen him," he offered, stunned by the resemblance.

Neville gave his victim a sideways glance and mused, "There is that likeness there, but… there's something else."

"He's Barney Fife, Woody. Look at him," Dell said again.

"Barney Fife… who's Barney Fife?" the amnesiac asked, giving Dell a queer look.

"He's a character on the Andy Griffith Show," Dell returned.

John Doe looked away for a second and then shifted back to Dell impaled with the same queer look. "Who's Andy Griffith?"

Dell looked to Neville, who shrugged. "Don't you watch TV?" he asked.

The young man hesitated as if analyzing the question. "I don't know."

"Well, in the show Andy Griffith, who's dead now, is really Andy Taylor the sheriff of Mayberry and he has a son named Opie, who's really Ron Howard the director these days. Then there's Aunt Bee, but she's dead. And Barney Fife is Andy Taylor's deputy, but really he's an actor named Don Knotts, who's dead too. So in actuality you look just like Don Knotts."

John Doe stared vacantly toward both men. "And he's dead you say."

Both Neville and Dell nodded. The door flew open and in walked Audrey. Looking up she stopped, surprised to see visitors. Her soft charm warmed the room as she swept by Neville and Dell, moving the food tray to the side.

"Hello Woody." Her eyes sparked with shy approval.

"Dinner was good, Audrey. Thanks," John Doe said.

Dell jabbed his friend with an elbow. Getting the hint, Neville interrupted. "Audrey, this is my friend Dell."

Dell extended his hand. "You're as lovely as my friend Woody said you were, my dear. I'm glad to meet you."

A red hue swept Neville's face, his eyes found the floor but he smiled at Dell's obvious flattery. Audrey, in a more professional approach, grinned obliquely at Dell's rather blunt praise. She quickly changed the subject.

"The neurologist was in this morning and agreed with Dr. Nichols. John Doe's amnesia is likely temporary. Over the course of the next few weeks, he'll probably regain his memory. The surgeon who operated on his leg gave us good news too. The leg is mending at a miraculous rate. Full flood circulation has returned and the repaired ligaments are setting at a fantastic rate. He'll have to wear a brace for a while but other than that, he's good to go."

"The police came in too," the amnesiac added. "Took my picture, but it didn't turn out...said something about bad film in the camera. Anyway they did take my fingerprints."

"They'll let us know if they identify him," Audrey said.

"Isn't that great," Neville said. The news brightened the situation for all except Dell. His expression changed to concern rather than relief. Noticing the grim lines across Dell's forehead, Neville asked, "What?"

"That name, John Doe, it's gotta go. He's not on a mortuary slab; he's a human being... a living breathing human being. John Doe's not right for him at all. He needs a real name, something alive."

Neville turned to his bedridden new friend. "What do *you* think?"

His shoulders shrugged. "I guess it's okay."

"What about Barney?" Neville started.

"That's no good. I never met a Barney I liked, except Barney Fife," Dell said.

"How about Don?"

Dell propped a hand to his chin. "Too plain."

"Ringo?"

Dell eyes narrowed at Neville's suggestion. "Don't be ridiculous."

"Harry?"

'No–no."

Feigning an air of deepest thought, Dell finally raised a finger in triumph. "Let's call him Phil–after the sheriff in your novel Woody."

Neville's face swelled with pride while Audrey approved the choice with a shallow nod.

"How's Phil sound to you?" Neville asked the amnesiac.

"I like it. Phil's a good name, at least until I remember my own," he said pleased by Dell's selection.

"Good, it's settled. Goodbye John Doe, hello Phil," Dell jibed.

Standing side by side near Phil's bed, Audrey's hand brushed against Neville leg–he thought he sensed the press of fingers. A warm adrenalin rush coursed through his veins and with his eyes shifting Audrey's way, she flashed a smile. Her long auburn locks arced along a flawless face, her lips red and moist, poised to speak. Neville felt a readiness long missing.

"I'll be back," she said, slipping toward the door. With Neville distracted, Dell silently signaled him, cupping his hands around his mouth miming, 'Go get her number!'

The hospital room door closed. Decoding Dell's message, Neville sprang into action swinging open the entryway. Once outside the room, he stood alone in an empty hallway. To his right across the aisle a lone nurse input data into a computer terminal at the station desk. Down the aisle to his left, he watched a male orderly cross at the intersection. A low buzz sounded from the overhead lights. Audrey had all but disappeared into the hospital woodwork. After several uncomfortable seconds scanning the halls, Neville returned to the room.

"Did you get it?" Dell asked.

Newly named Phil looked on from his bed. "She *is* very pretty."

Confused, Neville answered, "I can't believe it. She vanished. I went out right after her, but she was… gone."

"Whatda yah mean…gone? She couldn't be," Dell said rushing to the door and slipping outside the room. The same empty halls greeted Neville's friend. He scratched the side of his head and returned.

"That's strange. It's like there's a secret passageway somewhere near the door. I always thought doctors disappeared all too quick when you're lookin' for them." Dell's appraisal put a smile on both Phil and Neville.

"With your injuries healing, you'll be out soon," Neville said.

"I guess. The surgeon said he noticed an old injury from the x-rays… a broken pelvis. Seems I've had an accident in my past."

"And you have no memory of it?"

"None."

"Have you been able to remember anything since you woke up?"

Phil's face flushed with a sense of familiarity. "Last night, actually… I had a dream. In it, I was swimming in a pool with an older woman. A public pool I think."

Phil's dream stirred long forgotten memories for Neville. The public pool in Rainard, Maine popped into his head, learning to swim as a child, and Sharon Thurber the woman who helped teach him the fundamentals so early in life. Years had passed since he had last thought of Sharon and those carefree days spent as a child.

"Did you know the woman in the dream?"

Showing obvious confusion, Phil's lips twisted in a crooked grin, his eyes bulged. Emotions seemed to transfer to his face instantly. What a terrible poker player he would be, Neville reasoned, but an amazing silent film star.

"I couldn't make out her face."

"Aunt Claire always told me dreams can help solve a person's past or reveal their future," Dell added.

"All I know is… I felt happy when I woke up," Phil said.

Phil remained unflappable as he continued to smile throughout the visit, showing remarkable composure given he was alone in the hospital, absent any identification. Without a memory, he lingered in a foreign world, foreboding, yet he displayed resilience, an inner strength. Or did this dilemma simply not register inside his wounded brain?

"So what's next?" Dell asked.

"For me?" Phil's expression showed a complete failure to understand the question.

"Yeah."

"I haven't thought much about it really."

Neville peered across the room beyond the window and in the distance he spied an incredible sight: the statue of a glowing St. Gabriel, wings fully unfurled, flying unbridled in spotlights mounted in the angel's namesake square. Night skies filled with shadows cast from his outstretched wings, projecting a sense of motion from the clouds drifting high above. He had never seen the statue this way.

"Look at that," he whispered, pointing. All eyes shifted to the awe-inspiring night display.

"An angel...is that how they look, Woody?" Phil's voice imbued a sense of wonder.

Neville took a long meditative look at the sculpture. "I guess it's how we see them."

As all three stared in silence, the door opened and in walked Nurse Audrey. She was holding a chart in her hand. With her sudden reappearance, all three men gaped like schoolboys caught smoking in the washroom.

Focused on the paperwork, her demeanor took on a much more serious façade. "You're going to be..." As she spoke, her eyes lifted and by the bed, three befuddled men watched mouths agape. "What's wrong?" she asked.

A silence ensued. Neville broke the impasse. "Where'd you disappear to?"

"Disappear?"

"I followed you out—not two seconds after—and you were gone. Vanished into thin air."

A crooked smile crept across Audrey's supple lips as she clamped both hands across the chart, holding it crossways. "I just went to find this—at the nurse's station." Lifting the paperwork, she showed them the chart. "I must have bent down, behind the desk when you came looking."

Neville thought back. Audrey's simple explanation seemed credible. The longer he stared into her hypnotic grey-green eyes, the easier it became to believe. How could those eyes, that chaste face lie?

Dell intervened. "You were saying?"

Phil's attention reverted to the statue outside his window, the shadows shifting with the clouds. The way it merged with light, a ghostly silhouette levitating above the square as if to say, *'I am here, I have arrived.'* It held him beguiled, this angel of stone.

Audrey's eyes returned to the chart. "Well it's good news and bad news. With Phil improving so rapidly and the hospital over-crowding, they have to release him tomorrow. Right now they're wheeling up a young man from emerg to take Mr. Eleazar's bed."

Preoccupied with the town cenotaph, Phil suddenly realized she was talking about him.

"What?"

"So where's Phil supposed to go?" Neville asked.

"That's the bad news. We've called St. Anne's Mission shelter here in Solomon and with Christmas coming they're full up. We also called three shelters in Minneapolis-St. Paul… the situation's the same. After Christmas they'll all have open beds but until then…" Her voice trailed off. Visibly shaken, Audrey's eyes found the chart. The way she ended, her eyes cast down, her shoulders slack, it was as if *she* needed rescuing not her patient.

The news, although hopeful, stunned Neville. As Audrey's eyes lost their light, Neville felt compelled to resolve the difficulty for her, and for Phil. Wrapping an arm around Dell, he pulled him off to the side for a private conversation. Huddled by the bathroom Neville whispered to his best friend, "What do you think?"

Dell peered back at Phil, at Audrey, set strands of black hair behind his ears, hunched closer and whispered back, "About what?"

Neville's eyes rolled. "About taking Phil in for a few weeks– he's got nowhere to go. I *am* the one who hit him. Dewey could bunk with me for a few weeks and Phil could take his room."

Dell peeked over Neville's shoulder scrutinizing this bulbous eyed, would-be houseguest. Phil had returned to gawking at Solomon's marble-winged monument, somehow blind to the urgency of his own predicament. Audrey interrupted the bedridden young man's steady gaze and in low tones explained the problem.

"I don't know. He looks harmless enough and it would give you an opening with this Audrey now wouldn't it?" Dell said infusing a wicked enthusiasm. Looking past Neville, he studied the amnesiac, amazed at how much he resembled the fictional Barney Fife. Finally, he called over. "Hey Phil, do you play gin?"

Phil's head spun round. "Play what?"

"Gin–do you play gin rummy?"

"What's gin rummy?"

"Seeing you'll be workin' all day, I just wanted to make sure I didn't have another gin rummy prodigy on my hands. Let's take him in," Dell whispered.

Neville gave his friend a pat on the back. He joined Audrey near the bed and announced the verdict: "We'll take him in."

Audrey's eyes welled up, her face beamed and she hurled herself at Neville wrapping both arms around him slapping the chart against his back. Startled, Neville returned the embrace, holding Audrey ever so softly as if she were smoke and gripped too tight would dissipate into thin air. His every pore tingled holding her near, a fantasy alive in his arms; embracing him as a savoir, her protector. His amazing moment lasted only seconds.

"So I'm going to stay with you?" Phil asked.

Dell moved in closer to the bed. "I guess– but we have rules at our house and you're subject to those rules," he announced projecting an air of authority. Neville shuffled away from the bed with Audrey, guiding her with a free arm.

"What kind of rules?"

Dell countered, "Well... rules. Good rules and that's all you need to know right now."

"Okay Mr... I don't know your last name."

"It's Willows. See– there's rule number one. It's Dell, not mister anything. I'm nobody's mister."

"I understand."

Dell's eyes shifted in their sockets searching his thoughts for his next kingly law. "Rule number two: no complaining about the food."

Phil readjusted himself in the bed. "I liked the chicken they had today. Will you be cooking chicken while I'm there?"

"Of course. We love chicken."

With Dell and Phil discussing the menu and the Wishwood house rules, Neville took the opportunity to speak with Audrey alone. His first private words stumbled from his mouth.

"Audrey have you got a phone?" As soon as he said the words, he knew. "Of course you have a phone..."

Audrey mitigated Neville's embarrassment by diverting her gaze. Still, it did put a smile on her striking face. Neville struggled to sustain eye contact. "What I'm trying to say, and not very well... I'm very attracted to you. I was wondering if we could meet for coffee some time... outside the hospital. Maybe get to know each other a bit better."

Neville's heart pumped extra beats as she reached into a pocket of her pink smock, retrieved a pen and wrote ten digits on the bottom of Phil's chart. Taking utmost care, Audrey tore the strip free and handed it to Neville.

"I'd like that Woody," she said and happily turned to rejoin her patient. Holding the paper scrap with both hands, Neville stared at the phone number. He reached back beneath the folds of his grey coat and stowed the number in the most sacred section of his wallet–behind a picture of Dewey.

"Rule number eight, all garbage goes into the trash can under the sink. I don't pick up after anyone."Dell continued to dictate the guidelines Phil would need to adhere to while living in the Wishwood home.

"Sounds like you have a lot of rules in this house of yours." Audrey stood, both arms wrapped around the clipboard as she took in the tail end of Dell's commandments.

Dell brandished a lopsided smile. "Without discipline anarchy reigns and Woody and I are definitely not anarchists."

"I'm glad to hear that." Chuckling, Audrey's once serious disposition had softened to relief and as Neville joined all three bedside, she flashed him a grin. Neville quickly reciprocated.

Neville intervened. "I think that'll be enough rules for now, Dell. You can get Phil up to speed when I get him home."

"Don't forget... there'll be a test later," Dell warned their newest charge.

"What about the camera?" Neville asked.

"I almost forget..." The young nurse stepped in and opened the bedside drawer. She handed the scuffed silver camera to Neville. He studied it this time and with a knowing grin, faced Dell.

"It's an... Acme." Neville spoke the words in disbelief mystified by the maker's name.

"What's that?" Audrey asked.

"The brand– like Cannon, or Sony or Kodak? This one's an Acme," Neville said.

"Acme, like in Wile E. Coyote, Acme?" Dell asked. He knew every contraption, every devious gadget Wile E. Coyote ordered in his hunt to capture the Roadrunner came from the Acme Corporation.

Neville removed the battery cover and slid the batteries out. A crusty white film covered the two 'AAA' power cells. Neville handed the camera to Dell who inspected the silver square.

"Must've gotten wet. It's digital, fairly new..." Dell's face took on a perplexed look. "But Acme? I'd never imagined they even existed, let alone made actual products." Dell continued to scan the small device. "If it's okay with you, Phil, we'll take it home and put in batteries. Maybe there's something you'll remember on it."

"Sure."

Audrey's face froze with a sudden realization. "Clothes– Phil hasn't got any. The paramedics cut away his pants and his other clothes were near rags when he arrived. We threw them out."

Dell and Neville turned their attention to Phil, sizing him up as to what might work.

"How tall are you?" Dell asked.

Confused once more, Phil answered, "I… I don't know."

"Can you stand up?" Neville moved closer to the bed to lend a hand.

"I think so." Phil curled the top cover over and swung his legs to the side of the bed.

"Easy now…" Neville put out an arm for leverage and Phil slid down to the floor. Uneasy at first, he balanced on his good right leg.

"'Bout the same size as Artie, I'd say," Dell said. Phil stood three to four inches shorter than both his new friends.

"Okay that works," Neville said, satisfied. "Dad's clothes may be a bit dated for a guy your age, but they should fit. I'll bring a change of clothes."

"Perfect. They'll be discharging him between ten and eleven tomorrow," Audrey said. "I won't be in until later so I'll leave your name with the head nurse." Her voice signaled an optimism missing earlier in the visit. "I'm glad Phil's settled. Now if you'll excuse me, I have rounds to complete." Audrey made her way to the door. Dell slid the camera into his coat pocket. With one final seductive glance, the nurse offered her last words, "Goodbye Woody."

The door closed with her holding a striking pose, staring Neville's way. Suddenly Dell remembered. "The latex gloves!" With a spastic hop toward the door, Dell caught a leg on the bed rail, spun and accidentally bumped the bed with a hip. Set off kilter, he launched himself into the door face first. He hit with tremendous force.

Phil and Neville watched mesmerized. Mumbling some

fatalistic curse, Dell finally flung open the entryway and bounced into the hall. The door closed behind him. Several seconds passed. The door creaked back open with Dell shuffling in wiping at a small blood trickle from beneath his nose. The overall look, the downcast eyes, his slow deliberate actions betrayed his bewilderment.

"That really hurt! I think my nose is broken." Dell's voice now had a nasal twang. Finally, he looked up. "She just disappeared... fffssttt!"

Phil stared eyes wide. "Fffssttt?"

"Gone."

"There's got to be some sort of rational explanation for it Dell," Neville insisted.

Dell grabbed a Kleenex and wiped the blood below his nose. "Yeah, I'm sure there is... like she's a witch and we're all damned to the seventh circle of hell. A beautiful witch mind you, but a witch just the same."

"Maybe she's a good witch," Phil said.

Neville settled for her phone number. "Maybe... for now we have to go Phil." Neville latched an arm inside his friend's arm and headed for the door. "I'll pick you up tomorrow."

"And don't forget the rules," Dell cautioned.

"I won't, but can you write them down for me Dell?"

As Neville dragged him toward the door, Dell scowled. "Sure you can read?"

Phil thought seriously about the question posed. "I think so."

"Get some sleep," Neville said as they too disappeared from room 221. Neville saw it as simple coincidence that both had missed her leaving the hospital room, but his optimism centered on having her phone number.

Dell's ideas were more involved. In Dell's world, witches were real, along with dragons and dwarfs and demons of every type, including the characters from Star Wars. Dell believed in faraway universes, hidden beneath ink-black seas of time and space cast off from unknown realms only fated eyes could see. Inherently, Dell remained a dreamer.

Arriving home, Neville walked in, greeting the Wardle boy in the kitchen while Dell made straight to the living room. Russell sat across the table from Arthur holding a handful of cards contemplating his next move. The remaining deck sat between the two.

"Who's winning?"

"Not me, Mr. Wishwood. Your father's teaching me how to play gin." Russell's eyes never left his hand. "We're almost done this hand."

"Dad… play fair now."

Arthur smiled crookedly.

Neville left the two to finish the game. After their lively discussion on the trip home Dell quickly retrieved two AAA batteries from the TV remote and inserted them into Phil's Acme camera. It powered up and he found the menu to begin a review of the pictures on the memory card. Neville watched as his friend tinkered.

"There's pictures alright, but they're corrupted. The first two are of the statue in the square." Dell paused as he clicked through more stored images. "Then a picture of a woman and a child… I think it's a little boy and they're walking downtown, but it's hard to tell. The last one's a picture of a woman. It's from the side and she looks older. Still I can't make out any features."

Neville moved in closer. "Scroll them again," he said peering over Dell's shoulder. He watched as the partial pictures blinked by.

"It is hard to make out who they are. The only clear image is the angel statue."

Dell clicked off the Acme Camera. "I'll take out the memory card and let it dry out for a few days. Maybe the pictures'll clear up."

"Good idea, and then we'll show them to Phil–see if he recognizes anyone."

Dell slid the access lid open removed the card and wiped it down. "Yeah, it's still a little damp."

Russell Wardle appeared in the hallway. Behind him, Arthur Wishwood stood grinning.

"I'll be going Mr. Wishwood," Russell squeaked pulling on his boots and coat.

Neville reached for his wallet and took out a twenty-dollar bill. "Here... and thanks Russell"

"Have you got change? I owe your father two-dollars and twenty cents," he said as his eyes darted to the floor. Dell snickered in the background.

Neville's eyes shot to his father standing, innocently watching the proceedings. "Don't worry about the two dollars Russell. I'll take care of it."

"Two twenty," Arthur piped up. As his eyes met his son's he glanced away.

"Thanks Mr. Wishwood."

When Russell was gone, Neville took aim at his father. "You took advantage of that boy."

"He owes me two dollars and twenty cents," Arthur insisted shedding the impish grin.

"He owes you nothing. You're turning into a gin rummy hustler and I don't like it," Neville said wagging a finger.

Arthur looked up. "He still owes me two dollars and twenty cents."

Dell intervened. "I'll put the two-twenty on my tab, Artie. Don't worry." Dell reached beneath his coat and pulled his notepad out. He scribbled an entry and showed the elder Wishwood.

"Okay."

With that, Arthur traipsed off into the living room.

"I can't believe he did that," Neville said.

In a half laugh Dell followed, "Believe Woody, believe. Artie's turnin' into a predator."

Dell zipped his coat and headed for the door. Flashing the peace sign, he took his leave. "See you tomorrow..."

Neville joined his father and found the hockey game for him. The Bruins were playing the Canadiens in Montreal, enough to pacify the elder Wishwood for the remainder of the evening. Neville sat at the desk and tried working on his newest novel while his father stared vacantly into the TV screen.

They both sat preoccupied but for very different reasons.

Neville packed a set of his father's clothes and pair of old shoes in a small gym bag for the following day.

Arthur slept soundly unaware of his slowly collapsing past while Neville struggled to sleep at all. Anticipation resurrected long dormant desires.

CHAPTER 11

RITA CHERISHED HER time away from the dental office. With her office closed on weekends, she added most Thursdays and Fridays as off days. Short one day this week, she was eager to pick Dewey up from school that afternoon.

Rita's twin sister Megan and Megan's husband, Richard arrived after dinner to salvage Rita's laptop from the junk heap. Richard, a computer science graduate and an IT supervisor at the 3M facility in Minneapolis, was uniquely qualified for the rescue. All four sat in the living room while Richard diagnosed the problem. Dewey curled up next to Richard and watched with interest as his uncle fingered the keypad in search of answers.

"It's been so slow," Rita said, sitting on the sofa with Megan. Although twins, they were not identical, but there was no mistaking them as sisters. Rita's hair shimmered strawberry red while Megan's grew to a blonde-gold mix. The same height and slim build, both women matured into natural beauties, inheriting their mother's radiant white skin and arched facial lines.

While Richard's fingers danced along the laptop keys, Dewey stared at the screen shifting from each overlapping page of programming. His eyes ballooned. "You type faster than my dad, Unca Richard."

"I've had more practice, Dewey," Richard said, continuing his focus.

"How's your dad doing, Dewey?" Megan asked.

Distracted, Dewey answered, "Good." He continued to watch the screen change.

"Your friend Derrick called last night. We talked for almost an hour. He seemed very nice, which begs the question, how could he possibly be a friend of Richard's?" Rita asked.

Richard feigned a laugh.

"I've never met Derrick... what's he look like?" Megan asked.

"He said he's dark haired, athletic, about six-one. I'm looking forward to seeing him tomorrow night," Rita said, a flicker of enthusiasm in her voice.

Richard leaned back in the sofa. "That's him, but it wasn't me who convinced Derrick to call, it was Gord Hymes. I just gave him your number."

"Gord Hymes... Gord Hymes. Why's that name ring a bell?" Rita's face twisted in mock anguish.

"Abscessed tooth–I sent him to you last summer. He works in our office. Gord told Derrick you were one good lookin' momma."

"Now I remember. Late forties, bald, bad breath," Rita said.

Dewey looked up from the laptop. "What's a good lookin' momma, mom?"

Rita let out a howl, "Whoa, that's not for you just yet, young man. Now, go brush your teeth and get your pajamas on–it's bedtime soon."

Dewey moaned but lifted up from next to Richard and traipsed off down the hall.

"He's learning too quickly as it is," Rita said.

"They always do. Speaking of hot mommas, I had Maryanne Marlowe ask me about Neville the other day," Megan started. In some sordid way, she looked pleased to bring up the subject of Neville to her sister. Megan worked as manager at a small branch of the Bank of America in Solomon.

"Maryanne, I know her. A teller at your branch, and she's what, eighteen years old?" Rita's voice held a certain twisting tone, amused yet disturbed.

"She's twenty-five, Rita. I think if Neville asked her out she'd jump at the chance." The more pragmatic of the two sisters, Megan always enjoyed Neville's company and his jovial way with people. She never understood Rita's unhappiness in her marriage given Neville's proven character. She saw Neville the way most did: a solid guy, a good father.

"I guess…" Rita's eyes shifted sideways. Instantly, Megan read her sister's discomfort. Being twins, they had shared their life's journey; the umbilical cord, the amniotic fluid, their mother's blood and this lifelong ability to sense each other's innermost feelings; an uncanny state both struggled with over the years. Today Rita felt stripped of her privacy. She stood, slipped by her sister and retreated to the kitchen. Megan followed, leaving Richard alone to work his magic on the laptop.

In the year since their split, Megan had questioned her sister's motives for divorce. Rita never pinpointed a reason other than her feelings had changed. What she once believed was love, was something less than love. Megan suspected Rita's true impetus remained locked in her past.

Reaching the kitchen, Megan confronted her sister. "It's Spikes isn't it?"

A long pause ensued. "No…"

Again, silence.

"Maybe."

"Honey, that's ten years ago. You were young and innocent. It's over accept it. Even if you had the chance, you're both very different people today," Megan said in a gentle voice.

"Alright, so I think of Spikes from time to time. What's wrong with that? What's wrong with wanting a prince? You haven't got a romantic bone in your entire body Megs, that's your problem."

"Rita—"

"It's true, you know it's true. It took me years to understand I didn't love Woody, not that way, and now I'm chasing what I know I can have, what I want and it's because of Spikes— what we once had. I'm not giving up on that, not now."

"Rita, men aren't princes they're just people, like you, me. It's rare enough to find a good man you can get along with and love, let alone this so-called–prince you think is waiting to be unearthed. That's in fairy tales dear."

Rita hesitated. "Well Spikes was my prince once."

Jerome 'Spikes' Spikowski remained the center of Rita's illusory life, and for Rita there were many viable reasons. A handsome, well-proportioned young man, Spikes was the captain of the football team. He led Solomon High School to the state AA championship game. Ten years ago Rita was his girlfriend and proud of it.

They started dating when Rita was sixteen-years-old. One year older, Spikes had already impressed his coaches with a physical prowess well beyond his years. As starting middle linebacker his junior year, he led the state in tackles. Major college programs began visiting Solomon to scout what many called an up and coming Dick Butkas.

Young and in love, Rita continued to date Spikes through their high school years. She was the captain of the football team's girl and he was the lucky guy dating the school's most popular cheerleader, a script from old Hollywood if ever there was one.

Heavily recruited by all the major colleges upon graduation, Spikes chose Michigan. On acceptance, Spikes received four years of free academic schooling and the chance to showcase his prolific defensive skills for a shot at the NFL. His life appeared destined for prime time and her life along with it.

Rita started her senior year of high school missing Spikes terribly. She anxiously awaited his weekend calls. But the distance had grown to be more than geographic. That September, after playing in his first college game as a freshman, he called Rita from a frat party celebrating a Michigan win over Northwestern.

Spikes sat lounging on a leather sofa, drunk and holding an attractive blonde co-ed on his lap as he spoke with Rita. Rita could hear the noise, the excitement all around her boyfriend. While he engaged his first love in conversation, Spikes stared wistfully into the young blonde's eyes, and not wanting to cheat on his high school sweetheart Spikes did the noble thing–he dumped her.

For the next year, Rita remained inconsolable. Megan's guidance and sisterly devotion piloted Rita away from the rocky shoals of unrequited love, but Megan never forgave Spikes for the callous treatment of her sister.

In her first year at the University of Minnesota, Rita met Neville–a man so exactly opposite of Spikes it was frightening. The contrast was too great to miss, at least for Megan, and she worried for her sister. Was he really the man for Rita? Had this relationship with Spikes so devalued her that she opted for exactly opposite of who Spikes was? This serious tangle of emotions happened well before Megan realized the man Neville would become. The more Megan learned of Neville the less she worried. As they grew to be friends, Megan discovered the man Neville was: a kind, gentle, sometimes-awkward sort of person who loved reading, writing, old movies, television reruns and her sister Rita. And when Dewey was born, Megan witnessed the transformation from devoted husband to devoted husband and father. Neville's loving interaction with Dewey removed any doubt of her sister's choice in a husband. Neville had won Megan over long ago and all by being himself.

Today, Megan sensed Rita had returned to a past where she was the captain's girlfriend and the exhilaration created there. She wanted to relive the dream, the fantasy: and if not with Spikes than with a man who elicited that same passion.

Neither Rita nor Megan knew what had become of Spikes. For both women, he remained an enigma yet he had affected each in very different ways.

As a matter of record, Spikes' first year at Michigan ended in spectacular fashion. After playing all eleven games, he placed first on the team in tackles, unheard of for a freshman. Spikes star was definitely on the rise. In the second game of his sophomore year, fate found Spikes and laid waste to his future. Playing Notre Dame and in just the game's third play from scrimmage, Spike's tore the ACL and NCL in his left knee. Medics carted Spikes Spikowski off the field that day. He never played another game.

After several seconds of contemplation, Rita again faced Megan.

She had denied her first love for so long it seemed impossible to verbalize the loss.

"In hindsight, when I met Woody I was angry at Spikes. In a way I still am. He was my first love, my first lover. He'll always be special."

"Special's one thing Rita, I get that. But life changes, he's moved on, you've moved on. This life you think you can have... it's not real, not now, not ever. No matter who you meet– Spikes, Derrick, that other arrogant prick you dated–Sean... it's never going to live up to this, this fiction you've fabricated in your head."

"You may be right Megs. It's just I can't seem to feel the way I want with Woody." Was this a failure on her part or was she disenchanted with the life Neville provided? Or both?

A loud "Ah-ha" sounded from the living room. Caught up in debugging, Richard remained unaware of the last few minutes of conversation between his wife and her sister. "I think your problem is solved for now." He made an emphatic last click on the keyboard.

"What was it?" Rita asked joining her brother-in-law. Megan followed. Both put on brave new faces for Richard.

Richard swiveled the computer around and showed Rita the screen. "A virus. It's gone, and I downloaded a new virus protection program, that icon there." He pointed to a small display on her desktop. "Try and run it at least once a week."

"That's it, a virus?"

"You really should buy a Mac. They cost more but you wouldn't have to worry as much about viruses," Richard said.

Rita flashed a coy grin. "I don't really worry about viruses Richard because my handsome, learned brother-in-law's a whiz with these computer things." No one argued with Rita's logic. She gave Richard a hug and thanked both for coming to the rescue.

Dewey reappeared dressed in his Spiderman pajamas just as his aunt and uncle were leaving. He dragged a ragged stuffed monkey behind him.

"Is the caputer fixed Unca Richard?"

Richard lowered himself to his nephew's eye level. "Good as new,

Dewey. Next time I come over, I'll bring this racing game I found. We'll download it... if your mother doesn't mind."

All six eyes switched to Rita. "I guess no's not an option." A crooked smirk crossed her face while one hand patted Dewey's blonde head.

"You're still coming on the twentieth, aren't you?"

"What day is that?" Megan asked.

"A Tuesday. Mom and Dad leave on Wednesday, so we'll have Christmas with them before they go," Rita said.

"We'll be here," Megan said, glaring Richard's way. "And Rita, just think about what I said." Megan gave her sister a hug and they all said their goodbyes. As Rita watched her sister climb into the car, she did think about their conversation.

Some of what Megan described certainly rang true yet inside Rita's soul; she yearned for that singular bond, an almost spiritual joining she once shared with her high school sweetheart. Still stricken by reckless devotion, Rita failed to recognize the power of time; how time's passage can blur our erstwhile emotions projecting a halo of light onto our histories, disguising what actually transpired with a wish and the hope of what can be possible, what is possible. Time muddies even the truest memories.

Rita lived in a flawed world, optimistic in her possibilities yet naïve in the reality of relationships. She believed in a love she once had and curling a blanket over Dewey that night, she envisioned the next man, this unknown friend of Richard's, as her new knight.

CHAPTER 12

THE NEXT MORNING Neville stood with Walter Hendry explaining his need to leave work. Roland watched from behind his partition near the front windows, amused as always. Today Roland wore a bright orange dress shirt, a pair of cream-colored trousers and instead of his usual floppy red bowtie; he wore a floppy black one. With his tall lean frame, Roland looked like a fledgling yogurt clerk in a shopping mall's center cubicle.

Nodding, Hendry retreated to his office. Roland, a smirk stretching his thin face, popped up from his chair and made his way to intercept his coworker. Roland had bested his nemesis the day before and felt it was time to rub salt in the wound. His patent leather shoes squeaked along the floor as Neville watched him approach. A malicious smile smoldered as he asked, "So another day pass for Wishy our part time employee?"

Neville feigned a grin, pulling his coat over his shoulders. "What's it to you Roland?"

Roland countered Neville hands on hips, circling to the side like a wrestler in the ring. His thin blonde mustache bristled. "If your father's that sick maybe you ought to put him in a home– for the sake of your job here at the Sentinel."

John Winterburn heard Roland's offhand remark. "Hey Roland, that's way outta line."

Sam looked up as Roland returned a sneer in John's direction.

Neville held back the urge to leap onto his nemesis and

strangle him. His eyes swept up and down Roland's lean frame considering the ill-bred remark, yet knowing Roland's unwarranted suggestion was close to truth. Still, he didn't need Roland DeWitt explaining his options. "I didn't think you could possibly be any more ignorant, or impertinent than you had been these last four years, but here again you've surpassed even that estimation Roland."

Neville's assessment put a smile on John's face. Roland winced and grit his teeth as the tension welled up. His struggle, as always, was keeping his mouth shut. What Roland could not fathom was Neville's devotion to his father, given his own situation. Seeing the attention he had garnered, Roland retreated to his window perch.

Sam joined John near Neville's desk. "What an ass," Sam whispered.

"Thanks John. I think at times Roland believes he owns the Sentinel," Neville said.

"What a disaster that would be," John said. As they turned their attention away from Roland, John began again. "Say, I read the first eight chapters of your book... very inventive, Woody."

"Thanks. I like to think Stephen King stole the concept but I know it happens. It's just he's Stephen King and I'm, well I'm nobody. " Neville's concept in *Seven Days* was a town trapped beneath an alien dome and its effects on both the people inside and outside the barrier. As Neville headed out, the elevator door opened. There, pushing his wheeled wire tray, Willis Ogland slipped onto the second floor. As Neville stepped in, they exchanged morning pleasantries. Willis held none of Roland's animosity toward Neville or their coworkers, finding life much easier getting along with people. As it related to work, Willis was happy at the Sentinel, filling his mornings running company errands, chasing down supplies and acting as the office gopher. His afternoons were quite different. After lunch, Willis Ogland worked hand and hand with the press operators, apprenticing at the printing trade in hopes of finding a worthwhile job at the end of his training.

Willis rolled his way down the center aisle dropping off mail, a printer cartridge and bundles of paper for the printers. After resupplying the journalists, he pushed his cart to the back windows and Roland's segregated world.

"Hey..." he started turning past the last partition.

Seated, Roland slid his chair out past his lover. Grimacing, he peeked out into the aisle, scouting what he deemed the enemy. Willis watched amazed at the drama involved.

"What's the matter?" Willis asked.

Peering out past his friend, Roland looked up. "Those Neanderthals, they rally around that Wishy as if he were some kind of saint. It'll be a happy day when I leave this place behind."

Willis set his cart aside and sat. "That's twice you've said that, but you still didn't say where you're going Roland."

Roland recognized the worry in Willis's voice and with it, his face transformed. The anger left and he focused back on Willis, relaxing his sharp stare. His thin bloodless lips bowed to a smile. In his innocence, Willis worried for his partner and their future together. Roland sat considering the trust they had formed as friends, as lovers and realized, except for Willis he would be alone. Roland decided to reveal his plans.

Willis listened while Roland explained the intrigue in which he was now involved. Sitting perched atop his office desk, Roland started with his plot's birth as just an idea, progressing rapidly to his meetings with Davis Jefferson, his former Princeton roommate. He described Jefferson's inventive Yo-Yo Trojan and relayed how easy it was to implant the program into the Sentinel's main computer. Finally, he told Willis of the offshore account in the Cayman Islands, their destination the day after Christmas.

"What if they find the program after?" Willis asked.

"They won't. Davis said after it sucks the money out the business accounts, the program self-destructs and fades into illegible code. It's his ass on the line too, so I know he's not lying."

"So we just stay in the Caymans? Won't people get suspicious if we just stop coming to work?"

Roland laughed. "For now, it's a vacation. When we arrive, we split the money with Davis, open a new account and enjoy the warm weather for the week. We come back to Solomon, but only long enough to avert suspicion. Maybe two, three months and then we're free. Free to leave, free to settle back in the Caymans. Free to enjoy our spoils."

Expectations ran high and it showed in Roland's glassy eyes. Willis, on the other hand, looked much more subdued. Many questions rattled through his head as he watched his lover peer triumphantly past him, out onto St. Gabriel's Square.

While Willis remained silent, his eyes screamed concern.

It was shortly after ten a.m. when Neville arrived at the hospital. The weather remained cold with a gusting north wind adding an edge to an already hostile winter day. Clear skies were the only consolation.

Neville huffed out a heavy breath as he carried the gym bag under his arm and into the hospital lobby. He made his way up to the second floor. Our Lady of Mercies was busier in the morning hours and he dodged a path along the second level reaching room 221 nearly worn out. He knocked, waited, caught his breath then opened the door. To his surprise, Phil was not in his bed. The center curtain was half drawn and a new patient lay asleep in the next bed.

Neville slipped back into the hall. He walked down the aisle to the floor's station on the left where three nurses busied themselves behind the counter. As Neville approached, the closest nurse, a short blonde haired woman was inputting data on a computer terminal. Neville read her nametag, Cheryl RN, and waited. Her coiled blonde hair bounced with every click she made on the keyboard. Leaning over the counter he started, "Excuse me Cheryl, I'm looking for Phil in room two-twenty-one. Audrey said he'd be released after ten a.m."

The nurse continued to type. Without looking up she asked, "Who's Phil and who the hell is Audrey?"

Neville grinned. "I'm sorry, John Doe, the patient in room two-twenty-one. Audrey said he'd be released right about now." He pulled up his sleeve and checked his watch, careful not to drop the bag.

All three nurses appeared swamped by their duties. Finally, the little blonde nurse looked up. "Who's this Audrey person?"

Taken off guard Neville hesitated. "Audrey? She's one of the afternoon shift nurses here on the second floor. She said he'd be ready to leave between ten and eleven today."

Nurse Cheryl stood leaned forward palms pressed against the counter shelf and faced Neville. With a practiced professional bearing she said, "There is no nurse named Audrey on the afternoon shift here, sir. And I don't know exactly where John Doe is at this moment. Give me one minute and I'll find him."

The nurse sat, went back to typing while Neville stood stunned. "Of course there's a nurse Audrey on the afternoon shift. I've seen her here all week. We've talked, she's shown me John Doe's charts... I've got her phone number."

She stopped typing. "Sir, I don't know who you've been talking to on the afternoon shift but I've worked here for over a year and we have no nurse named Audrey on any floor, on any shift at this hospital."

The two nurses working the station heard her loud denunciation and joined their coworker across from Neville. Both wore vacuous stares.

"I'm sorry sir... did you say something about a Nurse Audrey here on the second floor?" the first nurse asked. An older black woman, she wore a small enamel nametag with Krissy embossed on it. Below the name, the designation read Floor Supervisor.

"Yes, I've seen her here every night this week."

"You must be mistaken, Mr...." Krissy said prodding for a name.

"It's Wishwood and I'm not mistaken. I think I'd remember her name seeing that we spoke right here in room two-twenty-one all this week."

Standing by the younger blonde nurse, the floor supervisor

stared across to the third nurse Janice, a woman in her forties. Both wore a look of incredulity. Something was definitely amiss.

Janice turned her back to Neville and whispered, "Isn't that the name Mr. Eleazar used last week? Said his nurse was Audrey?"

Krissy nodded remembering the reference. With all the medication Mr. Eleazar was on no one took much of anything he said too seriously. The little blonde nurse saw the expression on her colleague's faces. "We haven't got any Audreys here, do we?"

The older nurses peered down at her, but stood silent for the longest time.

"What's going on?" Neville asked.

The floor supervisor ultimately began. "We don't have a nurse named Audrey working here now but we did have. Audrey Timmerman was her name."

Neville interrupted. "Audrey Timmerman, that's it. We've talked every day this week."

The two older women exchanged a glance. Janice rolled her eyes. "Auburn hair, not too long, greyish-green eyes... very pretty?" Janice asked.

"That's her," Neville said.

A sudden tension rose in the air around the nurse's station as if someone or something had joined them. "This is going to be hard to believe but bear with me Mr. Wishwood. I knew Audrey Timmerman; she was a beautiful girl inside and out. Janice knew her too," she glanced to her partner. "She worked here at Our Lady of Mercies over two years ago in ICU. Audrey found a lump in her breast. They found it was malignant and that's when she began treatment here on the second floor. They performed surgery, a double mastectomy. She was undergoing chemotherapy when they discovered the cancer had metastasized into her lungs and spine. Audrey Timmerman died here at Our Lady of Mercies almost two years ago. She passed away in room two-twenty-one."

Neville knees buckled. He leaned against the counter for support. His thoughts raced to the conversations they had, the personal histories they exchanged and even the physical embrace they had shared. The woman he met in room 221 was a living breathing human being. Both Phil and Dell had seen her, interacted with Audrey just as Neville had. He stared off into space, immersed in his own calculations. After several seconds he asked, "What are you trying to say? This Audrey I met here... is a ghost?"

All three nurses glared across the counter just as confused and unsettled as Neville. The station telephone rang; all three nurses ignored it. In the lull that followed, the temperature on the second floor seemed to drop substantially and a chill shrouded all four standing at the station.

The floor supervisor broke the silence. "The story I told you is true, Mr. Wishwood... it happened. That's all I'm saying. There is no nurse named Audrey currently working at Our Lady of Mercies hospital, on any floor, on any shift. The Audrey Timmerman I knew died bravely. I was in the room when she passed."

This once simple trip to the hospital had become a predicament. The second floor aisles were busy. Nurses, orderlies brushed by, a doctor hurried past followed by a security guard on a path to the elevator on the opposite side of the intersection. Neville looked sideways and suddenly spied Phil in a wheelchair approaching the nurse's kiosk. A volunteer was pushing him down the aisle. As he came nearer, Neville pointed. "Ask him, he saw Audrey too."

The wheelchair slowed and Phil greeted his newest friend. "Hi Woody. They gave me this new brace." Phil lifted his light blue gown and showed Neville the gray plastic cast was gone, replaced by a black fabric knee brace. "I'm ready to go."

All four stared at the man in the chair. Smiling, he thanked the old woman who had taken him to the second floor sitting room and she left.

"Phil," Neville said. "Who was the afternoon shift nurse on duty whenever I came to see you?"

"Audrey, of course. Very pretty, I liked Audrey."

Neville faced all three nurses and beamed a grin of vindication. But Phil's own history was sketchy at best. He had sustained a serious head injury and now suffered from amnesia. The women looked to each other for an answer.

Neville dropped the gym bag in Phil's lap. "Clothes, for you." He continued to monitor the nurse's reaction while they whispered, nodded, even shrugged the occasional shoulder, but shared little with their visitor.

"I really don't know what to say, Mr. Wishwood," Krissy confessed. Phil looked up into four blank faces, holding tight to the cold gym bag. He was lost as to what their discussion involved. The floor supervisor motioned to Cheryl. "Can you help him get dressed please?"

"Sure."

Cheryl moved expeditiously. She circled the counter, grabbed hold of Phil's wheelchair and rolled him down the aisle. Phil lurched back in his seat but held on. Arriving at the door, she stopped abruptly nearly ejecting him into it. It was as if this duty constituted a reprieve from the Audrey dilemma.

If this fantastic story were true, who was this nurse on the afternoon shift? From what Neville could determine, the only credible explanation was that the Audrey he met and spoke with appeared to him as an apparition, a ghost harbored here on the second floor of Our Lady of Mercies hospital yet alive in some weird spirit dimension. Frustrated, Neville reached behind, pulled out his wallet and removed the torn slip of paper with Audrey's number on it.

"Audrey tore this off Phil's chart last night. That's her phone number on it."

He handed the paper to Janice. She took it, looked to Krissy and when the floor supervisor nodded, Janice retrieved Phil's chart from a line of clipboards sitting in angled slots on the wall. She walked the chart to Krissy and they checked the first page. Neville could see Janice measuring the torn strip as her supervisor watched intently. Neville saw both women's eyes widen and without a word, they lifted their heads in tandem to face him.

"This number, you say Audrey gave this to you last night?" Krissy asked.

"Yes."

"It fits the sheet, but…"

"But what? I'm not making this up. She gave me the number so I could call her after work sometime."

"Do you mind if I call the number, Mr. Wishwood?" Krissy asked.

"No, not at all. Let's get to the bottom of this right here, right now." Neville's frustration was growing.

Krissy lifted the desk phone and punched out the number etched on the slip. Her eyes stayed trained on Neville as she listened. Less than ten seconds later, her lips twisted to a frown and she hung up. She punched Redial, and handed the receiver to Neville. He listened as one short ring sounded followed by a click and a woman's recorded voice. *'The number you have dialed is not in service. This is a recording.'*

He leaned over the counter and checked the number scrolled across the phone screen. It matched the number Audrey had given him. Neville handed the receiver back to the floor supervisor.

She returned the torn strip. "Our two primary afternoon shift nurses on the second floor are Cathy Quinn and Rachel Bellmore and neither of them have even the slightest resemblance to Audrey. I'm sorry, Mr. Wishwood."

Neville stood profoundly confused. A sense of defeat overwhelmed him. He peered down at the ripped piece of paper and turned, half-expecting to see Rod Serling.

He recalled following Audrey out of room 221 and his failure in finding her. Suddenly Dell's attempt at finding Audrey the night before made sense, in a cock-eyed way. It made sense if you believed in ghosts. He deliberated for several seconds. Aunt Claire believed and she might even understand the rationale. For now, Neville held on to that.

From down the hall, Phil's door opened and he appeared dressed. Cheryl pushed the wheelchair and in a somewhat slower pace, they approached the station. As he sat, the shoes seemed right, brown suede tie-ups, even the denim pants were at least okay, but the green and black plaid shirt hung like oversized drapery on his meager frame. Even his scrawny physical build resembled that of Barney Fife.

Phil appeared pleased with his new wardrobe. "Great clothes, Woody. Thank you." Obviously, Phil had very little fashion sense. He looked like an onion farmer after a long day in the field.

Still stinging from the disappointment, Neville failed to match Phil's enthusiasm. "Courtesy my father, Arthur Wishwood." Distracted, Neville smiled and whether Audrey existed or not, Neville continued his support of Phil. "Is he going to need this wheelchair for long?"

"Not at all, Mr. Wishwood," Cheryl said. She circled back around the station counter and retrieved a grey handled cane. "This is courtesy of the Red Cross. Just return it when he no longer requires the help. The wheelchair is just a formality. We'll have one of our volunteer's take him down to the front doors and he's on his own from there."

Neville waved his hand. "I can take him. We're parked close to the front anyway." He shuffled sideways behind the chair, avoiding the pedestrian traffic on the second floor. Before he could leave, Cheryl interjected, "The bill, Mr. Wishwood. You need to pay the bill." She waved a wad of papers in Neville's direction.

He stopped. "The bill... what do you mean the bill?"

Cheryl leafed through the first few pages, finding the final tally. "Yes, they sent it up this morning. It's seven thousand, six hundred and forty-four dollars. First floor to the right of the elevators... the glass enclosed booth there. It says cashier."

As she handed Neville the paperwork, Neville stuttered. "I... I had no idea I had to pay his hospital bill."

The floor supervisor heard the flap, saw the bill in Neville's hand and approached again. With a smirk, she plucked the papers from Neville laid the document on the counter and pulled up the last page to show Cheryl.

"It's been paid."

A signature showed and a black stamp reading, Paid in Full. Method of Payment box checked off indicated Visa. Neville leaned in to read it and breathed a sigh of relief. The signature appeared skewed.

Unable to decipher the name he asked, "But who? Did a family member suddenly show up?"

Krissy laughed. "Not unless he has a black prince for an uncle."

Neville stood confused. "A black prince? What's that mean?"

"The man who brought this up was a black man dressed in purple robes. He conducted himself like a Prince of Africa, carried a small wooden staff in his hands and wore this wonderfully colorful knit cap."

Krissy clung to a hospital clipboard with both hands, her eyes lost in the ceiling lights, obviously taken by the appearance of this strange and mysterious benefactor. Janice, her partner heard her dissertation and joined the trio.

She laughed. "He wasn't black, or a prince Krissy," she said staring with astonishment. "He was noble for sure, a count or a duke but he was dressed in white. White suit, tie, shirt, everything was white except the red band on his fedora. That's the man I saw bring the bill up. How can you say he was black?"

"Because he was," Krissy said sharply. "And he was a prince!"

"What happened to your eyesight? Certainly a gentleman, but black? I don't think so."

Neville listened while the two bickered back and forth wondering himself who and what these women had seen. Yet he steered clear of the fray. Temperatures were rising at the second floor kiosk as both nurses continued to argue vehemently.

"What have you suddenly gone blind?" Krissy asked.

"Me? I think we should get you up to the fifth floor so you can have your eyes examined," Janice fired back.

Tensions mounted. People walking the aisle stopped to witness the excitement. Some wore hospital gowns, some colored fatigues and one hospital doctor lifted his glasses to watch adding to the congestion near the station. Krissy Holliwell, the head nurse on two, had an avowed fiery nature. Cheryl handed Neville the paper work and he stuffed it in his coat pocket as hostilities escalated.

"He was white…"

"Black, a man of color…" The argument continued, out of control.

"You can go Mr. Wishwood. Good luck Mr. Doe," Cheryl whispered. The gathering was four deep as everyone on the second floor turned their attention to the ongoing argument. Neville took the cue and slipped Phil through a growing audience. The decibel level continued to rise. It was getting ugly.

Nearing the intersection, Neville heard a loud, *Thwack*. A chorus of groans ensued. Phil turned in his chair to see. "Don't look now, but I think the head nurse just whacked her partner with a clipboard."

Neville glanced back. "Let's go."

They crossed the hallway and into a waiting elevator. He left the wheelchair near the front exit and helped Phil to his feet. Handing him the cane, he asked, "Can you walk?"

"I think so." He let out a short moan, leaned against Neville and with his cane firmly locked in his left hand took the first step. Phil gave a wide grin and hobbled through the doors. His jacket was light so Neville hurried him to the car.

The weather remained cold, blustery but still no snow that day. The ground was slippery making it imperative to plant the cane properly with every step. Somehow, Phil's expertise with the cane grew in leaps and bounds on their trip to the car and by the time they reached it, his limp seemed imperceptible.

Neville started the car, banged the dash for heat and slipped it in drive. Settling into the front seat, Phil asked, "That was strange back there. What were they arguing about Woody?"

"I don't really know. Something about who paid your bill, what he looked like."

"Must be the stress, people sick and all," Phil said.

Neville drove off, quietly reassessing this discovery that

Audrey, this nurse he admired, the only eligible woman he had met since Rita, did not exist— at least not in a natural state. These thoughts continued to circle inside his head holding him hostage on the drive home.

They arrived at Neville's home twenty-five minutes later. Phil carefully lifted out from the car and hobbled to the front steps. Neville guided him from behind. With their houseguest limping up the three porch steps, the front door opened and Dell greeted the two.

"Home, sweet home. Come on in," he said. Neville's father watched the action, peeking out from behind Dell.

"Hi Dell," Phil said as he surveyed the porch, the house and inside the front door. "What a nice place."

Neville followed Phil and helped him off with his coat. Dell yanked Arthur front and center for introductions. "This is Artie, Phil, Neville's dad."

Phil extended a hand, "Hello, Mr. Wishwood. It's very nice to meet you."

Arthur's impudent look registered his disapproval. He waited, studying Phil with his wonky eyes. Finally, a hand jabbed out and he shook with a grunt.

They headed into the kitchen. "Thought you'd be hungry," Dell said, extending an arm to show soup and sandwiches laid out on the kitchen table. "Dig in boys."

Neville drew Dell aside while Arthur and Phil began to scoop out soup. "You won't believe what happened," he whispered.

As Dell waited, Neville walked down to the hall opened his bedroom door and dropped the hospital paperwork on his dresser. The pages unfolded and last page opened, revealing the signature from the unnamed stranger who had paid Phil's bill. Reflecting in the dresser mirror, the name became legible. The signature was in mirror script.

Returning to the kitchen, Neville lowered his voice and recounted for Dell the nurse's tale on Audrey's fateful end.

"Whoa... are you saying Audrey isn't real or even alive?"

"I'm not saying it," Neville said. "They are."

"I mean, I put-on about her disappearing and all, but... they said she died two years ago?" Dell whispered, spooked.

"And the phone number, she called it– not in service," Neville said.

Dell reached behind grabbed a sandwich half from the platter and swallowed back most of it in two quick bites. Dell always thought better while eating. Phil and Neville's father slurped soup, eyed each other with reservation jousting elbows as they ate. Dell noticed the back-and-forth and intervened. "Hey you two cut it out!"

Both peered up sad-eyed and stopped sparring. From there, Dell put the predicament into perspective. "Well, she would've been one hell of a date."

"Be serious. You saw her, and Phil said the same. It can't be my imagination so what's going on?"

Dell lifted one finger in triumph. "I don't know, but maybe there *is* someone who might."

"Who?"

"Aunt Claire– you'll see her tonight," Dell said.

"Tonight? Why would I see her tonight?"

Dell flashed a disappointing frown. "You forgot..."

Neville was at a loss. "Forgot? Forgot what?"

"It's Friday, the Psychic Fair starts tonight. And Aunt Claire's there right now setting up her booth," Dell said.

The Psychic Fair was an exposition held just before Christmas every year. Local soothsayers joined with a troupe of travelling mystics renting booths in the Landsend Auditorium for a long weekend of fortunetelling, mysticism and extrasensory perception, all to the delight of adoring fans of the pseudoscience. If past practice were any indicator, there would be near one hundred booths set up for the public visitation. Once there, spiritualists in all the sorcerous arts would try uncovering their futures, their murky pasts and possibly reconnect them with long lost relatives. It was all available for a price.

Aunt Claire was one of many local mediums to rent space at the event. She read clients past or future by touch alone, preferring a hand-to-hand connection or at times, the simple touch of the face but then only to clarify an ambiguous vision. Aunt Claire used only one prop; a lit candle to help her concentration. On a good weekend, she could clear well over two thousand dollars and attract new clients in the process.

"The Psychic Fair... I did forget. But why aren't you helping her set up?" Neville asked.

"Grant's helping her this year. He's got that truck so it makes the set up that much easier."

Grant Balfour was Aunt Claire's next-door neighbor. A widower, he and Aunt Claire had been friends since she arrived in Solomon. Since the death of his wife Pamela three years ago, Grant seemed much more attentive to Dell's reclusive aunt. Both Neville and Dell believed he had a crush on her and mentioned it on many an occasion, teasing her mercilessly. Aunt Claire considered his thoughtful nature only a sign of their friendship, preferring to remain ignorant of any other motive.

"It should be a good one this year," Dell said. "They've got Ella May Hardacker as the feature medium. Even Aunt Claire wants to see her in action."

"Who's Ella May Hardacker?"

Of course, Dell knew the answer. Through his relationship with his aunt, he had maintained an interest in the occult. To a point Neville shared their enthusiasm, having lived with both for five years. Although he shared many such beliefs, Neville's understanding was nowhere near what Dell had acquired.

Phil shifted his chair away from Neville's father. Arthur stared at Phil as he munched on a grilled cheese sandwich. From the onset of the disease, Arthur continued to exhibit a serious mistrust of strangers.

Dell went on to explain the origins of Ella May's dubious powers. A corpulent woman in her forties, she was the granddaughter of Alvin Hardacker; a U.S. army barber in the nineteen-fifties. His only claim to fame was, on occasion, he had cut Elvis Presley's hair. Knowing the King's popularity at the time, Alvin was savvy enough to save the clippings and store them for generations to come. By chance, a young Ella May came across the plastic bag containing Elvis Presley's hair clippings and as a matter of legend these days; she promptly opened the bag and a vision of the deceased King of Rock and Roll appeared. In the vision, Elvis prophesied events to unfold in Ella May's near future. When the events transpired in her life, Ella May Hardacker claimed it a miracle and her career path was set.

According to her press releases, Elvis contacts Ella May with news from the spirit world through his shorn hair. It seems the long departed Elvis now converses regularly with the dead spirits of, not only her clients, but also world figures now residing with him on heaven's big stage. It was quite a story.

"Are you kidding me?" Neville asked. "I've never heard of her."

Dell smiled his usual gratified smile. "Not many people have. She's what we call an underground phenomenon in the business. She doesn't attend many functions like this, that's what makes it so special."

Neville was dumbfounded, but Dell's history lesson had veered Neville's muddled thoughts away from Audrey and the problems her appearance or disappearance had created.

"I've gotta get back. We'll talk later." As Neville said his good-byes, the gap between Phil and his father's chair had grown to three feet.

"Thanks, Woody," Phil said. Except for Arthur's steady glare, Phil seemed quite at home in the Wishwood kitchen.

Neville's relief did not last long. He still had doubts.

On his way back to the Sentinel, he hatched a plan to end the Audrey dilemma one-way or the other. Arriving just after noon, the office sat empty. With everyone at lunch, he took his place in front of his desk computer and punched in a password. Once on the Sentinel private network, he brought up the archives, from there, obituaries.

Neville peered around the room while the network honed in on the records. With his senses piqued, he could hear the low buzz of the fluorescent lights. Stories and pictures of a newsworthy past lined the newsroom walls. Second World War news, Ike's election and re-election, JFK's assassination, Robert Kennedy's assassination, Nixon's ouster and a local fire in the '70's that devastated the west wall of buildings in St. Gabriel's Square and of course 9/11.

He thought of how time had changed lives, and cities, even the world in just these last decades. How quickly life can shift with the altering of one perfect fact, one miniscule detail. It was all there, against the wall in black and white, a message from the past; no matter what, no matter who, the world goes on and on and on...

The program opened. Neville input dates around the period Audrey supposedly died. He clicked enter and a series of names appeared in a column. Audrey Timmerman was one of the names.

He hesitated. Should he look? Did he really want to know the truth, whatever it was? As a newsman, he had to know. He double clicked on her name. A picture of a beautiful young woman appeared in full color. Prominently displayed below the picture were the date of birth and the date of passing. She was twenty-five when she died.

The picture was a perfect depiction of the Audrey Timmerman he met in room two-twenty-one.

CHAPTER 13

DELL LOADED THE last of the lunch dishes into the dishwasher watching his newest charge intently as he interacted with Neville's father. There seemed to be tension between the two, unspoken yet palpable. During lunch, Dell noticed the distance between Phil's chair and Arthur had grown to several feet.

"Let's go check out your room here Phil," Dell started.

"He's staying?" Arthur asked, looking annoyed.

Dell pointed an accusing finger toward the elder Wishwood. "For a few weeks, until he gets his bearings, so you be nice. He's had a rough go this last week."

Arthur's eyes narrowed. "Do you know how to play gin rummy?"

"Not at all," Phil said, thinking it a good thing.

"Wanna learn?"

Dell made his way toward the hallway. Phil picked his cane off the empty seat and followed. "Maybe later," he said.

They left the kitchen. Arthur burped and joined the line. Dell took him to the last door on the right, Dewey's bedroom. Neville had cleared out most of Dewey's belongings, changed his Batman bedding, but left his son's clothes in their drawers.

Dell flicked on the light. The first thing to catch Phil's eye was an elaborate mobile suspended from the ceiling light itself, a glazed yellow ball shaped to mimic the sun. From its center, a series of thin black rods cantilevered out in arcs, nine in all, and from the rods small colored orbs dangled in space. Their sizes varied and only two flickered light from within. The inside bulbs on the other seven were obviously burned out. All nine were set at various positions around the center light-sun, the distances set to scale. Several twig-like projections branched off the main rods lowering tiny white lights as stars. Most were out. Even in disrepair, the limp display hovering above Dewey's bed remained a magnificent depiction of our solar system.

There was a time when it rotated the planets around a bright yellow sun but the small drive motor had burned out. Dell had taken it apart years ago and found the motor was an import from Taiwan and unavailable. The lights were also a special buy, again only available overseas.

"That mobile is wonderful," Phil said amazed. The painted planets were in colors associated with each. Mercury a dusty orange, Venus blue, Earth was green and blue, Mars a deeper red and on up to tiny Pluto colored iron-grey.

"We found it at a garage sale in St. Paul," Dell said. "Woody thought it would be nice for Dewey growing up. I tried to fix it but the parts were too hard to find."

Arthur swept by both to look inside even though he had seen the room a thousand times. Today he discovered it anew and his eyes searched the space as if discovering hidden gems. The room, other than its impressive centerpiece, was a typical boy's bedroom. Next to the dresser, toys were stacked on all four levels of a bookcase. Posters of comic book characters plastered the walls; Ironman, Spiderman and Batman all prominently displayed. Beside the bed, a white night table held a lamp made to replicate a rocket ship, a clown faced coin bank and a portable video game player.

On the bed propped by the pillow, Dewey's most sacred possession sat staring back: a ragged stuffed monkey named Wilkie. Rita had an identical Wilkie with her so Dewey was never without.

Wandering inside, inspecting its every nook and cranny Arthur finally asked, "Where's the bathroom?"

"It's not a hotel room Artie," said Dell. "The bathroom's down the hall."

Arthur scurried past both and disappeared down the hall.

"Is he alright?" Phil asked, whispering.

"Neville's dad has Alzheimer's."

"Alzheimer's… what's that?"

Dell paused to think. He wanted to phrase his answer judiciously so as not to offend Phil. "Well, like you he has problems remembering the past. In his case it's never coming back."

"Never?"

"Never. The Artie we've all known is fading fast," Dell said with a hint of emotion.

"Oh…"

Phil pondered the information while Dell led the way back into the hallway. Turning left Dell pointed, "Here's the bathroom. And this is Artie's room and of course, Woody's bedroom on the end. Dewey'll be bunking with him while you're staying here."

"Dewey's Woody's son?"

"Yeah, didn't he mention Dewey? Usually he's all Woody talks about."

"He might of… I can't remember."

The telephone rang. The bathroom door flew open and Arthur dashed down the hall in a blur, disappearing into the front room. Dell rolled his eyes and Phil watched him dash down the hall behind the hard charge of Neville's father.

"Hello?" Arthur asked. Hearing a woman's voice, he immediately dove into his diatribe. "Angela, it's late and we need you home. God knows…"

Dell snatched the phone from Neville's father, meting out a rebuke with his eyes.

"Hello?" Dell answered. It was Rita on the other end.

In pantomime, Dell directed Arthur to the general direction of his room. Arthur, showing his disapproval, sneered, grumbled something inaudible and wandered off slumped shoulders and all. Phil stood by taking in the scene.

"Sorry Rita. Artie still thinks Angie's coming back someday."

Rita's call concerned Dewey's Nintendo DS. Dell promised to drop it by later that night and he finished up their short conversation.

"What happened there?" Phil asked.

"Whenever the phone rings and a woman answers, Artie's mind drifts back to when he was married. Angela– his wife and Woody's mom– deserted them over twenty years ago. Haven't heard from her since. The Alzheimer's, it's stirred all that up inside Artie's head."

"That's kind of a sad story, Dell."

"I guess, but Woody seems okay with it all. Never really talks about it much. And he says neither did his Dad until he got sick."

Passing by Arthur's open door, they saw him on the bed rustling through the small tin box he kept in his lower drawer. He looked up, a smile brightened his face and he asked, "Gin?"

A roguish grin dimpled Dell's cheeks. "We have another project for today, Artie. Come on let's get busy."

Neville's father closed his little box and deposited it back inside the drawer. These days, he took Dell's direction without much prompting. Dell, as caregiver, found a willing conspirator in Arthur for his ventures. "You can help too, Phil."

Neville sat at his desk, spellbound, continuing to study the portrait of Audrey, a graduation picture from the nursing school she attended. The only disparity was the hair, shorter with fewer streaks.

The first one back from lunch was Sam Charters. He strolled off the elevator staring into a folded newspaper, unaware of Neville at first. Neville appeared pale, his dazed eyes fixed on the monitor, a lost soul in a lost world. Feeling a presence, Sam peered up from his paper. He watched his colleague for a few seconds. "Are you alright Woody?"

Neville awoke from his self-induced trance. "Yeah… yeah, I'm okay Sam." His appearance contradicted the statement.

"You look like you just lost your best friend. What's up?"

Sam's appraisal was closer than even he could imagine. He dropped his paper on the desk, unbuttoned his coat and approached. Neville's look concerned Sam and he prodded, "Is it your dad? Is he okay?"

Neville clicked off the picture of Audrey and forced a smile.

"Dad's okay… for now. It's not that." Neville pushed back from his desk. "I… I got some bad news. An old friend died."

"Sorry to hear that. My condolences," Sam said. "Life's just too damn short."

"It is, and thanks Sam for asking."

The evidence he mustered left Neville few options. Either he, Dell and Phil were losing their collective minds, or something incomprehensible, something off-the-charts eerie was happening. His thoughts cluttered with the *ifs*, the *hows*, the *whos* and ultimately ended with one implausible question: *why?* The situation dominated his entire day. Near quitting time, he brought up the archives again and printed a color portrait of Audrey Timmerman. He left the Sentinel fully immersed in uncertainty and questioning his own recollections, wallowing in the disappointment of meeting and losing a woman he thought might finally fit into his life situation. It had taken him a year to reach this point; to accept someone other than Rita as a possibility, a candidate willing to fill the void he felt. Audrey seemed almost too perfect and now he understood why. Because she wasn't real, at least not in the present.

He arrived home disillusioned and once again doubting his future. Dell came in from the front room and sensed his friend's mood immediately. In the living room, Phil sat on the edge of the sofa pen in hand, focused on something laid out across the coffee table. Neville's father sat cross-legged on the floor his back to the entryway also preoc-cupied with Dell's latest project. Both seemed content.

Neville yanked the picture of Audrey from a coat pocket but before handing it to Dell, he noticed the activity in the front room. Dell turned toward his industrious charges smiling. Both huddled about the coffee table busily working with felt tipped pens. Staring down, Neville realized Dell was holding something in his hand– a plas-tic coated cord.

"They seem happy. What are they doing?" he asked.

"I got this idea for the Psychic Fair. Thought I'd kill two birds with one stone. Keep them busy and help Aunt Claire. We went to the dollar store and I picked up a couple of Bristol boards and Sharpies and voila, instant advertising. And I found out Phil can read."

Neville brushed past his friend, walked into the living room and read the boards. Dell followed, wrapping the plastic cord around his fist. Seeing Neville, Phil and Arthur looked up from their duties. "Hi Woody," Phil said and went back to work.

Arthur's accomplished grin greeted his son. "Dell says this is gonna help Aunt Claire," he said with pride. "Who's Aunt Claire?'

"A close friend Dad," Neville replied, reading the first sign. "SEE THE AMAZING CLAIRE THE CLARVOYANT – NOW AT THE PSYCHIC FAIR. FRIDAY THROUGH SUNDAY – BOOTH 34..."

The two boards were sitting flat on top of the coffee table. Phil was crafting the letters in block form on one while Arthur filled in the lettering with black magic marker on the other. Arthur's dexterity had indeed faltered these last few years but for the most part, he stayed within Phil's outlines. A slip of paper Dell had written up sat beside Phil as he copied it out onto the cardboard. His three-inch lettering was neat and tidy considering his limitations.

"Where are you going to put these?" Neville asked.

Dell lifted the plastic rope to show his friend. "I'll tie the two boards together with this, and make a sandwich-board sign for in front of the auditorium."

"And who, pray tell, is going to be strutting around with that lashed to their back?" Neville asked, his voice dripping with sarcasm.

"Phil said he'd walk it around for a while, and maybe Artie can give him a break on and off," Dell said with a virtuous smirk.

Neville's laser gaze hit Dell like a lightning bolt.

"Phil said he was okay with it. I asked..." Dell defended. "And it'll only be for a couple hours. Besides, it'll probably be good exercise for that leg."

"Dell, he's just had surgery– and its freezing out. He can't be marching around that plaza all night in the snow. And my father, he'd get lost! What are you thinking?"

"Honestly, I thought the limp might get a few sympathetic customers to visit. It's just a few hours... to help Aunt Claire."

"Dell, come on!"

As Neville settled down, he held out the photo. "Look at this!"

Dell opened the page and stared for a second. "That's her... that's Audrey, just like you said." He looked up, astonished. "What the hell's going on?"

"I don't know but whatever it is I'm caught in the middle."

Neville grabbed the picture and walked away. With his newest endeavor nixed, Dell stood above his two sign-makers. He left them to finish seeing that, if nothing else, it gave them a sense of usefulness. He followed Neville to his bedroom.

"What about Audrey?" Dell asked.

Neville tossed the picture onto his dresser next to the hospital bill and looked back. "I don't know."

"What about tonight, are you coming? I'm picking up Bob and we're going for seven. Why don't you get Russell for a few hours and come with us? Aunt Claire might have an answer to this Audrey business."

Neville's thoughts returned to the disappointment "this Audrey business" had resurrected. "I have to work a half-day tomorrow. You go and I'll see Aunt Claire after I get off work."

After dinner, Dell retreated to his apartment and readied for the Psychic Fair. Neville settled in to watch *The Munsters* reruns on cable. Having had a long day, Phil thanked Neville and proceeded to bed. Tonight he wore a pair of Arthur's pajamas but Neville assured him they would find some clothes that actually fit.

Arthur sat quietly, content to watch television while Neville contemplated working on his novel. That seemed all but impossible. The Audrey situation and the mystery surrounding it had swirled an imperfect past into view. Instead, his own life reruns began as he recalled the pain and ultimately the bond that grew from it. His harsh remembrance, these recent events lingered making for a long night.

In the hours that passed his father grew tired. His day too had been one of change and discovery with the addition of Phil to their household. After putting him to bed, Neville retired for the night.

A restless first hour he spent reviewing the entire Audrey dilemma and as he transitioned into sleep, the gulls appeared flying high above the beach. He saw the waning sun, the red racer and Jennifer sitting with the fat man and the dream took hold. Neville squirmed beneath the sheets as the nightmare unfolded, a merciless attack on his defenseless psyche. His legs pumped beneath the covers as if to run, to hide but there was no escape, no running from the past. No benediction from what he had lived. The truth lay bare and when he cried inside the dream tears dampened the pillow upon which his head flailed. Twisting furiously he screamed aloud, '*No...No...No...* '

The dream had won again. That night Neville returned to the beach and once more the car, the fat man and the Jennifer apparition reappeared. Again, he watched little Lily rise to the heavens, brightest among the sky's night stars.

CHAPTER 14

D ELL ARRIVED AT the Wishwood front door just before
seven o'clock. Neville sat drinking coffee in the kitchen
while Phil and his father slept. His tired eyes skimmed
yesterday's newspaper. A persistent ache throbbed at his temples. Dell
came round the corner, his face red from the morning chill and his
hands scrubbing each other for warmth. When Neville looked up, he
saw a strange glint in Dell's eyes. The look was familiar. A sheepish
'I-might-be-hiding-something' glint. Or the ever popular 'I've-done-
something-stupid-and-I-don't-want-to-talk-about-it' glint.

Either way, Neville knew something had happened.

"Morning," Dell said, searching for coffee along the counter.
Neville watched and waited, putting aside the newspaper. In pronounced perfunctory actions, Dell shifted past his friend avoiding eye
contact and with his back to Neville asked, "Everything okay?"

"That's what I was going to ask you. You're agitated this morning... is everything okay with you?"

Dell mixed his coffee, slipped around the table and sat. He continued evasive maneuvers and picked up the newspaper hiding behind
it. "Sure, why wouldn't it be?"

"Dell!"

The newspaper rustled. "There's a sale at Gurney's– two for one."

Neville reached across and pulled down the paper.

Dell's impish grin switched to concern and he blurted out, "It
wasn't our fault! It just happened."

"What wasn't your fault?"

"Uhhhhh…the fire, you're gonna hear about it anyway."

"What fire? Where?"

"Last night at the auditorium. But it was an accident and…"

Dell waited. "And what?"

Dell began the tale branded the Physic Fair fire, reported on by all the local news outlets including The Sentinel. As a result of Dell's participation, Neville heard the facts few in their community would ever know.

After dropping Dewey's Nintendo game at Rita's Friday night, Dell had picked up Camouflage Bob at his bachelor apartment on Melrose just east of St. Gabriel's Square. They arrived early for the opening presentation by the Physic Fair's primary attraction, Ella May Hardacker. A public display of her physic abilities was set to begin at eight o'clock.

Before visiting Aunt Claire, Dell and Bob toured the cubicles lining the four spacious aisles inside the Landsend Auditorium. They found the headliner's center stage area near the hall's front elevated a few feet off the auditorium floor.

Last year's headliner, the Snake Whisperer, used three huge snakes to probe the mystical world of the unknown purportedly using mental telepathy. The claim was that his snakes possessed a preternatural connection with the beyond. After his largest snake, a nineteen-foot python, went missing two security guards found it looped around a pop keg near his stage kiosk. In their attempts to subdue the creature, the one guard had his leg nearly amputated by the coiling action while the second guard tasered the mammoth reptile. It did not go well.

Adding to the commotion, a patron's toy terrier dog disappeared near the booth, leash and all. They barred the Snake Whisperer from this year's event.

The auditorium aisles began to fill up as Bob and Dell circled in and out of the congested rows. Neon signs blinked discover your future here, or uncover past secrets there, and in between, the flags and pennants of hungry profiteers staked claims on calculating fates yet to unfold. Royal blues, majestic purples and regal reds sprouted through the crowded venue however the dominant color of the attending mediums remained basic black and mostly in velvet or satin. Black was forever the universal frill of occultists everywhere.

Kiosk owners crammed their aisle tables with occult books and trinkets ranging from ornate inlaid onyx, jade and opal jewelry, to simple silver rings and bracelets. Few gold pieces appeared on the stands for retailing, this crowd inclined to barter in silver.

With the influx of visitors, drink carts emerged offering refreshments to the teeming public, selling ice-cold pop to hot coffee and every potable option in between. People from all lifestyles roamed the concrete corridors searching for that one seer, one prodigious soothsayer to guide their future decisions; an experience in the occult, a unique night outside their normal routine or merely natural curiosity. The mix was indeed eclectic.

They found Aunt Claire sitting with a client inside her private canvas anteroom. The thinly veiled entrance disguised little of the activity and when she saw Dell waiting near the front of the booth, she excused herself. Aunt Claire wrapped her waifish arms around his neck for an extended hug. That night a black lace shawl covered her head and shoulders and beneath, a simple black silk blouse and floor length skirt. A silver pendant hung from her neck, a cameo of mother and child. Weeks had passed since they had last seen or spoken and she was excited to see Dell. She greeted Bob clasping both hands around one huge mitt.

She stopped mid shake. Her smile waned. "Bob," she said. "Tonight might be a good night to be home."

Her insinuation was blunt.

In a gruff half-laugh he replied, "I'm not home Aunt Claire, I'm here with Dell." There was a coy witlessness in the response. Bob missed the inference. Unfortunately, the subtlety of language was lost on Bob. Sarcasm, innuendo, at times even sincere pleading jammed up in Bob's filters. He needed uncomplicated descriptions. No, there was nothing subtle about Camouflage Bob.

As Bob rearranged the black toque on his head, Dell winked to his aunt. He understood.

"We won't be here long Aunt Claire. We're taking in Ella May Hardacker and we're gone."

"Be careful, that's all," she cautioned. "I'm getting a strange foreboding."

"We will."

Dell spent the next few minutes briefing his Aunt Claire on the Audrey dilemma and its effect on Neville. He assured his aunt that Neville would be calling on her the following day. From there, Dell and Bob made their way to the event bar, a rather innocuous little nook at the far end of the hall. Eight o'clock was still forty-five minutes away, so they drank beers while waiting. After two beers, Dell and Bob wandered back through the aisles checking out booths and books along the way.

Ella May Hardacker's stage area was now ready. Folding chairs were set along five rows in front of her elevated platform. The stage itself was fully dressed. A long table sat in the center decked out heavily in red, white and blue streamers. Behind it, a multi-colored canvas shelter housed what would be Ella May Hardacker's private-sessions booth. Books sat stacked on each end of the table. Flanking the presentation table, gas-lit torches sat fixed atop bronze-burnished pillars. Flames glistened off pewter fire-bowls flickering up into open black space. Near the right side fire-pillar, a small table held several more books for sale. To the left, a live size cardboard cutout of Elvis performing in a bejeweled white jump suit peered out to the growing crowd.

The melodic sounds of Elvis Presley's *Love Me Tender* began playing from the stage's corner speakers. Dell and Bob found seats in the front row. As Dell anxiously waited, Bob picked lint from his camouflage coat.

The Elvis song ended and the theme from 2001: A Space Odyssey followed. The music hyped up an eager assembly. The Elvis cutout lit up, his cardboard eyes flashed red then white and finally blue. The curtain opened and an overweight, overdressed Ella May Hardacker traipsed out, hands waving, greeting the fair faithful with zealous self-assurance. She waddled onto center stage wearing a purple velvet half-cape overtop a black velvet pantsuit. Shimmery rhinestones carved out star designs along the sleeves and pant-legs. Ella May carried the goods in one hand high above her head: a silver plastic bag no bigger than an oversized envelope. Stenciled across the silver bag's side were the initials E.A.P. (Elvis Aaron Presley) in old English lettering. She plopped the bag containing Elvis's shorn hair onto the presentation table and waved to the crowd, smiling back a wide toothy grin. With all the seats full, several people stood on the sides to view the Physic Fair headliner in action.

Enduring a merciless headache and short of patience, Neville stopped Dell's frenetic telling. "Dell no more set up. Tell me what happened."

"Okay, okay…" Dell paused, shifted sideways in his seat relaying a serious posture.

"So we're waiting and after the applause dies down, she requests a volunteer for a free reading. I look around and several hands shoot up. Her eyes zero in on the front row and I see Bob waving wildly in her direction. Unbelievably, she picks Bob. Bob jumps on stage and she asks his name. Facing the crowd, he proudly announces Bob, just Bob. Ella May Hardacker leads him to the presentation table, opens the silver bag and tells Bob reach in and handle the hair clippings. Bob's all smiles at this point. He pulls his hand out. She reaches in the bag after Bob, sifts around the Elvis hair and puts the bag back on the table. Closing her eyes, she lifts her hands to her temples and starts mumbling gibberish. After several seconds of this, her eyes suddenly pop open and she glares at Bob. Startled, Bob backs away. Then she announces to all in attendance, 'You've served our country faithfully and you now have the scars from your patriotic duty.'

"And nodding her head, she peers across to Bob, who nods along with her. Personally speaking, anyone in the place could have figured that one out seeing that the only piece of clothing Bob wore that *wasn't* U.S. military issue was his toque."

"Dell, cut the commentary."

"Alright… so I'm sitting there watching and I hear the vendor's call coming closer, getting louder and louder. Within seconds he's behind us and a sharp voice cries out, '*Ice cold pop, coffee, root beer, tea and...*'"

"No! Not..." Neville gasped.

"Yes... '*and eggnog!*'"

"No..."

"Bob's eyes wobbled," Dell continued. "His feet slid together and his hands found his hips. Lifting one leg he extended both arms and whirled himself around in one perfect pirouette. Bob's leg knocked over the torch and sent it flying onto Ella May Hardacker's presentation table, lighting up the contents. Books, ribbons, streamers and the silver plastic bag...poof, gone! Ella May Hardacker smashed into the flaming table launching the blaze into her canvas booth. It lit up like a fourth of July rocket. Screams of "fire" went out across the auditorium, so I jumped up on stage and grabbed hold of Bob, who was just coming out of his trance, dragged him off and we ran up the aisle toward Aunt Claire's booth. "

"Oh-my-God! Dell that's worse than last year's Snake Whisperer fiasco. Was anyone hurt?"

"I haven't heard. We grabbed Aunt Claire and hotfooted it outta there. The last I saw the whole stage was on fire and it was spreading fast to the booths nearby. By the time we got to the exit the sprinklers turned on."

"What about Aunt Claire, and Bob?"

"They're okay, but Ella May Hardacker may have to find a new line of work."

Neville shook his head. "Naw, she's probably got sacks of Elvis hair."

"He wasn't a monkey Woody. Where would she get sacks of Elvis hair?"

Neville stood up and placed the coffee cup in the dishwasher, eyeing Dell with dubious assurance. "There will always be sacks of Elvis hair Dell."

"Oh, I get it."

Neville checked the time, took two Tylenol from the cupboard and chugged back a mouthful of water. "What a mess. You should've listened to Aunt Claire. She always seems to know. Now I've got to get to work."

As Neville made his way to the front door, Dell followed.

"She won't be at the fair any time soon so stop by the house. She wants to talk to you," Dell said.

"I will."

Neville's car radio aired the latest news on the fire. By some miracle, no major injuries resulted from the blaze. Smoke inhalation sent one firefighter to hospital and only a few minor scrapes and bruises resulted from the evacuation. Other than that, the cost of the mishap was measured in dollars– an estimated half million dollars.

The general atmosphere in The Sentinel office remained subdued Saturday morning. Roland and Suzanne were off. Sam came in to work on an article pertaining to the upcoming election. Walter reviewed feedback on his editorial column and John covered the auditorium fire in Minneapolis. He had written up several eyewitnesses accounts. In proofing his colleague's story, Neville read one woman's version stating the man who started the inferno was an angry Russian ex-military who swore vehemently at the crowd and violently kicked the torch across the stage screaming anti-American epithets.

So much for eyewitness accounts.

Neville plodded through the morning finalizing loose ends from his previous day wasted in preoccupation with the supernatural. Adding to the matter, thoughts of his mother came back into view. Details of their relationship resurfaced. Issues he long since thought to be resolved replayed inside him. Neville realized that wound from childhood, his mother's choice to abandon her family, cut deeper than mere disappointment. It left a lasting scar.

He held onto what his father had said only minutes after her desertion, '*It's her loss today, not ours.*' And he believed his father for all those years. It was her loss and he *was* okay but– today he felt different, reconnected to that pain.

He failed to understand his loss was of innocence, a child's only defense and in losing that connection his future hurts, his failures cut deeper, stung longer. For Neville the only option available was to forget. Forget her, forget his life with her, forget the pain. It was her loss and always would be.

Today, he pushed it down and moved on.

Shortly after twelve, Neville left The Sentinel and drove to meet with Aunt Claire. His hope was that she could shed light on this manifestation of the dead and its meaning. Always a guiding influence, Aunt Claire was a surrogate mother to both him and Dell; a woman wise in worldly ways. But Aunt Claire's true talent was her ability to unravel the mysteries of life hidden behind the veil of time. To her, the future embodied not only our lives to come but also what lay beyond the physical world.

He pulled into her driveway and immediately felt a sense of coming home. After a quick knock on the door, Aunt Claire greeted him pulling her wrap up around her shoulders. Her face was fresh and white, her cheeks dimpled. Hugs followed and Neville joined her inside.

"I'll make some coffee," she said as she scampered into the kitchen. Neville sat at the dining room table. He looked around, remembering his time living with Aunt Claire and Dell. A book sat open on her favorite chair. A nearby light was on and he wondered what she was reading. The room was warm with memories.

She joined him across the table her hands clasped and ready. "So you're okay. The fire didn't cause any problems?" Neville asked.

"Just my little tent, a few books, but nothing of any importance. But you, Dell tells me you had a visitation."

"A visitation… is that what it's called?" Neville sat befuddled, unable to describe meeting what all evidence showed to be a ghost. "She was so real, so… alive. Dell saw her, and Phil, we all saw her, spoke with her. And then I find out she's been dead for two years."

Aunt Claire's smile grew. "Is it Audrey? Was that her name Woody?"

"Yes."

"That's because Audrey *is* alive… somewhere. At least the essence of what Audrey was here on earth." Leaning in she cozied up closer.

"Woody– you, Dell, this friend Phil have experienced what few living beings can attest to... a visitation from beyond our physical realm."

Unable to fathom the weight of her words, he slowly shook his head. "I don't know. As far-fetched as that sounds let's say your hypothesis is true, then what does it mean? Why did she come here in the first place?"

Aunt Claire eased back in the chair, her eyes vigorous, alive. "Spirits return to our world for different reasons. Perhaps it's to impart a message, or complete unfinished business. And there's always the possibility she appeared to guide someone in a specific direction. Did she give any advice, any message during your visits with her? Remember, it could be incidental, a subtle comment or some vague reference."

Exasperated, Neville exhaled and took a hasty mental survey of their conversations.

"None that I recall... she just tried to be helpful."

Her mind abuzz, Aunt Claire stood solemnly. While deep in thought, she left to retrieve their coffee. Her actions took on a mechanical cadence and as Neville watched a dimpled grin emerged, a sign she had come to a resolution.

"Since you three were the only witnesses and she left no clues, my guess is she came to guide one of you toward a destiny. Who had the most contact with this Audrey?"

"I'd say Phil. She was his nurse, at least that's what we thought."

"And Dell?"

"I don't think so. He only met her that last night."

"What about you?"

Neville's eyes strayed. He squirmed, picked up the cup and wondered his role in this possible spiritual intervention. While Phil was asleep those first few days, he engaged Audrey in conversation and even after Phil came to, he interacted with her much more than her patient.

"I spoke with Audrey all four nights. And I did feel an attraction from the very start, I won't lie about that. But even if I did what possible connection could I have in all this?"

"That I can't say but it's a certainty this Audrey was sent to expedite a specific outcome. Maybe something good, maybe bad, who can know. You say you were attracted to Audrey?"

"Yes... very." Neville bowed his head as if ashamed.

Her spindly fingers reached across and patted Neville's arm. "There's no shame here, Woody. You're not the first, nor the last to be swayed by a woman's charms. Was there a direction she might have tried to steer you?"

Neville knew the answer. Audrey's charms, not her words, had indeed motivated him to offer Phil a reprieve from homelessness. In an awkward way, Neville sought to impress this beautiful prospective partner. Not that he failed to feel compassion for Phil's plight. Neville saw this truth clearly yet felt uneasy conveying it to Aunt Claire. Pride reared up, and not wanting to appear weak, easily manipulated, he avoided the question.

"I really can't say. Mostly our conversations just felt natural. She seemed like the perfect nurse, the perfect friend."

"Maybe too perfect," Aunt Claire added.

"I guess, yes. This— this explanation, it's all speculation. No one really knows. I don't, and I know you mean well Aunt Claire, but..."

She interrupted, "Woody, look at me." Aunt Claire's face flushed; her eyes blazed an intensity Neville had never seen. With one exacting look, she commanded his every sense.

"You've always had doubts haven't you?" she asked.

Hesitating, he stared across the table. "Yes..."

A rapturous smile continued as she considered Neville's doubt. "For me, I believe in a force behind all that we are, all that we do. It's there to guide us. At times, we feel it: an overwhelming sensation that someone, something is pointing us in the right direction. Most times we don't. We miss the signs.

"Some call it God, some Allah. Some see it as this spiritual connection to all that lies beyond. Whatever it is, whatever it's called, it's there as sure as there are stars in the sky. We, as humans, have known it since the dawn of time. It's in our histories. We are born into it. A belief in gods, beings wiser, more powerful than us, centers the very foundation of man. It's our one universal truth. From these gods our plea has never varied; give us guidance and protection. And if there is a God, then there is a world beyond."

Neville shifted uncomfortably while Aunt Claire continued.

"I was given a gift. To some small extent, I get glimpses of what may happen or has happened. That gift could only come from beyond our world. I can't explain why any more than you can but I believe because I've lived it. In my many years of practice strange, even miraculous outcomes have occurred. People's futures redirected by something unseen yet all-powerful. I take no credit there. So what does all this imply? Is that what you're thinking?"

Neville nodded as Aunt Claire beamed back a smile. "It means that each life has meaning, purpose and each purpose differs. Yet they all share a common thread; in some small way they change the world in which we live. And when people begin to believe in change, wondrous things happen. This apparition, she came here with a purpose. It was no mistake, no coincidence Woody. That I believe."

Neville sat in silence. He raised his cup again and drank a swallow of coffee. His eyes refocused. She shared powerful beliefs, beliefs he struggled to grasp yet from her passion he realized this faith she so freely expressed was completely real to her. It worked in her life. He envied Aunt Claire's clear conception.

In the years he lived with her, Neville had seen Aunt Claire counsel clients and witness their devotion. They sought her advice on all aspects of daily life. They came often and at all hours. They came crying and left happy; they came happy and left troubled. Whatever the message imparted, it was evident they believed.

Even with all this before him, Neville wrestled with Aunt Claire's truth.

"Do you think I'll see her again?"

Her dimples disappeared beneath a somber façade. "That I can't say. If she's accomplished what she set out to accomplish, I suspect you'll never meet again... at least not in your time here."

Distracted, Neville's fingers spun his cup as he studied Dell's aunt. "If nothing else, you've given me plenty to think about."

"You're still my second love, dear, whether you believe or not."

She slid her frail arms across the table clasping both his hands with hers. "Let me do a reading for you. It's been years."

His hands flinched. It *had* been years. Eleven years since Aunt Claire had last looked into Neville heart and deciphered his will and his way. Her fingers curled into his palms with firm but gentle pressure. Her eyes closed. She angled her head toward the ceiling and in seconds fell into a trance. Her eyelids fluttered. After several seconds, her fingers stiffened fighting for release. Suddenly Aunt Claire's eyes popped open.

"That's odd. I read that same strong Pisces, nothing but water, torrents of water. All these years and nothing's changed."

Neville showed indifference to Aunt Claire's reading. He expected it. Water had played a major role in his life and left an ugly connotation for the ensuing years. He hugged Aunt Claire and thanked her for the reading and the motherly advice. The talk of water, the past sent Neville's thoughts spinning back to Bishop's Bay and its impact on him.

As he stepped onto the porch, the sun was high in a cloudless sky much like the beach that day. Today was cold, but that day it was hot and muggy; a perfect beach day.

The day Neville's life changed forever.

CHAPTER 15

I T BEGAN WITH Neville's second sitter, Sheila Babcock, leaving to marry a man in Boston. She was twenty-two, dependable and unfortunately for Neville and his father, happy to leave Bishop's Bay. It was two years after his mother had left when Sharon Thurber entered Neville's life.

Arthur had hired Sharon only weeks before to work in his hardware store. She seemed dedicated and responsible, and she possessed one irrepressible trait. Sharon was outspoken, which on its own would have worked out, but she seemed hard pressed to keep her thoughts to herself.

Her first day on cash a seemingly offhand remark to one of the store patrons, Earl Horvath a retired plumber, set Arthur to thinking. Largely unaware, Sharon told Earl he could easily have his barber shear off the hair growing from inside his ears. Earl stared back stunned and marched out mumbling.

The second issue happened two days later. Melody Jenkins, another long-time customer, approached Sharon at the till. Melody was wearing a purple blouse embroidered with dark violet flowers, a black wool skirt and purple suede boots. A woman in her early forties, Melody looked overdressed for the hardware store, but fashionable. Sharon stared for several seconds. In a sudden fit of honesty, she declared the color purple served a better purpose in caskets and on Catholic priests. Melody left in a huff.

If nothing else, Neville's father possessed an uncanny

ability to identify a person's limitations. Always the businessman, Arthur Wishwood cared about two things: that customers came in and that customers came back. Sharon's candid personality had become a detriment to his retail operation. After training her for two weeks, Arthur recognized Sharon's talents suited a higher calling. He knew of Sharon's struggles so instead of firing her, he offered her the position as Neville's sitter. And there were reasons for his decision.

A woman in her early thirties, Sharon had arrived in Bishop's Bay fresh off a tumultuous divorce. Arthur heard of her recent past from the cousin Sharon came to visit. Prior to Bishop's Bay, she lived in Cleveland, Ohio. Two years earlier a car struck and killed her seven-year-old son on the street in front of their home. The tragedy put undue strain on her marriage and eventually she and her husband divorced.

While visiting, Sharon decided to stay in Bishop's Bay and her cousin, Mary Lou Weaver, called Arthur about employment for Sharon. Arthur had known Mary Lou most of his adult life. He fished with her husband Marty on weekends, and knew their son Travis from Neville's hockey team. Mary Lou was quick to explain the circumstances behind Sharon's stay, and Arthur wanted to help.

With Sharon struggling in the hardware store, Arthur satisfied both his need for a sitter and Sharon's need for employment. Thus began a long and rewarding relationship for Neville and his caretaker, Sharon Thurber.

It took only weeks for Arthur to recognize Sharon was truly a mother at heart. He watched their relationship blossom from strangers, to friends, to trusted guardian to his young son. Nights he worked late, Sharon and Neville watched old movies at home, sharing popcorn, diet Coke and engaging in playful banter. She enjoyed the role of caretaker: the cooking, the cleaning, the overall planning for a child just as any mother and as much as it filled an emotional gap for Neville, it too fulfilled her.

Their growing trust fostered the more difficult conversations to follow. Sharon spoke openly of her son, Isaac's, tragic death; how Neville helped fill the void. Neville spoke of his mother's desertion and his father's stoic response. A rapport developed in their relationship that each realized early on. For both, each filled the other's need. When they reached that point they became more than just child and sitter, they became mother and foster son.

Sharon excelled in her duties, and Arthur felt comfortable working longer hours. This laid the brunt of Neville's upbringing on Sharon wide shoulders. Not that she was overly large, but Sharon was certainly no waifish young maiden. She held an athletic build, sturdy rather than fat. Her shoulder length blonde hair draped a round clear face and a little makeup actually emphasized Sharon's pretty features.

With Arthur working Saturdays, Sharon began driving Neville to his hockey practices in Rainard, a larger town west of Bishop's Bay. The winter drive was an hour each way but Rainard was the closest center with an ice rink. He knew Neville loved it and the distraction had served to bond father and son in a sport they both enjoyed. Sharon took to Neville's hockey from the onset. Sundays Neville played his hockey games and most game days saw Sharon and Arthur travel together to watch. Like most small town hockey arenas, the stands were cold and the coffee was awful. It did little to deter the ever-faithful parents. Most Sundays the stands were full. Mothers, fathers, brothers, sisters all congregated to cheer on their little hockey-stars-in-the-making.

For Sharon, the games became the highlight of her week and she cheered Neville's every move boisterously from the stands. With his subdued personality, Arthur was prone to be less rambunctious, often staring at the wild antics of his son's sitter muttering guarded comments so as not to offend the other parents nearby. Sharon took no heed and continued on, often reminding Neville's father, *"He's your son, cheer damn it!"*

But that was Sharon; whatever she thought came out.

In her first year, Sharon discovered the complex across the parking lot from the Rainard Arena. It was a public swimming pool and she took the time to look up the schedule. Neville was now ten-years-old and living so near the ocean, she thought he should learn to swim. The following spring she implored Arthur to enroll Neville in swimming classes. Arthur complied. Thus began Neville's odyssey into the world of competitive swimming. The change did not happen overnight.

THE LIFEGUARD

Neville took several years and Sharon's steadfast guidance to make it happen.

Sharon learned to swim at an early age. As a teenager, Sharon joined the high school swimming team and became a standout. She wanted Neville to share the joys she experienced from swimming and the friendships made. Neville, excited about his new endeavor, worked hard to emulate his guardian's success.

He was tall for his age, thin and lithe with a swimmers long arms and legs. He took to it as the proverbial duck to water. Under Sharon's supervision, Neville mastered freestyle swimming. Neville's father soon took an interest in his son's newest undertaking, finding a fatherly pride in Neville's passion for the sport.

Those first years learning to swim instilled a sense of accomplishment in Neville. For Sharon, she saw Neville's confidence grow providing her what she relished most: the opportunity to teach, to care, to make a difference in the life of someone she had truly grown to love.

Neville's abilities in the pool continued to improve and at thirteen, he dropped out of hockey. Although he loved the sport, by that time it was clear he would never perfect its finer points. That along with the introduction of body checking convinced Arthur of its possible dangers.

In his first year of high school, Neville tried out for the swim team. He failed to qualify. His second year, Neville made the team. His junior year, Sharon Thurber, his coach and mentor these last six years, took leave of the Wishwoods. The decision remained difficult, having grown to love Neville and her extended family in Bishop's Bay. Sharon's mother, living back in Cleveland, had suffered a setback. A cancer diagnosis resulted in radical surgery and a lengthy convalescence. Now fifteen, Neville was old enough to care for himself and well on his way to becoming a competitive swimmer.

In an emotional parting, Neville hugged his surrogate mother and held her for several teary minutes. Sharon's athletic arms wrapped him with a passion unequaled in Neville's young life, hiding the tears streaming off her cheeks. Neville's tears slipped onto her shoulders as he labored to release her from his grip. Sharon had become the parent he never had. A mother and coach, his fiery mentor spurred Neville on to achieve what he once thought unachievable. She had given him goals and ultimately passed on her competitive spirit. By giving of herself, Sharon Thurber had imparted Neville with a true sense of his own potential.

The train arrived on time that day in Rainard. Typical fall weather, cool with a slight breeze wafting in from the coast. Even Arthur knew he would miss his friend and confidant of these past six years. Although they had argued on what was in Neville's best interest on many occasions, he saw the woman she was, and in his quiet way loved her for it. Arthur realized Sharon was the only other human being who loved his son as he did, without judgment, without reservation.

Finally releasing Neville, Sharon kissed him. Arthur Wishwood stepped forward and with his own grateful hug, whispered two words in her ear, "Thank you." Arthur slipped an envelope into Sharon's jacket pocket. It was extra money for a friend is all he thought. With a parting sniffle, he kissed Sharon. Boarding her waiting train she called back one last time, "You'll always be my second son Woody...always. We'll see each other soon."

She disappeared into the train car.

Neville would never see Sharon Thurber again and he would forever wonder why. While taking care of her ailing mother in Cleveland, Sharon took the advice of doctors and tested for the disease. They discovered Sharon had cancer. Sharon Thurber died less than a year later while her mother made a full recovery. A cruel irony to be sure.

Neville's junior year of high school found him captain of the swim team. Along with his promotion, Neville's twelve-member chess club elected him president. Adding to an already full schedule, Neville took on the responsibility as editor of their high school yearbook. That year Neville learned the delicate art of living a balanced life, but it kept him centered. What little time he did find, Neville squandered on old television reruns.

His junior year passed and Neville attained his goals, but his senior year is what propelled him to new heights. He remained captain of the swim team, maintained a straight-A grade, was re-elected president of the chess club, and again asked to lead the yearbook staff as editor. His responsibilities left little time to pursue what he wanted most, a girlfriend. To a degree, Neville felt the satisfaction of his successes but in many ways, it seemed hollow. He knew his father was proud of him, and there were benefits to being popular in school, still Neville bore a loneliness; missing someone special to share his accomplishments.

In April of his senior year Neville's high school swim team won the county swimming meet. His 100-meter freestyle time was the fastest ever recorded in the state. His 200-meter freestyle time was only point five seconds off the state record, and his 200-meter backstroke won the event final. His long hours in the pool finally paid dividends.

Over a three day weekend in June, Neville swam for the Atlantic States title in all three events. With his father sitting in the stands, a nerve afflicted Neville finished second in the 100-meter final, just behind the winner by a mere one second and his 200-meter backstroke garnered a solid third place finish. For a small town like Bishop's Bay, Neville's efforts catapulted him into celebrity status. He returned home the conquering hero.

That summer town fathers recognized Neville's achievement by awarding him a coveted job patrolling the beach as one of their primary lifeguards. Neville and five other fortunate candidates took their place in shifts atop the two towers spaced along the pristine beach fronting the resort town of Bishop's Bay.

The early sixties saw the town fathers invest in the community by not only transforming the beach property but building twenty one-bedroom beach cabanas along a shelf of land once used as a railway siding. Pine trees dotted the grounds where once trains cars lined up for fresh fish. That stretch now housed the original twenty cottages and dozens more built in the years since. These rentals, the pristine beach and the overall laid-back attitude of their small town drew tourists from all over the state and well beyond. People trekked here from as far away as Boston and New York for their summer getaways.

Tourism had become the town's primary revenue source since the late nineteen sixties. Fishing, once the primary source of income for residents, continued only as a recreational activity and centered at the small marina built just north of the beach.

That fateful summer, Neville stood guard.

Sitting atop a lofty tower perch enamored by a newfound confidence, he surveyed the crowded summer seashore armed with binoculars he paid for himself. Anxiously, he waited to be of service.

It was early August and half the summer had slipped away without incident. That day the beach was alive with activity. Sea-scent drifted in with every ocean wave, a mix of salt, sea – weed and hot, humid air. Near Neville's tower, a radio played an oldies station; Bachman Turner Overdrive rocking out one of their classics, "Let It Ride". A leash-free toy collie ran by below, a yellow Frisbee clutched between his toothy jaws. Blankets and beach towels covered the sandy grounds painting the shoreline in squares of rainbow bright color. Children, parents, teenagers scurried in and out of the frothy white mix rolling in from the bay's unending churn.

Glassing the shore thirty yards out, Neville's gaze crossed a sea-nymph lifting demurely from the surf. A young girl his age, her black hair flattened against her head dripping of seawater and sensuality. She wore a white one-piece suit trimmed in black and as she moved up the sandy incline, the sway of her slim hips hypnotically compromised Neville's somewhat limited attention. Her curves shifted in esthetic rhythm with her arms. Her lean figure accentuated small, firm breasts, sitting proud. The young woman's legs were long and tanned and as she marched toward him, her blue eyes seemed focused on Neville alone.

The glasses dropped and dangled from the strap around his neck. He stared out as she continued her trek in and gulped a nervous gulp. He had no idea who she was.

Out past the rolling breakers to his left Neville missed seeing the fat man holding the two oversized inner tubes: one Jerry Kavanagh, a banker from Providence. In front of him in the shallows, his six-year-old son pleaded for him to come closer. Jerry laughed, teasing his son to venture further. He held tight to the oversized tubes, blocking the view from the beach. Two young girls frolicked in the waves behind the fat man and his son, unseen by anyone on the beach. The older girl was Campbell Prentice and with her companion, Lily Delysle, they had come to vacation here these last four summers.

Lily's mother, Janet worked in Boston and the last four years she had rented a cottage in Bishop's Bay. Today she sat soaking up the sun unaware. Lily was twelve-years-old, just graduating into eighth grade. Only Campbell saw her slip beneath the ocean surf that day. Neville should have, but he sat atop his tower distracted. Realizing her companion had succumbed to the water, the second girl screamed for help. Her voice dwindled in the sound of breaking waves, the giddy laughter of vacationers and children's excited screams.

In one quick motion, Neville returned to his field glasses and gazed upon the innocent beauty once again. Her smile widened as she came in closer. Neville failed to see the struggle playing out behind the fat man with the oversized inner tubes. No one did.

Another wave came in smothering Campbell's screams, tossing her headlong into the murky green waters. Jerry's inner tubes screened all sight lines from the beach itself so when Lily's mother looked up and saw nothing, she lay back down to feel the warm spray of sun.

Neville continued to follow the path of this mysterious young nymph as she closed the distance to his tower. Neville was indeed, immersed. Bachman Turner Overdrive continued to play nearby and at twenty feet from his post; the sea-sprite took on a name as he recognized her from school. Jennifer Capaldi, a member of his chess club and somehow transformed from the bespectacled seventeen-year-old geek he had known into this ravishing young nymphet.

As Lily drifted beneath the waves, Campbell struggled to remain afloat.

Neville stepped down from his tower. "Jen, what happened to you?" he asked befuddled and obviously without thinking.

"So you *can* see me," she returned sarcastically. "My parents gave me a birthday present is all. I had my eyes lasered– no more glasses." Her hand sat proudly on a hip as Neville stepped down another rung. Yes, Jenny had certainly changed, and what a change. Not only had she relinquished the glasses but beneath those dowdy plaid skirts she wore, a newly sculpted woman had formed.

Neville took the final step onto sand and leaning against the tower support began a conversation with Jennifer. A scream suddenly let out from the shore near Neville's lifeguard tower. The radio went silent and with a second scream piercing the air, he turned and saw people running to the water's edge. Neville bolted from Jennifer's side and ran past several onrushing tourists.

He broke through the crowd and watched as a man dragged a young girl onto the beach. It was Jerry Kavanagh and the girl was Campbell. He held onto his own son with his free arm. Breathing in spurts, she screamed frantically, *"Lily... Lily... she's still out there..."*

Neville shot past a winded Jerry Kavanagh, dove into the water and swam straight to where he had last seen the man. Waves curled in his path as he sped to deeper water. He dove down and within seconds Neville found an arm drifting with the current, pointed out into the bay. The arm appeared detached, a ghostly remnant lost in the murky green froth. He yanked it. Lily's face appeared through a cloud of hair. She seemed at peace with the world, angelic. Her tiny frame drifted into his arms and as he clutched her Neville darted to the surface. With his heart pounding in piston beats, he hit warm air. He adjusted her head and swam as hard and fast as his body allowed.

Near shore, he stood with Lily's frail lifeless body draped across his arms. She weighed less than air in those few steps up the beach yet she hung heavy as lead in his arms. A crowd gathered and a steady disconsolate murmur eked out. All watched as Neville placed her down on the sand and began CPR. His partner lifeguard called out for someone to call an ambulance. Someone did.

Lily's mother knelt in the sand nearby with both hands covering her mouth, in shock. Tears streamed from her wide eyes. Neville breathed for Lily and switched back to pumping her fragile chest. Back and forth he went, breathing, pumping. Lily's eyes stayed closed. Dribbles of water drained from her nose and mouth. Neville continued compressions.

Eight minutes elapsed. The ambulance arrived with no signs of life still from little Lily. They carried a large grey case onto the beach parting the worried crush of onlookers. Her mother stood as the attendants took over. Neville pulled back and sat stone-faced in the sand allowing the paramedics to continue. It was too late. Jerry Kavanagh's efforts, Neville's efforts, the paramedics efforts were all too late.

Little Lily Delysle died on that beach in Bishop's Bay the sixth day of August. She was twelve-years-old. Neville wandered off the beach late that sunny afternoon never to return, at least not in person. He cried, knowing the truth and his responsibility in Lily's demise, yet he spoke of it only once. Neville confessed the sin to his father, Arthur and only because he needed his help.

Neville took the balance of his summer off and with Arthur's blessing looked to escape Bishop's Bay and the guilt of little Lily's death. His next three weeks were the longest of his life. The endless hours amounted to torture and in them: he relived that dreadful day repeatedly.Arthur tried mitigating Neville's involvement or lack of by constantly reminding him that accidents happen all the time. Neville would hear nothing of it and vowed never to swim again and to drive the point home, instead of entering Boston College as intended he enrolled in a university far from any ocean, from any beach. He found an opening at the University of Minnesota. Having saved his entire life for Neville's education, Arthur quickly agreed.

The last week in August, Neville moved to Minnesota and began his life anew. A virtual prisoner in his own home his last month in Bishop's Bay, he found the move liberating. Neville fought to be free of guilt and at first believed he had accomplished his escape. He soon discovered the truth.

Within months of moving to Solomon, the dream made its first nightly manifestation. Sleep became the conduit for Neville's haunted past to return. It visited on a regular basis.

For Neville dreams became the enemy, his shame the ammunition.

CHAPTER 16

MINUTES BEFORE NOON Saturday, Willis Ogland arrived at Roland's condo carrying a tray with two hot drinks. He buzzed and waited. In time, Roland answered. A lethargic voice called through the intercom, "Come on up."

Roland greeted his lover wearing only the bottoms to his night-wear. He yawned, gave Willis a brief hug and retreated to the living room to sit. Willis followed placing the tray on the coffee table.

"There's a coffee here for you." He unzipped his coat, pulled his own drink from the tray and sat across from his friend. Roland glared stone-faced as he slumped forward to pull out the drink.

"I'd prefer a latte, but…" He grumbled.

"Up late?"

Leaning in, Roland hesitated. His eyes and head shrugged toward the end table and the e-book reader lying next to the lamp. "Yeah, well… I was reading and before I realized it was two o'clock."

Willis slid across the sofa and picked up Roland's electronic reader.

Although he played the innocent fop at times, he was no one's fool. He suspected Roland had done little reading the night prior. Unbeknownst to Roland, Willis had visited his condo the night before and had called his home phone. If Roland were home, surely he would have answered especially for his closest friend and lover.

Willis suspected his lover had found another, more pleasurable pursuit in a Minneapolis club they had visited weeks before. The venue,

The Fall Staff, was an exciting distraction for both and one of its more stimulating aspects was the abundance of eligible gay men in attendance. Of course, Willis wanted what he, himself offered– fidelity, and to this point in their relationship, he assumed Roland's loyalty. Now he had doubts. Still, he hesitated to accuse Roland and instead Willis held onto hope and acted the part of Roland's dutiful but dim lover.

He clicked on the e-reader. *"The Fall of Hyperion,* by Dan Simmons. What's this... science fiction?"

Roland let out a laugh. "What surprises you most? That I enjoy a good book or that I read at all?"

Willis shut off the e-reader and placed it back on the table. "I don't know. You just never seemed like the science fiction type."

"There's a lot you don't know about me Willis." Roland flashed a sly smile and sipped his coffee.

"They were talking in your office about a book Woody wrote. Apparently it's science fiction... from what I heard."

A scowl invaded Roland's once playful demeanor. "I've seen it. John had it out on the desk last week... *Seven Days of Sun* or something. Knowing Wishy, it's probably trash like those Star Trek books. Twenty years from now he'll still be writing obituaries for The Sentinel."

On some level, Roland's prediction failed to strike Willis as all that bad. Twenty years of secure employment meant a place to live, a weekly paycheck and vacations away from the cold Minnesota winters. No, Willis saw Roland's contemptuous observation as something that might work in his life. Willis had no grand plans like his lover Roland. Instead, he saw this scheme to rob the accounts of Sentinel advertisers as an outrageous gambit fraught with consequence. Willis found contentment in a simpler way of life.

"Maybe he will," Willis said, turning away.

Roland detected his discomfort. "What is it Willis? I know something's bothering you."

Unable to face Roland, Willis muttered back. "This plan of yours worries me. Your college friend Davis...what if he turns on you?"

"I told you," Roland started. "Davis has got a lot more to lose than I do. He's the one who should be worried. Besides, what can go wrong?"

"Famous last words…"

Roland stood, joined Willis on the sofa and wrapped an arm around him. "Our little plan here, it's harmless really. Who's getting hurt? These companies? They have plenty of money and anything we get, insurance will reimburse. It's a victimless crime all done from a distance. No one gets hurt, no one suffers."

Roland lifted his lover's chin kissing him on the cheek. "The plan is perfect don't worry. Three months from now we'll be sipping margaritas on a beach while this town is still digging out from the winter snows."

A cautious grin crossed Willis's lips. "If you say so."

Roland's plan sounded harmless. His scheme left everyone involved on the sidelines away from the actual theft. No guns, no threat of injury, just the slick manipulation of numbers in a series of bank accounts. No fuss, no mess and a fortune would be theirs to enjoy. At least that was the sell from Roland's end.

Willis wanted to believe his friend but the stirring in the pit of his stomach told him a very different tale. No amount of antacid could settle the churning inside. Willis said nothing and drank his coffee unwilling to voice his concerns. He knew Roland preferred it that way.

After visiting Aunt Claire, Neville returned home to find his father sitting bolt upright in his favorite leather lounger, smiling broadly. Arthur's chest puffed out proudly displaying his new blue two-pocket button-down shirt and matching blue corduroy pants. Unable to contain himself, Arthur exclaimed, "Dell bought me new clothes. And he bought the new guy some too."

"Phil?"

Dell pounced from the hallway wild with energy. Both hands directed Neville's attention behind him. As if introducing a circus act he announced, "Ta-da…"

A pleased but reluctant Phil walked out dressed in a tan version of Arthur's buttoned, two-pocket dress shirt. His pants were matching tan with a wide black belt. Phil's shoes were black lace-up half-boots. On his hip, a small black pouch hung from the belt, an imitation cartridge holder. Phil, whose looks resembled the fictional Barney Fife, stood before Neville dressed as his double. The only thing missing was the badge.

"What do you think?" Dell asked.

At first dismayed, Neville watched Phil model his new wardrobe. He seemed all too honored to show them off to his new friends. Neville moved in closer examining their houseguest. "How do you like 'em Phil?"

"They're great, and they fit much better than your father's clothes."

Dell beamed a proud grin.

"You don't mind looking like a television character?" Neville asked.

"Not at all. I've got new clothes that fit and feel comfortable. What more could I ask?"

Arthur climbed from the lounger and stood next to Phil. "Me too."

Although initially annoyed by Dell's antics, Neville watched both men display an odd allegiance to their benefactor. Their smiles convinced him Dell's unorthodox care must be therapeutic. Outnumbered, Neville let out a laugh. "I guess it's a job well done."

Pleased by the outcome of the morning shopping spree Dell again directed his attention to their houseguest. "I got him a pair of jeans and a black shirt too, but this... this is my masterpiece."

"You sound like Dr. Frankenstein, '*look, look what I've created,*'" Neville quipped.

"No monster here," Dell said rearranging the shoulder epaulets on Phil's shirt. "Just a good lookin' guy in uniform."

Their light-hearted banter helped soften the severity of Neville's last few days. Dell's timing was impeccable. As Neville took stock of both men modeling their newest fashions, Dell retrieved a plastic bag from the coffee table.

"I picked up Dewey's Christmas present this morning. Look at this." Dell pulled out a small box– an Apple i-Pod.

"He'll love it Dell."

"I think so. I'll load it up with music before Christmas. Lots of Beatles, a few Rolling Stones, maybe some Queen and a dash of old Soundgarden. That'll get him started."

Phil and Arthur stood side-by-side sizing up the other's new look. They could easily have passed for father and son in their contrasting blue and beige outfits. Neville retreated to the kitchen.

"What about Aunt Claire?" Dell asked. "Did you see her?"

"Of course…"

Left out of their conversation, Arthur whispered something to his surrogate son. Phil nodded and the two hurried from the living room.

Neville went on to explain Aunt Claire's rationale on the appearance and disappearance of Audrey; her thoughts on the intervention by the now departed young nurse and how it appeared related to either him or Phil. Dell saw how his aunt's explanation seemed far-fetched to his friend. At this point in the conversation, Dell interrupted.

"Do you believe in God?"

"I guess…"

"Do you know what he's thinking?"

"Of course not," Neville said without thought.

"Neither do I. And neither does Aunt Claire or anyone else for that matter. That's her point Woody. Who are we to try and make sense of something so extraordinary it defies human logic? We can't. And do you know why?"

Neville took a feeble bite of his sandwich. His eyes focused on Dell. "No."

"Because human logic doesn't apply past these boundaries. Out there the rules are different," he said waving a hand above his head. "… and so are the reasons for the rules. If Aunt Claire says she came with a purpose, you can believe she came with some purpose we can never know."

Frustrated, Neville placed the sandwich back on his plate. "But why? Why did she appear here?"

"All I can say is… to be determined," Dell said with the same self-assured smile Neville saw on Aunt Claire.

The conversation had soured Neville's tuna sandwich. He pushed it aside. Never one to waste food, Dell picked up the sandwich and took a hearty bite. "I'm going out tonight with Bob. Why don't you come with us? Have a few beers, a few laughs, maybe meet a few women… it'll be fun," Dell said swallowing back the last of Neville's lunch.

"I don't know," Neville said as he fingered the plate. "Maybe another time Dell."

"Woody this thing with Rita… at some point you have to let it go. I know you love her; I love her too. But Rita's just not seeing your life together the same way she did when you first got married. It's not your fault. You've tried. I keep telling you: you've been a good husband and a terrific father. Something in Rita has changed and *you* can't change it back.

"It's time to move on. Come on out with us, meet a few women and you'll see. Life goes on. We can get Russell to watch Phil and Artie for the night. Besides, Bob said he's willing to wear something other than his camouflage outfit tonight. That alone'll be worth the price of admission."

A crooked smile swept across Neville's face. He knew his friend meant well but…

"I know what you're saying makes sense but I'm just not there. Not yet, anyway. Give it a few weeks and I'll see where I'm at. But I appreciate the offer, Dell."

"Boy, ain't love grand," Dell jested.

"I know…" Neville shot a pained look toward his friend.

"Hey, I almost forgot. The weather's supposed to get hostile next week. I thought we'd go up and get our tree tomorrow. Shaner's Mountain should still be passable and Willard'll be waiting."

"Sure." Neville thought for a few seconds. "I'll call Rita. I'm sure she'll be okay with letting Dewey come."

What began that first year after the fire as a tribute to his dog Willard, had morphed into an annual pilgrimage and every year since,

Dell visited his former forest home near Shaner's Mountain. Dell and Aunt Claire buried Willard near the site of the burnt out log cabin. While visiting the gravesite, Dell found it therapeutic to cut down a Christmas tree from his father's three-acre lot. Every year since, Dell returned to visit his dog's grave on or near the date he calculated Willard was born: two weeks before Christmas. Dell vowed to celebrate Willard's life not his death. He continued to stay true to that promise.

In the years since Neville, Arthur, Aunt Claire and even Rita had accompanied Dell to pay homage to his loyal dog and return home with a tree in remembrance. This year they planned to introduce Dewey to the ritual.

As they made plans for an early morning departure, Arthur and Phil silently appeared in the kitchen doorway. Neville glanced up.

"What's this?"

"What do you think?" Phil asked with obvious excitement. The two men had exchanged clothes and faced their caregivers with wide exemplary grins. Phil's once perfectly tailored look in tan transformed to baggy blue while Arthur's tidy blue appearance now had him resembling a bronze overstuffed sausage. The shirt buttons stretched the fabric to a point nearing liberation. Although they stood roughly the same height, Arthur's round shape made the switch weirdly comic.

Neville and Dell stared for several seconds and suddenly erupted. After the laughing settled, Dell approached shepherding the two men toward the bedroom.

"Come on! You two can't stay in each other's clothes… you'll wreck them. And then all that money I spent'll go to waste. And I'll get mad and do something I'll regret."

Dell's voice faded as all three disappeared down the hall.

Neville sat alone in the kitchen. He resisted moving on as Dell suggested all because he still loved his ex-wife. As he held out hope, he called Rita and arranged for her to drop Dewey off early the next day. Having once partaken in Dell's ritual return to Shaner's Mountain, Rita recognized the trip as a wholesome experience for her young son.

That afternoon they settled in for the night. The sun dwindled along the rooftops across their neighborhood street, the air stiffened with a crisp cold wind leaving only the sound of leafless trees chattering in their wake. The western sky grew bright from a half-moon radiating winter white into the cloudless reaches.

Dell had returned to his upstairs apartment after dinner to prepare for his night out. Neville turned on the television. The Bruins were playing the New York Rangers. Arthur had joined Phil on the sofa and they waited for the game to begin. Tonight, for some unexplained reason, Arthur abandoned his usual place in the leather lounger.

"Do you like hockey Phil?" Neville asked.

Phil telegraphed a blank stare. "I don't know. Is it like football? I remember something about football."

"Not really, but it's just as competitive and a lot faster. I've got tickets to a college hockey game this week. If you like you can tag along with us."

"Okay."

The game began and Neville opened his laptop as he sat preparing to catch up on his writing. A glance across showed both Phil and his father intently following the play by play. He smiled and left them alone to retrieve the dictionary from his bedroom dresser.

Neville approached the dresser and noticed the folded picture of Audrey. His thoughts spun back. While he reached to pick it up his eyes caught a reflection in the dresser mirror. Next to Audrey's picture lay the hospital bill half-opened and now reflected the signature of Phil's benefactor. The name, impossible to read in the hospital, translated in reverse image.

Neville picked up the bill and studied the signature. The name remained indecipherable as written. He turned the page around and flashed it toward the mirror. In a startling discovery, the reversed writing spelled out the name *Camillus De Lellis*.

He stood before his dresser and wondered aloud, '*What the hell's going on?*' He heard the front door rattle and rushed into the hallway to see Dell enter. With his dark hair still slick, Dell sported black dress pants and shoes adding a grey patterned shirt. Over top, he wore a long black coat. He was dressed for his night on the town.

"Dell, come here!"

As Dell approached, Neville pushed the signature into Dell's face.

"What's this?" Dell asked backing away.

"Read the signature!"

Dell held the document steady and tried to decipher the written words. "I can't, it's just mumbo-jumbo."

Neville took his friend's hand dragged him into the bedroom and held the bill before the mirror. "Read it now."

Dell's eyes refocused in Neville's bedroom light and he read the results. Shocked, his mouth popped open. "Oh my god it's mirror writing– like Da Vinci! But who's Camillus De Lellis?"

Neville sat on his bed stared up at his friend and gathered his thoughts. He remembered the argument by the two nurses the day before; their insistence that each had seen a very different man and how he had attributed their dispute to stress. Now he wasn't so sure.

"I have no idea."

Pulling the bill from Neville's hand, Dell studied the signature and after returned to the dresser mirror. He read it again. "Camillus De Lellis."

"Google," Neville said. "Everyone who's anyone is on the internet."

They made their way to the living room.

Arthur groaned as Neville sat at the desk. Phil followed with a groan of his own. New York had scored. Dell watched from over his friend's shoulder as he punched up the Google website. He entered the name Camillus De Lellis, and waited.

A Wikipedia reference came up first. He clicked on the search result and a web page popped into view. Dell hovered over his right shoulder as he read the results aloud.

"St. Camillus De Lellis, born 1550, died 1614, an Italian priest who founded a religious order dedicated to the care of the sick."

Further down the page Neville read with surprise: *"Canonized by Pope Benedict XIV in 1742, he is known as the patron saint of the sick, hospitals, nurses and physicians."*

Neville turned to face Dell, both stunned to learn that a saint had paid for their awkward, sometimes misinformed houseguest's hospital bill. And not just any saint but one, who by all accounts, had been dead for four hundred years.

Dell picked up the bill and studied the information once more. "Says here he paid by Visa. Wonder what he put on the application for occupation– dead saint?"

"Dell…"

"Just saying. I had to lie to get mine," Dell said.

Neville sat frustrated. "Maybe he lied too…who cares."

"Saints don't lie. That's why they're saints."

Neville gave his friend a cease and desist glare. Both turned their attention across the room. "Phil, do you know who Camillus De Lellis is?" Neville asked.

He looked over. "Pardon?"

"Camillus De Lellis, do you know who he is?" Dell asked.

As he stared vacantly toward his two caregivers, Phil pondered the question at great length. "Does he play for the Bruins?"

"No, but you're close," Dell returned.

"Who is he?" Phil asked.

"He's a goalie for the 1961 Montreal Canadians," Neville's father inserted and returned to the hockey game

"Close too, Dad, but no. He's just a man from a long time ago. Sorry to interrupt." Neville closed his laptop. In their confusion, Neville and Dell retreated to the kitchen. This newest wrinkle had both men confused.

"How does this fit into any of this?" Neville asked.

Dell lifted the back of his coat and sat across from his perplexed friend. "Maybe this guy's dyslexic. Or he could have forged the signature… scribbled a name he knows and took off."

"Yeah, let's scribble a name in mirror script and see if anyone figures it out. It doesn't make sense. The nurses, Dell, they each saw a very different man and both were so convinced of what they saw they had a fight over it. It just doesn't make sense."

Dell hesitated. "Not to us. Isn't that what Aunt Claire was trying to say, Woody? Just because we can't figure something out, doesn't mean it isn't significant to someone, somewhere."

This was not what Neville wanted from his friend. In the wake of yet another strange encounter, he wanted Dell to agree that this conundrum had a rational explanation; that they could interpret this newest twist within the boundaries of physical science. At that moment, Neville looked to Dell for such reassurance but found another barrier instead. The most logical motive seemed to center on what Dell said previously– to be determined.

As they sat in silence, Dell popped up from the kitchen table. "Saint or no saint, it'll all be here tomorrow. Tonight it's time to play and I'm not letting St. Camillus De Lellis ruin my first real night out in a month."

Dell made his way to the refrigerator. Before Neville could respond, Dell squatted and peeled off leaves from a head of lettuce. Neville watched him move on to the celery and snap off a long stalk. From there, Dell plucked a carrot from the crisper and sliced off several shards with a knife. He followed by snipping the celery into smaller sections.

Staring back inside the refrigerator, Dell asked, "Have you got any radishes?"

"No, but there's a couple tomatoes in the next drawer."

"Tomatoes are too messy… same with onions. This'll have to do."

Dell ripped the lettuce leaves into lesser squares and with the celery and carrot slivers stuffed them into an inside pocket of his overcoat.

Mystified, Neville asked, "What on earth are you doing?"

Dell looked over, finished with his collection. "What… this?" He pointed to the pocket. "It's my opening for tonight."

"Opening for what, a salad bar?"

Snickering, he closed the fridge door. "Of course not. It's how I meet women," he said.

"You meet women by offering up a salad snack from the inside pocket of your coat?"

"Not exactly…"

"Well then what exactly?"

Dell sat next to his friend. A smile crept across his face as he began to enlighten Neville on his unorthodox views to meeting women in a public forum.

"First I scope out a woman I want to meet. Without her seeing me, I'll walk by and sprinkle the mix on the floor by her seat. On my way back, I'll act like I just spotted it, bend over, pick some up and show her. Then I'll ask if it's hers and with most women, they get a little embarrassed lending to a more talkative frame of mind. That gives me a chance to throw in a compliment or two, like... *You must eat a lot of this salad stuff to maintain that slim figure of yours,* or, *They say eating salad makes for a pretty complexion just like yours.* From there the conversation takes off. Works every time."

"*That* works every time..."

"Every time. Sometimes I'll use small potatoes, even green beans, uncooked of course... anything one might considered odd in a nightclub setting. The odder the better. It makes for great fodder, conversation-wise."

Whatever he thought of Dell's methods, Neville knew his friend was onto something. He had witnessed a number of attractive women Dell dated over the years even with his inordinate share of quirks. Dell possessed a strange, ingenuous appeal. Women seemed drawn to his inner child like cats to cream. One could only guess why he never settled down. Perhaps, like the gambling it was more about the chase than the actual achievement.

Nearing the hallway Dell turned back. "Tomorrow, early... Shaner's Mountain. See yah."

He heard the front door open and close. Neville sat and examined the hospital bill again. This time the mirror written signature of a long dead St. Camillus De Lellis struck him differently. He smiled at what Dell pointed out as the method of payment, Visa, and his attitude toward the entire gambit switched to one of absurdity.

A long dead saint paid the hospital bill with a Visa card. It sounded ludicrous, far-fetched. His smile widened and he came to terms with the entire illogical mess. Dell was right; saint or no saint, life does go on and if something were to come of it, what could he do anyway? Yet it added to the mystery.

He folded the bill, replaced it on his dresser and grabbed the dictionary he initially came for. Neville joined his father and Phil in the living room. Both sat quietly staring at the television while the game was at intermission. One of the game announcers interviewed the New York goal scorer. They seemed transfixed, weirdly attentive as if caught in a spell cast by the television.

Neville went back into the kitchen and microwaved a bag of popcorn. The popcorn interrupted their spell instantly as they broke eye contact with the screen long enough to gobble most of the bowl's contents during the break. The second period started with Neville announcing the next day's plan.

"Day trip tomorrow and we're all going," he said.

Finishing a mouthful of popcorn Phil asked, "Where?"

Arthur continued to eat.

Neville explained the ride to visit Dell's dog and the circumstances surrounding the dog's death. He added the ritual procurement of a Christmas tree for the holiday season as part of the trip. Phil appeared excited by the adventure while Arthur continued to munch the last of the popcorn, gazing ahead with a vacuous stare. If he understood any of it, he kept it to himself.

The game played on and Neville tried to ignite his inner muse. The writing, his ambitious plans for the night, withered in a whirl of reflection: his father's plight, Audrey, and of course, his failed relationship all circled like feeding vultures inside his head. Add to that the appearance of an impossible signature on a hospital bill. Neville gave up on writing and closed his laptop for the night.

As all watched the game, the Bruins finally scored. "It's in the net!" Phil said excitedly.

Neville smiled, seeing Phil enjoy the action.

"The net, the net…" Arthur said stabbing a finger toward the TV screen. Something clicked and his head slowly shifted toward Phil. "I sold nets. For years I sold nets. People like to fish and I sold them nets. In Bishop's Bay. The store. Nets."

Arthur eased back and returned to watching TV. Phil looked on puzzled.

"You sold nets," he said.

Arthur peered over and nodded. Neville had seen his father revisit the past on many occasions. For Arthur, memories were like rafts set adrift upon the abyss. Every so often one would wash ashore. The memory would pass and a new subject taken on.

"At times things come back to him. He'll be alright," Neville said.

"So it's a part of what you said he had…Alzheimer's?" Phil asked.

"Unfortunately, yes."

Arthur, unaware of their conversation, continued to watch the hockey game. The Bruins scored late in the third period giving them a two-one victory. Arthur flashed a satisfied grin, somehow understanding the result. With the game over and only the uncooked kernels left of the popcorn, Phil and Arthur went their separate ways.

Neville made sure his father found his bedroom. He said his goodnights and Phil followed suit, voicing his enjoyment of the game and the possibility of seeing one live. Phil retired finding Dewey's room inviting after a full first day in the Wishwood home.

At ten o'clock, it was still early. Neville sat in the living room thinking of Dell and Bob, and their night on the town. He remembered such nights before Dewey and fatherhood, before Rita and marriage. Dell remained as he always had, unaffected by circumstance. He saw the world through his own prism, this attitude based more on enjoying life rather than enduring it and nothing interfered with his array of diversions. Yet he stayed true to his principles of friendship and loyalty. Neville knew Dell would always be there; always remain committed to him and his family no matter what.

Although Dell took so little of life seriously, on many occasions he counselled Neville on taking Rita's rejection to heart. He pointed to Neville's efforts as a husband and father, the hours he worked, the dreams he tried forging into reality. Dell emphasized, if Rita's choice was to divorce, he saw little more his friend could have done to prevent it. He highlighted Neville's all-abiding devotion to his wife and his son, never showing bitterness toward Rita for her choice to dissolve their marriage. And when Neville was down, Dell would point to Dewey and how truly special their son was.

Neville closed the front room drapes and turned out the lights. Morning would soon be here and their pilgrimage under way. As he made his way to the bedroom, he heard a stirring in Dewey's room. A light shone below the door. He walked by but decided not to disturb Phil.

Neville closed his bedroom door and went to bed. While he thought of the possibilities behind these strange apparitions of Audrey and Camillus De Lellis, he heard the bathroom door open and close. Phil must be up. Arthur Wishwood rarely woke. After several seconds, he heard the door open again.

Business done, he thought.

That night Neville struggled to sleep. Again, he heard a door close.

In time, Neville began to doze off. Suddenly he awoke to a loud clatter from the front of the house. Footsteps sounded on the porch and a woman's high-pitched squeal. Dell was home and he had company. The steps shuffled off and faded into night. In the next few minutes, Neville heard the floor above creak ever so slightly.

As he tried a new sleeping position, he heard the muted beginnings of Wagner's "Ride of The Valkyries." Neville knew it wouldn't be the movie, *Apocalypse Now*, tonight but the music alone, more for mood than anything else.

And Dell's mood surely involved love.

CHAPTER 17

NEVILLE WOKE TO the sound of a car horn. The clock read seven-thirty-two as he swung the covers back and lifted his tired body from its warm nest. As he tottered into the living room, he heard footsteps clatter across the porch. Half asleep, he opened the curtain and saw a woman slide into the back seat of a taxi. Dell waved from the front steps. Neville closed the curtain and shuffled toward the kitchen.

The front door opened and Dell came bounding in cold and excited. He flipped off his snow-covered sandals. "I keep forgetting how cold it is this early," he said brushing his hands together. Neville went straight for the coffee maker.

"No coffee yet?" Dell quizzed.

"I just got up…"

"Is Dewey coming?"

Neville looked at the kitchen clock. "She said she'd drop him off at eight." He sat down, yawned and stared up at Dell, still disoriented. "How was your night?"

"Great… met a wonderful young lady, Jennifer Gilchrist. And I think she's a keeper," said Dell, plunking two slices into the toaster. After a few seconds, Dell's comments registered.

"So you're officially in a relationship… with a girl?"

"I guess you could say that. I like her and we did have a lot of laughs."

"What about Bob? Did he meet anyone?"

Dell sat down. His enthusiasm waned. "Bob... I'm starting to worry about that boy."

"Why?"

"He did meet someone but she was older. Rhonda, Rhonda..." Dell gazed into the ceiling. "...Billington, Billingsworth. Anyway, she works at a bank somewhere. All she talked about was money, and how to invest it. Bob was mesmerized."

"What's wrong with that? Older, good job..."

"She's married," Dell added abruptly.

"Oh... that's not good."

The toast popped up and with the coffee brewed the conversation ended. As Neville poured out two cups he said, "I didn't get much sleep last night, maybe you should drive today."

"No problem. Car's all gassed up and ready to go. Besides I have heat."

Dell buttered and ate his toast. Neville gulped down a mouthful of coffee. "We better get dad and Phil up. Dewey'll be here any minute."

"I'll wake 'em."

Dell went down the hall, first to Arthur's room. He banged on the door, pushed it open, flipped on the light and called in, "Up and at 'em Artie. We're off to magic mountain."

Arthur stirred and sat up somewhat dazed.

Dell followed the same routine and banged on Phil's bedroom door, opened it and he flipped the light switch on. With it, the room transformed. Bright light flickered from the planets orbiting the room's center sun. No longer dormant, the spheres rotated in symphony above the bed. A dark projection shone across the ceiling to mimic far-flung star fields and all nine planets glowed with new life and color. The mobile sparked an amazing display as it circled the sun-like center of the simulated solar system. It was more incredible than even Dell imagined it could be.

"What the hell happened here?"

Phil turned beneath the covers. He sat up. "How do you like it, Dell?"

Distracted, Dell called, "Woody come see this."

Neville came down the hallway and saw Dell staring inside Dewey's room. As he joined his friend, he looked in. "Oh my god. Is that the same mobile we put up?"

He watched spellbound as the planets traced a circular route around the yellow sun. The lights, once dead, now shone and shimmered in a remarkable recreation of their celestial home. The ceiling backdrop flashed light streams casting alien shadows of worlds too far to know. A subtle whirr sounded from the light's base and the once latent motor set the entire display in motion.

"But, but how..." Neville stuttered.

Phil swung his legs out of bed. He appeared small in Arthur's old pajamas.

"I cleaned it up last night." He pointed to the wastebasket. Inside it lay several blackened tissues and on the dresser an open jar of Vaseline.

"You did this... last night?" Neville asked.

"Yes, I thought Dewey would like it."

"Like it, he'll love it! But how'd you get the motor working?" Dell asked.

"I don't know. All I did was clean it."

Dell stared at the mobile then back to light switch on the wall. "I can put a dimmer switch in now and regulate the light."

Neville looked up at the working solar system. How could this scraped and scarred mobile look so pristine? As he stared, Arthur walked in and immediately noticed the newly activated light fixture. "Batteries," he said. "Double A's is all it needed."

"Right again, Artie," Dell said, looking into simulated space. They all stared into the void created within Dewey's bedroom

Dell shut off the light and all four headed to the kitchen. The doorbell rang and while Dell continued on to the kitchen, Arthur and Phil followed Neville to the door. Two silhouettes appeared through the front door curtains, one short, one tall. The door opened and Dewey scurried in.

"Hey how's my big guy?" greeted Neville.

"Good dad. When are we going?" Dewey's eyes widened as he stomped his boots on the carpet. Blond locks sprouted from beneath his knit cap.

"It's all he's talked about since you called," Rita said from the half-opened doorway.

Neville introduced Phil and she offered a polite handshake.

"You're just as pretty as Woody said you were, Mrs. Wishwood," he said. Rita flashed a smile. She turned her attention to Neville's father.

"How are you, Arthur?"

Rita's greeting was unusually tepid. They had remained close yet for some reason today she faced her ailing former father-in-law with reticence. Her hands remained folded in front and she stood at a distance. Arthur smiled, stared as if deciding a course of action.

As Dewey removed his backpack and coat, Rita backed out onto the porch. "Have fun… I'll see you in a few days."

"Bye Mom."

Rita climbed back into her SUV. After watching his ex-wife drive away, Neville introduced Phil and explained the sleeping arrangements for the next few weeks. Dewey would bunk with his father, leaving Phil to recuperate in Dewey's room.

Neville took his son's hand. "Phil has a surprise for you."

"What?"

"Come with me."

Neville led Dewey to his bedroom. Phil followed close behind. Once inside, Dewey eagerly inspected every dark corner and seeing nothing changed, he asked, "What is it?"

Neville switched on the light and suddenly the bedroom flooded with light. Dewey's eyes steered up as he gawked at the newly glowing planets orbiting his room. He studied the star fields gleaming across the ceiling and stood, mouth agape staring into the world created within the very walls of his room. Both Neville and Phil watched a small boy lose himself in the wonder of the universe.

"Wow!"

"Like it?" Neville asked.

"It's like all of space right here in my room."

Neville shut off the light and again guided his son out into the hallway.

"That's Phil's present for letting him use your room."

"Thank you Phil! It's awesome," Dewey said, peering up at their houseguest.

"You're welcome."

In the kitchen, Dell prepared breakfast. Pancakes cooked in the larger skillet while another pan browned sausages. Arthur sat ready for his serving. Except for Dewey, they all ate a full breakfast that morning. The thrill of his transformed room and the upcoming trip curbed the boy's appetite. At nine o'clock, they piled into Dell's Ford Taurus and began their day-trip to Shaner's Mountain.

Neville joined Dell in the front while Dewey took a seat between Phil and his grandfather in the back. A familiar track, Dell had travelled it twice a week for ten years. He knew with good weather they would arrive in less than four hours.

On the drive, their conversation jumped from Audrey, to Rita, to Dell's newest girlfriend, Jennifer. They avoided talk of the signature found on the hospital bill, yet it hung there like a murky haze, distorting their view.

The back seat stayed mostly quiet. Dewey asked Phil the occasional question about his personal life, nothing rude just the curiosity of an inquisitive boy. As each answer came back with an *'I don't know,'* or *'I'm not sure,'* Dewey gave up.

The skies dulled to soot grey and the white ridge to the west grew irregular like the profile of an amusement park ride. Snow erased the blacktop leaving the route less defined and the only outline came from those who last passed. Every bush and branch wore the distinctive mark of ice.

Dell turned off the main road to the northwest, down a little used logging road. Here the route remained indiscernible except for a decided lack of trees. Buried beneath a foot of new snow the gravel surface lay undetected. In the years passed, the logging companies moved farther west leaving the roads left behind unserviced. During the winter months, storms would often uproot trees and block the path. Today they hoped for a reprieve from that eventuality.

Dell slowed and continued on the winding track. His Taurus handled the snow well but with the road covered in white a downed tree would be difficult to spot. They bounced and swerved their way for thirty minutes or more. The woodlands deeper in grew thick and their once broad roadway narrowed to a width not much greater than the car.

Above, the skies remained a listless grey. On the forest floor, the path had transformed and a gloom dominated the land. The taller trees blocked out the overhead light and the road took on the properties of a tunnel. They wound their way deeper into this mine of wood until a clearing appeared.

The Taurus came through the forest tunnel into a shining white stretch of snow spread out across the clearing floor. To the far left, an old trailer sat grounded on axles and buried in snow. Nearby icy timbers, blackened lower fragments formed into a square were all that remained of Dell's former forest home. The chimney, now just several rows of rock, sat piled up into empty space. The charred wood timbers, the home furnishings lay scattered about in ruins just a foot or two above the clearing floor. The forest had reclaimed Dell's log cabin.

Dell parked near the old trailer. His father had felled an acre of trees to build the cabin and with the structure destroyed; the clearing took on a wide airy feel. The day remained cold and dull as they piled out from the car. Ice encrusted mesh fencing sprung from the ground on what was the cabin's east wall. To the right of the wire fence a large pine vaulted into grey sky, its trunk scarred from the fire. Beneath the tree, a makeshift cross memorial marked the spot where Willard lay. A rusty steel studded collar hung from the center of the cross marking who was interred. Twelve years later, the cross still stood.

Dell walked around to the back of the car and removed a small box from his trunk. He carried the box to the cross he had erected years ago. Everyone followed. The box contained Willard's favorite dog treat: cereal bones. Dell pulled out a handful and planted them near the rusting marker.

"He did tricks for the bones," Dell said staring into the ground.

"Was he trained Unca Dell?' Dewey asked.

Dell's face brightened. "I don't know about 'trained' Dewey, but he could sit pretty or shake a paw for a biscuit. Sometimes he'd roll over."

Phil and Arthur stood behind Dell, near the cabin remnants. Neville looked up the path behind the clearing toward Shaner's Mountain. Years later, the trail had all but disappeared beneath the overgrowth. The mountain itself was really a hill and not a very big one at that, but to a boy growing up it all meant adventure.

Dell stood staring at the marker, a smile overtaking the sadness. "He was my closest friend back then."

Arthur heard a stirring behind him and turned to investigate. Phil heard the same stirring. The two walked toward the rubble, Phil using his cane on the icy gravel. Dewey tagged along behind.

Neville walked up the path a ways and stared into the woods. Some trees still showed wounds from the fire. Firefighters had hacked down several damaged trees and their stumps were sprouting new branches. New life sprang from the ashes and now coated in white, it gave the woods a virgin glow.

"It must have been terrible the day of the fire," Neville said.

"The smoke, that charcoal smell, yeah it was awful but all I could think about was Willard and how he must have died," Dell said.

Neville rarely found his friend in such a pensive state. Dell was never one to meditate on a loss for too long, even one this huge. Today it all seemed different. Brooding over his dog's death, Dell appeared transfixed by that time in his life and the overwhelming emotions that provoked the separation from his parents. Neville wondered about his friend's state of mind.

"Dell, the fire… is that why you decided to stay with Aunt Claire?"

Looking up from Willard's grave, Dell drew a deep breath. "The fire and a few other things."

In behind Dell, Arthur moved closer to the logs strewn along the former cabin wall. Phil and Dewey followed. As they approached the outer rim of what once was a wall, a hiss swelled from inside a nook formed from the ruins.

"What things?" Neville asked.

He looked up at Neville with a peculiar smile. "My parents weren't bad people Woody, but…"

Dell stalled and Neville prodded. "But what?"

"At times they made bad decisions. The week before the fire I heard them talking about insurance. I didn't understand then but later, after I saw the cabin in ruins, I realized it wasn't an accident."

"You mean they set the cabin on fire?"

Dell laughed. "They had written a book on building a log cabin and the book's success was based on how well the finished product turned out. They insured the cabin for over a million dollars. My father was good friends with the forestry service superintendent at the time. I'm sure he did the investigation, if there ever was one. Probably no one ever suspected. After he realized Willard was dead, my father couldn't look me in the eye. That's how I knew. And then it hit me. They didn't think about me, or about my dog for one second. All those years they shipped me off to Aunt Claire and why? Because they didn't want to deal with me."

"Does Aunt Claire know?"

"I've never told Aunt Claire. She doesn't need to know," Dell said.

"Your parents, they're still in Colorado."

"Yeah, they're really into skiing from what I understand. Now they've got the money to do it."

It all made sense. Dell's choice to live with Aunt Claire was the aftermath of a tangled childhood. After the fire, he recognized Aunt Claire was his only advocate in life. Given the circumstances, Dell's decision seemed somewhat sounder than it first appeared.

As Neville and Dell continued their conversation, the other three squatted on haunches in front of the ruins and the nook. Phil poked his cane into the recess. A loud hiss came back, warning the three curious interlopers. All three sat peering into the log alcove. Arthur grabbed the cane from Phil and with a forceful poke jabbed it into the burrow. The hiss sounded louder yet and a small furry head popped out. A series of shrieks followed and all three jumped up. Arthur fell back onto Dewey, dropping the cane. They yanked Dewey up and all three beat a path to the car.

Hearing the commotion, Dell and Neville swiveled to see the animal leap from its nook-nest and their three charges in hasty retreat. Identifying the charging creature, they joined the chase. Doors opened and closed in a matter of seconds with all five sitting winded in their seats. The beast was closing in. Dell locked the car doors.

They peered out to watch a skunk waddle a path toward the car. Two baby skunks, still too young to wear the distinctive white markings, tumbled out from their nook home. The mother skunk pivoted, looked to its young but soon resumed her watch on the car and the people inside. While her pups wandered in and around the cabin debris, the skunk sat on its haunches and stood guard.

Dell turned on the car hoping to scare the skunk away. The skunk maintained her station between them and her two offspring.

"Now what? We still haven't got our tree," Dell said.

"We'll wait… it can't stay there all day."

Four grown men and a boy, held hostage by a rogue skunk, waited in a forest clearing in northern Minnesota. Ten, fifteen minutes passed, and the skunk remained true to her duty.

An eerie wind rose up. Above, the mass of grey clouds began to race spinning the world faster and faster. Sky-steered pines twisted in the mounting gusts. The forest dulled to a monochrome mix of shadows drained of color and with it, the winds set branches into motion jangling like a chorus of chimes. Clashing evergreens echoed out along the forest track when suddenly Neville's father croaked from the back seat. "Wolf."

The skunk mysteriously abandoned her post and scampered off to join her brood inside the nook. Arthur pointed over his son's shoulder. "Wolf."

Near Willard's grave, bushes wavered clattering out icy clicks and the snout of a new beast pushed through. Two oily black eyes followed. Amazed they watched the animal skulk from the clearing's edge, cautiously approaching the grave. Covered with sleek fur, grey and black, it slipped slowly into view. The animal surveyed the scene without a look in their direction.

A car door opened and Dell stepped from his seat, wide eyed. Pulling his toque from his head, he let out a call.

"Dell what are you doing?" Neville screamed.

In a glance, Dell looked back inside the car. "It's Willard! He's here... now," he said excitedly. As he rushed toward the grave, the animal's head cocked up. The dog sat and let out a low familiar howl wagging its tail wildly brushing snow aside as it waited. His paws padded the ground until Dell reached and with a sudden leap, he sprang up to his master's shoulders.

"Willard... how, how can you be here?" he asked amazed. He rubbed down his dog with both hands. Standing on his back paws, Willard stood as tall as Dell and while licking his face, the dog howled his delight.

Neville opened his door and walked across the clearing to where Dell had reunited with his dead dog. The back doors opened and the others joined in behind. Neville looked up, around into spinning skies, the color-blunted forest trees. Ice spines jangled in the rare wind and with renewed awareness, Neville smiled.

As Dewey approached, he watched his Uncle Dell enthusiastically interact with the dog. "Dad, I thought Unca Dell's dog was dead?"

Neville looked down at his son. "He is."

"But..."

"I know Dewey. I don't have the answers. Just let Uncle Dell enjoy his time with Willard," Neville whispered.

And they all watched Dell enjoy his dog this one last time. In the excitement that followed, Willard took time to gobble down at least a half dozen of the dog treats Dell placed by the grave. Dell watched with great pride as his dog barked and pranced and played in a circle around his master, kicking up snow and adoring the man who had raised him from a pup. Dell's attention stayed fixed on Willard, wrestling and patting down his one-time pet.

Arthur tugged on his son's sleeve. "It's not a wolf?"

"No Dad... it's Dell's dead dog."

After several minutes of play, Dell tried leading Willard to the car. He walked away, patting his leg, prodding Willard to follow. "Come on boy… this way."

Willard made no attempt to follow and again padded the ground above the grave. Dell tried once more and again the dog refused to move. Instead, he howled low and long. Willard turned back toward the clearing's edge and the bushes from which he had come. His paws padded the snow and with one quick look, Willard turned to see Dell, barked one last time and quickly scampered into the forest brush. Within seconds he was gone, a grey and black spirit merged in the grey and black woods.

Mesmerized by the miracle a silence engulfed the travelers. The clack of branches from above was the only sound heard. On his knees, Dell peered up at his friend and asked, "How does any of this happen, Woody?"

Neville placed a hand on his friend's shoulder. "I wish I knew."

Dell climbed up from his knees, placed his cap back on and wiped away the tears. He wandered up the trail toward Shaner's Mountain alone, lost in the magnitude of what had occurred. Until now, these strange events were merely a diversion, impersonal and distant. Today they became all too real and all too personal.

Neville looked along the path to see his friend staring up into the treetops, into grey sky. They shared the same questions that day and in their bewilderment, received the same answers each in their own indefinable way. In the end, they realized there was no answer, at least not now. These miracles with Willard, with Camillus De Lellis, with Audrey were beyond their ability to comprehend, beyond their human limitations and as Aunt Claire had so insightfully decided– all to be determined at a future date. Yet, within each, an indefinable sense of trepidation filled their hearts.

The winds ebbed, that ghostly grey pall lifted and returned life to lifeless woodlands and in that moment the wonder passed. Dell's gaze leveled, his eyes set along the trail into the stand of trees beyond a bend in the path. His friends stood milling near Willard's grave giving Dell time to regain himself. After several minutes, Dewey broke from the group and trudged up the slope to his uncle. With Dell focused on the woodlands, Dewey slipped his hand into Dell's, surprising him.

"It's okay Unca Dell," he said. "Willard came back to say goodbye."

With glazed eyes, Dell lowered to one knee and wrapped both arms around Dewey. "I know Dewey. It was just nice to see him again."

Dell stood and he whispered, "Let's get the axe… I see our tree."

A quiet quintet felled a tree that afternoon. They carried it off to the car and stowed it inside the trunk for the trip home. It remained their final act before leaving that day. Without speaking a word, Dell and Neville passed a glance between them realizing the miracle that occurred. As for Dewey, he knew something very strange had indeed happened but he had no name for it, no understanding of what to call it. And Arthur? Who really knew what he could discern at this stage of his illness.

That left Phil, their amnesia riddled houseguest, the only coherent connection to the apparitions. Phil appeared central in these mysterious goings on. His self-effacing manner seemed innocent enough, yet who truly knew the man's motives or his capabilities?

Early that afternoon Dell guided the Taurus back through the northern Minnesota woods to Solomon. For the first hour, the journey remained solemn with little conversation. At their first rest stop, Dell broke his silence: "That's the way I want to remember Willard," he said. "Full of life."

Neville thought of how Aunt Claire and Dell must have felt burying Willard's charred remains; the lasting memory it created in his friend's psyche. Dell now had a new memory to replace the anguish of their final time together. Neville understood from that moment on they would never return to Shaner's Mountain. Dell received a wondrous gift that cold day in December, a remembrance of a life once lived and no matter the source, he cherished that last chance meeting.

They settled in the car for the last leg on their journey home. Daylight was fast fading and from the northwest, an all-obscuring veil continued to advance. A winter storm chased the Taurus south toward

Solomon. They arrived home in darkness, the mood much more jovial than it had started.

It was after six o'clock when they unloaded the tree. Neville placed it in the basement to thaw for the night with a plan of decorating it the next night. As Neville checked the phone book for dinner, Dell called Aunt Claire from the kitchen. With Dewey, Phil and Arthur warming up in the living room, he wanted a conversation away from their houseguest.

He spoke of the miracle appearance of Willard, his playful demeanor and his unchanged look after all these years. Although excited Aunt Claire took the news rather stoically, citing a case in which she counseled a client visited by a beloved nephew who passed away in an auto accident. And it wasn't the only case she had heard involving spiritual visitation. She spoke clearly on the subject, stating that these cases almost exclusively associated a positive outcome for those interacting with the spirit world. Her optimistic outlook buoyed Dell. Just as Neville and Dell suspected Phil as the catalyst for this intervention, she agreed in principle but cautioned, "He may be the agent or the subject of the anticipated outcome. In either case, there may be fallout."

Dell hung up. Aunt Claire's caveat circled inside his head. And like most of what came to mind he absent-mindedly asked, "Do you think Phil might be some sort of evil doppelganger?"

As he spoke the words, Dewey walked into the kitchen, hungry and tired. "What's a doppelganger?" he asked.

Dell quickly backtracked. "Well it's like a friendly ghost Dewey… like Casper."

"But you said evil."

"Did I? I meant playful, in a devilish sort of way."

"Oh…"

Now off the phone, Neville asked, "What's this now?"

"Nothing," Dell said, shooting a cautious look Neville's way. "Just talking about Phil."

"Yeah, he's a doppelganger," Dewey added innocently. "Are we having dinner soon?"

"Pizza's on the way…" Neville said as he rubbed his young son's head. As Dewey returned to the living room, Neville asked, "What was that doppelganger remark about?"

"Slip of the tongue. I didn't see Dewey and I asked if you thought Phil might be an evil doppelganger– it was stupid."

"Something's going on and I'm pretty sure Phil's at the center of it."

"Aunt Claire thinks the same thing– I just talked to her."

Dell relayed the conversation he had with Aunt Claire and her prudence on how to proceed from here. Whatever the situation, it was gaining momentum. A dead nurse, a long dead saint and now Dell's dead dog signaled an escalation. The visitations were becoming increasingly intimate.

The pizza arrived, they ate dinner and after settled in to watch television, tired from the daylong trip and very much preoccupied by the questions that remained unanswered. But where could they find the answers? Who do you ask? Their best resource was Aunt Claire and she had no firm grasp of the matter, no clear direction to take. It all came back to wait and see.

With bedtime nearing, Dewey asked Phil if he could see his room and the orbit of the planets before retiring. Phil led the way and as he switched on the light, the room flashed into motion. Phil watched Dewey's face as the planets spun slowly around the center light. The smile made Phil's efforts worthwhile.

Unexpectedly Dewey asked, "Are you a doppelganger?"

"A what?"

"A doppelganger."

"What's a doppelganger?" Phil asked.

"Unca Dell said it's a friendly ghost."

""I really don't know who or what I am Dewey, but you can be sure of this… I'm a friend."

Dewey stared after hearing Phil answer. His doubting eyes switched to acceptance and a smile broke out. "I believe you."

With a quick turn, he traipsed down the hall to his father's bedroom. Dewey gave a tired look back and disappeared inside the room.

Phil did the same, closing Dewey's door behind him. Not long after Arthur turned in Dell left for the comfort of his own bed. Neville joined his son who had already fallen asleep. The day had turned out to be quite eventful. All inside the Wishwood household witnessed a remarkable return from dead, if only for those few minutes. It served to stir up hopeful dreams that night and anticipation of what was to come.

The winter storm that chased them home arrived after midnight and with it, the power went out. Darkness descended across Solomon. Streets once clearly defined were lost in the shadows of portentous clouds. An ice rain pelted the town and all before it bowed to its white dominion, all save St. Gabriel's Square. There, with power sustained, an angel soared above the city its marble wings set billowing against the winds. Bathed in light, St. Gabriel flew impervious to all elements cutting a path through nature's white fury.

CHAPTER 18

GREY LIGHT CREASED the curtains as Neville pulled himself up from beneath the covers. The room was cold and his clock was blank. No power. Dewey slept soundly beside him. Without waking his son, he slipped out of bed and quietly dressed. After calling upstairs, Dell came down a few minutes later.

The battery operated kitchen clock said it was just before eight o'clock. Neville was late again. Outside, wind driven snow strafed the streets of Solomon. One look told the story. Six to seven inches of snow accumulated and still no letup in the storm.

Meeting in the kitchen their conversation was short.

"No school for Dewey today," Dell offered as he pulled aside the kitchen curtain.

"No, but I've got work and I'm late again."

"You won't be the only one Woody."

As Dell had indicated, Neville was not the only one late at The Sentinel. Suzanne stood alone in the office, shaking the snow off her coat. Over the next hour, Roland slipped in followed by Walter and John. Sam was the last to arrive. John Winterburn settled himself and after putting his coat away, he approached Neville's desk.

"I'm into chapter seventeen, Woody. So far, I like it…especially that Kennedy reference. That was a stroke of genius," he said.

Neville's face lit up. "Thanks John."

"I'll have it done by the weekend… maybe sooner if the weather stays like this."

Neville sat, hoping to hear a word or two of encouragement from The Sentinel's senior reporter, Sam. Neville's eyes shifted surreptitiously to his mentor. Sam, seemingly focused on his own work, continued preparing for another day at the office. Neville followed his lead and re-engaged in his work. Sam flashed a grin. He had heard John's comment on Neville's manuscript, *Seven Days*. He decided to say nothing, knowing suspense was a trait any good writer would appreciate.

And what would a day at The Sentinel be like without at least one argument with Roland DeWitt? Roland sauntered over and stood menacingly in front of Neville's desk.

Neville hesitated, finally peering up at his workmate. "What?"

Roland blurted out a burst of venom. "You took my parking spot!"

Easing back in his office chair, Neville replied, "How could you tell?"

"I can tell– mine's closer to the back door!" Roland waggled his hips impatiently waiting for an explanation.

"I guess I missed the yellow lines, maybe because they're buried beneath a foot of snow! Now if you don't mind, I have work to tend to."

Neville attention returned to his desk, ignoring Roland's sour smile, his metered hip sway and a general look of disgust. Roland continued to stand defiantly over Neville's desk, his hands planted firmly on his boney hips.

Offended by Roland's pettiness, Neville peered up ready for the coming confrontation. "Anything else, Rolly?"

With teeth clenched, Roland squared himself, curled his fingers into fists, looked up and realized an audience had formed. Sam and John were both staring his way, and Suzanne stood watching by her office door. Exasperated, Roland marched back to his desk mumbling incoherently, pumping his fists into empty air.

The storm continued to batter the town. Shortly after one o'clock, the power went out in St. Gabriel's Square, shutting down the Sentinel with it. After thirty minutes of imposed darkness, Walter sent everyone home.

Dell had cleared their small sidewalk and driveway with the snow blower that morning, saving Neville the trouble. Neville arrived home to a surprised lot. All four sat huddled around the kitchen table when he came in, cold and hungry. Dell and Arthur were engaged in their customary gin rummy match while Phil and Dewey watched. Candles burned in tea saucers on the table. Try as he might Dell had failed to glean any clues from their suspect houseguest who pleaded ignorance at every turn. He was beginning to believe Phil was indeed oblivious to the strange conjuring.

Looking up, Dell asked, "No power?"

"Yeah…" Neville said giving off a shiver. "Who's winning?"

A sour smirk flashed across Dell's face as he surveyed his cards. Kneeling on a chair, Dewey joyfully returned, "Puppa's winning and he already won the first game." He pointed to Arthur's red peg well ahead of Dell's blue.

Neville smiled, circled the table and gave Dewey a quick squeeze of the shoulder. From there he searched the refrigerator for lunch. Phil smiled and said hello, but stayed engaged in the card play. As both men played their cards, he watched as if trying to determine the rules or the intricacies of the play itself.

After Neville's arrival, the game continued for another forty-five minutes. After it ended, Dewey and Arthur joined Neville in the living room while in the kitchen Phil studied Dell as he added his day's losses to the notebook.

"What's that?"

"What, the book?" Dell asked.

"Yes."

"It's what I owe Artie, why?"

"Just wondering. How much do you owe him now?"

Dell pulled the book back and closed the flap. "Enough." He walked away shoving the notepad back into his pocket. As he retreated to the living room, Phil followed. Passing the foyer, Phil saw someone in silhouette through front door curtains. Curious, he approached the door and slid aside the curtain. Through the winter slick glass, he could see someone standing on the sidewalk near the end of the driveway. Whoever it was, they held something in one hand.

"Woody there's someone out there," he called.

Neville came in from the living room. He slipped the curtain sideways. Alone behind his car stood a woman and she was staring into his car bumper.

"There is, but what's she doing?"

The living room emptied. They queued in the foyer all wanting a look at the mystery woman. Neville opened the door and stepped out onto the porch for a better view. The weather was savage; a fierce wind peppered ice pellets about the porch and car. Neville folded his arms across his chest and walked down three steps onto the front walkway. He squinted against the dying light and seeing only a silhouette, shielded his eyes for a closer look.

Through driving snow, he recognized the visitor at the base of the driveway. It was the neighbor, Mrs. Wardle, Russell Wardle's mother. Neville hadn't seen her since the summer and all the trouble. Standing in the driveway was a wisp of the woman he knew, gaunt and deathly thin. A tattered blue housecoat hung from her withered frame adding a zombie-like element to her appearance. Mrs. Wardle's one hand held tight to what appeared to be a golf club.

Phil stepped onto the porch and waited. Wind-driven snow skewered the woman's terrycloth robe yet she stood unyielding, preoccupied with Neville's parked car. Neville inched closer. Her steely eyes shifted in his direction and she raised the club as if to warn him. Neville stopped.

Although he knew the answer, he asked in a quiet voice. "Are you okay Mrs. Wardle?" Mrs. Wardle was definitely not okay.

She said nothing. Her eyes intensified, stayed focused on him. She stood twenty-five feet from where Neville waited. Phil marched down the porch steps and joined Neville watching the woman's every move. Neville inched another few feet closer. Mrs. Wardle's other hand clutched the handle and she held the club in an axe grip arms raised and ready. Ice clumps knotted her hair like dirty-blonde dreadlocks.

Again Neville stopped, held himself against the cold and pleaded, "Mrs. Wardle, it's cold. You're going to freeze to death if you don't come in from the weather."

Phil slipped closer. "Who is she?"

Neville leaned back and in a low voice said, "Mrs. Wardle, a neighbor. She's got... problems."

In twilight, the scene morphed into colorless grey. Mrs. Wardle stood defiant against the elements and Neville. Unafraid or unaware, Phil hobbled past Neville across a white lawn in a line toward the woman. Her hostile gaze switched to Phil. As he approached, the club hoisted higher in an unspoken threat.

Madness flashed about Mrs. Wardle's face. Eyes narrowed, nostrils flared, her perfect teeth clenched and with a weighty swing the club came down. It arced through wind and weather. Mere inches from Phil's head the club suddenly stopped mid-swing. June Wardle stood petrified as if impaled by an arrow of time. Her eyes shifted in their sockets puzzled, locked onto him. Edging closer, he extended an empty hand. "Mrs. Wardle it's going to be alright. Trust me."

Their clothes rippled in the winter furies. Her head cocked sideways as would a dog's hearing a command from her master. Phil's eyes glowed with unspoken compassion, soft, accepting and as he crept closer, a smile cracked her sullen lips. Somehow, she understood. In this silent accord, Phil reached up and slid the club from her hand.

With Mrs. Wardle disarmed, Neville made a cautious approach and placed his arm around her shoulder. Phil took her frozen hand in his and together they guided the stricken woman toward the porch and a warm place inside the house.

Seeing the rescue party returning, Dell, Dewey and Arthur dashed inside to wait. Dell retrieved blankets from a hallway linen closet. Neville sat Mrs. Wardle on the vestibule bench, her bare arms and legs, her face shining with the texture of wet glass. He wrapped the woman in a thick wool blanket.

Arthur peeked out from the living room and Dewey, spooked by the whole ordeal, poked his head from behind his uncle Dell. Dell took the golf club from Phil and made a quick inspection. Twisting it in his hand, he announced, "Nine-iron, and it's got blood on it."

Mrs. Wardle continued a vacant gape. Without warning, she blurted out, "Brad Pitt's on TV tonight. Fight Club, channel six– eight o'clock." She was seriously lost in the world.

Dell made a few short swings with the golf club. "Never could chip," he said to himself.

Melting snow dripped from those who had braved the storm. Neville retrieved the club. Wrapped in the blanket, he crouched before a troubled June Wardle and showed her the club. In this subdued state, she seemed ready to speak. "Mrs. Wardle, whose blood is on the club?" His tone was mollifying but direct.

She continued to stare, unaffected. Phil approached, dropped his blanket and leaned in cradling her face with both hands. In a sudden shift, her eyes reacted searching out the source of contact.

"It's okay... it's all going to be okay Mrs. Wardle," Phil said. She suddenly smiled. In that instant, she appeared to rediscover something relevant. She softened, that harsh edge dissipated and she seemed fully aware of her misdeeds that day. A semblance of contrition overwhelmed her and her head dropped. She began to sob as her quivering hands clutched her face, hiding from those prying eyes all around her.

Neville stood, clasped Mrs. Wardle shoulder and left her to cry. He proceeded to the living room, looked up the Wardle number and called. A frantic voice answered.

"Have you found her?"

"Tom. It's Neville Wishwood from down the street. Your wife's here. She's a bit of a mess right now but she's okay. I knew you'd be worried."

"Thank God."

Tom Wardle went on to explain the circumstances of his wife's outing that winter day. They were sitting quietly in the living room watching Jeopardy! when June began to fidget in her chair, the brown lounger near the living room fireplace. Their children, Russell, Julie and little Astrid were busy in their rooms. Bessie, their toy poodle, scrambled out from the hallway carrying a pink slipper in her mouth– June's slipper. June Wardle hopped from the lounger and tried grappling the slipper from the dog's teeth. The dog, sensing her master's playfulness, jogged and jumped away down the hallway, happy to engage in the sport of keep away. But June was not playing. Something snapped inside and she headed for the nearby closet. Finding few real weapons, she opted for one of her husband's golf clubs. By now, she was seething. She cursed Bessie up and down and pursued the dog against her husband's shrill protests.

Hearing the commotion, the children spilled into the hallway in time to see their mother thump Bessie two-handed with the golf club. Tom Wardle arrived to the screaming anguish of their three children. Bessie lay breathless on the hallway floor.

June Wardle plucked the slipper from the dog's mouth, put it on and proceeded to her bedroom to find the second slipper. Tom picked up Bessie. The children huddled around their father and when June reappeared from the bedroom, her eyes told the terrible tale. Transmuted by deed, she emerged a vixen-witch set to battle all in her path. Her family shrieked and all four ran to the basement door. Tom and the children scrambled behind the safety of a locked cellar door. Tom went on to explain they hid there for several minutes and when he felt it safe, he returned upstairs to find his wife gone. That was when he called police.

A sad and sordid affair, Neville thought.

Tom Wardle arrived shortly after the phone call fully equipped with a winter coat, a hat and a pair of winter boots for his wife. Twenty minutes later the police arrived and escorted a broken June Wardle into the squad car. She left quietly, still sniffling with the understanding of what she had done. They took her to the hospital, the sixth floor psychiatric ward.

In the following hour, the storm abated and the Wishwood household returned to normal. The power returned less than an hour later. They talked of June Wardle, the dog and its injuries and finally Phil's unselfish reaction to the situation.All Phil would say that night was, "She was afraid. She just needed someone to understand, that's all." He maintained a laiser-faire attitude toward the entire ordeal and made little of his heroics. Dewey sat between Phil and his grandfather on the sofa that night and they watched television. Every now and then, he would peer up at Phil as if to study him. Phil returned his stare at every instance with a smile and a quick return to the television.

Yes, even Dewey had his suspicions.

While everyone watched the television, Neville carried up their Christmas tree from the basement along with boxes of Christmas decorations. In the hours before bed, they happily decorated the tree. All five helped to choose the right mix of color and clarity for the family tree. That night they found the Christmas spirit. For Phil, he found a sense of peace with Dell and the Wishwood clan.

Megan worried that night, not for her sister Rita but her mother and father. Living in Minneapolis, she was unsure of the storm's effect in her parent's home town of Solomon. With the power restored, she called her parent's home. Annette Fording answered.

"Mom, is everything okay there?"

"It's okay… now. The power came back on thirty minutes ago."

"And dad, he didn't go out in this did he?" Megan asked, concerned.

"No, we stayed right here, lit a few candles. I tried reading but you know your father, he roamed around house like a lion in a cage. Checking this, adjusting that…finally he was making me so nervous I told him to go downstairs. He's down there now watching the news."

"Good, I was worried he might get caught out in the storm."

"Have you heard from Rita?" her mother asked.

"No. She told me she'd call after her date and she hasn't called yet. And I didn't want to call her and look like I'm prying. We got into a little… discussion earlier this week and I don't think she appreciated my point of view."

"About Woody again?"

"Woody, her attitude… a lot of things mom."

Rita's sister Megan was one of Woody's staunchest supporters, even while being Rita's closest confidant. The Fordings, Annette and

Will, were also at odds with Rita's choice to divorce a man who had endeared himself to both. They too saw Neville as a solid man, a good husband and a loving father– attributes missing in the men Rita had dated before.

"You might be waiting a while," Annette told Megan. "I watched Dewey the night of her date. She came home before nine-thirty and she wasn't in any mood to discuss why. I asked her how it went and she just stared at me. Then she checked on Dewey."

Megan hesitated. "That was Matt, Richard's friend from work. She was certainly excited about meeting him. They had talked on the phone and according to her he seemed a perfect match."

"From her look that night I'd say she's over it. I just wish Rita would come to her senses before Woody moves on and she loses him forever," Annette confided.

"Maybe I'm getting too involved, but I found out something last night. It's just I'm not sure if she's ready to see it. You know how bull-headed Rita can be."

Annette Fording smiled hearing Megan's worries. "No one's as close to Rita as you are dear. You're twins, it doesn't get any closer. I know you have her best interests at heart but she's never been the practical one.

"When she wanted a white pony for Christmas, you wanted clothes; when she couldn't live without 'N Sync concert tickets, you merely wanted the CD. It never ended, all through high school, and now her husband doesn't seem to measure up. I don't understand any of it or where it comes from."

"Oh, I understand it," she started. "…at least some of it, and I've tried to tell her…" Megan's voice trailed off. "I'll just have to wait and see."

Annette and her daughter finished their conversation with the announcement of an upcoming promotion for Megan's husband, Richard. The news swelled Megan's pride in her husband and it showed in the way she spoke of him. Annette felt fortunate to share the same stellar opinion of Megan's choice in a man as she had shared in Rita's.

The Wishwood Christmas tree stood erect and newly festooned. Painted bells and balls hung from the boughs with silver tinsel dripping from its branches. Strings of colored lights adorned every limb, some blinking on and off while most maintained a steady glow adding a warm festive ambiance to every corner of the living room.

Dell had retired to his own apartment and Dewey was fast asleep. Arthur meddled with his tin box and inside Dewey's room Phil curled beneath the blankets after another long day.

Upstairs, Dell brushed back the covers to his bed and suddenly noticed the camera on his dresser. The Acme camera he had taken from Phil.

He picked up the camera, the memory card and batteries now dry from days of sitting out. Reassembling the unit, he clicked on the power and went directly to menu. He clicked the review button and up popped the first picture on the screen. It was the angel flying above St. Gabriel's Square, brighter than before and completely clear. The dry camera and card had indeed improved the picture quality.

The second picture was a full frontal view of the angel, this time a night version and clear as a bell. He clicked the review button once more and the third picture appeared bright and intact. Dell gasped at the sight.

"It can't be…"

Dell raced downstairs and banged hard against the locked door. He stood near panic as Neville opened it.

"Hey, what's up?" Neville asked.

Dell pushed his way in and lifted the camera's view screen. "Remember the camera, the pictures we couldn't quite make out?"

Neville eyes leveled on the image, his brows furrowed and he gasped.

The picture on the Acme camera was a photo of a woman and child walking in snowbound St. Gabriel's Square. The woman was Rita and the child, Dewey.

CHAPTER 19

TUESDAY MORNING DAVIS Jefferson woke up with a hangover. He had too much time on his hands. As he sat in a Minneapolis hotel room Davis occupied the hours drinking, reading the newspaper, watching television and surfing the Internet. Adding to his glut of mindless time, he sat thinking. Thinking of Roland, the plan he had concocted and the work Davis had input into the project. The more he thought, the more he realized the inequity of his expended energy versus that of Roland's. After all, it was his expertise providing the tools to extract what both believed would be a substantial amount of money.

Ideas were cheap, especially ideas from a dolt who had locked himself into a meaningless job, in a meaningless town, surrounded by meaningless little people, like Roland himself. After days of unending internal chatter Davis reached a conclusion: his asinine one-time roommate was cheating him. The more he drank, the more he read, the more he watched and surfed, the greater his resolve to remedy what he believed was a personal injustice. He needed to settle Roland for the last time. Roland the gay Princeton graduate, Roland the sharp-tongued antagonist, Roland and his vacuous understanding of what it means to function in business at any level. In that sense, Davis saw Roland as no match for his experience or business acumen.

His internal dialogue denied bitterness had anything to do with his decisions. *"It's just business,"* he told himself. That was the lie. The lie he held away from his lips and any conscious thought. In that respect, he was much the same as Roland although he refused to see it. Each lived in their own distinct narcissism and afraid of the world, each hid behind a separate shield of self-centeredness. They had grown to be brothers of the lie and resentment ruled their decisions.

Davis realized he had a new act to add to their play. Hung over, he picked up his i-Phone and texted Roland, *Tomorrow nite-9:30, Trillium Bar. Need to talk about the split. 50-50 no good. DJ.*

Roland sat alone checking invoices from last week's advertisements. Willis had just left his cubicle with an agreement to meet for dinner at seven o'clock. Roland, in his usual contentious manner, took out his growing trepidation on an unsuspecting Willis. Although bullied once again, Willis went on his way happy, knowing he would join his lover for a night alone. He saw Roland differently than most. He saw the gentle loving side. Not that he denied Roland's character flaws, but he accepted his faults with the optimism that Roland would change. Time would spin its magic spell and Roland would realize the error of his ways. But that was Willis; ever hopeful, ever loyal.

As Roland switched screens on his desk computer, he heard the buzz of his i-Phone. He tapped open the newest text, read it and in a fit pushed his swivel chair back from the desk. Davis Jefferson had thrown down the gauntlet and now awaited Roland's response. He stared into his phone reading the message again and again. As he did, his every thought worked the solution. Roland swung his chair around and stared into the square. An ice film tempered the glass and below a yellow snowplow scraped the storm's deposit from the cobbled court road.

It was simple: Davis wanted more and if he got more Roland got less. Roland didn't like less, didn't like the sound of *less* and that was when a solution emerged. Roland met his partner's challenge and quickly jotted back his own text, *Trillium Bar-9:30 tomorrow-I'll be there.*

Simple enough, challenge received, challenge met. It took all of ten minutes to conjure but Roland's easy answer to this test of wills was much more involved than it appeared. After sending Davis his answer,

Roland made a quick call to his parent's home. He needed what only his father could provide and arranged to see him after work. The man he most despised was about to present Roland with the answer to the Davis problem.

Roland leaned back and watched the plow cut through white drifts driving road snow into curls. The plow pushed the slush mix into shoddy mounds. Cleanup was a dirty business. Now he had his own clutter to clear-up.

As much as the events of the last week had disoriented Neville, the pictures on the Acme camera launched his concerns to new heights. Rita and Dewey were the two he loved most, and they now represented pieces of an unfathomable puzzle. Only one man had the answers. After another restless night, Neville reluctantly went to work, leaving Dell to question the amnesiac about the pictures on his camera. They believed the subtle approach seemed best, leaving accusations aside. Restraint may be the better solution to discover the end goal. After dropping Dewey off at school, Dell returned home brewed a pot of coffee and waited for Phil and Arthur to wake up. After his third cup of coffee, Dell greeted Arthur in the kitchen. "Sleep okay, Artie?"

Disoriented, Arthur sat down. "Is Angela up yet?"

"She may be, just not here."

Phil arrived in the kitchen shortly after, his thinning hair set wildly about his head. "I had the same dream again last night. The one where I'm in the swimming pool with an older woman, and she's holding me up in the water. All of a sudden, the roof caves in on the pool and we have to escape. I wonder why I dreamt that?"

Dell sat across from Phil and with a sudden jerk, he pulled the camera out from inside his hoody sweatshirt pocket, blurting out, "And what about this picture on the camera!"

After three cups of coffee, all subtlety was lost. Startled, Arthur peered at Dell. Phil's eyes bugged at the sight of his camera. Dell held the small silver camera out over the table.

The picture of Rita and Dewey showed in the camera's screen. Phil studied the picture. "It's Dewey, and Rita," he exclaimed.

"Yes, I know. But why?"

Several seconds passed. Phil's head waggled sideways. "I don't know. I can't remember any of this."

"It is *your* camera," Dell said.

"Yes, I guess."

"So they're your pictures."

"I suppose…"

Just as Dell was making his point, Phil clicked the camera's review button forward. Another picture appeared in the view screen, an older woman with shoulder length dirty blonde hair obscuring her facial features. Phil recognized the photo. "That's her! That's the woman in my dreams. The woman in the pool!"

"No…" Dell grabbed the camera back.

"It is Dell, I swear it!"

"And you don't know why you took that picture of Rita and Dewey?"

"I don't remember any of it."

Arthur sat next to their houseguest staring out into space. All he wanted was breakfast to be served. His issues were much simpler.

Instead of answers, he had carved open another elusive facet. Who was this woman and how did she figure into their ever-expanding puzzle? Later that morning he called Neville at work and updated him on Phil's interrogation. They agreed on one thing: their approach would be cautious from here on.

As the afternoon progressed, Phil joined his new housemates in the kitchen to follow their gin rummy tournament. It became apparent that Phil openly sided with Arthur. He sat next to the elder Wishwood studied each move and cheered his continued success against Dell. Arthur's initial mistrust of their houseguest faded. Memory was clearly an issue for both, and in sharing that loss they formed a kinship.

They acted as teenage boys reveling in Dell's every misfortune. Late in the afternoon, Phil began whispering in Arthur's ear as if to explain a ploy that could confuse or cajole their caregiver into a mistake.

For the most part, Dell found it amusing, but nearing the end of that particular afternoon, he seemed annoyed at his losses. He ended the daily tournament with a stern announcement that he needed to pick up Dewey from school and added the day's debits to his accounting. All three piled into the car. How, he wondered, did he continue to lose to an old man with Alzheimer's whose only aid came from an amnesiac? He settled for the easy answer– dumb luck.

Roland finished work and headed to his parent's home in Minneapolis. Having served in congress for well over two decades, Gregory DeWitt had accumulated a rather plush lifestyle. Their home was a healthy sixty-five hundred-square-foot featuring five bathrooms, six bedrooms, two sitting rooms, a large open kitchen, a games room and a den. Roland met with his father in the den, a museum more than a workspace.

The wood paneled walls displayed the weapons of war. As a collector, Roland's father had amassed an impressive assortment of weapons, many of which were gifts from grateful lobbyists. Shields with companion spears and swords hung from all four walls, one set dating back to Roman times, all marred by time and tumult. Knives, smaller blades set inside sheaths, tarnished helmets all sat on display along the far wall near a bookcase.

A glass cabinet stood by the corner desk and inside Gregory DeWitt displayed his most prized possessions: guns from every age. The flintlock musket was his first purchase some twenty years prior followed by a single shot carbine from the Civil War. Just last year he added a single barrel Remington pump-action shotgun from the early 1900's.

With his long guns, Gregory DeWitt had also assembled an assortment of handguns– all in good working order. His oldest handgun was a Colt 2-shot .22-caliber derringer from the late 1800's, the weapon of choice for most gamblers. He held a British No.2-MK1 revolver made by Enfield, a P .08 German Luger and a rare Smith and Wesson .38 caliber revolver, U.S. Navy issue circa 1900. All highly sought after, his collection came more from military issued firearms than commercially built guns. The case stored in excess of two dozen handguns from every country and combatant of twentieth century wars.

The den itself was a trip back in time right down to the desk where his father worked, old teakwood a design reminiscent of Victorian elegance and propriety. One lamp lit the room. Warped shadows stretched across the history of timeless conflicts. Gregory De Witt sat punching keys on his laptop.

"Still busy at it, father?"

He looked up. "Roland, I was surprised to hear from you. Changed your mind about Costa Rica?"

Roland shot him a glare. "No, Dad. I just wanted to know when you, Mom and Freddy were leaving. It is Christmas and I do want to wish you all a happy holiday."

"You're a little late for your mother...she flew down Monday. Fredrick and I are flying out tomorrow." He leaned back in his chair.

"How convenient for you and Freddy," Roland replied, adding an acid inflection to his tone.

Roland's father pulled himself up in the chair. "Let's not start that again."

"What? Freddy, the son my father always wanted, or Freddy, who's not gay, the older brother of my other very gay son."

"Roland..."

Grinning snidely, Roland interrupted his father. "No. That's it isn't it father? Freddy *is* the chosen one and I'm the afterthought, or afterbirth. Either way it means the same thing."

"Roland that's enough," Gregory De Witt bellowed. He leaned in closed the laptop and calmed himself sufficiently to address his son. "It's never been that way. Gay or not we've always loved you just as we've loved Fredrick. Except..."

Roland's father paused as he pulled himself erect.

"Except... that I was gay and you couldn't stomach *that* about a son of the great and powerful Gregory DeWitt," Roland fired back.

Gregory DeWitt shook his head as he looked away. "Except for the gigantic chip on your shoulder blinding you to whatever good did come into your life."

Gregory DeWitt had heard his son's contemptuous rants for as long as he could remember. He had tired of Roland's inability to see through the self-pity he heaped upon himself, of his constant complaints of paternal partiality, of his parents rejection of him for his sexual preferences. He had heard it all. No, Gregory DeWitt resigned himself to one simple edict: that without psychological intervention he and Roland were destined to be at odds with each other. As it was, this family that had begun with such promise continued to splinter over Roland's incessant bickering.

Roland planted himself in a chair across from his father. Gregory DeWitt's cell phone rang to end the round. He took the call. "Hello…"

Roland relaxed and sat back in the leather armchair in front of the desk. With eyes locked, he waited to pounce, and use that Princeton education, his acerbic wit and put his much-accomplished patriarch in his place. He waited as his father listened to the caller.

The elder DeWitt turned his back to Roland. "Just a minute, Harry…"

His hand covered the phone. "I have to take this Roland, it's private."

Roland shrugged his shoulders, smiled but stayed put. Exasperated, Gregory DeWitt pushed his chair away and strode out of his den. Roland kept his eyes fixed on his father. He heard the click of shoes fade into a carpeted sitting room at the end of the hall.

Roland popped up and made straight for the cabinet near the desk. He tried prying open the cabinet's glass doors to no avail. He stared into the glass cabinet wanting to smash it open, but thought better of it. Under his breath, he cursed his father. He had only minutes, if that.

Moving on he checked the top drawer, locked. The second drawer was unlocked but inside he found only ammunition. The third drawer was open. Inside he found the object of his search, an old handgun and knowing his father, it was likely in firing condition. The pistol was a

Walther designed Mauser P.38, German made and rare. Designed to replace the Luger, the Mauser remained a more reliable field firearm.

Roland pulled the gun from inside and checked it, popping out the magazine. It had ammunition in the clip. Roland and his brother Fredrick were both proficient in the use of handguns. As teenagers, both sons received instruction in their care and use. Roland had visited the gun range several times while in high school.

Inspecting the gun that deadly impulse returned; the one he felt as a boy firing round after round into a man-target. The gun imbued a sense of power; an energy Roland savored. Its intent meant one thing alone: he held the all abiding lethal force when and if he needed it.

The gun's cold black metal weighed well in his hand and he realized the balance of power had shifted. Roland did a quick inspection and recognized why his father had yet to exhibit the gun. It had a bent trigger guard and his father would never display a specimen that was less than perfect. Like the gun, Roland felt shut inside the drawer much of his adult life.

He heard his father's approach, slipped the pistol in his coat pocket, and slid the drawer shut. Before Gregory DeWitt reappeared Roland had reseated himself in front of the desk.

"So you're not going with us I take it," Roland's father restarted.

Having accomplished his primary mission, Roland stood facing his father, who now looked quite pleased. Whatever the phone call entailed it appeared to have brightened Gregory De Witt's day.

"No dear father, I believe I'll be passing on the invite," he said lending a sarcastic edge to his words. Roland left the fight behind and headed for the door. "But wish mother and Freddy a Merry Christmas for me."

His father followed him out and before Roland reached the exit he called out, "Roland, we do love you son. Merry Christmas! We'll see you in the New Year."

There was no teary sentimental scene, no hug. As Roland opened the door he looked back and mustered a lukewarm, "Merry Christmas, father." He had what he wanted. The door closed on the life Roland once lived and he was happy to say goodbye. Roland left his father's home with an answer to his problems and a way to pursue the future he so richly deserved.

At home, he coddled the gun in his pocket before putting his coat away. Was it for action or merely intimidation? Willis buzzed the intercom shortly after. Roland greeted his lover with a wide smile, a hug and a kiss on the lips, a huge sign his mood had indeed switched. Taken aback by his friend's over-zealous humor, Willis made a wary entrance into the living room.

Discarding his coat, Willis glared at his usually pensive partner. Roland's eyes burned with a rarely seen fervor. "So, what's gotten into you? At work you seemed anything but overjoyed."

"I know," Roland confessed. "Sorry if I was rude this afternoon, but that's all changed." Things had changed. Tonight, Roland felt empowered and ready to deal with his nemesis, Davis Jefferson.

He took Willis by the hand and led him into the kitchen. "Let's stay in and cook. I've got chicken, there's vegetables in the freezer… I can make a stir-fry for two. You and me, and then…" Cupping a hand against Willis's cheek, Roland's face flushed and as he smiled the blonde whiskers above his lips bristled. His sensuous smirk invited only one response: yes.

Roland set about to make dinner while Willis sat mystified by his lover's good humor.

"Now I get it… you got a visit from the ghost of Christmas past," Willis quipped.

Roland smiled. "No, nothing that dramatic. That Neanderthal, Jefferson texted me today," he started, busy preparing the food.

"About…"

"What else… the money. He's wants to renegotiate the terms."

Again, Willis sat confused. How could this latest wrinkle cause Roland such elation? Any impediment ordinarily sent Roland over the edge. "That's why you're happy? Because Davis wants more money? I don't get it."

Roland laughed, wiped his hands on the dishtowel and gave Willis a knowing grin. "Of course not. It's my resolution that's made it tolerable and if I do say so, brilliant."

Roland walked past Willis and disappeared into the living room. He opened the closet, pulled the handgun from his coat pocket and stood admiring the gun for several seconds, enamored with its weight, its power. As Roland returned to the kitchen, Willis spotted his solution. A wave of panic struck him and horrified he leapt from his seat, pulling the firearm from Roland's easy grip. "No! You can't! I won't let you!" Willis cried clutching the gun with both hands. He backed up, keeping the gun well away.

"What are you doing, Willis?" Roland cried out. Enraged, he stepped closer, his eyes locked in, his fingers taut.

"You said it was a victimless crime... no one would get hurt," Willis stammered, holding the gun close to his body. He backed away as his lover approached. Willis read the resolve in Roland's eyes and frightened, he slid further into the kitchen corner.

He was running out of room.

Holding out his hand Roland commanded, "Willis, the gun."

Willis cowered against the counter. "It won't work. You'll get caught and I'll lose you."

Roland was beyond reason and fully fueled by a need to succeed. The fates demanded he act and the gun was his only answer– the gun and steely ambition. He lunged toward his lover and their hands grappled for the gun. Twisting against the counter they wrestled the pistol in circles each gaining an advantage and losing it in micro-seconds.

"Let go!" Roland screamed as he pushed Willis, wresting the gun his way. Roland made one final all-out yank; a crack echoed out. All tension subsided. Roland took hold of the gun and Willis slipped down against the counter, his body bent trying desperately to stay standing. A whisper squeaked out, "Roland..."

"Willis!" he screamed. Attempting to upright his lover, he dropped the firearm. Willis continued to slip; his glassy eyes aimed straight ahead, past Roland. His weight shifted and Roland could only guide him to the floor. Blood spewed from a wound in his chest as he tried to speak. No words came. His eyes wandered.

"Willis!" Roland cried, huddled next to his lover. "I'm sorry, I'm so sorry! Don't die, don't leave me."

Propped against the cupboard doors, Willis stared out unable to focus. The light in his eyes dimmed, color drained from his face and his head bobbed as if held up by strings. Roland drew him close, laid his head across his chest and hugged him. He heard a last sigh and his head collapsed upon his shoulder. Willis was gone and with him, a piece of Roland died.

Roland's only friend, his conscience lay dead on the floor.

CHAPTER 20

A T HOME, NEVILLE readied for the big game. Wisconsin was visiting Minneapolis to play his beloved Golden Gophers with the overall lead in the Big Ten conference at stake. Minnesota trailed the Badgers by one point but had lost the two previous tilts between them, both close games. With pen and pad in hand, Neville led the way.

A cold clear night greeted the Minnesota faithful. Thirty minutes before game time the parking lot remained a hive of activity. Droves of Gopher fans queued before the entry gates excited and anxious to find their seats inside Mariucci Arena. The long lines ensured a capacity crowd and partisan support for the underdog Golden Gophers.

Once inside, Neville and Dell guided Dewey, Phil and Arthur to their seats near the top of the lower bowl. Twenty-three rows up and just right of center-ice, they had a perfect view for the game. After sitting, Neville took Phil to help at the concession. The mood was festive inside the arena and together they fought through the congested aisles and loaded up with pop, nachos, hot dogs, popcorn and Dell's favorite, peperoni sticks. Someone sang the anthem with the Minnesota faithful standing restless yet confidant.

A whistle quieted the crowd, the referee dropped the puck and the game was underway. Nearing the four-minute mark, Wisconsin got a lucky break and a puck dumped into the Minnesota end hit off a stanchion, bounced to a charging Wisconsin forward Kruger who skated in alone on Minnesota's goalie, Cary Waimes and scored–advantage Wisconsin.

The packed house fell silent. The first period ended with the score 2-0 for Wisconsin sending a disconsolate Minnesota crowd into the break, hushed. Neville sat with his entourage discouraged but hopeful.

"Good game," Phil said. His compatriots shot a loathsome look his way. Immediately, he understood the untimeliness of his words.

The second period started and Minnesota had made adjustments to tighten up the defense, but the offense was sputtering. Nearing the ten-minute mark Minnesota got its first break and Schaffer, their leading scorer, intercepted a rink wide pass skated in and scored on a backhand.

The arena went wild. Minnesota was back in the game. With the partisan crowd now into it, the on-ice play picked up. Two minutes later Wisconsin's defenseman, Powell, powered a point shot past Waimes to put them ahead by two goals once again. Mariucci Arena fell silent. The second period ended with the score 3-1 for Wisconsin.

Again, patrons went to break with the arena mood at an all-time low. Still they swarmed the concessions, the restrooms but overall it remained an unenthused assembly. Minnesota was down 3-1 to their inter-conference rival with no foreseeable signs of life in their offense.

Neville looked down the aisle at Dewey munching popcorn, excited and happy to be there, his father eating nachos and Dell smiling, a pepperoni stick in hand. Next to him, Phil stared out onto the scores of fans as they returned for the third period. It started slow, much the same as the first period. Neither team gained a competitive edge, a big plus for Wisconsin. Six-minutes in Wisconsin scored their fourth goal on a redirected shot from the point. The goaltender had no chance to save it.

The crowd sat deathly still. You could hear the low hum of the arena roof ventilators. Gopher supporters began a rush for the exits. Neville sat and scribbled something into his notepad. He seemed destined to write a disappointing hockey column. With less than ten minutes left in the game, play resumed. Minnesota continued their hapless effort.

With the score four to one, time became a huge factor. As Schaffer took the puck at center ice, the Wisconsin defenseman Stilson promptly tripped him. On the power play, Minnesota took possession from the faceoff. Their right defenseman wound up and when he let it go, the shot hit the Wisconsin goalie in the right shoulder. The puck dropped in the crease and Schaffer, wrestling with two Wisconsin d-men, whacked the rebound in for Minnesota's second goal.

There was hope.

With just over six minutes left, the play became frantic. The goal had re-energized the team and the building and Minnesota went on all-out attack. The next two minutes saw all the action stay in the Wisconsin end and their goalie, Mattick, made several game saving stops. Then the unthinkable—a Minnesota penalty called for an inadvertent high stick in the offensive corner. A collective groan uttered out from the entire building.

The next two minutes played out with everyone on the edge of their seats. Wisconsin took control in the Golden Gopher's end. But here, the Minnesota goalie shone and on one sequence made three spectacular saves from in close. Time ticked by and nearing the end of the penalty, Zack Bolland iced the puck to kill it off. It was now up to the Minnesota offense.

With just over two minutes left in the game, Wisconsin played all defense and tried everything to scramble the play at center ice. Seconds ticked off and still Minnesota struggled to get the puck into the Wisconsin end.

The once raucous crowd quieted, whispered a steady babble of optimistic rants. Prayers ran through the stands from the ever-faithful fans. A horn sounded from the upper bowl. Wisconsin pushed the play up to the Gophers end but the whistle blew.

Neville checked the clock. His team had made a game of it but it was still 4-2 for Wisconsin and time was running out. The arena clock showed 1:12 remaining. He wrote down the time so as not to forget to include this turning point in the game. Next to him, Dewey sat swinging his legs chewing on popcorn caught up in the excitement generated by the crowd. Next to Dewey sat Arthur, mouth open and his hands still planted on his knees staring out onto the white ice surface. Neville collected himself and whispered, *"They're coming on... if they only had more time."*

Phil heard Neville's lament. With play stopped and the players lined up for a face-off, he stepped into the aisle. No one saw Phil tread down the stairs, walk past the exit sign and stand at the boards. No one except Dewey. All eyes were fixated on the ice. Dewey watched as his new friend Phil reached up head high and placed his hands against the glass. In seconds, the scene transformed. A white mist began to seep from the ice surface rising from every corner of the rink. The linesman, ready to drop the puck, stopped and looked at the referee. They stared at each other and shrugged as the ice mist morphed into a rink wide haze. After huddling with their partner officials, they stopped play.

The players relaxed, skated in circles and waited for an outcome. Some searched the ice for an answer, several watched the benches for direction and others looked grimly to the stands. The mist thickened, transformed into a steadily rising white fog and engulfed the suspended center scoreboard. The fog rolled up into the silent seats of Mariucci Arena.

Within minutes, the players and the on-ice officials were mere shadows moving inside a fishbowl of white. Dewey stopped eating the popcorn fixated on Phil who continued to hug the glass as the fog spewed over the partitions into the stands. The arena patrons sat in awe as the mist billowed into their midst. A stick clicked on the ice and echoed out across the venue. Skate blades scratched the ice surface; no other sounds.

Lost in the power of the white vapor all attending stood mute, disoriented in time, yet it felt good and clean and right. Phil removed his hands from the glass and began a trek back up the steps. Dewey's wide eyes followed Phil's return. The mystery fog swirled and began lifting, climbing and dissipating into the arena rafters. It left a feeling of bewilderment in its wake. Gone–and below without notice, without comprehension, the game clock now read 5:12 remaining.

Time had realigned in favor of the Minnesota Golden Gophers and not a soul present detected the change. The listening audience, the people watching on cable TV all came under the same spell and in it, an amnesia of sorts took hold. The game circumstances were restructured and with it the memory of those events.

A slow uncertain muttering restarted within Mariucci Arena. Dell stood, leaned in and called along the aisle to Neville. "What the hell just happened?" His hands clutched the sides of his head. By now, Phil had returned to his seat. He smiled and looked down the aisle at Dell. Chomping on his popcorn, Dewey glared spellbound at Phil, wondering.

Neville gazed around the building awestruck. "I don't know... I really don't know."

"Well, whatever that was... it friggin' blew my mind!" Dell bellowed. Arthur stared out onto the ice, his hands locked on his knees. His head shifted to Dell. "Great game, eh?"

Dell peered down laughing with excitement. "Artie, for once you took the words right outta my mouth."

Reenergized by the fateful fog, the arena faithful returned to cheering. The noise level hit fever pitch. With over five minutes remaining there was still time for the Golden Gophers to strike, and strike hard. No one suspected the change, no one knew yet there was an overall sense of euphoria, blind faith that a miracle was about to happen.

It already had.

The officials gathered at the Minnesota blue line, the whistle blew and the skaters lined up for a face-off. The game was on. The partisan Minnesota fans ramped up the noise. Horns blared from the upper bowl. It was hard to hear. One man in front of Neville held a cell phone against his ear to hear the radio broadcast. The linesman dropped the puck.

Schaffer won it and the puck trickled back to the left defenseman, Dallard. Schaffer, Elliot and the right-winger, Tulluck chased in toward the net. The Minnesota defenseman took up stations at the Wisconsin blue line.

Schaffer battled the Badger defenseman, scooping the puck and skated along the back wall behind the net. He crept out and passed to Dallard. He one-timed the black disc, firing it end-over-end and Mattick, the Wisconsin goalie, caught his right pad on it. The puck trickled to the side. Schaffer was there, and fighting through a check by a Wisconsin d-man, he kicked the puck to the hard charging Elliot in the slot. Elliot slapped it, and with Mattick moving, the puck found a lane through his legs. The red light fired and the arena erupted. It was chaos. The clamor thundered out through stands into the stadium parking lot. Those who had rushed to leave began to race back in.

It was now 4-3 with just under four minutes left in the game.

The goal had emptied every seat in the house. The entire arena was on its feet cheering wildly, stomping, crying, laughing, high-fiving–including Neville's row. The tension had created an infectious excitement. Even the staid Arthur Wishwood joined in, waving his arms with gusto. How much of it he understood who knows but at that moment, he seemed truly happy. Neville was ecstatic as he jumped up and screamed along with his row of family, friends and fans, still clutching his pen and pad. The only one not taking part was Phil, yet he watched with a prideful grin, satisfied at the contagion let loose.

Amid the roar, the players aligned at center ice. The second bowl, mostly occupied by the Minnesota student body, boomed down the chant: Go Gophers Go. Suddenly a new chant overran the first: Badgers Suck.

The building thundered electric–a madhouse. They dropped the puck and when the arena announcer broadcast the goal not a soul in the arena heard it. Recharged, the Gophers went to the attack. Minnesota hemmed the Wisconsin defense deep in the offensive zone, cycling the puck along the wall playing keep away. Nearing the three-minute mark, they managed to stop play to the left of the Wisconsin goal. That was their job– keep the play in the offensive end.

Minnesota sent out their number one line once again. Rested, they were ready. Schaffer took the draw. The puck hit the ice and with a clever move, Schaffer slipped a shoulder into the Wisconsin center-man and flipped it back to his right d-man, Jamie Warren. He skated along the blue line until he found an open lane to the net, wound up and shot. The puck careened off a leg into the corner. Elliot retrieved the disc and fired it back to the point. Again, another shot, this one through, but Mattick made the save.

The crowd was in frenzy-mode. The puck bounced to Schaffer, he shot and again, another save. Elliot found the rebound and fired it back to the Wisconsin net– another save. Wisconsin players littered the ice in front of their goalie, trying every conceivable way to stop the puck. Three more shots, three more saves. Minnesota was playing like a team possessed. With three players covering the ice near the crease, Tulluck found the stray puck and instead of shooting fired a pass to Schaffer at the side of the net. His first shot hit a sliding Mattick. With the puck loose, Schaffer slapped at it again. It hit the outstretched goal pad popped up and over the besieged Wisconsin goalie across the goal line. The red light rang up and the referee pointed to the puck–a good goal.

The building exploded in a one gigantic roar. They had tied the game, and if the arena was a madhouse before, it now detonated into utter pandemonium. The aisles clogged with shouting dancing, kissing, hugging fanatics racing up and down the angled steps. The celebration in Neville's row matched the entire building with even Phil taking on high fives from the strangers around him. With wide eyes, he too joined in the bedlam.

It was Schafer's third goal, a hat-trick and the frenetic Minnesota faithful inundated the ice with hats of every size and description. Programs, cups, food trays, food; anything loose in the stands found its way to the once white surface. As they celebrated, a cleaning crew poured onto the rink and began the job of clearing the venue for the last one minute and thirty-eight seconds. The Wisconsin coach gathered his players by the bench and with hands flailing, delivered a scathing rebuke of their play. Even without words, there was no mystery in the message. Play harder, play smarter.

The delay served to calm the devoted Minnesota supporters but nearing the re-start of play the clamor again grew to fever pitch. The entire house rose to their feet; clapping, screaming, cheering, whistling–it all came out with less than two minutes left. A thunder of thousands deadened the sounds of play. The referee dropped the puck.

Wisconsin sprang first with Ian Traner, their star center, pulling it back. He moved up and dumped it into the Minnesota end and all three Wisconsin forwards gave chase. The adrenaline fueled Minnesota defense met them in the corner.

1:25 left.

Minnesota's Bolland found Traner digging for the puck and with an outstretched arm rammed him into the glass. Traner hit face first and dropped to the ice. The referee's arm went up. Minnesota had taken a penalty at the most inopportune time. The clock perched high above center ice read 1:19 to play. The capacity crowd let out a pitiful groan. They would be lucky to keep the score tied.

They lined up in the Minnesota end of the ice with the home team down a man. It was crunch time. Neville stared left toward the play. He held the pen and pad crushed in a solid fist, whispering, "*Hold 'em, hold 'em now…*"

Dewey spied Phil again leaving his seat. Ducking in front of his preoccupied father, he watched him trail down the steps and take up a position at the glass. Once again, Phil placed his hands against the partition. This time nothing seeped from the ice. Caught up in the excitement, no one except Dewey noticed him standing there. Unwittingly, all in attendance had already seen a miracle. In the next seventy-nine seconds, they would all be witness to what would grow to be legend.

The puck dropped. Traner swept it back to Powell at the point. The hulking Wisconsin defenseman faked a shot, slipped sideways, wound up and fired the puck. It ricocheted up and off the right post. A loud ping echoed out. Two Wisconsin forwards pounced on it and using one man as a screen, the second forward fired it hard. Bodies were flying all around the goal crease and it struck something, a leg, a stick and deflected to the net. The puck hit Waimes on the pad and kicked out in front. Moving in from the blue line the defenseman pounded it toward the net. A loud clank echoed out across the arena along with a frightening chorus of moans as it rang off the crossbar hitting the back glass. The entire building watched the action unfold from a standing position. Traner curled in fighting off a Minnesota defender and with a sweep of his stick threw the puck in front of the goalie. The Wisconsin winger, Decaro fired it and Waimes threw out his right leg deflecting it into the right corner. A miracle stop from that close in.

With his hands firmly planted against the glass pane, Phil watched the play to his left. His fingers twitched on the cold, slick surface. The surrounding glass wall flickered, glowing with a strange electric hue just as energized as the crowd behind it.

Wisconsin continued the assault while the seconds ticked down—less than forty left in regulation. Waimes had already stopped six shots in the last minute not counting the one post and crossbar hit. It was as if Waimes pads had grown wider, his goal stick longer in the face of the Wisconsin barrage.

From the left corner, Traner again found Decaro in front and fired a pass. Decaro one-timed it and Waimes, playing possessed flicked out his blocker deflecting the disc into the right corner. Minnesota seemed one-step behind their rivals.

Less than twenty seconds to go. With the puck retrieved, a closely checked Traner passed it up to the point. The left d-man sent it across the ice to Powell. Schaffer and Connors were the penalty killers up front and they challenged each possession. Powell again faked a shot, but this time Schaffer sniffed it out, and when he moved left to find an open shot, Schaffer followed.

Ten seconds left.

Powell wound up and Shaffer took a defensive stance to block the shot. Powell's blast boomed off his stick. The puck careened off Schaffer's shin pads and out to center ice. Connors saw the break, and although dead tired from the penalty kill, he jumped up the side alone. Schaffer shot by an off balance Powell, who made a desperate grab at the Gopher forward. Powell tugged at his arm. His hand slipped down and with no other recourse, the defenseman pulled Schaffer's stick from his hands. The referee's hand shot up, but Schaffer fought back and pushed past the flat-footed Powell, kicking the puck up to his partner Connors in the clear.

Six seconds… the crowd was ecstatic.

Connors took the pass and raced over the blue line, in alone on the Wisconsin goalie. Mattick set himself, aligned with the hard charging Connors, who shifted left with the puck. Mattick slid with him, opening up a space between his legs.

Three seconds… the building held its collective breath. One thought swept the building like a virus, *It was Connors, their best defensive forward, skating in on a breakaway, not Schaffer, with his soft scoring hands; Connors with one goal on the season and the game on his stick.*

In those last seconds, Connors slapped the puck, it rang off Mattick's inside pad and wobbled and wobbled and with just enough momentum, the puck slipped across the goal line. The red light fired and the building erupted for the last time.

The game clock read one point two seconds left.

It ended amid mayhem never before seen in Mariucci Arena. The Minnesota Golden Gophers had come back from an impossible deficit and beaten the number one ranked team in the nation. It took time for the crowd to realize the impossibility of what transpired. They stood cheering for what seemed forever. The Minnesota faithful met a cold windless night happily unaware of the real circumstances. And Neville had a whale of a story for The Sentinel's sports section.

The talk all the way to the car was of a game to end all games. Neville, holding Dewey's hand, walked a slow unfocused path along the snow-covered concourse, jawing cheerfully with Dell while Phil and Arthur trailed behind. Dewey turned several times and stared back to see Phil. His second trip to the glass had aroused Dewey's suspicions and even a five-year-old understood the implications.

A biting cold invaded the confines of Neville's sedan. Neville and Dell continued to chatter on about the game in the front seats. Neville turned up the fan and all five sat shivering, waiting for the car to warm up. He banged the dash.

Dewey's eyes followed Phil's every move. Arthur leaned back and relaxed. His smile, his gloved hands locked on his lap indicated an overall contentment. The car pulled out and Neville and Dell continued their excited chatter about those last eight minutes. Dewey suddenly turned toward Phil. The wool tendrils of his knit cap whipped around with his head. In a small voice he whispered, "You did that."

Distracted, Phil's eyes lowered. "I'm sorry, what was that?"

Continuing to stay focused on Phil, Dewey said in the same small voice, "What happened... in the game. You did that didn't you?"

"Did what?"

Dewey's lips pursed and in a whisper said, "Helped them win."

"Did I?' he said with a cryptic smile. His gloved hand reached across, curling around Dewey's knee. Arthur sat beside them unable to decipher their conversation.

"And if I did Dewey, was it wrong?"

The woolen tendrils of Dewey's winter cap dangled near his pant legs as he considered Phil's admission. Of course he didn't really say he had a hand in the outcome, but he didn't deny it either. The little blond brows furrowed, hardening his look. After several seconds, his intensity transformed to easy comprehension. "No... anything that makes that many people happy must be okay."

With a wink and a squeeze of the boy's leg, Phil returned, "I agree."

In their secret exchange, a trust formed between Dewey and the houseguest Phil. They understood a wicked truth only they shared–a confidence.

It was near midnight when they pulled into the driveway. The cold, the late time and the excitement had drained all except Neville. While it remained fresh in his head, he had a story to write. As they exited the car, Dell said his goodnights and walked toward the side entrance of his upper apartment. He stopped, turned and faced Neville. "It all changed after the fog, Woody. That weird white fog."

Neville, struggling with the front door lock looked up. "The game?"

"Yeah... funny." Dell swung around the corner and disappeared along the side. Neville knew what Dell said was true. It did change after that mysterious fog–dramatically. He returned to the door, jiggled the key and forced it into the frozen lock.

The first floor was dark but warm with only the spray of porch light jutting in through the open front door. He found the lights and all removed their winter gear. Before closing Dewey's bedroom door, Phil called back, "Thanks for the ticket Woody. The game was exciting right to the end. And the people, they were going crazy. I know what hockey is now."

"It was a great night. I'm glad you enjoyed it," Neville said as he ushered Dewey into the bedroom. Phil's door closed. Arthur stood at his own bedroom door locked in some desperate search for understanding. A tired Dewey changed for bed and Neville approached his father.

"Dad, it's your bedroom. It's late... go to bed." He placed a hand on his father's slumped shoulders. Arthur's head swiveled, his eyes, his face seemed set with worry.

"I think we forgot your mother at the game," he said.

Neville shook his shoulder and smiled. "She'll be by in a while. Don't worry."

His face eased. "Will she?"

"Of course. You'll see her later." Neville knew the lie would pacify him.

"Good, 'cause we have to talk."

With his conscience alleviated, the elder Wishwood opened his bedroom door and disappeared into the dark. Neville acted amused by this easy persuasion, yet it only reminded him of the damage his father had suffered. He returned to his room where Dewey sat waiting, his legs beneath the covers. "Is Puppa okay?"

"Puppa's fine Dewey, just a little confused. Now you get to sleep–it's late." Neville leaned in and kissed his son.

"What about you? Aren't you coming to bed?"

"I have a bit of work to do first. I won't be long... go to sleep," he said brushing Dewey's blonde hair with a hand. He switched off the bedside lamp. A dull glimmer shone from the night light.

"Night dad."

"Goodnight..."

The kitchen was dark. Neville switched on the stove light and sat with his laptop at the kitchen table. With the events fresh in his thoughts, and his notes nearby, he started the column.

He quickly fashioned the dismal play by the home team in the first two and half periods. How Wisconsin had built up a three-goal lead and the dire situation that had left the Golden Gophers in. How the fans expected a home loss, how well Wisconsin had played–and then the fog. That mysterious mist that filled the arena instilling the entire venue, players and fans alike, with a new found sense of belief.

It was here Neville referenced his notepad again. He read one notation aloud several times: *One-twelve remaining, fog appears on the ice.*

He read it again and yet he could not remember writing it. Inspecting the written words, the writing– they were his. Staring into the dark with only the laptop's glow illuminating his face he checked what memories he could muster. One specific thought came back and it clearly told him five-twelve remained in the game.

It was in the darkened kitchen an eerie calm swept over him. This thought that something had changed that night, a fact or a detail inside the facts themselves; something secret and wonderful yet he was at a loss to retrieve it in his recollections.

Incapable of forming a sensible explanation for the conflict between his notes and his memory, Neville finished his story with what he knew and what he saw. Still a sense of déjà vu nagged at him. One piece of a jigsaw puzzle seemed pressed into an opening it did not fit.

Neville sat for a few seconds, finally e-mailing the story to his work computer. Joining Dewey in bed, his son's small voice broke the silence. "He did it Dad." His eyes gleamed like little blue glow balls.

Neville looked over. "What are you doing awake? You're supposed to be asleep."

"I know... I couldn't."

"And who did what?"

"Phil did. He helped us win the game tonight. I saw him," Dewey whispered.

Neville rolled sideways. "How could he help win the game Dewey?"

"Remember the fog? He was standing at the glass when the fog came up. And when he came back the fog stopped."

Neville loved that Dewey possessed a keen awareness. At this point he realized his son's perception may well be true, yet he played it down so as not to frighten him. "He probably went down to get a better look... that's all son."

Dewey processed his father's explanation. "Maybe, but he went down again—at the end of the game. He was standing alone with his hands on the glass when we scored the winning goal. I saw him, and I don't think anyone else did. It was almost like he was invisible to everyone but me."

Neville had no real answer to his son's speculation. "Well, if Phil helped us win that game tonight, I for one, think it was a good thing."

"I think so too. Even Phil thought so."

"Now let's get some sleep champ."

Dewey's disclosure resurrected those doubts he sensed just minutes before. That same uneasy feeling crept over him. Were Dewey's suspicions that misplaced puzzle piece? Why couldn't he remember if Phil was sitting next to him, or standing near the glass? It all reminded him of the conversation he wanted to have with Phil about the camera, the picture of Rita and Dewey. In the excitement, he had forgotten and now it was too late. Yes, there were issues but tomorrow would be soon enough, he thought. Tonight, enjoy the win.

That night remained a welcome distraction for Neville and he let go of Audrey and Rita, his father's illness and settled himself with thoughts of a remarkable Minnesota win and a great story for The Sentinel. Son and father both dreamt of hockey, of victories and victors and of being that player with the game on his stick, as Connors did. They dreamt of games played only in dreams. They dreamed alike, father and son.

CHAPTER 21

ROLAND'S TEARS SLOWED and he retraced the events leading up to Willis's sad demise. In them, he narrowed the options. His twisted logic saw only one villain in this tragedy: Davis Jefferson. If not for his outlandish demands, Roland would not have needed a gun and Willis would be alive. And because he loved Willis, Roland too was a victim. It took little time for Roland to reinforce that notion and plan a direction forward.

Only one solution seemed plausible. He took Willis's body, removed his clothes and carefully discarded everything except the car keys. It surprised Roland how little Willis actually bled from the wound. Only smears of blood made their way onto his kitchen floor.

Placing him on his dining room table, he sponged down a naked Willis with warm water. Why is anyone's guess, but he did take meticulous care in cleaning the body. He removed an onyx ring from Willis's right hand ring finger and in exchange, Roland unhooked a gold chain with its gold cross from his own neck. He latched it around the neck of his lover. Love seemed all but a lost venture now. Roland was well past the tears as he plotted an escape from this responsibility. He thought of dismembering the body but that seemed too macabre, even for him.

With Willis laid out on the table, he took the bag of bloodied clothes and went shopping. The bag he dropped in a dumpster. Christmas meant stores were open late and he found a sport shop near St. Gabriel's Square open. There he purchased an oversized hockey bag and a set of weights.

Adrenalin powered Roland through his deeds that night and stoked the anger growing inside. Retribution became his focus. Roland borrowed a baggage carrier from the underground parking garage and took it up with him to his condominium. Once inside he locked the door and set out to ready Willis for disposal, his only viable option. No one would understand and see his innocence in Willis's fatal accident, so he plotted a way around the situation.

Roland took a bed sheet, the light green one Willis so loved, and swaddled his lover in a tight mummy wrap. Before covering his face, Roland kissed him one last time. Willis was losing the human texture, his lips cold, dry, his skin firming up. Roland realized the enormity of death. Willis was gone, never to return. As he finished the wrap, his thoughts returned to Davis fueling an ever-mounting rage. Roland's hands worked faster in his state of hate as he taped shut the loose ends of Willis's burial bonds.

In death, Willis remained the same as in life: a smallish man with smallish features. His limbs still pliable, Roland easily slipped him inside the black hockey bag. Before lifting him onto the baggage carrier, Roland sat and stared into the night. Lights flickered in the black beyond the windows. He spied the statue sitting high and bright above the square and out past the Sentinel building, the ice forming on the Snake River. That was it, the place to go. So resolved he sat back and waited.

From a distance, the square looked different at night. Darkness hid the people, the bustle of their busy lives as they scurried about the shops and stalls searching for something bigger, better, something smarter, smaller. From his perch above it all, the square took on a tranquil aura untouched by human strain, free of the chaos the world indulged and silent, so very silent. For a moment, Roland sensed a calm amid his rush for revenge, a certain inspiration as if transported to a higher level beyond the reach of mortal men, beyond the gods themselves. Sitting alone, watching light filter through the gloom, a wicked smile cracked his lips and he understood the duty before him. Willis Ogland was gone; a black bag on the table. Justice demanded an advocate and vengeance a champion. Roland accepted his place as that almighty crusader and prepared to fulfill the obligation inherent in the role.

Davis Jefferson must die.

Midnight came and Roland lifted the bag onto the baggage cart. He placed three 20 lb. weights in a pillowcase and set them beside the bag. From the elevator he proceeded out the back door. There it was in visitor parking: Willis's beat up Volvo. Only one overhead light worked the other out leaving the lot dark for easy flight that night.

After loading the bag and weights in the trunk, he set out for the Sentinel. There were two roads into the Sentinel parking lot, one from the square itself, an alleyway seldom used by anyone other than employees of St. Gabriel Square's shops, and a riverside road that ran directly into the parking lot. He took the Snake River road the five blocks from his condominium.

The lot remained deserted when he arrived, as were the buildings and the square itself. Well past closing time, his only concern was the Sentinel pressmen who began their day at 3 a.m. After backing the Volvo into the space nearest the Snake River, he stepped out into the cold, crisp night.

With no wind, the only sounds were the crackling ice and the Snake's surly burble. After a survey of the silent grounds, he slipped on his gloves, opened the trunk and lifted the bag onto a small berm. A coating of snow topped the ice formed over the land between the lot and the river. The only impediment remained an orange plastic barricade fence. He dragged the black bag to the fence, lifted it, slid the bag under and pushed it to the river's edge. A solid ice sheet spread out into the river for some 25 feet. Beyond that, the Snake continued its rush downriver.

Roland returned to the car, pulled out the bag of weights. Back at the river, he zipped open Willis Ogland's tomb and dumped in the ballast. For good measure, Roland added the steel jack from the Volvo's trunk.

A crescent moon and several stars occupied the night sky. He leaned in and pushed the bag toward the raging river. The lumpy river ice made the exercise an ordeal but he remained determined. Ten fifteen feet out he heard cracking below his feet and quickly stepped back. Roland retreated to shore and watched the crack encircle the bag. Separated from the frozen shelf, the bag and the berg below it drifted slowly into the river's flow.

He heard something, a hum and startled he turned and saw two lights driving in from the square. Roland pulse pounded. Survival took over and he scrambled to the Volvo. He slid himself into the trunk of the car and pulled the lid down but not fully closed. He could see light skimming the river ice and his heart dropped; the bag teetered on the ice flow, water flushing over its edges.

'*Drop you bastard,*' he whispered. The metal studs on the black bag reflected the light. The light drew brighter, closer; he could hear the engine hum louder, the crunch of snow. Roland pulled the trunk lid tighter. A crack of winter white shone in. A voice crackled, a radio hissing and he knew who the interlopers were. St. Gabe's security for sure he thought and they had stopped to see the parked car. Had they noticed the bag in their headlights? He pulled the trunk ever nearer to closed.

The bag wavered on the ice, fluttered as it drew into the river current and in a sudden shift, slipped into the murky swells unseen. Gone, and with it any trace of Willis Ogland.Roland laid still, he heard a door open, the crush of footsteps and he held his breath. A lifetime passed, or so it seemed. Was this the end of the plan, his vengeance?

Waiting breathless, the steps retreated, a car door closed and Roland let out a heavy sigh. Seconds later the sound of car tires pressing frigid snow echoed along the riverbank. They were gone. He remained statue-still for several minutes and when he felt it clear, he opened the trunk and hopped from the claustrophobic space. Sweat beads had formed on his face, his hands felt clammy inside the gloves.

Roland closed the trunk, pressing it down instead of slamming it. The night seemed much brighter, cleaner. Of course it did, especially after his term in the trunk. A quiet descended along the riverfront. The crackling ice, the river's torrent hushed. Roland peered in every direction, searching out the soundless premonition. Reconsidering his position alone in the lot, he searched his pocket and reclaimed the gun. Protection, yet it failed to yield that same sense of invulnerability. Its weight remained heavy but its fascination, its power had faded. Spooked, he wound up and pitched the firearm as far as could, finding the river. After a look around, Roland locked up the Volvo, tossed the keys in the river and set his feet on a path home. Blocks later, he stopped combing the darkness for the ghost he wholly expected to see. Willis was gone, he told himself, and no power on earth could return him. Roland was right.

Back home that night Roland showered twice, once to rid himself of a long day's filth, the second to wash away the sin. Roland would soon learn sins have a way of lingering.

The next morning Roland came in late to work. Head down, he hurried past his coworkers as Neville recounted the prior night's Gopher game and the mysterious white fog that had interrupted play. They had read his account and found the story so impossible, so compelling in how this disruption signaled an all-out reversal for the home team. Suzanne, no diehard hockey fan by any means, stood by the printer attentive to Neville's every detail. John and Sam listened keenly from their desks. Walter Hendry, a big Minnesota supporter, leaned in from his office doorway as Neville laid out the last few minutes and the pandemonium set in motion.

Their comeback story and the mysterious way it evolved had hit newsrooms nation-wide, with every state newspaper calling it The Miracle at Mariucci Arena. Indeed, no one knew just how miraculous the game actually was, yet it sparked the imagination of every sports fan across not only the state but the country. Neville beamed in the afterglow of such an improbable win that day, happy to be a hockey fan and a Minnesota Golden Gopher alumnus.

While all this transpired, Roland found his place behind the blue partition. His second shower failed in absolving the guilt and he now suffered the effects of too little sleep and too much conscience. Fear had taken hold, quieting his normally rambunctious babble. He sat absently enduring his own thoughts along with his previous night's actions. They ran nonstop inside Roland's head, like an old vinyl record skipping, repeating the same verse over and over.

It took two hours for anyone to notice Willis was not in. Sam mentioned he had seen his car parked in the lot, so a worried Hendry asked John to investigate. Roland's ears perked up upon hearing the development and when John returned with nothing to report, he heaved a sigh of relief. Roland realized John was not about to find his dead lover, still he seemed relieved.

Roland's day muddled along and after lunch, he managed to supplant his internal upheaval with righteous indignation. Davis was the real culprit he told himself. He was the one responsible, the mastermind behind Willis's unfortunate end. If not for Davis, all would be well. It all came back, his status as judge and jury, his inalienable right to decide and his place as Davis Jefferson's executioner. Nearing the end of his shift, it had all switched inside Roland's head. Satisfied, Roland swiveled back in his chair and watched the busy lives of the St. Gabriel Square patrons through his prism of pomposity. Roland was again in charge.

That afternoon Dell too was busy identifying culprits in his life. As he sat across the kitchen table from his adversary, Arthur, he watched their resident amnesiac continue to whisper strategy in his ear.

"Hey, it's not like I'm winning here," Dell said. "What are you tellin' him?"

Startled, Phil said, "Nothing. Just to keep winning is all."

"Yeah, I'll bet."

"It's your play, Dell," Arthur said. However tenuous his medical condition, Arthur continued on track when it came to gin rummy, and that frustrated Dell more than anything. Gin was a card game involving both skill and luck. It was getting to the point where he believed neither existed for him, at least against his nemesis.

The last game finished and Dell added the losses to his notepad. While Dell cleaned up the kitchen, Phil and Arthur migrated back to Arthur's room. After their first apprehensive meeting, a bond seemed to form between these unlikely cohorts. Seeing them from behind, they could easily be mistaken for father and son, especially dressed in their Dell-bought uniforms; same height, same short-legged walk, but from the front there was no mistaking Phil's bulbous eyes and thinning hair so distinctly opposite from Arthur's plump, natural facial features.

Dell's cell phone rang. On the other end Jennifer Gilchrist, his newest love interest, distracted him with details of their date that night. His outlook brightened while his charges sat on Arthur's bed waiting. Dewey's school day would soon be done and they'd be off to get him.

"I've got things…" Arthur started.

"What things, Artie?"

Arthur bent down, pulled open his lower drawer and retrieved his tin box. "Look…" he said, lifting the lid.

Phil leaned in. A stack of Christmas cards lay on top. Below the cards were documents and at the bottom trinkets from a life lived lay scattered about: Arthur's two medals from Vietnam, the Purple Heart and the Silver Star; several keys, some loose others on key rings. A rifle bullet rolled atop a collection of old coins and pictures from a past long forgotten, dog-eared and scuffed from age. A gold-edged pocket-watch filled one corner of Arthur's tin memorial.

Arthur pushed aside several items settling on a picture. He lifted it out and showed Phil.

"Angela…" he said.

Taking it in hand, Phil looked at the picture, a photo of a young attractive dark-haired woman leaning over a boy, both smiling for the camera. The boy was Neville at five-years-old; the brunette was Angela, Arthur's long lost wife.

"She was pretty," Phil said.

Arthur took back the picture and pulled the Christmas cards from the box. He handed them reverently to Phil. "She's coming home," he said smiling.

Phil opened the first card dated nine years ago and silently read the inscription. The card was signed "Angela Wishwood". Phil continued opening all eight Christmas cards, one for each year since and all addressed to Neville, all signed by his mother, Angela. The current year's Christmas card had yet to arrive. The cards and their significance induced a sadness in Phil yet he managed to smile. He understood his new friend was incapable of determining their relevance. Arthur took the cards and placed them back inside his tin box.

"You have nice things Artie."

With a certain childlike pride, Arthur returned a grin. He placed the box back in the drawer and as he did, a call came in from the kitchen.

"Okay you two mongrels, let's get going." Dell's call had ended and he was ready to pick up Dewey. That afternoon Phil learned a little more about his sponsors, both father and son.

Neville arrived home ready for Dell's dinner of spicy chicken and rice along with a side of green beans. After dinner, Dell disappeared upstairs to prepare for a night out with Jennifer Gilchrist. She possessed a certain special quality, a quirkiness he rarely came across. As he explained to Neville, "She's one of those women… the longer you talk to her, the prettier she gets."

A monumental compliment if you considered Dell's track record with women. While Dell prepared for his date, Neville readied for a night out with Dewey. The town scheduled public skating every Wednesday at Solomon's only arena just east of St. Gabriel's Square and Neville took the opportunity to teach his son the basics. His plan was to sign Dewey up for hockey the following year. His own experience made him realize the better the skater, the easier the game.

Neville packed up Dewey, Phil and his father and they drove off for a night at the ice rink. At the arena, Neville helped Dewey with his skates while his father and Phil took up stations in the stands. After lacing up his own skates, Neville searched and found a chair for Dewey. It would help to balance his son on the ice and keep him upright as he mastered the skating stride. The sparse crowd that night made it easy for Dewey to find lanes to skate.

At five years old, Dewey was still learning. Neville followed his progress around the rink, on guard for others skaters and any missteps.

They skated the circuit and with Neville's constant encouragement, Dewey pushed faster, harder. He was making progress. Soon Dewey would no longer need a chair or a hand for stability.

Phil and Arthur sat huddled near the top level watching as Neville and Dewey circled the ice. A bitter stillness hung in the arena stands. Few endured the cold. The bench seats were hard and unforgiving. From their high perch, they watched in silence and shivered inside their winter coats.

"Do you want coffee, Artie?" Phil asked.

Arthur's head swiveled round. "Coffee? We don't sell coffee or live bait. I've got toasters on aisle three though."

Realizing Neville's father had drifted back, Phil waited. After several seconds, he stood and tried again. "Artie, would you like a coffee?"

Arthur looked up and smiled. "Sure."

Phil found his way to the snack bar, through the double doors and waited in line. A rush of heat blew down from overhead making the anteroom much warmer than the ice rink. The arena kiosk was slow and he stood second in line. When his turn came, an older man greeted him. The clerk's manner was gruff, as if he had worked too long, for too little. Phil ordered two coffees and the man asked, "What size?"

Phil stared, dumb stuck by the simple question. After several seconds Phil finally answered, "Big…"

The clerk returned a grim smile, shifted left and poured coffee into two Styrofoam cups. He plunked lids on both and handed them across the counter.

"That'll be four-fifty," he said.

Again, Phil stood stymied. He had no money.

Neville had watched Phil enter the snack bar from the ice and realized neither of the men had money. Concerned he watched the transaction from the rink. Through the glass partition, Neville could see the clerk hand Phil the coffees and wait. From his vantage point, it appeared Phil was talking to him. The clerk appeared none too happy.

"Wait here Dewey." He reached for the gate handle and just as he opened the door, he saw Phil nod and the clerk's once sour expression switch to a smile. He began nodding in unison with his customer. At this point in the discussion, Phil turned and walked out of the kiosk. Neville stepped out from the ice. Phil approached the stands and confused, Neville asked, "How did you pay for the coffee?"

Phil grinned as he reached the bottom tier. He seemed quite pleased with himself. "That nice man in there gave them to me," he said pointing back to the concession. "Must be the season."

Neville glanced back to the kiosk. The concession clerk looked more inclined to bath in coffee than give it away. Phil climbed back up to the top tier coffees in hand. Neville, dubious as he was, watched Phil reach his father and share the plunder. He joined Dewey on the ice but kept one eye on the pair in the stands as they cradled their cups and drank. Armed with a rather pensive grin, his father waved down from the stands. Neville watched and wondered; whoever this stranger was he seemed to exert a positive influence on his ailing father. For that, he was thankful.

Roland DeWitt woke up from a nap. Refreshed, he readied for his meeting with Davis Jefferson. His message had said nine-thirty and he did not want to disappoint. However, the plan had changed. The gun now lay at the bottom of the Snake River and his original resolution had become more a mandate.

Roland dressed and searched the kitchen for the right way to end his partnership. He came upon a carving knife, sharp and sturdy. That would fit, he thought. Messy, but it suited the plot. He remembered the story John Winterburn covered of the car-jack victim found in the parking lot adjacent from the bus terminal. How it baffled the police even to this day.

Once settled, his actions became robotic. Roland set the knife on the counter and pulled on his coat. He wrapped his colorful knit scarf around his neck and slipped on gloves. He took a dishtowel, wiped the knife blade and handle, slipping it inside his coat pocket and called a cab.

A heavy snow fell as he reached the University of Minnesota

campus. The driver stopped and let Roland off a block from the Trillium Bar. The winds picked up. Store signs swung in harmony with the ever-rising gusts. At 9:15, he crossed the street and entered a coffee shop directly across from the Trillium Bar. After ordering a coffee, Roland sat near the window. He had a perfect view of the bar's front entrance.

Within minutes, Davis appeared walking toward the bar, head down, coat wrapped close to his face. Roland checked his watch and took a gulp of coffee. Davis had come from a lot in behind the corner bookstore. It made for the perfect rendezvous– dark and isolated.

The winds continued to pick up driving the snow sideways. The street remained free of cars and people. Only one other person sat inside the coffee shop. Roland felt alone in a desolate world yet he remained governed by his edict. He checked his watch and with one last gulp, he finished and stood. He rewrapped himself, slipped on his gloves and set out into the weather. The sting of wind-blown snow hit him first.

The time had come. Davis would soon be out, angry at Roland's absence and impaired by however many beers he had drank. He nestled in near the bookstore's back door by the dumpster and waited. He could see Davis's Buick from there and all angles of approach. Light from nearby streetlamps did little to illuminate the lot.

Roland stood shivering, his thoughts spinning, spiraling out of control. Willis – Davis – the money – it all circled inside his head pushing him over the edge. Twenty minutes in, a figure emerged from the winter haze. It trudged toward the Buick. The sound of crushing snow flooded the small lot. Davis had finally arrived and Roland stepped out to meet the challenge. The Buick's door opened, the figure sat and the car started. Roland hurried to the Buick's passenger side, banging on the window. Davis flipped the locks and Roland jumped in.

Davis wasted no time. "You're fucking late!" he barked.

Roland brushed the snow from his clothes, his head. "Car wouldn't start and I had to wait for a cab."

Through the Buick's shadowed interior, he saw Davis's skeptical sneer. Roland struggled to keep his composure while he groped the

knife handle through his coat. His mind screamed, *Hurry, hurry...
NOW!* In a sudden rage, Roland jerked the knife from inside his coat.
The interior blue of the car flashed across the blade, he swung down
landing the point into Davis's leather coat.

"What the..." Davis shrieked.

A sharp pain slashed through his shoulder. Blindsided by the
attack he instinctively pulled away. Roland became a haze of flailing arms, again missing the throat but catching bone. Injured, Davis
yanked open the door and rocked toward it. "Are you fucking crazy!"
he screamed.

Possessed by demon will, Roland leapt up and onto his wounded
nemesis. Both landed in a heap outside the car on snow. Roland's arm
cocked again, the knife came down plunging into his chest. Davis was
helpless. His eyes ballooned as he lay prone fighting off Roland's frenzied attack. Giddy with power, Roland sank the knife in again and
again.

Roland stopped and stared at his vicious work, lifeless and bloodied. The wind continued to blow shifting snow into pockets. White
eddies swirled nearby. A new task remained and he prepared to finish it. Roland searched the dead man's pockets, stealing his i-Phone.
Still wheezing from his deadly workout, he leaned into the car and
popped the trunk open. Roland stood and scanned the parking lot.
A car passed on the adjacent road. When it was gone, he dragged the
body to the car's rear.

Roland lifted the body into the trunk, closed it. He swept up
handfuls of snow, washed his face with it letting the icy chill reinvigo-
rate him. After a quick shake of the head, he took his place behind the
wheel. Time and falling snow would soon erase his night's exploits.

Well after eleven o'clock Roland reached Solomon. With traffic
light, he drove the outskirts of St. Gabriel Square watchful for potential witnesses. Adrenalin continued to fuel his actions and after several
minutes, he found it safe and parked the Buick in a deserted corner
of the lot adjacent to Solomon's bus terminal. It would be days, if not
weeks, before someone discovered the derelict car. What would be left?

Another car-jack victim dumped in the same Solomon parking lot; one more body frozen in time.

Before abandoning the Buick, he looked inside. Roland surveyed his surroundings and finding nothing amiss, he made a dash for a darkened side street. He threw the keys into a bank of plowed snow. It took only twenty-five minutes to reach his condominium.

Under the intense lights of the lobby, he noticed the gleam of blood on his black coat– no red color but slick spots. Everything slowed as he worried his way up the elevator and into his condo. Roland undressed, bagged the clothes he had worn and showered. With the deed accomplished and alone inside his condo walls, he felt a wondrous rush of excitement. Justice, righteousness had prevailed against tyranny.

Roland retrieved Davis's i-Phone and sat on his sofa to examine it. He punched up the menu and found his phone unprotected. No password was required. Under folders, Roland discovered the file Yo-Yo and opening it, a number of bank accounts came into view. These were the accounts already traced by Davis's ingenious Trojan software. Four numbered accounts aligned and at the file's end, the numbered Cayman account currently reading zeroes. In a week and a half that would all change. The numbers would all click in and the amounts would add up to his big payday.

Roland set aside the i-Phone and poured vodka into a green glass tumbler, mixed it with cranberry juice and drank the concoction in one guzzle. Roland embraced the warmth vodka provided; it mingled with his euphoric blood-rush together forming a coat of invulnerability. An insatiable sense of power rippled through his veins as if the act of murder enabled his noblest part, a right fundamental to those who lead, who champion, who rule the masses.

However irrational, Roland's festering logic took root and like a virus, it spread to where he believed he could not, would not be defeated, or denied. Sadly, any thoughts of Willis were quickly dismissed, a casualty of Roland's grandiose vision of life.

Roland slept soundly while two men lay in their wintry tombs.

CHAPTER 22

WITH HIS LEGS curled beneath him, Dewey waited at the kitchen table with Arthur and Phil for a customary winter treat: hot chocolate. Neville poured packets of chocolate powder into four mugs, adding hot water and creamer. Dewey added an ice cube and all four slurp-tested the chocolate mix. Satisfied sighs soon replaced the slurping and they gulped back their nighttime treat.

It was off to bed for Dewey soon after. Neville led him to bed, turned out the lights and kissed him goodnight. "Mom'll be picking you up from school so I'll see you next week."

Both loved their son and worked hard to make his life as normal as possible. Living apart their lives changed little, only now each faced the world alone. Dewey fell asleep dreaming of hockey, and his parents watching him play from the stands.

Within the next half hour, a tired Arthur followed and headed for his bedroom. As Neville guided his father toward his room, the phone rang. Rejuvenated by the bell, the elder Wishwood raced past his son back into the living room.

Arthur plucked up the phone and hearing a women's voice, started, "Hello... Angela it's our bedtime and you should be home. Where have you..."

Neville pulled the phone from his father's iron grip. He pointed down the hall and in a quiet voice said, "Dad... bedtime."

Phil watched wide-eyed from the sofa as Arthur slunk away.

Holding the phone against his chest, Neville watched him leave. Finally, he took the call.

"Hello?"

"Hi, Woody." It was Rita.

"Hi."

"Is Artie okay?"

"He fine Rita. Just a blip every now and then."

"I know it's late but I just wanted to know if you were going to the school Friday."

Friday was Rita's day with Dewey and his last day of school before Christmas. His grade one class had planned a Christmas party and an impromptu career day. Parents were encouraged to attend and volunteer information on their chosen career paths. Only a fraction of the parents usually attended.

"Yeah, I was thinking of going. What about you?" Neville asked.

"I told Dewey I'd go, so I'm committed," she said laughing.

Neville sensed something different in Rita's voice. Was it friendliness? Up until now, Rita had presented a stoic tone in all their conversations. Tonight she sounded playful.

"Great, I'll see you there," he started. "...and whatever you do, don't wear your white dental coat."

Rita made a giggly noise. "I won't, I promise. See you Friday."

A short call but interesting, and with it Neville's heart surged with renewed optimism. She was still the only woman he had ever loved; his first and he had always hoped his last love.Phil watched as Neville disappeared down the hallway to settle his father. To Phil, it was evident Neville's mood had lightened. "You seem pleased about something," he noted on Neville's return.

Neville sat in the lounger. "I guess..."

"You still love Rita don't you?"

"Is it that easy to see?"

Phil folded his hands on his lap. "She's very pretty, your Rita."

In his short time with the Wishwoods, Phil had made strong connections with both Arthur and Dewey. As for Neville and Dell, they were decidedly different; they had suspicions and rightfully so.

"She is," Neville said, leaning in. "But that brings us back to the camera. Dell said he asked about the pictures on it... Rita and Dewey's picture."

Phil's head dropped, his eyes averted Neville's gaze.

"He did ask but I told Dell everything. I can't deny the camera's mine, but I don't remember taking the pictures, Woody. It seems I must have but..."

Phil's words trailed off while his hands fidgeted in his lap. He found it difficult to face Neville. "At least I don't recall it yet. I'm hoping it comes back and if it does, if I remember why, I'll tell you right away."

Neville sensed an authenticity from their amnesia-impaired lodger. His answer was simple enough, and it matched his symptoms. Up until now, Phil had only a vague memory of a woman in a swimming pool and the glimpse of disaster all from a dream. Neville knew all too well about dreams: how they twisted truths into caricatures. Yet within dreams lie a veracity, this honesty hidden amid the riddles.

Neville tried a different approach. "What about the game last night? Dewey seems to think you had something to do with the outcome."

"I don't know." Phil lifted his head to face Neville. "I heard you whisper a wish Woody... for a chance to win the game. I just wanted what you wanted– your team to have a chance, that's all. And they did. Was I wrong to want what you wanted?"

Neville smiled, finding no real fault in Phil's logic. Yet once again, Phil had evaded a direct answer to the question asked.

"No, I guess not."

A short silence followed.

"Dell told me about your mother. She left you and your father long ago, he said. Does Artie still believe your mother's coming home?" Phil asked.

"It's the disease. Something about my mother seems trapped inside Dad's head. Some days he doesn't mention her, and some days his every thought revolves around their early life together."

"It must have been hard growing up without a mother."

Neville hesitated as if travelling back in time to relive those early years. "I was lucky…" he started. "Dad was there and fortunately, he chose wisely in who to trust. I guess it wasn't the worst thing to ever happen to me."

"No?"

"No, not at all…" Neville left the rest unsaid.

"Have you heard from your mother since then?" Phil asked.

As Neville stood, he broke eye contact. "Not a word. "

Sensing the disappointment in Neville's voice, Phil felt pangs of guilt. He knew the truth. Neville's mother Angela had indeed tried to contact her son. Phil had read the inscriptions on the cards in Arthur's tin box. To tell Neville meant betraying Arthur's trust. So, Phil made a decision to remain silent that night.

Carl and Sylvia Ogland were simple people. They loved their son Willis and knew of his sexual orientation, readily accepting it as only a part of who he was as a person. Before Roland, Willis had become involved with an older man. The affair ended badly and they had watched Willis suffer through its final act. They understood his naivety could lead him astray and they worried. They also knew he was currently in a relationship but had no idea with whom. After two days, Willis was still missing.

Early Thursday morning Carl Ogland called The Sentinel and Walter Hendry. It was out of character for Willis to neglect a call from his parents. In that respect, Willis had always been conscientious. They asked if their son had been to work these last two days. Walter was quick to inform the Oglands that he had not, and that Willis's car sat parked in the Sentinel parking lot. The news was not what they had hoped for and the Oglands called police.

Dell picked up two dimmer switches at the hardware store after dropping Dewey at school and spent the next hour installing them in Dewey's room. Once fitted, the dimmer switches controlled the intensity of the mobile's center sun-light and the speed at which the planets revolved.

After lunch Dell, Arthur and Phil sat at the kitchen table to begin the gin rummy tournament. Dell sat alone on one side while Phil joined Arthur across the battle lines. Dell took a much more serious approach that day but after his first hand yielded a quick gin, his smile reappeared.

As the game continued, Dell's smile dimmed. Soon the eyebrows arched and his hands clutched the cards with steely resolve. Arthur's red peg outdistanced him on the board. He stared unflinching when Phil would whisper a word in Arthur's ear, hoping to catch a phrase or read his lips just to see if they were bending the rules.

The next hour went badly for Dell, losing all six games. The last hand finally broke him. Halfway through the last game, Arthur reached for the deck to retrieve a new card. His partner tugged his shirtsleeve, leaned in and whispered something in his ear. Instead of drawing from the deck, Arthur shifted his hand to the discards and picked one up.

Dell dropped his cards and blurted out, "Okay that's it. As if I wasn't havin' enough trouble...you two are ganging up on me here. What are you telling him?"

Dell's outburst startled both his opponents. They hesitated, staring back in disbelief. After several seconds, Phil croaked back a reply. "I just told him the six he needs is the second card from the top. That's all Dell, honest."

"That's cheating! You can't tell him what card is—" Realizing what Phil admitted, Dell stopped. He lifted from his seat and glared at his two opponents. "The cards are face down. How do you know what the second card from the top is, Phil?"

"Well, I just spin time ahead in my mind and I see what turns up... then I tell Artie if the card helps," he said with all innocence.

Stunned, Dell sat back down. "You spin, what... time ahead and see what cards play?"

"Yeah, is that cheating?"

Arthur watched the exchange between Phil and Dell in silence.

"So you know what card is on top?" Dell asked.

"Well, yes. The nine of diamonds, but he doesn't need the nine of diamonds he needs the next card, the six."

Dell reached across and flipped the top card on the deck. The nine of diamonds appeared. He turned the second card and the six of clubs showed. Dell sat dumbfounded.

"He needed the six," Phil started. "Show him your hand Artie."

"That's cheating. He'll know what I've got," Arthur argued.

"Just this time," insisted Phil.

Arthur tipped his hand forward revealing the cards he held. He had three jacks, three fours, a king and three sixes. The second card from the top, the six of clubs, would have given Arthur gin. Dell studied the hand and sat back flabbergasted.

"And you can do this anytime?" he asked.

"I don't know, I guess," Phil said.

Unconvinced, Dell gathered up the cards, shuffled and placed the deck on the table between them. "What's the top card?"

With Arthur looking on, Phil stared at the pile. "The ten of spades..."

Dell rolled the card– the ten of spades. "...And next?"

"The queen of hearts."

Again, he rolled the top card. The queen of hearts. Phil correctly guessed the next twenty-eight cards Dell peeled off.

"Are we done here?" Arthur asked.

Deep in thought, Dell gathered up the cards. "For today, Artie."

The elder Wishwood slid out of his chair. Phil did the same, until Dell clasped of his arm.

"You said you spin time forward in your head?"

"Yeah..."

"So you see what happens before it happens?"

"I guess. I never really thought of it that way." He realized Dell was no longer angry and his simple smile reappeared. Phil seemed oblivious to the implications. As Dell gathered up the cribbage board, the cards and their drinking glasses, he recognized the importance of this fantastic discovery and with it, a plan formulated. Before Phil made it out through the kitchen doorway, he whispered, "Phil..."

"Yes, Dell?"

"Let's not say anything about this to Woody just yet, okay?"

"Sure."

It was one of Dell's great gifts, the application of someone else's talents. He spent the afternoon ruminating about the details.

On his way to work that morning, Roland picked up a pack of cigarettes. After breaking the habit his senior year at Princeton, he found relief in lighting up once again. Adding to his discomfort, that morning Hendry informed the staff of a probable visit by the Minnesota State Police in regards to Willis Ogland's disappearance. Until now, no one had taken Willis's absence too seriously.

After lunch, Roland stood in the cold just outside the Sentinel's parking lot twin doors. With no smoking in the building, Roland braved a biting wind sweeping in off the Snake River. He was first to see the State Police car enter the lot. The car parked next to Willis's snow covered Volvo. A uniformed officer exited, checked the license plate and circled the vehicle inspecting every detail in his walk. Roland watched with grave interest.

A second unmarked police vehicle arrived shortly after. Roland picked up the shovel near the back entrance and skimmed snow off the short walkway to the Sentinel's employee lot. He placed the shovel back beside the doors and lit up another cigarette. Roland made himself useful as he tried to determine if they had found any real clues from Willis's car.

The detective looked all business. Square jawed, no smile with brows furrowed, he held his hands inside his topcoat pockets walking over to the uniformed officer. Roland could see the detective's hairline, an army issue crew cut. They spoke for several minutes. Roland watched the detective nod while the other policeman pointed as they circled the back of Willis's abandoned Volvo. Roland drew a long drag from his cigarette.

Halfway through his second smoke, Roland flicked it into the snow and retreated back inside. It wasn't long before the detective appeared on the second floor news room. Roland watched his progress from behind the blue partition wall.

Hendry was first and they spoke for only a few minutes. John Winterburn's interview took even less time. Suzanne, Sam and Neville followed in turn leaving only Roland. He heard the squeak of shoes coming ever closer to his cubicle. As he slid his chair into the aisle, he could see his office coworkers standing in the background. All eyes were on Roland. A rattle of nerves hit him first– his stomach churned. Roland was fortunate to be sitting.

"Mr. DeWitt?" the detective asked extending a hand.

Roland popped up from his chair and shook the officer's hand. "Yes, Roland DeWitt."

"I'm detective Hoyer, Minnesota State police. How are you today?"

"Good, but I don't know where Willis is, if that's what you're here for." His upper lip twitched into an uncomfortable smile.

"I'm sure that's true." The detective gave Roland a long steady glare. "...but I'm here trying to piece together a timeline of when Mr. Ogland was last seen and by whom. I'm told you and Willis Ogland were in a relationship of sorts... is that true?"

Roland's eyes dropped to the floor, averting the detective's full on stare. 'Well, yes... I guess that's what it was. Nothing serious but we were seeing each other."

He pulled a spiral notepad and pen from his overcoat pocket. "You two... are gay?"

"Yes..." Roland answered with an air of indignation.

Hoyer smiled. "I'm not here to judge you Mr. DeWitt. I really don't care about your sexual preferences, but it might be important in finding Mr. Ogland. It seems he's been missing for several days now."

"That's true. I haven't been able to reach him since, what... Tuesday night." Roland tried planting his hands in his pockets as he swayed in the aisle. "Can I sit down detective Hoyer?"

Hoyer, writing something in his pad looked back and smiled. "By all means. I'm not trying to sweat the answers out of you Mr. DeWitt." He followed with an abrupt laugh.

"Now, is that when you last saw Willis Ogland? Tuesday night?"

"Yes. He came over for dinner, we ate and Willis left. I'd say around nine, nine-thirty. I've tried to get a hold of him since but there's been no answer to any of my messages. I've been worried myself, detective."

Hoyer leaned on Roland's desk propping a leg across the corner and again wrote in his notepad. "What was his mood that night, Mr. DeWitt?"

"Willis? He was in good mood like always. It was just his nature."

"You two didn't have an argument or disagreement Tuesday?"

"Not at all. We got along well. That was one of the attractions… Willis was so even tempered."

Hoyer eyes lit up and he smiled again, this time much wider.

"You said: *Willis was so even tempered,* Mr. DeWitt. *Was* is past tense. Care to explain?" Hoyer had caught Roland in a simple slip of the tongue. He could feel the blood boiling in his veins as the detective continued to stare, steely eyed and alert.

"I didn't mean Willis in the past tense only that my attraction started in past tense before we actually started going out," Roland returned, trying to limit the damage.

Hoyer continued his silent, steady gaze while Roland flushed as he tried to extricate himself from the slip. "Surely you don't think I had anything to do with Willis's disappearance? He was my best friend… I loved Willis."

The detective said nothing. Roland had raised a red flag in the initial stage of his investigation. A long-time detective, Hoyer understood why people disappeared. The list was simple; personal gain, revenge and love or as novels portrayed it, crimes of passion. So far, Roland remained his only link, being what appeared to be the last person to see Willis alive, or his only suspect. He kept that information to himself. Roland went on to explain their night together and Willis's eventual departure after dinner.

"Can I have your address and phone number Mr. DeWitt, in case I need to get in touch with you?"

Roland provided the detective with both. He shook Roland's

hand and as he left, he said a few words to Hendry on the way out. Roland heaved a sigh of relief as Hoyer departed. Later that day, while Roland took a smoke break near the back doors, he watched a tow-truck load Willis's Volvo onto a flatbed. What caught his eye was that the two men involved both wore latex gloves.

His thoughts reverted to that ill-fated night; how cold and dark it was, back to the security guard, the black bag and the end of Willis Ogland. Sadly, Roland's only concern remained for his own wellbeing.

With Dewey at Rita's for the weekend, after work Neville joined Dell, Phil and his father for dinner. Spaghetti, meat sauce and rolls. Cleaning up, Dell began the conversation.

"I've got to pick up Aunt Claire for six-thirty. They towed her car into the Ford dealership this morning. It'll be ready for seven."

"What now?" Neville asked.

"The starter… and two hundred and ten bucks," Dell said.

"She should buy a new car, or a better old car."

"I wish I could find one for her."

"What about my dad's car. He doesn't need it. It's just as old but at least it runs." Neville continued clearing the table, handing plates and flatware to Dell.

"Maybe… I'll ask her. For now hers is running."

"What about your date last night? How'd that go?"

Dell's face lit up. "Great. I really like Jenny. She's got this warped view of things. It's funny; we seem to see the world the same way."

Neville laughed. "Now that could be trouble." He opened the dishwasher and slid the plates into place.

"You know what they say Woody, great minds think alike."

"Yes, but they also say sanitariums are filled with minds that think alike."

"Ha-ha…" Dell found his friend's retort somewhat offensive. He wiped his hands and headed for the door. Dell made one more point. "After dinner tomorrow I was thinking about taking Phil down to St. Gabriel's Square. Maybe the sights might stir up some memories."

"I guess it couldn't hurt," Neville said. "You want us to go with you?"

A panicked look came over Dell. "No, no you stay home... take it easy. Maybe I'll just get Bob to come. He could probably use a night out."

"Okay..."

Before leaving to pick up Aunt Claire, Dell called Camouflage Bob and arranged for him to pick them up at seven o'clock. The rest of Dell's scheme was on a need to know basis.

As far as Neville's night, he settled in with Phil and his father, turned on the television and set about to work on his novel. Meanwhile his two housemates watched the Boston Bruins play the Detroit Red Wings at home. Buoyed by his latest conversation with Rita, he worked on the computer and watched the two interact on the sofa as they sat side-by-side. What seemed odd to Neville was they said so little yet they communicated in such easy fashion; a hand motion, sometimes a nod of the head, or a whisper and a smile. Both appeared content.

For that simple fact, Neville felt grateful.

CHAPTER 23

A T THE SENTINEL, the mood remained somber yet hopeful that Willis would reappear. Three days had elapsed and there was still no sign of their missing colleague. Roland's usual animated demeanor morphed into impassivity a sign his coworkers attributed to concern for Willis's sudden vanishing. These last three days Roland quietly went about his business, a definite change from his scatter-shot intrusiveness.

That same insight slowing Roland's often-reckless behavior had quickened his uneven thoughts. Discovery of his grisly conduct and ultimately the judgment of others had become a primary anxiety, shaping his conduct. He had ridden the tempest to desperate action and a backlash now stirred those around him. The pressure mounted. Conversations, office sounds and activities took on new relevance and piqued his already heightened senses. Real detectives were asking questions. People wondered the whereabouts of Willis. Unlike Roland, Willis had endeared himself to those who knew him. With this realization, Roland sat alone behind his wall– alone with the truth.

Ten o'clock came and Neville headed out for the Parent's Day Christmas party at Dewey's school. He arrived on time greeting Dewey's teacher at the classroom doorway. Rita, who had arrived earlier, watched Neville's interaction as she stood behind the class with three other parents. A buzz of small voices sounded as the class of nineteen grade one students cackled, continuing to turn and stare at parents lined along the back.

Miss Gillette quieted her class with a whispered, "Children," and placed a finger to her lips. Neville had met Miss Gillette the final week of Dewey's kindergarten year this last June.

Last year Elizabeth Gillette was a dark haired, slim figured attractive twenty-five year old teacher in her first year. This year she maintained that same attractiveness however, a newfound poise had emerged. Rita's stare persisted, making a close study of Neville's smiling, simple contact with the charming young teacher. As Neville passed by his son, he brushed a hand across Dewey's blonde mop. Rita's smile brightened as Neville approached.

"Hi Rita, glad you made it." Neville sat on the bench along the classroom's back wall. Rita followed suit.

"Woody," she started. "Dewey's teacher, Miss Gillette seems quite taken by you. How well do you know her?"

"Miss Gillette? It's only the third time I've met her."

"Third?" Rita's voice registered a jealous twang.

"Yeah... the first time was last June and after the Caribbean cruise we took last summer..."

Rita jabbed an elbow into Neville's ribs. Although it hurt, he could not help but let out a muffled laugh. Rita swiveled toward the front and unable to contain herself, laughed along with him. Several students turned hearing the commotion. Neville noticed Rita's eyes; how they lingered a bit longer, how her smile settled into gentle approval. That same smile he had seen when they dated, an unmistakable connection, shy yet inciting a response. As the last parent arrived and Miss Gillette closed the classroom door, Neville made a brave request.

"Listen Rita, the Sentinel Christmas party is next Friday. If you're not busy I'd like very much if you would come with me."

Rita's eyes answered first, blazing two blue indelible marks on Neville's heart. Her seat suddenly became uncomfortable and she shifted forward lowering her head away. "I– I'm not sure if I should do that, Woody," she said. Neville's request had caught her off-guard.

"I'm not asking for anything permanent. Just a night out before Christmas is all... nothing more. It's at La Scala."

As she thought, her eyes traced the smile-lines curling near Neville's lips, his beard-stubbled cheeks and chin and the aquiline nose he had imparted their son Dewey. Neville still held those same strong features.

"La Scala. I love their pasta primavera. Let me think about it," she said.

"Good enough."

Neville saw something familiar. An involuntary twitch, this special little one-eyed wink she made when excited. For Neville, Rita's maybe seemed a much-improved result than the chorus of no's he had heard for so many months.

Miss Gillette called the classroom to attention and introduced the children to Rita Wishwood. Rita clenched her hands amid a smattering of applause as she stepped to the front and began. She introduced herself and her occupation as a dentist and spoke first on the importance of dental hygiene while the class of five-year-olds squirmed in their seats. In less than five minutes, Rita summarized her talk by answering two questions after which she handed out new toothbrushes to every student.

The next parent, John Delaney, Owen's father, came up to explain his work as an auto mechanic. John displayed a car starter he had brought with him and using a pencil, he pointed to the broken teeth on the starter's gear ring and tried explaining the importance of vehicle maintenance to five-year-olds. After fifteen listless minutes, Miss Gillette intervened.

Karen Wolfe went next. Neville recognized Karen, a mid-forties realtor, as the agent who sold Arthur Wishwood his duplex six years ago. Her daughter, Kayla sat proudly paying attention from a front seat while her mother described the duties of a real estate agent in simplistic terms.

Naomi Stennis followed, a woman who worked at the same bakery where Dell once worked. Her son, Brandon, had become one of Dewey's closest friends and had slept over once during the summer break. She spoke about the baking process only briefly and she too handed out a sampling of wares. She left two dozen donuts on Miss Gillette's desk for the class's lunchtime treat.

The last parent to speak was Neville. Wearing his varsity jacket unzipped, Neville's nerves forced him to plunge his hands into his pants pocket jangling the change and his car keys in unison. They were only children he told himself and forged ahead. He stared out at nineteen sets of studious little eyes their attention riveted on him and him alone. To his left, Miss Gillette stood leaning on the doorframe. Dewey straightened in his desk and looked on with pride while his father explained his profession as a writer at their local newspaper and his duties there.

A hand shot up and waved enthusiastically. Neville nodded and Nathan Killops stood from his classroom seat. "Did you write Harry Potter because my mom's reading Harry Potter to me at night? He's awesome."

Low laughter swept the room. Nathan looked around warily while his classmates giggled. Stepping closer, Neville grinned. "I wish I had, but no. An English woman wrote Harry Potter... J.K. Rowling."

As he timidly shuffled side to side, Nathan asked yet another question. "Is there really magic and wizards Mr. Wishwood?"

The classroom grew silent. All nineteen five-years-olds awaited the answer. Even the adults anticipated an answer, especially Rita. Neville folded his hands, drew a great breath and addressed them all in a whisper.

"Magic is such a mystery, but it surely exists. It's within us all in one way or another. But for it to work you have to believe... then it's up to us to discover the magic that lives inside each of us. All I know is magic can happen for anyone at any time. No one knows how or why, just that it can happen for anyone.

"As far as wizards...well, wizards don't always have wands like they do in Harry Potter. Look at Mr. Delaney. If I had a problem with my car, well, he's the wizard I'd want working on it." John Delaney sat up proudly holding his car starter in a rag as the children peered to the back of the classroom.

"And Dewey's mom; if I had trouble with my teeth, she'd be the wizard I'd want fixing that. And what if I needed a place to live? Then I'd need a wizard like Mrs. Wolfe to help me find a home. And Mrs. Stennis, if you were hungry wouldn't you want a wizard like her around. So wizards do exist it's just they're not always like Harry Potter. Who knows, maybe someday all of you will be wizards in someone's life."

The children gazed up, all nineteen little minds spellbound. Nathan still had one more question. "What about you Mr. Wishwood? Are you a wizard like the other parents?"

Neville paused giving Nathan's question much scrutiny. "Me... I'd say my chance at wizardry has yet to come, but I'll be ready when it does."

Miss Gillette intervened and thanked Neville for his thoughtful answers and all the parents for their time. The attending parents said their goodbyes to the class as a whole on the way out.

Rita stopped and waited for Neville. As he met with her in the hall, she offered her approval. "That was sweet Woody. The kids, they loved hearing that magic is real. I loved that you kept their dreams alive."

His small part in the day's proceedings seemed to break the ice. Neville watched her leave that Friday morning sustained by the fact she had not crushed his ambitions.

At the Wishwood home, the day went by as it usually did with one exception. While Dell and Arthur engaged in their afternoon gin rummy routine, Dell enforced a new rule: their audience of one could not speak. To administer his newest edict, Dell plastered a length of duct tape across Phil's mouth.

Even with the change, Arthur continued his dominance. The duct tape did little to hide the smile Phil formed after every win by his cohort. Dell, to his credit, maintained an optimistic outlook and played on. Enamored with his upcoming plans, he played the game haphazardly knowing he would soon find solace in a much more beneficial setting.

Consequently, when Neville came home, Dell was ready for a night out with Bob and his newly anointed financial advisor, Phil. A bitter north wind had driven the temperatures below zero. Wisps of snow sifted through the shroud-like skies when Camouflage Bob arrived out front. He honked the car horn. The Wishwood's front door lurched open and Dell, huddled in his winter black slicker tramped out. Phil followed down the steps bundled in his fur lined black bomber jacket.

Phil took a back seat while Dell rode shotgun in Bob's weather worn Crown Vic. Bob turned to the back seat after greeting Dell. "This is Phil, our houseguest," Dell said. "Phil– Bob one of my best friends.

"Hey…" Bob's eyes flared with dull understanding. "Haven't I seen you somewhere?"

Phil leaned in closer from the back seat. "I–I don't think so…"

"Sure… you look like someone. Were you in Iraq?"

Of course, Phil did resemble someone Bob had seen. The dim light inside the car added a certain maturity to his facial features and with his hair slicked back Phil took on an even greater resemblance to the fictional deputy Barney Fife.

"Bob, it's just the light," Dell said getting Bob back on track.

"Okay, where to then."

Bob, a man easily distracted, was also easy to appease. Phil diagnosed Bob's guileless innocence and he liked him straightaway. With his sturdy build and size, Bob could have projected a menacing front yet he wore no conceits. Instead, Bob played the role he was born to play, a simple man with simple pleasures. After introductions, Dell delivered the destination.

"Where fortune awaits us my friend– Mystic Lake."

Dell leaned back in his seat, comfortable in his decision and no wonder. Mystic Lake was a nearby casino. Dell calculated Phil's extrasensory abilities would be best served in a casino. Given Phil's proven talents, the prospect of a most bountiful harvest seemed certain.

Dell insights concerning Phil's perceptive nature had gone no further than this misanthropic expedition. He saw only an opportunity to enhance his bank balance. Dell's thoughts shot past those somewhat deeper implications attached to Phil's gift. Beyond the glitter of gold, a mysterious force was announcing its presence. Whatever numbed his perception, Dell missed the obvious allusions.

Mystic Lake casino stood on the outskirts of Minneapolis, a forty-five minute drive from Solomon. On the drive, Dell explained the simple rules of Blackjack to Phil and Bob. How much either understood of the game remained in doubt but a confident Dell forged ahead anyway. They parked and followed into the casino itself excited for the adventure before them.

They entered into a grand atrium. Massive ivory columns stretched to a domed ceiling. Cast figurines danced in naked glory along the coffered edgings rounding a circle of majestic white panels. On the floor, dark marble stretched in all directions. To the left it led to the hotel lobby where a tuxedoed concierge stood guard. To the right, the swirled marble stepped down a flight to the casino level. They turned right once more into the gaming room. Once inside brassy lighting and a menagerie of sounds assailed them head on.

A gaudy maze of multi-colored carpet attacked their senses, as if their casino hosts had set a coven of Himalayan goat herders loose on looms to weave the abstract covering. It spread out in kaleidoscope colors across the room. Raucous sounds filled the space; the chinking bells and steady clatter of coin, the beep and buzz of fiercely vivid machines as they echoed mind numbing musical ditties. An eclectic mix of people sat and stood and mingled animated by the machines, searching the spinning wheels for a number, or symbol or series of symbols to align and announce their good fortune.

Bunched together, staring keenly about the frenetic scene, they ventured further into the belly of the Mystic Lake Casino. A sickly sweet smell suddenly struck; the perfect additive to quench the far harsher odor of cigarettes and stale beer. Walking along a bank of slot machines the three turned a corner and found Dell's Promised Land. Spread out before them lay a sea of green felt tables each meticulously attended by a uniformed employee. They were the gatekeepers, the guardians of fortune and to walk away with a profit one must defeat these minions of lady luck.

All three stood across the threshold of the blackjack den; all three loosened their coats as if preparing for an old-fashioned showdown. Like Wyatt Earp at the OK Corral, Dell led his crew to an empty table. Bob took his spot in first position by the dealer. Dell left a space and took the third seat with Phil parking himself in seat four, next to Dell.

The dealer greeted all three with a wide smile and a friendly, "Welcome to Mystic Lake."

Bob and Dell each changed in cash for casino chips while Phil gaped openly at his surroundings. Chips of various colors sat perfectly aligned in the dealer's tray, a shoe sat stacked with blue backed cards and out past the rows of semi-circular tables blinking, chinking machines whirred out their musical call. To his left a table busy with patrons extolled the ifs and buts of the last card played. Behind, he saw a board lit with numbers as its wheel spun below. Another oblong table stood encircled by players throwing dice and keeping watch along the sideboards. A rush of adrenalin pulsed through Dell. For Phil, this was indeed a world unseen and unknown.

After swapping the cards in the shuffle machine, the dealer asked for a cut and they were under way. Lost in the casino atmosphere Phil sat mystified by the action. Dell called him to attention. "Well…" Dell said.

Phil looked back. "Well what?"

Dell whispered back, "The cards, what about spinning the cards in your head."

Phil refocused while the dealer waited patiently for a bet from Dell and Bob. Phil set into action. "Right… Umm, Bob's gonna get a king and a ten, you're gonna get a nine and seven and the dealer, a jack and a four."

The table minimum was set at ten dollars with a max bet of three hundred. Dell put out ten dollars to start. Bob followed suit. Like a magician's trick, the cards came out just as Phil predicted. The only card not showing was the dealer hole card. Bob, although not overly experienced at Blackjack, knew enough to stay.

The dealer turned to Dell.

"Well, what's the next card?" Dell whispered.

"Another jack." Phil whispered.

Knowing the dealer would have to hit his fourteen, Dell waved off the hit. The dealer turned over the unseen four, and again as Phil predicted he took the top card, the jack, and busted out. Dell and Bob collected their first win.

After several hands and several correct predictions, Phil whispered, "You're getting an ace and a queen, Bob's getting two kings. The dealer's gonna have an eight and seven."

Dell pushed out two hundred dollars in chips for his bet. He whispered across to Bob, "Up your bet."

Bob, again not schooled in the gaming sciences pushed his ten-dollar bet closer to the dealer and smiled back at Dell. After the hand, Dell collected one and half times his bet for the blackjack, three hundred in chips and Bob took back his ten dollars with pride, nodding over at Dell, "It worked!"

All three laughed while the dealer flashed a grin and collected the cards. Well into the swing of things, Dell ordered drinks for all. And so it went for the next forty minutes. Dell and Bob did lose the odd hand, but with Phil knowing the cards to come, Dell identified when to increase his bets and when to decrease them. Camouflage Bob bet a steady ten dollars every hand, failing to make use of Phil's future information. Doubtless, Bob never did grasp Dell's explanation of what the inside track meant, but he was winning.

With their blackjack booty piling up, the pit boss made a special effort to stay close to their table and monitor the proceedings. He realized the three were not counting cards because the bets were too random but still he watched and waited. The relief dealer made his way to their table replacing the original dealer. He politely introduced himself as Dwight and acknowledged all three at the table, but his gaze hesitated at Bob. Dell noticed immediately.

Bob rarely identified the subtle signals people so often disclosed. Innuendo and sarcasm went undetected by Bob along with physical tells such as voice inflection or an over long look. All went well beyond

Bob's limited abilities. For Bob, irony was something you did to a shirt before wearing it.

Dell, on the other hand, immediately recognized this new dealer's rapt attention to Bob; how his eyes slanted suspiciously toward Bob: how Dwight's brow knotted when facing Bob, yet his smile returned when facing him. And then the voice: definitely more direct when addressing Camouflage Bob, yet quite congenial when speaking to Dell. These intricate human behaviors reflected the emotional temperature in their situation so Dell kept a close eye on Dwight's actions and reactions. Phil sat unaware of the growing tension.

The waitress returned with their second round of drinks and Dell tipped her with a five-dollar chip. Meanwhile Bob scooped up his beer and gulped back half that bottle. On his third beer, Bob was having a good time. On the end, Phil sat quietly sipping a Pepsi. He had tried beer but found it bitter.

The regular dealer returned and Dell watched keenly as Dwight lingered, joining the pit boss in short conversation. The pit boss, a short stocky man, diverted his eyes to their table and Bob in particular. Dell read the signals and realized something was definitely up.

After Dwight left, the short stocky pit boss made a phone call still eyeing Bob from inside the circle of blackjack tables. They played on and within minutes, a uniformed security guard made an appearance next to the pit boss. Bob and Phil sat unaware as both casino employees kept a steady gaze their way.

Dell gathered up his chips and shoved them into his coat pocket. "Let's try something else," he announced eyeing the pit boss warily. Flipping the dealer two five-dollar chips, Dell offered a "Thanks," and slipped from his seat.

"Where we going?" Phil asked.

"Just over here," he said pointing to the roulette table behind them and plucked his beer from the table. "We'll try our luck on that. Come on Bob."

However, Bob was winning and because it was so foreign he wanted no part of moving. "I'll stay here. The cards are going my way."

Dell looked inside the blackjack pit and he saw two more security guards walk their way accompanied by two rather large police officers.

He made one more plea. "Bob it's time to move!" Phil looked on from the side and followed as Dell shifted his winnings to the roulette table.

Bob smiled back stupidly. "The luck's over here, Dell, my boy."

The guards approached and Dell countered, "No it's not Bob… trust me on this one."

Seconds later security and the Minneapolis Police arrived at the blackjack table. Dell watched and wondered if by some inexplicable means the casino had discovered his plan and was now wreaking their revenge. How could they know?

What had happened was no accident. Dwight, the relief dealer, had attended a convention the week prior at the Landsend Auditorium—the Psychic Fair. When Camouflage Bob accidently kicked over the flaming standard and set the building on fire, Dwight was witness to the event. Dressed in his customary camouflage gear, Bob would be hard to forget. Dwight knew the police were still on the lookout for the man involved and he alerted his pit boss who called police.

With one eye on Bob's predicament, Dell pointed to the numbers lit up in sequence on the roulette wheel tote and asked, "What's the number gonna be Phil?"

In shock, Phil watched the two police officers approach their friend Bob across the aisle. Taking defensive positions an arm's length from Bob, one officer held a hand to his gun. Bob was a big man and they were taking all the necessary precautions.

"What about Bob?"

Dell turned and glanced over. "He'll be alright." He knew it was a lie. Dell edged toward the open aisle afraid and ready for a sprint. At the blackjack table, the first officer called to a seated Bob, "Sir, we'd like to speak with you about something. Stand up and put your hands above your head."

Defiant, Bob stayed seated. "I didn't do anything!"

Casino patrons swiveled in chairs, those standing turned to

watch. Bob's simple smile had changed to a scowl. Determined, he sat adamantly refusing to move.

"Sir, stand and place your hands above your head," the officer repeated in a more forceful voice. Three casino security guards jostled into position. Surrounded, Bob folded his arms and stared vacantly ahead. The vast expanse of the casino floor grew surprisingly quiet and in it, people stared to that section where Bob sat in revolt. Fearing the same treatment, Dell looked on from his place across the aisle. Phil scrutinized the entire police process, mesmerized by the situation.

The second officer moved in and clutched at Camouflage Bob's arm. A sudden swarm of uniformed men pounced, taking Bob to the carpet. They forcefully rolled him face down. The move was quick and brutal.

"Dell!" Bob cried out.

Bob was down and Dell turned to run. Phil grabbed his arm. "Dell– we've got to help Bob!"

Shaking his head, Dell countered, "No we don't..." Prying at Phil's fingers, Dell tried pulling away. This was one area Dell knew his limitations. Fighting had never fit with his peace-nick lifestyle. Most women would make short work of Dell let alone five trained security types. No, Dell had always extricated himself from situations like this with his tongue and right now, that tongue remained tied.

Bob was down and one police officer pulled at his arms. A second struggled to snap handcuffs onto his oversized wrists. A casino security guard leaned a knee into Bob's back and tried desperately to tame the beast Bob. Two guards held tight to his flailing legs. Trapped in a network of brawny arms and bodies, Bob wriggled but made no headway.

"Help me..." Bob pleaded.

"You're under arrest," the first officer muttered. A circle of patrons formed and beyond the first line heads bobbed to see the action. Phil yanked on Dell's coat sleeve stopping him before he could flee the scene. He saw Bob now lying powerless across the casino carpet. Phil let loose of Dell and in measured strides walked to where Bob lay. Phil's face transformed. His smile glowed of self-assurance and he approached the first officer. His first words were slow, sincere and spoken with clarity and conviction.

"Let Bob go."

The besieged officer looked up and saw Phil standing next to this human dog-pile. His eyes caught Phil's. The tension in his face eased. His hold on Bob loosened. The second officer struggled with a still wriggling Bob and without his partner's assistance he called, "Need some help here…"

He forced a look up and saw his fellow cop staring spellbound at Phil. "Eddie," he yelped. His focus shifted, his eyes locked onto Phil's and the same daze engulfed him. Caught unprepared, he stopped, released his grip on Bob and relaxed alongside his partner.

Both men stood and stared at Phil, the deputy extraordinaire. The casino guards soon realized this overwhelming force and followed suit. A silence unknown on the casino floor took hold while the Friday night crowd stood in awe. Dell watched the drama unfold from behind his blackjack benefactor.

Uncompromised, standing over the two policemen, Phil directed, "There's been a terrible mistake. Take the handcuffs off this man."

The first officer repeated Phil's command. *"There's been a terrible mistake. Take the handcuffs off this man."* The second police officer complied and both men helped Bob up from the floor. Camouflage Bob brushed the dirt from his camouflage pants and his camouflage coat.

Phil's eyes continued their eerie glare. "We apologize for the trouble," he said.

Both officers stood bolt upright like robots and repeated, *"We apologize for the trouble."*

As Dell observed the room, he realized the overtly quiet crowd had failed to move a muscle. He walked up nose to nose with one man nearby. There was no reaction. Then another, and as he walked the circle of patrons they continued to act and react as statues might, stone still, immobile. The only 'live' people, besides Phil, Bob and himself, seemed to be the police officers and they responded only on Phil's command. Dell touched one man's face. It was human flesh.

As Bob finished brushing off the dirt, he offered his hand. "Thanks little buddy."

"I think it's time to go," Phil said.

"What about all these people? Are they okay?" Dell asked.

"They'll be fine."

Phil led a path through the human pylons while Bob and Dell followed. Remembering his chips, Bob dashed back and retrieved his winnings from behind the five frozen guards. They walked along the carpeted track turned right and miraculously, when out of sight, the casino action restarted. Everything awoke with a sudden clatter of machines, coin and of course people.

With their perpetrator now gone, the Minneapolis police officers stood in front of three casino security personnel. One officer held a pair of empty handcuffs.

"What's going on?" The first cop asked.

"I– I'm not sure," the second one said as he surveyed the area. Behind them, the guards looked at each other skeptically. The patrons searched here and there for the reason they had assembled. Soon, all involved found their way back to doing whatever they were doing before this embarrassing moment arrived.

The pit boss entered in and immediately asked, "What's going on?"

The security guards, the police looked lost. There was no logical answer or even any specific recall to fall back on. A sense of something remained, like ashes or a shadow in the mind yet the allusion played on, barking a familiar refrain inside the picture world the subconscious can be, like a song that won't end, a guilt that won't die. In time, as with all human affairs, the feeling faded.

As for Bob and Dell, they found a cashier near the lobby entrance and cashed out. Bob made a hefty four hundred and ten dollars while Dell struck the mother lode: two thousand three hundred and forty dollars. Satisfied, they left Mystic Lake a happy crew.

But Dell, he had many questions.

CHAPTER 24

WITH DELL AND Phil gone for the night, Neville set up to work on his novel once more. Editing was a tedious job but with practice, it added life to a manuscript. Before starting, he turned on the television and found a game for his father. Not his beloved Bruins, but a hockey game to occupy his attention. At times, he wondered if any of it mattered: if his dad really understood the different teams or his Bruins or even if the game itself made sense. In some way, Arthur did seem to enjoy the action and for that reason alone, cognizant or not, Neville resolved the time spent was worth the effort.

Arthur settled in on the sofa, his interest centered on the TV. Heading for the kitchen, Neville called out to his father, "Dad, you want anything to drink?"

Arthur's head swiveled his way. "A beer, I want a beer."

Neville thought it odd. Since stricken with Alzheimer's his father had rarely asked for anything, let alone a bottle of beer. Alcohol remained a restricted item on his father's diet, so at first Neville refused. "How about a can of Pepsi?"

Unaffected, Arthur again said, "Beer, I'd like a beer."

Neville thought again, *Why not? One bottle of beer certainly won't kill him.* He came back with two beers and placed one in front of his father. Arthur grabbed the beer, gulped back a mouthful and let out a loud belch. *Dell's corrupting influence for sure,* Neville thought.

As he sat idly at his desk, he remembered the day and Rita's seemingly shifted attitude. A face appeared in his head– her face. Something vital had changed in Rita's life– but what? Why was she suddenly more attentive? He let the thought lie.

Having written for years, Neville realized the importance of editing but on occasion, his mind would slip to avoidance. Whether it was a conscious or unconscious decision, Neville forestalled his editing duties and revisited the events from earlier that week. June Wardle came to mind.

Distracted and somewhat curious he called Tom Wardle. In their short conversation, Tom explained that his wife remained in hospital but had made significant progress since the Monday intervention in the Wishwood driveway. Following a full day of teary confessions in the psychiatric ward, she miraculously found a sense of herself, what she had done. Instead of her usual silence, June was contributing to her own recovery. For once, Tom saw new hope in his wife's eyes and the great possibility of rehabilitation. Tom Wardle ended their exchange with a heartfelt thanks to Neville and his family.

The development with the Wardles caused Neville even more bewilderment. He was happy for June Wardle's prognosis yet how she had arrived at this healing place concerned him. He went over the details of the encounter and remembered only Phil had touched the woman, adding his encouragement and compassion. Had his interaction influenced June Wardle's healing?

He glanced across at his father sitting comfortably, sipping beer, content in his ever-shrinking world. In some small way, Phil had altered his life. With the onset of Alzheimer's the friends his father had made since arriving in Solomon had all drifted away. Henry Colquitt, Jerry Langraff, Bernie Wolcott, none of them called or dropped by anymore yet Neville realized this was the unavoidable verdict of the disease. The separation it produces not only inside the sufferer but also in their associations. Few friends remained.

Phil's arrival prompted a newfound fraternity for Arthur, a friend suffering a similar fate. However true, Neville was never quite sure his father even knew of Phil's amnesia or could understand its parallels. Neville's only concern was that his father appeared much happier since Phil joined their household.

As Neville got up and headed to the kitchen for a second beer, the phone rang. As always, Arthur leapt across the sofa and quickly picked up the phone. Before Neville could react, his father started, "Angela, you've got to get home right this minute. It's too late for…"

The voice on the other end interrupted. "Hello, Arthur…"

Neville stopped. His father's face had suddenly paled as if a hand had clenched his soul. He held the phone out away from his ear and stared into the device. Moments later, he willingly handed it off to his son without a fight.

Neville took the phone. "Hello?"

A short silence followed and a voice, measured and sure said, "Hello, Woody."

Neville stood bewildered. "Mom?" Her voice endured, indelibly etched in his brain even after two decades.

"Yes. How are you son?"

"I… I'm good. A little surprised to hear your voice, but good," Neville said, reeling from the conflict coursing through him. Confused, Neville asked, "And you mother, how are you?"

"Today, I'm in a good place."

"And where's that?"

"I'm in Clearwater, Florida. I've lived here for quite a while now. It's where I took my treatments," she said. For Neville, memories flooded back, good and bad.

"Your father, how is he?" she asked.

"Dad… Dad's had his issues. He's a bit confused but right now, he's okay. What treatments were you taking?"

"Will he be okay?" she asked.

"We'll see. They're trying a new medication." Unsure of what he wanted to divulge Neville hesitated. Finally, he said, "Dad has Alzheimer's."

Angela Wishwood sighed. "I'm so sorry to hear that Woody."

"What about you– your treatments?" Neville again asked.

"I've been in treatment for Lupus for almost ten years. There's a wonderful clinic here in Clearwater that specializes in the disease. They've helped greatly."

"Is that why you called? To tell us you're doing better?" Neville's question was set with a bitter edge. He struggled for a way to react, to respond to a mother who had absented herself from his life twenty-two years ago.

"No, not at all," Angela returned. "I called because you wouldn't call me. I understand your anger but I still want to make my amends– apologize to both you and your father for what I did. Being sick was no excuse for abandoning you, Woody. You deserved better. You deserved a better mother and a better future. For my colossal mistake, I take full responsibility and I'm so sorry. My hope is that somewhere in the future I can make it up to you and your Dad."

Hard seconds elapsed. Neville considered what his long lost mother had disclosed and looked across at his father. Arthur struggled to follow the conversation from his seat on the sofa. Sadness seemed the root of his empty stare and yet he persevered as he had done his entire life. Neville saw his father's will, his strength of spirit

"Why would I call you of all people?" Neville asked.

"I understood you might not, but still I prayed you would. Every year I left my number on the Christmas cards and hoped one day you might try to understand. Maybe forgive a little and make the call, that's all."

Neville hesitated, confused. "Christmas cards, what Christmas cards?"

It was Angela's turn to pause. In time, she understood.

"That father of yours, God bless him. I've sent a Christmas card each of the last eight years Woody. Each card had my number. All this time I thought you were just too angry to call. Maybe you are but at least now you know."

This newest revelation dumbfounded Neville, however, the intrigue and the manner of its undertaking puzzled him. He gave his father a seditious glance as he turned his attention back to his mother.

"I don't know what to feel right now, it's all pretty sudden." In his confusion, he searched for a response. He found a simple exit. "I should tell you though, you're a grandmother. Dewey's five-years-old, just so you know."

"Dewey... a little boy. And what a wonderful name. He's happy, healthy?"

"Very much so."

For all her faults, Angela Wishwood recognized Neville's reticence. Why leap blindly back into a relationship with someone who had betrayed him so tragically? Instead, she offered a truce. "You'll need time to digest all this, I'm sure. Can we at least agree to talk after the holidays?"

Neville agreed. "Sure..."

"Good... for now have a Merry Christmas, tell your father I'm sorry and give my grandson a big kiss from me."

"I will...Mom." Neville wrestled with acknowledging his mother still he said the word.

"Woody, I love you son and I *am* sorry."

Conflicted, he ignored her last words. "We'll talk soon."

Inside an emotional ambiguity tore at him. The call revived his mother's betrayal, welling up anger from deep within. Sins acknowledged remained sins and although his mother freely admitted her mistakes, the damage was irrevocable.

Yet Neville held no malice. He saw his mother's innocence in her confession of ignorance and she had offered to repair at least some of the fallout. He accepted her apology with Zen-like tolerance knowing she too struggled with life's burdens. Neville saw how fear could pray upon a young, preoccupied mother. His battle raged between vying emotions.

Arthur gazed blankly. "Is she coming home?"

Neville spoke the lie. "Tomorrow dad– she'll be home tomorrow."

Arthur smiled, took another draw of his beer and returned

to the hockey game. Neville knew when tomorrow came his father would forget. It was sad but he understood the situation. Arthur Wishwood never could grasp the inner workings of his own heart let alone someone else's. Neville closed up his laptop and posed a simple question to himself. Could he forgive his mother and accept her back into his life?

All three shivered in the cold car. After their hurried exit of Mystic Lake, Dell swung around to face Phil. "Those cops just kowtowed to your every word. And the crowd– they stood there like statues. The whole building froze. Who are you– Obi-Wan-Kenobi?" Dell asked, flailing his arms.

"What do you mean?"

"What I mean is, no one puts an entire building in a trance and directs Minneapolis police to 'Let Bob go.' It doesn't happen… not here, not in the real world."

"Are you angry?" Phil asked.

Dell suddenly realized his overzealous reaction had unsettled Phil. "No, no… how do I put this?" He settled back in his seat. "What you did back in the casino, it was unbelievable. I just want to know how– how you did it?"

Phil's bulbous eyes searched the car as he sat wondering. "I don't know. I saw Bob in trouble and I wanted to help is all."

"And Bob's grateful…"

Bob nodded while he drove. "I'd have spent the night in the can."

"But how did you do that?"

"Honestly Dell, I'm not sure how I did it. I wanted them to stop hurting Bob and I thought, I've got to do something… so I did."

Dell soon recognized their conversation was going nowhere. That night it became evident Phil possessed unearthly powers; powers that bent men's will, powers that fractured time and suspended the arc of future events. Greater powers than even Dell anticipated. Dell saw no easy answer and because of his beliefs; because of Aunt Claire he realized Phil was no ordinary man. These realizations swirled inside Dell's thoughts. For the first time in Dell's life, he was left baffled as to what to do. How could anyone believe what Dell and Bob had witnessed? Instead of pursuing his questioning, he decided they deserved burgers and beers. Bob welcomed the idea. But Bob was simple enough to believe any explanation put forth.

Dell's theory was Phil had entered their lives for a reason and it wasn't to defraud the Mystic Lake casino. Did Phil even know why? And what should he tell Neville?

They made their way back to Solomon, arriving at Hank's Burger Heaven just after ten o'clock. They sat by the front window overlooking the municipal parking lot and across from that, the Greyhound Bus terminal. A favorite among locals, Hank's Burger Heaven was a main street staple, situated just outside St. Gabriel's Square.

Dell ordered three Cloud-Nine burgers with the works, a 'gaggle' of Heavenly Fries, his words not the menu's, two Buds and a Pepsi for Phil. As they sat waiting for food, Phil was first to notice the commotion across the street. Through a wispy snowfall, a strobe of blue and red signaled from the municipal lot across the street. Two police cars parked at angles near the lot's corner engaged a snowed in Buick sedan. Three police officers stood outside surveying the vehicle while a fourth sat inside his car.

As Phil pointed Dell mused aloud, "I wonder what's up?"

The food arrived and as they dove in all three watched the action unfold across the street. After the grisly discovery a week earlier, people remained vigilant and so the night shift clerk at the Greyhound terminal reported the abandoned car. From their vantage, very little action was taking place.

They finished the Cloud-Nine burgers and their Heavenly Fries and watched as two more police cars joined in the parking lot. Streaks of red and blue flickered across the terminal building, the main street shop fronts like a laser light show. Bob and Dell enjoyed one more beer while they studied the situation unfolding in the lot across the street. They said little inside the restaurant intrigued by the developing story. As all three headed for the door, they saw another unmarked car enter the now crowded lot.

"That's where they found the dead carjack victim last week," Bob said as they approached his car at the other end of the lot.

"That's very sad," Phil said.

"Certainly not the way I want to go," Dell added as they jumped into Bob's Crown Vic.

Phil absently replied, "I don't think you'll ever have to worry about that Dell."

Wondering if Phil might possess inside information, Dell turned toward his new friend, unsure of how to respond.

It was well after eleven o'clock when they pulled up to the Wishwood home. The ground floor lights were out so Dell suggested Phil sleep at his place for the night. They said their goodnights to Bob and quickly made their way through the sifting snow up to Dell's apartment. Dell gathered blankets and a pillow for his guest, laid them out on the sofa and sat next to Phil.

"For now, let's not tell Woody what went on tonight," he said.

Phil shifted uncomfortably on the sofa. "Are you sure Dell? Woody's been good to me and I certainly don't want to start lying to him. It doesn't seem right."

"Don't worry. I plan on telling him, just not right now."

"Okay... just for now."

While Dell readied for bed, Phil laid out his blanket and took a visual tour of Dell's apartment. The flat-screen television stood across from the sofa where he sat and below the TV, DVD's stocked the shelves. Next to it stood two towers of CD's and to the right in the corner, Dell's pride and joy, a glass cabinet full of bobble-headed figurines all colorfully painted standing face-out on five glass levels. Hundreds of beady little eyes stared back at Phil while he wrestled the blanket around his shoulders.

Dell said goodnight, turned out the living room light and disappeared into his bedroom. Phil stretched out along the sofa completely covered. The blanket shielded him from a cold breeze leaking in from the window above. The panes gave a slight rattle with every gust but his true discomfort lay in his disloyalty.

CHAPTER 25

OVERNIGHT A DUSTING of snow had carpeted Solomon lending a veneer of purity to the town setting. While Neville readied for a Saturday half-day of work, he heard the front door creak open, the stomp of snowy feet on the hallway carpet followed by Dell and Phil rounding the kitchen corner.

"It's a cold one today, Woody," Dell started, rubbing his bare hands together.

"Morning Woody," Phil said.

"Coffee's on." Neville pointed to the kitchen counter. "You guys had a late night."

"Yeah, and not much luck," Dell started. "I think we'll try again tonight."

Surprised, Phil swiveled in Dell's direction. This was the first he had heard of Dell's new plan. Still consumed by the conversation with his mother the night before, Neville failed to see the disbelief register on Phil's face.

"Guess who called last night?" he quizzed.

Dell swallowed a gulp of coffee. "I don't know… Gandhi?"

"Close… my mother."

Choking, Dell spit coffee back into his mug. "No way!"

"Yes way… we talked for about ten minutes. She said she wanted to make amends for what she had done."

"Was she, you know, serious?" Dell asked.

"Seemed like it."

Phil sipped coffee and stared. Dell sat and thought over Neville's dilemma. "Well... how'd you feel?"

Neville stood, placed his mug into the sink. "Angry... confused. And in a funny way I felt sorry for her."

"Sorry? Why?"

"I don't really know. Something tells me she's had it pretty hard." His thoughts drifted for a few seconds. "You still care about your parents don't you Dell?"

Dell straightened in his chair. "Yeah, I guess I do."

"Still talk to them?"

"I get an e-mail every few months, yeah."

"And they certainly didn't handle everything perfectly."

"No, but..." Dell stopped. Suddenly he understood. No matter the circumstances, they would always be your parents. "What about Artie?"

"Dad, he took it okay– a little stunned but okay."

"That's pretty crazy, especially now at Christmas," Dell said.

"Yeah, and that's another strange detail. She said she's been sending me Christmas cards for the last eight years. Have you ever seen one?"

Phil's face flushed, but he said nothing.

Dell paused. "Not that I can remember."

"Yeah, who knows? We ended it agreeing to talk after the holidays. Hopefully I'll be better prepared."

Neville set out toward the front foyer. Dell followed. "I nearly forgot. We ended up at Hank's last night..." Dell started as Neville pulled on his coat. "There was quite a commotion in the parking lot across the street. At least four police cars."

"What was up?"

"Don't know, but it looked big. It's that same lot where they found the dead carjack victim. If you hear, give me a call."

Neville arrived for work and discovered John Winterburn already at his desk fully immersed in his notes punching out a story on his computer. John rarely worked Saturday unless a story took precedence.

Before removing his coat, he approached. "Must be big for you to be here."

John looked up, "Oh, hi Woody." He stretched his arms, arching back against the chair. "They found another abandoned car in the same Solomon parking lot last night. A man's body was in the trunk. It's got the State Police and the Minneapolis Police baffled. They were both there last night and neither one seemed too thrilled. From what I could gather, they don't have much to go on. The car's a rental and the victim lives out of state... that's all I've been able to get."

"Jesus..." Neville muttered, walking back toward his desk.

John swiveled his chair back into place, but before Neville had walked too far, John reached into his valise and called, "Woody, I've got something here."

He pulled out Neville's manuscript and flopped it on the desk. "I finished it last night, and Woody... it's pretty good. I really liked what you did with the ending."

Neville picked up the manuscript. "Thanks John, I appreciate the encouraging words."

"And... I couldn't help myself. I did add a few comments. Nothing much, just something to think about," John added.

Neville smiled and tucked the manuscript into a desk drawer. So far, the reviews were all positive. Now all he needed was Sam's verdict.

Behind the blue partition, Roland had rolled his seat closer to the aisle. He heard the short conversation between his coworkers and knew they had discovered Davis's body. Unnerved, he reached for his cigarettes, pulled on his overcoat and fled downstairs for a smoke.

As he stood on the walkway fumbling for his lighter, he found Davis's i-Phone in his coat pocket. He pulled it out warily and turned on the device. He clicked over to the main screen and stared at the rows of icons. *Should I keep this,* He thought, *or throw it away?* It remained the only connection to his former roommate, a key piece of evidence and if found certainly a major worry. As he studied the display, one icon went unnoticed– the i-cloud icon.

Yet it represented something powerful to Roland: his dominion over an adversary, the ultimate battle trophy. That morning he made the decision to keep the phone. As he stood by the Sentinel parking lot door, he clicked off the phone and slipped it back inside his coat.

Rita and Dewey spent the morning Christmas shopping. Now home, she set up a movie for her son to watch that afternoon. The night prior, while decorating their Christmas tree Dewey had gone on and on about the involved workings of the Wishwood home in his week with Neville.

He talked incessantly of Phil and the hockey game, of Uncle Dell and their trip into the Minnesota forest; the resurrection of Willard, and Puppa and the card games played. Lastly, he spoke of his father with Mrs. Wardle in the driveway, and their time skating and of course, sharing his father's bed. In Dewey's descriptions, Rita could sense the awe in a little boy's exploits, the inflection of wonder in his words and a growing concept that a five-year-old's dreams would always be a delicate balance based in not only reality but also whimsy.

She realized Neville would always provide for her son's imagination, and how ill equipped she was in this area. Hers was a mother's love– practical, careful, enduring.

Adding to her confusion was this ambiguity over Neville's invitation. On one hand, they were divorced and Rita feared leading Neville on. Yet witnessing Neville interact with Dewey's attractive teacher Miss Gillette wrought an unfamiliar possessive pang– jealousy. Something inside her had changed and Rita was at a loss to identify what it was. While Dewey sat watching his movie, Rita called her closest confidant. "Hello, Megs…"

"Well, if it isn't my long lost sister Rita," she quipped.

"I know… I was supposed to call. I'm sorry."

"How'd it go?"

"With Matt? That was a disaster. That's not why I'm calling."

"What about details, what happened?"

"Come early Tuesday... I'll tell you then. Right now, I'm stuck and I don't know what to do."

"About..."

"Woody invited me to their Christmas party next Friday and I don't know what to say."

"Just say yes," Megan said.

Rita stayed silent. Could it be this easy? 'That's it, say yes."

"In case you haven't noticed Rita, Woody still loves you."

"I guess, but I'm not sure I love him... that's why I'm torn. What if I don't love him? I've already hurt him enough."

Megan was quick with her rebuttal. "You didn't love Matt and you went out with him. Isn't that why we go through this whole dating ritual in the first place– to find out if we can love someone? Rita, take a chance, just say yes."

Rita's sister stopped short. She had uncovered a sad but meaningful secret, one she wished stayed secret. For Megan, she hoped Rita could come to a proper conclusion without hearing her discovery.

Once again, Rita took her time. "I don't know... in some way it seems callous."

"It's not callous Rita... you have a child together, you have history. Most of all, he loves you and that's not all that easy to find."

Fretting over her sister's advice, Rita ended their conversation. "I'll think about it."

Joining Dewey on the sofa, she watched the movie play in full HD on the flat screen. It took Rita only seconds to realize the main character in Toy Story was, of course, Woody. Smiling ironically, Rita caressed Dewey's silky blonde locks and wondered.

That afternoon, Neville called home and relayed the details of John Winterburn's story. Dell felt what most in their small town might feel; how can such a thing happen in a quiet community like Solomon?

Along with Willis Ogland's disappearance, the body found in the car remained a mystery.

After three days and no word from Willis, Hendry entered an

article into The Sentinel's third page asking for the public's help in locating the missing Sentinel employee. The small story would appear in the Monday edition along with headline news of another grisly murder. No one had, or could connect the two at this early juncture, still Roland, unprepared for the emotional toll, squandered his nervous energy smoking cigarettes and agonizing endlessly about the possible consequences of discovery.

Unwittingly, Roland had underestimated his own capacity for compunction even though he remained singularly occupied with himself. His thoughts never strayed to his victims or their suffering, only his own self-serving escape survived the litany of questions inside his head. In some small way, Roland relived the agony of sin and moral turpitude in those days leading up to Christmas.

After discovering the body inside the derelict Buick, the Minneapolis Police working in conjunction with the state police, identified him as Davis Jefferson. A quick check with the rental car company and they found Davis Jefferson had been staying at the Marriott Hotel. That afternoon they obtained a search warrant for his hotel suite and descended on the site to glean whatever clues possible. The focus of their search fell on Jefferson's laptop computer, which they secured as evidence. As per procedure detectives checked in the laptop to the evidence room. Subsequently Abby Guinard, a forensic computer analyst, took possession of the laptop and began the arduous task of hacking into Davis Jefferson's computer and files.

Late that afternoon, Dell and Phil again left for a night out with Bob. Dell's newest strategy involved the same elements: a casino, their money and Phil's prolific power of foresight. Blinded by the possibilities of easy money and enabled by his gambler's heart, Dell looked no further than these paltry prospects.

They arrived at the Treasure Island casino after six o'clock and played as they had played at Mystic Lake, with one great exception. As

Dell raked in pot after pot, uneasiness brewed within. He remembered the stir the night before, the people locked in place, their easy escape from an impossible situation. While he played and Phil read the deck, his discomfort increased. Dell became overly watchful and suspicious. The dealer's smile, the unhurried walk the pit boss made around their table, the excitement of other casino patrons all seemed cause for worry.

A scuffle broke out at the table next to theirs. Two men fought over a five-dollar chip dropped on the floor. With his attention directed toward the struggle, Phil asked, "Why are they fighting, Dell?"

"Well, it's five dollars," Dell said.

"Is five dollars that important?" Phil asked.

The question caught Dell completely off guard. In a flash of pure clarity, Dell understood Phil's innocent observation. His eyes switched back to the two men wrestling on the carpet and he saw the absurdity. As he watched security break up the scramble, a strange truth hit home. Suddenly, none of it made sense. Money, was it only about money?

Nearing forty-five minutes of play, Dell unexpectedly announced to his two partners, "Let's get outta here."

Dell realized a greater good was indeed at work within these powers Phil exhibited. When Dell's intention switched, Bob asked, "What's wrong Dell?"

Dell stopped and smiled a wide toothy grin. He pulled Bob close. "Nothing's wrong Bob my friend. It's more about what's right."

They drove home in silence. From his backseat perch, Phil watched a whitewashed landscape whisk by happy to be on his way home: home to Neville, Artie and their staid and steady life, leaving behind the casino and its lure of excitement and riches, a world far too surreal and intimidating for Phil.

Bob dropped them off at the Wishwood house after nine o'clock. Neville and his father were rummaging through old photos from a shoebox when they came in. Scattered across the table were remembrances of times past, still a blur for Arthur. After joining Neville and Arthur in the living room, they sat across the coffee table and Dell stoically began his confession.

"Woody, there's something I've been keeping from you."

Neville peered up at each individually. Phil averted his look.
"What's that?" he asked.

Arthur stared at a picture of his ten-year-old son in hockey gear.

"I found out Phil here has a gift for reading cards." Dell hung his head as he continued. "I, uh, I used it to make a few bucks at the casino. That's where we've been these last two nights– with Bob."

"Reading cards? What's that mean?" Neville asked.

Phil sat silently while Dell explained. "He knows what cards are coming before they're turned over."

Neville listened still in a quandary. "Like how?"

"I don't know how, he just does. Wait…" Dell lifted from the loveseat and disappeared into the kitchen. He returned with a deck of cards and handed them to his friend.

"Shuffle them."

Neville hesitated but did as Dell asked.

"Put the deck on the table," Dell said and with a dramatic flip of his hand invited Phil to continue.

Phil looked across at Neville and called, "Six of spades." Neville turned the card, the six of spades appeared.

Somewhat surprised, Neville shrugged. With another flip of his wrist, Dell invited Phil to carry on and with each correct call Neville's concentration hardened. After half the deck, Neville stared across at the two, stunned.

"Phil, how do you do this?"

He squirmed in his seat. "I can't really say. Like I told Dell, I just spin time forward to see the cards fall. I didn't know I could until this week."

Neville paid strict attention to what Phil described. Stone faced, he collected the photos strewn across the table and placed them back inside the box. After deliberation he asked, "Mrs. Wardle, did you help her?"

"I wished for her to see clearly, to understand her actions, yes."

"And Dell's dog?"

"Dell seemed sad and I thought of what he had missed all these years, and suddenly Willard appeared."

"And what about Audrey... was she a part of it?"

"And Camillus de what's his name..." Dell injected.

Gazing back innocently, Phil intoned a surprising authenticity. "Honestly, I have no idea how that came about Woody. I had nothing to do with them."

"So what do we do now?" Neville asked.

"Something's up, that's for sure," said Dell. Arthur handed the photo back to his son.

Suffering from amnesia, even Phil failed to comprehend his peculiar talents or intent. His arrival seemed directly connected to Neville and those in his earthly sphere. Yet, what agency deals with the issues at work here?

Only one name came to mind.

"What about Aunt Claire, have you called her?" Neville asked.

Dejected, Dell followed. "She's in Duluth at a small fair up there. Her and Grant left Friday and they won't be back until Monday night."

As he placed the lid on the box, Neville studied all three. Outside a cold wind swept snow across the neighborhood lawns. White drifts formed across the silent streets isolating them in a world made intensely surreal by their predicament. What powers were at work here? And for what purpose? The answers remained buried deep inside one man's mind beyond a forgetfulness forged by Neville's front bumper. What they understood as impossible seemed eerily real and attainable through the auspices of their houseguest Phil. One question remained unanswered for both Neville and Dell– why?

After Dell left and Phil and his father had retired to their bedrooms, Neville too tried sleep as a distraction. His thoughts strayed from his mother's confounded call to the possibilities of a second chance with Rita and now this issue with Phil. They fought for space between warring emotions. At first sleep seemed impossible yet as his thoughts settled and made peace with his worn body, Neville slowly drifted into restless slumber.

Once there, he rose above the clouds and joined the seagulls as they arced in flight down from the sky, down to the beach– the beach and the bay; Bishops Bay. In his dream, he stood again on the tower and watched the red racer, the fat-man and Jennifer Capaldi. He saw little Lily Delysle rise high into the dusky night taking her exalted position in the celestial sky. He saw the crowds crying and at the last, his final vision, the flicker of one special star.

Sound asleep Neville cried aloud, "*No... No... No...*" until finally he sat up in a cold sweaty heap. Blankets tangled around his legs, and his eyes searched to find a bearing. In a fog of half-sleep, he found the alarm clock glowing out the time, 2:02 a.m., and past the clock, a hazy figure appeared in shadow by the door.

CHAPTER 26

THE BEDROOM GREW cold. A frosty mist exhaled from Neville's nostrils. Breathing became difficult. His hands braced against the mattress and lifting upright he stared at the dark form alarmed and unprepared.

"What do you want?"

The shadowy figure shifted sideways. "Are you okay?"

The voice was Phil's and Neville breathed easy. Somewhat groggy, Neville rearranged his position on the bed. "I'm good," he offered. "But what are you doing up?"

"I heard screaming and I wanted to check and see if you were okay."

Neville brushed his tired hands across his face. "It's just a dream…"

"Sounded more like a nightmare."

"Yeah, I guess. I have it every now and then," Neville said not quite awake.

Concerned, Phil asked, "What's it about?"

The chill forced Neville to notice he had left his window slightly open. Pulling his blankets aside, he shut the window and quickly jumped back into bed.

"I'm alright Phil… go back to bed."

Neville wrapped himself in blankets and turned away. Phil came in closer. His simplicity and unsophisticated way with words won most people over and Neville was no exemption. In a quiet unobtrusive voice, he asked again, "What's your nightmare about Woody?"

Neville hesitated but in his delirium, he whispered the words he had never spoken before this night. "I–I dream about a little girl, a little girl that dies."

Phil moved closer. "In your dream how does the little girl die?"

Neville stirred uncomfortably in his blankets reluctant to face the question. Even now with half his secret out, he paused to think of an excuse for his dream and the responsibility he shared. An impulsive fit of honesty took hold and he relented.

"She drowns– because I didn't do my job."

Although simple in many ways, Phil was not so simple that he failed to recognize the guilt oozing from Neville's words. "It's something that really happened isn't it?"

Neville twisted back around and sat up while Phil studied him. "It did happen and a little girl died because I was… distracted," Neville said.

"How old were you?"

In the dull light, Phil could see Neville trying to evade his stare.

"I was eighteen…"

"I have a hard time believing you caused anyone's death Woody, and if you were distracted, you were only a boy. I'm sure it was no one's fault really."

"No, I did it," he said, rubbing his eyes, straining to avoid Phil's constant gaze. "You once said my mother's leaving must have affected me." Neville paused as if identifying something relevant, something terrible. "I remember telling you it wasn't the worst thing to ever happen to me. This was it; this was worse by far. And the nightmare, I have it ever since."

Hearing Neville's confession, Phil watched his eyes well up and for the first time in his life; Neville sensed a release from his pain. What he believed as truth had finally escaped and there was relief in admitting it to another person.

"You were just a boy. Besides, who knows the result even if you weren't distracted?"

Neville's mention of his mother stirred Phil's feelings of guilt. He held his own small secret. Neville's honesty spurred his own confession of sorts and Phil shifted the conversation. "I heard you talking to Dell about your mother. You mentioned something about Christmas cards," Phil said.

Neville looked up. "Yeah, she said she had sent me a Christmas card the last eight years, but I never saw them."

Phil peered back sheepishly. "You didn't get the cards because your father has them. They're in his tin box in the dresser. He showed me them last week."

Neville shot up erect. "What?"

"Artie's been keeping them in his box for years I guess."

Unraveling his blankets Neville stepped into a pair of leather slippers. "You're sure..."

"Yes, they're with all your father's keepsakes. I saw them."

Neville wiped his eyes clear and headed toward the darkened hallway. Phil followed. Starlight shone in from the living room window setting a dull glow along the short corridor. The house was dead silent. Neville stepped quietly to his father's bedroom door and listened, hearing an easy wheeze of breathing. Phil stood behind him observing from a distance. As Neville disappeared inside the room, Phil heard the slight drag of a drawer. Seconds later Neville reappeared holding his father's treasured tin box.

He whisked the prize off into the living room and with Phil trailing in silence, Neville clicked on the lamp nearest the Christmas tree. The light set off an array of shimmers from the tree's silver tinsel. Phil sat on the sofa while Neville took up one side of the loveseat. He flipped open the lid. Documents sat on top and when Neville dug deeper, the Christmas cards appeared from beneath. All eight bunched together.

He checked the dates. Neville decided to read each in chronological sequence, beginning with the first. Dated nine years ago, the card pictured a winter scene with Joseph, Mary and the baby Jesus huddled inside a straw strewn animal stall.

He opened the first card to a note written inside:

My Dearest Woody,

*I hope you and your father are well. I'm writing to first, wish
you both a Merry Christmas. The second reason is to make my
amends. I don't expect you to forgive me because I ask, my hope
is to show you. I realize my terrible selfishness. I abandoned you
when you needed me most. It has taken me years to see it but
I understand all that now and I am so sorry. All I ask is that
you try to forgive me my thoughtlessness. I have been very sick.
My lupus returned disabling me and I was recommended to a
wonderful clinic in Clearwater, Florida, the Haimes Clinic for
Lupus Research and Treatment. They explained my drinking was
aggravating the disease. I tried quitting but eventually ended up
in a treatment center for alcohol dependency. It was there I began
to understand the impact of my decisions. While in treatment,
they asked me to find a God and pray to him, to find a faith and
follow it. I have put all my effort into doing just that. Today I'm
ready to take the next step and beg for another chance to be the
mother I should have been. I know it's too late for much of it but I
am willing to try if you are.*

My phone number is 813.555.2122. Please call.

I love you very much, Mom.

Neville finished the first card and confused, stared across at
Phil. Neville wondered of the mother who had abandoned him; how
she now felt the pain he once felt. Yet he survived, as she now must.
Nine years had passed since this card had arrived and his thoughts
turned to his father. Why had he kept it from him? What was he
afraid of? Losing his son to a long lost mother, to a ghost?

Neville turned his attention to the cards left in the box. He
read them in sequence. The next several cards were less descriptive,
begging for forgiveness and always leaving the same phone number with a heartfelt request for a call. After each card, he studied
the images on the front. They all showed the same biblical scene

depicting the birth of a child on a star lit night. The same thought expressed through different angles. The voice inside the cards all carried the same message: Forgive me, call me.

Neville came to the last card from just a year ago. Phil watched as he opened and read this last communication. It told of his mother's struggle with Lupus, which had once again returned after a long period of remission. Hospitalized at that time, she remained in treatment, and he sensed the worry in her written words. At its end, she again begged for his forgiveness and left her phone number.

Neville closed the last card and like all the previous cards, he considered the angelic face of a child in his mother's arms camped beneath a sparkling night star. Mother and child, together at this most joyous moment of life.

The cards were a compelling testament to his mother's regrets and her admission of guilt. That cold hand of conscience had forced a renewed sense of responsibility, or lack of it, into life's forefront. Her past had finally eclipsed whatever future she was striving towards and Neville held her sentence in his hands. He sat staring across the living room, beyond the life he now lived back into the same past alluded to in the cards.

As Phil watched from the sofa, Neville peered out across the years and replayed what he had lost in his world. Etched indelibly on his heart was his missing mother, little Lilly Delysle, his father's deadly struggles, and of course, Rita. Emotions thundered within and near tears, he suddenly saw Dewey and a smile curled the corners of his lips. Dewey, his one triumph, forced all his agonies to mere slights.

"Are you okay?" Phil asked stirring Neville from his thoughts.

Neville wiped his eyes. "I'm good Phil, and thanks for telling me about the cards."

He closed his father's tin box and stood. His hair flared out at angles. He seemed strengthened by a rediscovered need. Still concerned, Phil asked, "What are you going to do?"

"After the holidays I'll give my mother a call and see if she's ready to meet her grandson," he said with a smile.

Although a gateway to his deepest disappointments, the Christmas cards gave Neville a different view of the mother he had resolved to forget. Her repeated attempts to make peace and settle their estrangement instilled new hope for at least a friendship between the two.

Reentering his father's room, Neville replaced the tin box in the dresser drawer. They returned to their beds that night forgetting the dream that had awakened them. The phone call from his estranged mother that had so confused Neville just days before now made perfect sense. After years of trying, she took the first fearful step at reconciliation.

The next morning, Neville sat with his father and Phil watching *The Munsters* reruns on the Televisionland channel. His once contemptible vision of his mother had changed overnight and he saw the human side of her flight from Bishop's Bay. A fearful reaction to her condition and a warped self-interest had forced her to flee her husband and son. He saw the woman not the evil caricature he had so carefully crafted over the years. Neville realized his naiveté. Painting his mother with this wide villainous brush was his attempt to wipe away the heartbreak. Perhaps the same brush his father had used and for the same reason. But life is much more complicated and he recognized that truth. She would always be his mother and if for no other reason he owed her the chance to make amends.

Just before noon, Dell arrived and they adjourned to the kitchen. Phil and Arthur stayed in the living room to watch television, quite content to follow the Munster clan in their wacky home adventures.

Their conversation centered first, on Phil and his extraordinary powers, then shifted to Aunt Claire, agreeing to consult her before doing anything. Of all the people they knew, Aunt Claire seemed the most likely to discern a path with regard to Phil and his unearthly abilities. Neville also updated Dell on the discovery of the Christmas cards and his mother's attempts to contact him these last nine years. Dell took the news with skepticism, harboring a somewhat jaded outlook in regards to Neville's mother. He saw Angela Wishwood without the emotional baggage the Wishwoods carried. Because of that, he remained cautious.

After a short discussion, Dell stood announcing his plans for the afternoon. He was taking his new girlfriend Jennifer Gilchrist public skating followed by a late lunch and a movie. A grimace crossed Neville as Dell prepared to leave. Noticing the change in expression he asked, "What's with the frown?"

Neville's brow arched. As he lifted his head to meet Dell's stare, a pause ensued. "I knew a Jennifer once."

Dell edged in closer and for the second time that day, Neville confessed his sin. He told his best friend the story that had led him to Solomon, the secret he had kept these last eleven years. And for a second time he confided the guilt over his distraction for one, Jennifer Capaldi and the resulting death of another, little Lily Delysle.

Once again, Neville felt a release from the telling yet the guilt remained all too real. Dell hesitated before offering a response. "You don't know that she still would have drowned Woody. You don't know," he said quietly.

"No. That's something I'll never know but..."

Neville's eyes drifted from Dell's steady gaze. His terrible secret was now out and although its weight lifted, his conscience continued its assault.

"I have this dream... some strange abstract of that day. I see Lily rise up into the night sky– heaven I guess. And then it always ends with me walking away crying."

"Woody, do you believe in predestination?"

"I don't know..."

"Aunt Claire and I have talked about things like this. Maybe things are just ordained... predetermined. No matter what we do, no matter how we act, many of our greatest triumphs, our greatest tragedies are unalterable. I believe death may be a big part of what's preordained in life. When Willard died in the fire that's how I looked at it. It was just his time. That helped me get over it. Maybe, just maybe it was Lily's time."

Realizing his friend was offering him a flight from conscience, he grinned.

"Thanks for trying Dell, but I can't believe that. What we do, how we live has to count for something or else why try? Why try to make a difference if it won't change anything? I can't believe we're all just numbers on a wall waiting to be checked off.

"As far as Lily's concerned, you're right about one thing... it was her time. But that doesn't mean I couldn't have tried. If I had, if I was paying attention that day, maybe Lily would be alive. That's the possibility I live with... my penance."

Dell laid a hand on his friend's shoulder and gave a gentle squeeze. In one of Dell's few profound moments, he understood his friend's deep regret and unexpectedly found a comforting thought.

"Sometimes the cost of conscience is too high Woody. It's time to forgive yourself."

A cold clear day, the winter sun shot spears of light in through the kitchen window. Neville could feel the rays warm his back as he peered up. His face was blank, wanting only a discharge from the guilt. "Maybe... you better get going. You'll be late."

Reluctantly, Dell made his way out the front door. He carried his friend's burden with him. In these last eleven years together, they had forged a bond as brothers. And while Neville had shared his tragic past, Dell knew now was not the time to dig deeper.

That Sunday afternoon Neville sat contemplating Lily Delysle, his long absent mother and of course, his strained relationship with Rita and the hope of reconciliation. He spoke only when spoken to and then only in terse one word answers. As all three watched old reruns, his charges took their lead from Neville and said little.

After dinner, Rita arrived to drop Dewey off for the night. The front door opened to an overly excited Dewey dragging his mother by the hand into the Wishwood foyer. Neville met them there.

"Hi Dad, I wanna show mom the solar system Phil fixed for me," he said, Rita in tow. Neville leaned down and gave his son a quick hug as they raced by. Fully dressed, Dewey flung his backpack onto the bench while Rita rolled her eyes and followed.

Neville managed a quick, "I love you too son."

They sped by the living room along the hall to Dewey's bedroom. He smiled at Dewey's show of boyish exuberance. Phil followed from the living room. Dewey opened the bedroom door and switched on the overhead light. Still holding her son's hand, Rita looked up, suddenly staring into the center sun, the LED starlights and the model planets glowing in bright colors slowly circling the room above the bed. Neville joined them while Arthur made his way there unsure of the nature of all the interest.

"Dewey," Rita exclaimed, "this is just wonderful. It's much more real than I thought it could ever be... and it actually works now." She turned her attention toward Phil, standing behind Dewey. "How did you get it to look so real?"

Before Phil could answer, Neville intervened. "Our Phil here has his own set of gifts Rita. It seems very little is beyond him when he puts his mind to something," Neville said tongue in cheek.

"I sold those in the store for years," Arthur added.

"You sold globes dad... not these," Neville said.

"Maybe..."

"Well it's just beautiful now." Rita leaned over and gave Dewey a kiss. "But I have to go so I'll see you Tuesday."

As she headed for the front door, Neville followed. Alone by the door Neville asked, "So, Friday... Christmas party? Yes...no?"

Rita held tight to the door handle. Her feet shuffled. "I don't know, Woody."

"Just say yes. It'll be fun."

"Can I give you an answer Wednesday? Is that too late?"

"Wednesday's not too late... as long as it's yes."

Rita looked away from her ex yet smiled as she closed the door. Neville watched through the glass. Although her lips were unsure, he saw hope in her smile.

Dewey raced in, kicked off his boots, flung his coat on the bench and ran back to his bedroom. Alone with Phil, he dimmed the center sun on the dimmer switch Dell had installed. The darkened room heightened the focus of the planets revolving above his bed. The ceiling lit up with a spray of light from the fixture base.

Pointing to the ruddy red planet, Phil asked, "What's that one?"

Dewey fixed his eyes curiously on Phil. "You don't know?"

"Maybe I did, but I forgot."

"That's Mars, the closest planet to Earth." Dewey pointed at the circling display. "That green and blue planet, that's us... Earth."

Phil found the orb to which Dewey had pointed. His eyes traced its path around the sun and with a profound look of awe, asked, "Where's the moon?"

Dewey's head cocked slightly. "I guess they couldn't fit it in."

Dewey and Phil stared into the planets circling just below the bedroom ceiling silently contemplating the missing moon and the wonder of far off worlds.

The moon captured Roland's keen interest also. Staring out from his sofa, he viewed a bright northern sky. The headphones he wore piped in music, yet try as he might he could barely hear it. The moon, framed perfectly in his patio window, held him mesmerized. His mind drifted. On the coffee table, a crystal candy dish his mother had given him sat brimming with cigarette butts. Two glasses stood next to it, the ice cubes long since melted. A half-empty bottle of vodka completed the table's contents.

Ripping off the headphones, Roland stood, walked to the window and in his trance traced the light from the orb moon to the square below, to the Sentinel and beyond to the Snake River. His sight settled on the spot where he had entombed Willis in an icy grave. He saw ice shifting near the river's edge where he had dragged the body from his lover's parked car.

Suddenly he turned from the window. Across the room, he saw the kitchen floor where Willis had died and yet another remembrance of that fateful night, the dining table where he had cleaned the body. To escape he rushed toward the closet and retrieved Davis's phone. Frantic, he punched up a screen showing twelve identification numbers from the Yo-Yo. Twelve and still counting.

Yes, that was why, the reason for the madness– to find an unfettered life, a life without the abstract judgments of impudent imbeciles. He held the phone tightly as this realization filled within. Once again, he rationalized his decisions. After several inner justifications, Roland made his way back into the kitchen, scooped up a handful of ice cubes and returned to his bottle of vodka. He sat on the sofa and drank to success. Still, his eyes avoided the patio window and the moon.

Conscience, a trait long thought absent from Roland's psyche, had gained a foothold and with it sleep was becoming increasingly difficult. Roland found a semblance of solace and sleep near the bottom of a vodka bottle and to his detriment, Roland's vodka intake swelled, further blurring the line between the rational and the irrational.

CHAPTER 27

NEITHER DELL, NOR Neville had any inkling as to how to proceed with their houseguest, Phil. Aunt Claire was unreachable so Dell left a message on her home phone to call as soon as she got in. Now they waited.

Monday morning Neville went to work and with Dewey off on Christmas holidays, Dell took charge of all three for the week. After breakfast, Dell attempted to teach an Alzheimer's afflicted old man, an amnesiac and a five-year-old the card game hearts. The result was predictable.

An hour of constant squabbling over the general rules followed and after several instructional hands, his pupils were no closer to understanding how to play than when they started. Dell gave up and settled on the simple game of war. It kept them occupied well into the afternoon.

Neville's day started slow, all until an altercation broke out. Across from Neville's desk, Hendry stopped Roland on one of his several trips downstairs to smoke outside the Sentinel parking lot door. He discretely pulled him aside. "Have you heard anything about Willis?"

Roland's eyes narrowed to tiny black darts, his hands became a flurry of uncoordinated motions and he exploded. "Why would I hear anything? You put the ad in the paper! I should be asking *you* that question."

"Whoa young man I'm just concerned."

"Keep your concern and shove it!" Roland fired back, pushing

Hendry aside and launching him into the editor's office door smashing the glass. All eyes watched in dismay.

Hendry regained his balance and caught Roland at the elevator door, yanking his coat. "You can't treat me that way. Get out and don't come back!" Hendry shouted.

Roland smirked. "*You're* firing *me*? Ha!" and followed into the elevator. The doors closed. Outside on the sidewalk, he made a phone call to his father's best friend and Roland's godfather, Carter Ellison. After their short conversation the Sentinel owner assured Roland his position was safe. After the call, Roland enjoyed a second, more satisfying cigarette.

Flustered by the incident Walter retreated to his office. Once seated, he reached for the blue Bromo bottle, muttering as he fumbled with the cap. Suzanne was already cleaning up the glass when Hendry's phone rang. Everyone heard Walter's side of the conversation.

"I *can* fire him and I did Carter."

A pause ensued.

"I'm not taking him back, not now. Not after today."

After a lengthy silence, Hendry erupted. "Then find yourself a new editor!"

Suzanne scurried from the doorway just in time as Walter pitched the Bromo bottle against the office wall near where she had stood seconds before. Mumbling incoherently, Walter pulled on his overcoat and trudged toward the elevator. All eyes stared dumbfounded as Hendry disappeared through the doors.

Later that afternoon, Carter Ellison called his senior reporter, Sam Charters, and asked him to fill in for Walter on a temporary basis. Sam agreed.

Abby Guinard finally broke Davis's password. She had spent the morning investigating his files and when she opened his e-mail account, it garnered a treasure trove of personal information. Between Davis Jefferson's received and sent correspondence she pieced together a list of people to contact in regards to his death. He had letters to and from his lawyer, e-mails from his father, a woman he was dating in Atlanta, a small internet company in Chicago and several friends. However, Abby's most interesting find came from someone in the Minneapolis-St. Paul area... Roland DeWitt.

Davis kept everything and although he posted mostly by i-Phone, all his e-mails automatically forwarded to his laptop by a function of a program called i-cloud. Abby discovered another interesting fact; they found no cell phone on Davis's body or in the rental car.

Early that afternoon while reading the e-mails, she ate a tuna sandwich from her bagged lunch. Abby still had student loans and in order to pay them off she held herself to a strict financial regimen.

Reading Roland DeWitt's first e-mail to Davis she stopped abruptly mid-bite. In it, Roland spelled out clearly Davis Jefferson's reason for his visit to Minneapolis. Abby put down her sandwich and read on to Davis's reply and Roland's second conformation e-mail. A secretive plan between the two had surfaced in the writings and the mention of a program called Yo-Yo. There, with this information, came a phone number– Roland DeWitt's phone number.

After the e-mails, Abby dug a little deeper and found the Yo-Yo program in a file on the laptop's C-drive. Dissecting the written code, it became apparent the program was a bug of some sort, malicious software. She called the detective in charge.

A man in his mid-forties, Billy Tofflemire was a seasoned homicide detective. He joined Abby within fifteen minutes of the call. After cursory introductions, Abby leaned over the desk showing him the e-mails, his biggest lead in the case to date, and Roland DeWitt's phone number.

Tofflemire looked over the correspondence, took copies of all the evidence, especially noting the phone number. "It's a good lead," he said. "I've viewed all the security video at the Marriot. It looks like Jefferson left the hotel Wednesday night just before nine o'clock and never came back. Maybe the phone records'll show something."

Abby finally returned to her tuna sandwich, took a quick bite and frowned. Returning it to the saran wrapping, she neatly folded the sandwich in the plastic wrap and tossed it into the wastebasket. "Bread's stale– now I don't have a lunch."

Billy scooped up all the copies, gave Abby a satisfied smile and before leaving quipped, "Ask me how many lunches I've had spoiled over the years, dear."

Abby, all business in her attitude swiveled her chair back away from Billy. Her frugal outlook took over. "I can't afford to throw away good food. Not on the salary they pay me here. That should get you your subpoenas Detective Tofflemire."

"It will and if it works out lunch is on me."

Abby stopped and watched as Tofflemire strode down the aisle. The likelihood of a free lunch supplanted the frown and she whispered to herself, *"One can always hope."*

It was after ten o'clock that night when Aunt Claire finally called Dell. She and Grant had arrived home late after waiting out a winter storm in Duluth. Although her weekend was prosperous business-wise, the long hours left Aunt Claire spent so she listened listlessly to her nephew's newest evidence of the houseguest Phil.

Dell spoke of Phil's ability to see the fall of playing cards, calling it spinning time forward to see an outcome. He described Phil's sudden immobilization of an entire floor of patrons at the Mystic Lake casino as they made their escape from the Minneapolis police. He explained confronting Phil about these actions and Phil's inability to account for his impossible actions and to having no real understanding of how he could muster such power.

Phil's amnesia had virtually robbed him of any comprehension.

Aunt Claire listened, yet in her state of exhaustion offered no real answers that night. Instead, she reminded Dell of Christmas dinner on Wednesday and suggested bringing Phil along for the celebration. After dinner, Aunt Claire would be able to take Phil aside, do a private reading and evaluate Phil's abilities and possible intensions.

Dell agreed and left the details up to Aunt Claire. She now

understood that he could not only predict outcomes, but also facilitate them. Her experience in the mystical world remained much more reliable than anyone else they knew so Dell felt a sense of peace leaving the details to his capable aunt. He followed up by relaying the information to Neville. Knowing Aunt Claire would be spearheading the effort to unlock the mystery of Phil's powers eased their load for the time being.

CHAPTER 28

TUESDAY WAS A busy day for Rita. Having invited her family for Christmas dinner Rita headed home after a full day. She had prepared a twenty-pound turkey the night before and returned home earlier that day to slip it in the oven. Now she worked on the final details of their holiday feast adding cooked cranberries at the last minute. She expected her parents in the next half hour. A trip to Paris, France, was their Christmas present to each other and they were booked to leave the next day. This would be their last chance to visit before the holiday.

Rita's sister and brother-in-law had arrived early and from her open kitchen, their conversation continued. Richard sat skimming a magazine.

"Where's Dewey?" Megan asked.

"Woody's dropping him off at dinner. Tomorrow's my last day so I'll take him back after everyone leaves. At least Mom and Dad can have a visit before they go. I'm sure they've got something nice for him. You know Mom," Rita said.

Megan turned to her husband. "When Dad gets here you'll have to move honey. You know how he likes the leather recliner."

"I know," he said flipping pages, "And when he's finished downing a quart of whiskey we'll have to listen to the snoring. Hope you've got enough Crown Royal for the old goat."

After several seconds staring down her brother-in-law, Rita broke out a wide smile. She walked over to a small cabinet next to the newly decorated Christmas tree and opened the doors. Richard glanced over. A variety of liquor bottles included two full bottle of Seagram's Crown Royal. Both sisters were well aware of their father shortcomings especially since his retirement ten years ago.

"Richard, try and be a little more considerate of Dad. Look at all he's done for us," Megan said. As wedding presents, the Fordings had given both daughters and sons-in-law a one-hundred-thousand dollar down payments on their homes.

Richard looked up at the sisters scurrying about the kitchen and offered a truce. "Okay, I know he's not really a bad guy, and he has helped us Megs, but there's no getting around the fact he drinks way over the limit. I don't know how your mother puts up with it."

"He didn't always act like this, Richard," Rita began. "You've only known him these last five years. Before all this, he was a good father and a good husband to Mom. She's said it many times. He's a bit overbearing these days… still he tries."

"It was that stock venture wasn't it," Richard said, folding the magazine. "That's when it all changed, according to what you told me."

Rita stirred sauce on the stove while Megan searched a cupboard for the dinner napkins. "He'd worked all his life, saved and invested for our futures. To his credit, he made some very wise financial decisions and we've benefited. Certainly money changes people, so I guess, to some extent that's when things changed."

Megan stopped dead in her tracks and glared. She seemed highly amused by what Rita had said.

Rita recognized her sister's smirk. "What?"

"You're talking about the Microsoft deal?"

"Of course… Why?"

"Wise financial decisions? Are you kidding me? Don't you know the story Rita?"

Rita stopped stirring and stared blankly at her sister. "What story?"

Megan laughed while Richard looked on from the living room. Now he was curious to the details. "Yeah, what story?"

"I thought she told you. We were in high school when Mom told me, and it's not Dad's, 'triumph of the ordinary man in America,' story. Believe me, the truth is very different."

Rita turned the burner to low and sat with Megan at the dining table. Richard's ears perked up as he helped himself to the dish of assorted nuts on the coffee table.

Annette Fording's narrative began in the early 1980's with Will Fording (before his financial windfall he preferred his given name, Wilbur) managing a grocery store in St. Paul. He worked with an assistant manager named Roger Binder, who at that time became heavily involved in the stock market.

For three years, Will heard his assistant extol the virtues of the free market system and the profits from his investments in the stock market. And for those three years, Will Fording watched Roger Binder's own stock rise as he exhibited startling gains. Roger drove a shiny new Cadillac, had moved into a newly built home in the suburbs of St. Paul's and dressed well above his station as a grocery store assistant manager.

Impressed, yet still somewhat timid to the idea of stock investment, Will– formerly Wilbur– began peppering Roger on the subject. He learned he needed to set up an account at a brokerage firm, find a promising stock and just jump in. Not exactly brain surgery.

It just so happens that in 1986 Will's mother passed away (his father had passed on years before) and to his surprise, he and his brothers and sisters each inherited thirty-two thousand dollars from the estate. Although a sad event, for Will it seemed an act of providence. With Roger Binder's encouragement, Will Fording set up his trading account, listened attentively to his assistant's advice on the market and chose a rising stock for investment. He settled on a little known technology startup called Microseal, its trading symbol, MSFL on the NASDAQ.

With his thirty-two thousand dollars in hand, Will Fording jumped in. After discussions with Roger Binder, Will wrote down the trading symbol on a slip of paper, stuffed it into his Kroger shop-coat pocket and waited until lunch-break. With Roger out for lunch, Will called the brokerage. While stuffing the paper inside his shop-coat pocket the 'L' smeared slightly and took on the appearance of a 'T'. Pulling the slip of paper from his pocket, he studied the company's trading symbol and called them out over the phone– MSFT, thirty-two thousand dollars, all in.

From here, Wilbur relied on Roger's verbal reports as to the progress of his investment. The stock Roger had suggested, Microseal, dropped off the trading radar within six months. Roger Binder transferred to another store shortly after and Will carried on with his. Knowing little of the markets, and even less of the statements his brokerage firm sent him annually, Will struggled to understand the meaning of the numbers appearing on his brokerage reports. He saw the word *split* on several statements and associated the action as something very bad. The word *split* itself, brought up painful images of ballet dancers stretched to the limit, muscles knotted too tightly to stand.

Being too proud and too ashamed to admit that he had squandered his inheritance, Will began to hide the statements from his wife, Annette. For several years, his fortuitous blunder went undetected. On more than one occasion he actually cursed his former assistant profusely for involving him in this, get rich quick scheme. Of course that was when he drank too much, or thought too much, or had worked too hard on a particular day and saw so little of his life changing in the way Roger Binder's had changed. Still he worked and saved and continued to complain. All the while, his wife Annette, the true steadying influence in their daughter's lives, managed to salt away reserves enough for the further education of their daughters.

With the brokerage firm's statement arrival in early January 1999, it all changed. Thinking the statement a tax receipt and with taxes being her household domain, Annette opened it. As she read the contents, her eyes ballooned. Immediately she telephoned the brokerage firm and they shared the glad tidings over the phone. The enormity of her husband's secret hit her like a gold plated lightning bolt. Will Fording's stock blunder had peaked to a value of nearly six million dollars. She dropped the phone and cried.

That night Annette confronted her husband, who at first denied the account, lying to save face. After learning its potential value, he fessed up. He lamented over the many years he spent whipping himself for such a callous move; how he stayed up nights plotting to hide the evidence of his naiveté; and his pounding resentment of his one-time assistant, Roger Binder.

Now as it turned out, he was the family hero, the man of the hour, the husband of the millennium and the wisest father in the northern hemisphere. But above all, a true man among men. Of course, his wife Annette belayed his omnipotent view of himself at every turn still it seemed to sink deep into Will's psyche.

Annette, being the more practical, had Will sell off all his Microsoft shares and invested the money in steady, safe bonds. The Fording's lifestyle changed. Will retired, Annette quit her job at a local restaurant and the girls, Rita and Megan, were given the princess treatment.

Will's drinking habits changed. No longer settling for the cheaper whiskeys, he switched to Seagram's Crown Royal, a more distinguished malt. Their father began thinking of himself a savior of sorts, an every-man prevailing over an oppressive world, a Don Quixote of the masses never seeing the true madness of fate. Where once a relatively shy man, he freely ministered advice to all in earshot willfully forgetting the blunder that made it all possible.

As Megan finished retelling her father's true history, it brought out the facts as they often are. Neville's namesake, Ozzie, steps into a bucket of shit, literally and his life ended as a result. Will Fording steps into his proverbial bucket of shit and rises in triumph.

Rita glared at her sister. Megan's story was unsettling as she realized the extent of their family's good fortune. "Mom told you that? Where was I?"

"You? Probably off with Spikes. And Dad had gone off to the club. I think they had a date night planned and when he disappeared she was a bit pissed."

Rita sat on her seat's edge and pondered this new family truth. From the living room, Richard jumped into the conversation. "Hey, speaking of dates… what about last week, my buddy Derrick. How'd that go Rita?"

Megan's eyes narrowed. Not surprisingly, she knew the answer to her husband's question. Armed with a playful smile, Rita patted both knees and turned toward Richard. "The date with Derrick... yes. That was an eye opener for sure." Rita's tone took on a coy, cocky tempo.

"Rita, it's not Richard's fault," Megan whispered.

"What, not good? I thought you two would be great," Richard said.

"Wait here. I want to show the outfit I bought for that date with Derrick, just so you understand that I did try to impress your friend."

Rita stood and quickly disappeared down the hall. Megan sat still, her eyes avoiding Richard's anxious stare. Rita reappeared in a sleek black skirt, knee high black suede boots with her arms folded across a fashionable long sleeved emerald green silk blouse, V-cut to expose just a hint of breast. The sharp green of the blouse offset her shoulder length red hair. Rita looked every bit the picture of elegance.

"Nice, very nice," Richard said.

"Yes... we were going to an early show, then a late dinner. He bought our tickets and each a pop and a small bucket of buttered popcorn. We ate the popcorn and fifteen minutes into the show this..."

To Richard's utter shock, Rita dropped her arms exposing five neon-yellow fingerprints etched across the green silk blouse. In a mocking mood, she pranced out in front of her brother-in-law, teasing him with a waggish dance, twirling as if to strip. Richard's stare soured as Rita continued to frolic ensuring his friend's fingerprints stayed front and center. The evidence was clear and concise. Megan laughed as her husband's smile vanished. Rita continued prancing about like some second-rate stripper. Finally, Richard raised his head and bellied out a hearty laugh, joining the Fording sisters in good-natured contempt.

"Yes, he's one classy guy. I hadn't known him what, thirty minutes and this," Rita said laughing as she pointed to the fingerprints.

"What a lout," Richard agreed.

While Rita left to change, Megan slipped alongside Richard cupping his head in her hands. In consolation, she planted a kiss along her husband's ear. A disappointed Richard acquiesced. "I guess men really don't know men. I thought he was a better guy than that."

"Not to worry, honey… most women are prepared for disappointment, especially Rita. She hasn't exactly run across Prince Charming in the last year. The last date she had the clod told her he forgot his wallet and she had to the pay for dinner, the tip and the parking. I guess they think she's a dentist, she's got plenty of money."

Rita returned dressed in red slacks and a pale pink blouse still brandishing a grin. "So that was that."

Richard leaned forward. "I guess replacing Woody won't be that easy."

"I never thought it would be." Rita lifted a pot-lid surveying the steaming broccoli. "Woody really is a good guy and a good father, but…" Her words tailed off.

Megan joined her sister back in the kitchen. "I guess," said Richard picking out another magazine. "…but I always liked him. Any guy whose goal in life is to have three sons and name them after Donald Duck's nephews can't be all bad. With Dewey already here all he needs is two more kicks at the cat."

"Kicks at the cat… how crude," Megan said.

"You know what I mean."

Rita's smile returned. She looked out at Richard scanning his magazine. "It wasn't a goal to have three sons really or name them after Donald Duck's nephews, Richard. It was more about recapturing an innocent age; a time when kids weren't expected to grow up too quickly, or be something other than just kids. That's what we talked about anyway, but that's all gone…"

Her voice trailed off again losing focus. She stood silent as if examining her thoughts written across the cupboard doors.

Suddenly Megan's voice shifted Rita's attention back to now. "I know Woody's never been the most exciting guy, Rita, but at least he's genuine." Richard sat thoughtlessly thumbing through a magazine, munching on nuts as the sisters busied themselves.

Rita never looked up. "I know that, Megs… but there's got to be more doesn't there?"

"Why's there got to be more? Do you get along? I mean is there anything that he does that absolutely drives you crazy?"

"No he's pretty stable that way I guess."

"Is he a good father?"

"Of course… he worships Dewey."

"Was he attentive in your marriage?"

Laying out the knives and forks, Rita returned to the recent past. "He'd be up late writing most nights and he'd be tired some days. Other than that, he always tried to pay attention to me. He always remembered my birthday. Stuff like that. But it's not just that Meg… I just fell out of love with Woody. He has great qualities but I'm not in love with him anymore."

Rita's last words stopped Megan's napkin folding in its tracks. With her eyes shifting in their sockets, Megan planted her hands onto the red silk tablecloth and leaned across at her sister. She coldly repeated her sister's words. *"You love him, but you're not in love with him.* You said that very thing last year, you said it again in a conversation we had three months ago. Rita I can't stay quiet any more. I know I should– that it's none of my business but I just can't. I hear that line on every second-rate soap opera at least once a week. What does it mean? Does it mean he's not exciting enough or he doesn't fulfill that idea of what you think a husband should be, or that he doesn't pay enough attention to you? Or is it simply, that sexual chemistry you once had is missing? What is it Rita?"

Megan's rebuttal stunned Rita leaving the cutlery frozen in her fingers. She stuttered back, "I–I guess that's it."

She paused, avoiding her sister's glare. "Or maybe it was the letter…"

"Letter? What letter?"

Rita leaned forward checking on her brother-in-law and his whereabouts. Satisfied, she shifted nearer Megan and hissed, "A letter from Spikes."

"When?"

Rita leaned over to check on Richard again. "Dewey was about three years old. Mom dropped it off. It was mailed to their house,"

"And what'd it say?"

In a whisper, Rita began again. "He said he was in rehab for drugs. Part of his treatment was to inventory his life and decide who the people were he had hurt and how he had wronged them. He said his first thoughts were of me. He went on to apologize for the way he dumped me. And Megs– he said he still loved me... after all these years."

"But Rita, he might not..."

Rita interrupted. "See, it wasn't *all* in my head. He did love me and according to the letter, he still does. I've wrestled with this ever since, and yet when I did work up the nerve to call I couldn't find any trace of him. I even asked Colin Redding, his best friend from high school. It's like he fell off the earth."

Megan's voice grew small. "Honey I love you. You're my only sister, my role model but I have to tell you, rehab doesn't always work. What he said in the letter he might have meant at the time but addiction is a powerful illness. Not everyone gets well."

"If only you'd read the letter, felt the passion in his words. He understands his mistakes, he wants to make a new start and for him, a big part of righting the past was to ask my forgiveness. I could almost feel the pain in the letter Megs. What's that say?" Rita asked.

"Of course forgive him. But you were teenagers when all this happened and whether you believe it or not life goes on– for both of you. It's the past Rita, you can't live there."

Rita appeared unconvinced. "Maybe..."

Megan hesitated as if debating within. "I wasn't going to do this, but now I can't *not* show you this." She took her sister's hand. "Where's your laptop Rita?"

Fumbling the dinnerware Rita dropped it on the table. "In my bedroom. Why?"

Richard looked up from his magazine after hearing the clink of knives and forks. "Hey what's going on in there?"

"Sister stuff... it's alright honey," Megan replied and Richard went back to reading.

Megan dragged her reluctant sister toward the bedroom. She spotted the computer on her dresser and quickly picked it up. Patting the bed next to where she sat, Megan prodded her sister to join her. Rita watched as she clicked onto the internet and signed in.

"Sit," she ordered and a rueful Rita sat.

"What's this?" Rita asked as she looked into the laptop screen.

"Facebook... I found Spikes last week."

"No!"

"Yes, and you need to see your prince as he is today."

"But I looked on Facebook. I couldn't find him," Rita confessed.

As Megan input Jerome Spikowski into the search window, his site appeared below. "You probably spelled his name wrong," she said clicking his Facebook page.

A picture popped into view of a large crowd sitting in endless rows. The scene was a stadium and in the foreground, a rather hefty unshaven dark haired man sprawled lazily across the laps of two spirited young women. Both women held tight to plastic cups of beer and the man in center focus. Looking closely, Rita recognized her former high school sweetheart Spikes Spikowski, his broad smile exposing a missing lower incisor. His unshaven face showed cheeks decidedly more full than his high schools days. A red vest stretched across his rotund chest and belly advertising Budweiser in broad white letters.

At first, Rita thought it showed one large outdoor party but reading the caption below the wide frame picture, she realized the venue.

JOIN ME, SPIKES, IN SECTION 126 OF THE BIG HOUSE FOR SOME BUDS AND DOGS... GO WOLVERINES!

In the picture's background, a sign announced Welcome to Michigan Stadium home of the Michigan Wolverines. Spikes' once bright future had evolved into this sad state leading him back to the very stadium he had once played football in, only now as a beer vendor. In so many ways, the outcome was heartbreaking.

Spikes football injury years ago led to several operations and ultimately an addiction to painkillers. Because of his injury, he was unable to play football again. Campus police arrested Spikes the following year for selling painkillers on campus. His full ride scholarship ended after the arrest and the University of Michigan expelled Spikes in his sophomore year.

Since his time at Michigan, Spikes had entered rehabilitation centers twice to treat his drug addiction. His issues were ongoing. Neither Rita nor Megan realized to what extent Spikes had fallen. All they saw was an aging former football star in decline. Other pictures on his Facebook page made it painfully obvious Spikes had never grown up. Rita stared, mesmerized by the evidence of a life gone astray.

The scales dropped away from her eyes. Those haunting whispers of a better life that had plagued her fell silent against the gale force of truth. Her ongoing fantasy shattered in such a way she could hardly breathe. Spikes could never be the man she once dreamed.

While she sat silent, her entire adult life played out. Those countless hours wasted contemplating what could have been; what she imagined should have been; how months, years of daydreaming had adversely influenced her marriage. How her misguided vision of the past had skewed the ways in which she viewed Neville.

Rita realized the wrongs she had inflicted in the name of love. Clearly, love had little to do with any of it. Her sin was living in a world that did not exist, living a life of illusion.

"Ever since high school you've had this vision that somewhere out there a prince is waiting– like Spikes." Megan pointed to a link on the Facebook page. "Here he is. Click that button. Send him a message if you'd like. Looks to me like he could use your dental skills Rita girl," she added with more than a touch of sarcasm.

Staring blankly into the screen, Rita witnessed her juvenile vision of life slam headlong into the reality of life itself. She had measured her husband against a romantic dream, a fiction created inside a hopeful heart and finding him lacking she had deserted him emotionally. It all came back in stunning clarity.

Rita shut the laptop screen. "Oh my God, I can't do this. Spikes may need someone but it can't be me. Not now, not ever."

Megan took her sister's hand. "I don't see much of Woody these days but any time I have he's always given me a big hug and asks how Richard is, and Mom and Dad. Then he'll say something like, it's time for me to add a little Richard to the world. Now that's sweet, Rita.

He even bought me a coffee a few weeks back at the coffee shop in St. Gabe's square."

"He did?"

"Of course he did. He's always been a standup guy–he hasn't changed. Can't you see that? Woody still loves you. It's time you did something about it."

A worried look came over Rita as she listened to her sister explain what she had so much trouble seeing. "How... how can he still love me? I've been so lost in all of this."

"Honey if there's one thing I know it's that Woody still loves you. Don't let guilt hold you back."

"He asked me to the Christmas party Friday," a stunned Rita said.

"And..."

"I told him I'd let him know."

"Rita what are you waiting for? Go!"

"I will. Maybe by Friday I'll know what to say."

Heaving out a relieved sigh, Rita embraced her sister and thanked her for not only the support but also the courage of her honesty. They were sisters, twins, and their bond remained as strong as it ever had. Megan knew Rita's heart as no one else could and because of the connection, she understood what worked in her sister's life. For Megan, the only answer for Rita had always been Neville.

Near tears, a call came in from the living room. "Hey what are you two doing?"

"Nothing," Megan yelled. The Fording sisters collected themselves.

"Sisters and secrets, they seem to go together," Richard said as they reentered.

Rita wagged a finger at her brother-in-law as she returned to the kitchen. "That will always be your cross to bear, Richard dear."

A knock sounded, the front door opened. Huddled together, Annette and Will Fording traipsed inside. Will carried a bag filled with Christmas presents. Richard, Megan and Rita met them in the foyer and the family exchanged Christmas greetings, handshakes and kisses.

As he shed his overcoat and shoes, Will started. "I need to shake off this cold. Is the bar open, Rita?"

Rita called over to her brother-in-law, "Richard, can you fix Dad a drink?"

"Sure," Richard said catching Megan's sly sure smile. "Ice, Will?"

"Please."

As Will headed for the leather recliner his wife asked, "So where's our little Dewey?"

"He'll be here anytime," Rita said from the kitchen.

Having given up his seat Richard took an unopened bottle of whiskey from the cabinet, added ice to a tumbler and poured out a drink for his father-in-law. Will took to the leather chair and as Richard handed him the drink quipped, "Now that's why you're my favorite son-in-law." He swallowed back a gulp of whiskey.

"I'm also your only son-in-law," Richard said.

"That too."

Will sat back to enjoy the rest of his drink and with the mention of son-in-laws a sharp knock came from the front door. The door burst open and Dewey raced in. Neville followed into the foyer behind his son. With Rita in the kitchen, Dewey ran first to his Gramma, wrapping his arms around her neck as she bent to greet her only grandchild. Will, Richard and Megan made their way toward Dewey for their Christmas hugs.

Silently watching, Neville stepped forward and gave his former mother-in-law a hug. Dinner was near complete and Rita stopped to survey the reunion from the kitchen doorway. Neville continued, hugging Megan and shaking hands with Richard and Will. She saw the interaction between her ex-husband and her family; how each cared for him and wished him well. How Neville seemed at such ease in their company. *He'd always fit right in*, she thought. *How did I not see any of that before?*

In some strange way, Neville looked very different. Megan's revelation, along with a bout of soul searching had resurrected the man she met ten years before. She saw the reasons she cared so much in the beginning: his bright smile, his genial way with people, his tender touch. Dewey ran up and while she bent to hug him, Rita heard Neville's call, "Have a nice night."

By the time she looked up the door had closed. Neville was gone and Rita had missed her chance to speak to him, to tell him yes to Friday night and the Christmas party. No one noticed her disappointment and Rita carried on with the dinner.

Soon after, they sat in the dining room eating holiday turkey, talking holiday blessings and having a rousing discussion involving French cuisine, the price of Francs on the open market and the upcoming adventure of Will and Annette's trip to France.

Will Fording continued to drink whiskey from a tumbler and expound on the currency markets and their effect on the world economy, a subject in which he had little to no exposure. After several drinks, Will liked to spout his philosophies, economic or otherwise and his family listened respectfully knowing a slip of the pen had made his fortune. As far as the subjects discussed, Will had few real insights. When Richard rolled his eyes at one of Will's outlandish claims, Megan was quick to jab an elbow into his ribs. Dewey watched the back and forth intently and giggled when his uncle winced in pain. Yes, even Dewey realized Grandpa Will was half-drunk. Yet they all made their allowances and loved him just the same.

After the Christmas banquet, the family settled into the living room. Rita turned on the television. Richard sat with his wife, Megan on the loveseat; Rita, Dewey and Gramma Annette snuggled across the sofa. Will kicked out the leg rest on the recliner and laid back to watch Frank Capra's holiday classic, *It's A Wonderful Life*. Less than thirty minutes into the movie, Will was snoring. Dewey, sitting between his mother and grandmother, paid inordinately more attention to the presents piled beneath the Christmas tree than the James Stewart classic. Yet even distracted, he heard the clatter of teeth amid the snorts erupting from his grandfather's late night snooze, quietly snickering to himself and to his uncle Richard across the coffee table.

As the movie neared an end, Rita's mother stood. "Rita what a wonderful dinner but we have an early flight."

Rita joined her mother standing. "Richard, can you help mom out to the car? Are you all right to drive?" she asked.

"I'm fine. He'll fall asleep again once we start driving."

Annette Fording gathered Christmas presents from her family and Richard helped Will to his feet. Somewhat stunned, Will mumbled an awkward approval of Jimmy Stewart movies and headed for the door. A round of hugs followed. After their usual best wishes for the holidays, Richard guided his father-in-law to the car. Richard and Megan readied to leave soon after. Megan hugged her sister and holding her at a distance stared directly into her eyes.

"Do the right thing Rita."

Rita knew exactly what she meant. Do the right thing by Neville, by her son and of course by herself. It was time to make a leap of faith and trust these emergent insights.

Rita was not about to let the moment pass and she decided to drop Dewey off at Neville's that night. Filled with fresh enthusiasm she bundled up her son and headed for the Wishwood home. She rushed up the snowy steps carting a tired Dewey along and knocked on the door. Dewey pushed in, dropping his backpack on the vestibule bench. Dell met both as they came in and seeing Rita, he began strumming his air guitar. *"Lovely Rita meter maid...."*

"Unca Dell..." Dewey droned, embarrassed. He unzipped his coat dropped it on the bench and wandered into the living room.

"Is Woody here?" Rita asked smirking at Dell's antics.

"He went out to the store for milk and cereal. He'll be back in fifteen, twenty minutes if you want to wait," Dell said.

Confused, Rita hesitated. Finally, she decided. "Just tell him I said yes."

Dell stared back blankly. "Yes to what?"

"The Christmas party Friday night."

"You're going?"

"I am," she said proudly. "...and tell him thanks."

Dell placed a pensive hand onto his chin and with arched eyebrows took on a look of concern. "Well that's not gonna work. He was supposed to take me. Now what am I gonna do?"

Rita's smile disappeared. She faced Dell without an answer for the dilemma. "Oh…"

Suddenly, Dell's face broke into a wild grin. "Just kidding. He wasn't gonna take me anyway. Last year someone said I ate all the shrimp at the buffet table. Of course it was all a lie– no one can eat that much shrimp. Believe me I tried."

Rita laughed. "I know you like shrimp Rita so be careful. They'll probably have someone watching the table Friday night," Dell warned.

"Dell you're still impossible," she said, turning to leave.

"Hey, who's gonna watch Dewey Friday?" he asked.

As she stepped down the porch, she called out with a smile, "Probably you."

Dell stared back. "You're probably right," he whispered to himself and closed the door.

A short time later Neville returned home. Dell broke the news of Rita's visit and her answer to his invitation. Neville was elated. Rita's acceptance opened up new inroads to a possible reconciliation. That night Neville had his most restful sleep in months.

Others were not as fortunate.

CHAPTER 29

NEARING ONE A.M., Roland drifted off into a half-sleep. Vodka, an effective numbing agent those first few days, had become less and less effective. Tonight he added an Ambien tablet to the mix. Lying naked beneath his sheets his two worlds collided. The world in which Roland wanted to live free, without obligation, and the world created by his attempt to achieve that goal.

A cold sweat coated his body, his legs and arms thrashed as a vision formed next to him in bed. Turning his face, Roland felt a cold touch along his cheek. He opened his eyes and there, staring back were Willis Ogland's eyes. Dappled with water, Willis's face, his matted hair nestled in the pillow next to Roland. He could feel wet fingers caressing him as he stared back speechless.

Without warning the vision spoke. "It's cold here Roland."

Transfixed by the icy blue eyes, his heart a mad flurry of thumps, Roland's fingers gripped the top sheet as if to brace himself against a blow. Roland searched for words and finally stuttered, "I'm– I'm so sorry Willis but you're dead."

"It's very cold here," the voice said sounding at a distance now. Yet the apparition remained next to him dripping water onto the pillow.

"Willis you're dead. You can't come back."

A shocked expression came over the Willis apparition as he placed wet hands against his greying face. His voice screamed from an even greater distance, calling out in panic, "Roland, I can't feel anything. Help me!"

Roland's eyes popped open and he bolted straight up in bed. Next to him was an empty pillow. His hands searched the empty space beneath the sheets. The sheets were damp and cold. He patted the pillow– it was wet. Confused, the vision fresh in his mind, he asked himself, *Was this real, a return from the dead?*

Roland eyes searched the dark corners of the room and his hands shot to his face. He wept. Suddenly he realized he had experienced a nightmare and stopped crying. Wiping away the tears, Roland jumped from the bed and ran to the living room. After a stiff swallow of vodka and a round of mental maneuvers, he settled the situation in his mind. *Just a dream,* he thought, *a bad dream. It was over, no harm done.*

After resolving the battle within, he curled into a ball on the sofa. Stuffed in a bag at the bottom of the Snake River, Willis lay buried, never to return. The dream had come and gone. As with all his difficulties Roland minimized the extent of its effect vowing to stay the course. For Roland, the end was in sight and his new life one short plane trip away. He continued to make plans passing yet another night without sleep.

Neville's unexpected luck continued into the next day. As he arrived on the second floor of The Sentinel, John Winterburn approached and pulled him aside. Before Neville had a chance to unbutton his coat, John started. "I called Sam last night Woody. My father-in-law had a serious car accident in Phoenix two days ago. We've had to move up our plans."

"Is he alright?' Woody asked.

"He's in ICU, stable but guarded," John said. "Sandy's mom's a mess so she's flying out today. I told Sam about the Phoenix job and the family emergency. I tendered my resignation last night. I leave next week."

"Family comes first. We'll manage, John," Neville said shaking his friend's hand.

Although a terrible tragedy had befallen his friend and coworker, the fallout provided an opening for Neville. Walter Hendry's sudden departure and Sam Charters unexpected promotion gave Neville his long awaited opportunity. Without knowing, Roland DeWitt had provided Neville his chance at advancement. He stood shaking the cold from his limbs when Walter Hendry's office door opened. Sam appeared in the doorway and one hand silently beckoned Neville into the office. "Woody, a minute please."

Before he could settle in, Neville joined Sam in his office. To his surprise, Suzanne stood by the desk smiling, her arms holding a folder up across her chest.

"John told you?" Sam asked as he sat.

"Yes, he's leaving," Neville said.

"It's your time now Woody. I have every confidence you'll meet the challenge. Suzanne has your paperwork. In it, you'll find a substantial raise reflecting an increased level of responsibility here at the Sentinel. Congratulations."

Suzanne stepped forward, opened the folder and placed it on the desk in front of Neville, adding her own congratulations. "You earned it, Woody," she said and pointed to the dotted line on the second page. "Sign here."

It all happened in what seemed whirlwind fashion. Inexplicably Neville's sworn enemy had somehow altered his destiny and once again, he sensed an odd symmetry to it all. He did as instructed and noticing his new pay grade, hesitated. A smile swept across his face. His salary was now near double. Suzanne gathered up the paperwork, handed him a slip with his new pay scale and left. Sam, somewhat perturbed by the circumstances, pulled in closer to his desk.

"One man's misfortune often leads to another's good fortune. Work with John. See if any of the stories he's written these last few weeks need follow-up."

"I will. And Sam, thanks for your confidence. Walter would never have given me this." Neville turned to leave still staring at the slip.

"Woody…" Sam stopped him mid-turn. "I've got more good news. I finished your book."

"And…"

"And I loved it. I made a few editorial comments, a few actual changes and I sent it on."

"Sent it on? Sent it on where?" Neville asked.

He hesitated, holding Neville in suspense. "My editor in Boston. I Fed-Exed it last weekend. She's probably reading it right now."

"What!"

"Yeah, I think it's good. And if I'm right, she'll be getting a hold of you."

"A publisher... in Boston," Neville said bewildered. "You're kidding, right?"

Sam stood and curled a fatherly arm around Neville's shoulder. "No, no joke. *Seven Days* is now in the hands of a publisher. Congratulations again, my friend."

It took Neville time to realize what Sam had done. In referring him to his editor, Neville gained an advantage most aspiring novelists could only dream of. In his euphoric state, he crossed the aisle and found his desk. The office space in which he worked, his entire world seemed transformed and in those few seconds. His eyes opened to the possibilities the future presented. A habitually productive and responsible employee, Neville found concentrating on his work a monumental effort that morning. His life, his destiny seemed headed in the right direction.

Roland rushed by on his way downstairs. He was now spending more time smoking cigarettes outside the main floor exit than he was working on The Sentinel accounts. Neville watched him pass. His slacks hung precariously from his hips, his cheeks hollow, grey. Overall, his face looked drawn, sapped of color. It was becoming readily apparent Roland was losing weight in the week following Willis's disappearance.

A biting wind blew in off the Snake River. Because of the weather, his usually pleasurable habit was uncomfortable today and forced Roland to stay buttoned up to his bowtie. One of the two double doors opened and Manny Duryea, a Sentinel press operator joined Roland on the concrete walkway.

Roland turned, and hunched from the cold, nodded grim faced.

Manny nodded back and lighting his cigarette he stepped closer. Over the years, Roland had made a point of not fraternizing with what he deemed 'the lowly working stiffs'. Everyone working at the Sentinel was aware of Roland's haughty attitude so it was no surprise when Roland moved away.

Sneering, Manny let out a laugh. "Too good for us pressmen, Rolly?"

Manny was one of the press operators who had taken Willis under his wing, apprenticing him in the workings of commercial presses. Manny liked Willis. He found Willis a willing and attentive student, humble and appreciative but most of all friendly, all traits absent from his closest friend and lover, Roland. As Willis grew closer to his first floor mates, he sensed safety in their company and confided his sexual orientation and his relationship with Roland. Although he didn't fully comprehend this attraction to men, Manny showed no sign of prejudice toward Willis and had never let it inhibit their working relationship.

Cold and tired, Roland moved nearer to the parking lot, his movements sounding in the crush of snow along the walk. "I just want to have my cigarette," he said turning away.

Unaffected by his rebuff, Manny asked, "Any word on Willis?"

Fumbling his cigarette, Roland peered back at the stocky press operator. "Nothing… and why would I know anyway," he barked back. Roland dropped his half-smoked cigarette onto the snowy walk. He cursed and kicked at it.

"Why so upset?" Manny prodded.

"Never mind," he mumbled and headed toward the back double doors. Manny grabbed his arm, startling Roland.

"We liked Willis. I hope he's okay," Manny said plainly, but his eyes said something very different. Roland turned toward the press operator and saw accusation in his steely glare. He brushed away Manny's hand. "Yes, let's hope."

Roland scurried back into the safety of the Sentinel.

Dell sat on the sofa in the Wishwood living room fitting a curved piece of wire into a small grey bead. His three custodies sat watching curiously while he formed the wire and twisted it in place with a pair of needle nose pliers. Dewey sat on the carpet across from his uncle mystified by the artistry involved in manufacturing a moon. The night before Dewey and Phil had convinced him the refitted solar system remained incomplete without a moon for the planet Earth. Dell was quick to rectify their concern.

"There," Dell announced. "…ready for installation, or should I say to join the rest of creation."

"What is it?" Arthur asked.

"It's our moon," Dewey said beaming proudly at his idea now realized. Arthur stared blankly at his grandson lost in the concept.

"Dell makes moons?" he asked.

"Today I do Artie," Dell said holding out his creation for all to see. "Let's go put it on."

The next twenty minutes passed with Dell perched on Dewey's bed attaching the wire and the moon to the green and blue ball they knew as Earth. His three apprentices watched as he twisted the wire in place, adjusted how the grey bead hung, ending the installation with a tap to ensure free movement. When he was finished, Dell hopped off the bed.

"Dewey, hit the switch."

Dewey flicked the light switch, the center sun grew bright and the planets started slowly orbiting above the bed. They all watched in amazement as Dell's moon wobbled in its own circle about the Earth.

"You did it." Phil said.

"Of course," Dell said. "You had doubts?"

They all turned as they heard the front door open. Neville had left work to join his family for Aunt Claire's Christmas dinner. Dewey ran to greet him and racing into the foyer, he grabbed his father's hand. "Come see what Unca Dell did."

"What?"

"The moon, Unca Dell made me a moon," Dewey said.

"Well let's go look," Neville said and led by his son, still bundled in winter wear, he made his way along the hallway, joining everyone in Dewey's bedroom. Neville looked up at the orbiting mobile. Dewey jumped up onto the bed and pointed at Dell's addition to his universe.

"Wow... Dell you outdid yourself this time," he said.

Still holding his pliers, Dell bowed in Neville's direction. "You expected less?"

While they readied to join Aunt Claire, Neville related his good fortune to Dell. His promotion, the pay raise, and of course, his book all made for exciting news and accordingly, Dell followed with an explanation for it all.

"It's the Phil effect, Woody. He's some kind of good luck charm."

Neville listened yet minimized the Phil effect. "Maybe."

Dell was adamant. "No maybe about it. Just look at what he's done."

Again, Neville hesitated. "Let's wait and see what Aunt Claire finds out before getting too wound up."

Neville said the words, but even that didn't truly convince him. They had witnessed too much by this amnesiac, Phil. The allusion Dell had suggested could certainly be true, but instead he wanted to believe in himself, in his own God given abilities as to the reasons for his destiny. He had worked tirelessly and as his father had always assured him, hard work produced positive results. Still, he struggled to understand Phil's influence and its impact on his life.

They chose Dell's heated Taurus for the short drive over to Aunt Claire's. After a somewhat quiet ride, they knocked at Aunt Claire's front door. Dell quickly opened it and all five filed into the foyer. Grant was standing near the kitchen with Aunt Claire and as everyone removed their winter gear, all exchanged cheerful Christmas greetings.

Dewey had visited on many occasions and considered Aunt Claire much the same way as his Gramma Annette. Hugs and handshakes followed. Grant, the next-door neighbor, joined in their celebration. After greeting her nephew and friends with heartfelt hugs, she faced off with the stranger in the group. Phil stood behind his new friends. A parting took place as Aunt Claire approached her guest.

"Hi, I'm Phil," he started, extending his hand. "Merry Christmas."

In her warm way Aunt Claire clasped Phil's extended hand, greeting him as if an old friend and as she did her eyes tipped up to his, squinting. She studied him with a calculating gaze and a smile crossed her lips. Still holding onto his hand, she continued to stare for what seemed forever. Finally, she released it quietly recounting, "There's an aura surrounding you, a warmth... I can feel it. You're very different than most I've met."

She paused, her eyes widened, her hands trembled and drew naturally to her face. In a show of uncertainty, she stared silently into the hallway carpet assessing the sum of what she had experienced. Something inside Aunt Claire clicked and with this sudden understanding, her eyes darted back to Phil. "You're someone quite unique aren't you?"

"I am?" Phil asked. His friends hung on her every word.

"Yeah, a guy without a name or a life," Dell injected.

Aunt Claire's face formed a knowing look and she whispered, "You're a seraphim."

"A what?" Dell and Neville asked in chorus. A saucer-eyed Dewey watched in amazement, waiting for the answer just as his elders did.

An uncomfortable silence landed between Aunt Claire and her guests. Phil added his astonishing response, "She's saying I'm an angel... a seraphim is an angel."

Struck by the odd reply Dell started. "You, who two weeks ago didn't even know what planet we're on– you know what a seraphim is? How's that work?"

"I really don't know how Dell... I just do."

"But not just any angel," Aunt Claire said. "A seraphim is the most trusted of angels, their highest order... and closest to God. Oh yes, this young man is special indeed... very special."

Aunt Claire's announcement stunned the group and while they continued to stand and stare dumbfounded an unaffected Arthur blurted out, "What's for dinner?"

That broke the silent standoff.

"Take off your coats, come in and get warm... everyone," Aunt

Claire said but her eyes continued to follow Phil as he made his way toward the sofa. "Dinner will be ready soon."

Dell gathered up the coats and put them in the bedroom. Neville guided his father over to the sofa. Dewey, Phil and Arthur sat there as they had in the back seat of the Taurus. Neville took the high-back chair while Dell joined Grant on the loveseat.

Dewey looked up at Phil and whispered, "Are you really an angel?"

"Me?" Phil appeared amazed himself. "I'm not so sure Dewey. Maybe."

Across the living room, Dell stared at Grant, sitting next to him. After several seconds he asked, "So, when you and Aunt Claire were in Duluth did you stay in separate rooms or did you economize?"

Grant stared back. "What?"

Stone faced, Dell returned, "You heard me."

As Dell waited for a reply Aunt Claire was quick to call him into the kitchen. "Dell, come carve the turkey dear."

"This is just a reprieve. We'll talk later," he said as he joined his aunt. Grant gave Dell a grin and a small wave as he left to help.

Everyone ate a hearty Christmas feast that afternoon. Turkey, mashed potatoes, stuffing, corn and green beans, and a cranberry mash filled the hungry crew. Neville talked of his promotion. Dell spoke of the moon he had made, and Aunt Claire and Grant talked of Duluth and the storm they encountered. Surprisingly absent from the dinner conversation was any talk of their special guest, Phil. There was purpose in their avoidance. Angels are, inherently, a difficult subject.

Yet it hung over the dinner table like a mist or the shadow of a truth once told. It was as if amnesia had infected the group. While Grant and Aunt Claire cleared the dinner table a new silence developed, a contradictory silence rooted in superstition and the oft mistaken idea that if ignored an idea, a statement or belief or even an angel, did not exist.

Still she had spoken the words and she definitely made the statement. Denial or ignorance was not enough to nullify the truth as implied by Aunt Claire's initial assertion. With Aunt Claire's innate ability, she saw what truly emanated from inside this stranger, identifying him as an angel of the highest order– a seraphim. While the adults sat quietly eating pumpkin pie, the youngest led them back.

"So, is Phil really an angel Aunt Claire?" Dewey asked with innocuous clarity.

With the exception of Arthur who continued to scrape the last crumbs from his plate, everyone at the table stopped. Curious eyes all, they quickly peered up at Aunt Claire waiting at her indulgence. She heard Dewey's question clearly and sat up, placed her fork on the plate and wiped her lips with a napkin.

"I think he is," she directed to Dewey. "…but let's find out for sure." All eyes followed Aunt Claire as she took her plate and set it on the kitchen counter.

"Everyone into the living room," she ordered. "Dell, turn the TV on and find something to entertain our guests." She turned to Phil and patted the empty seat next to her. "And you young man come sit by me."

Like an obedient child, Phil joined Aunt Claire while the remaining guests filed silently into the living room. Dell did as directed and switched on the television finding an appropriate movie. Charles Dickens, A Christmas Carol was in the opening scenes introducing the famous story's main character, Ebenezer Scrooge. With its time-travelling ghosts and homespun sincerity it seemed the perfect movie for an afternoon laced with intrigue.

Outside, a grey day was in transition. Night shadows crept up walls, covered snowbound streets and swept into the lands surrounding the town of Solomon. Street lamps sparked on creating islands of illumination within the grid of roads. Winter white had given way to the dusky cloak of night. Above a slowly shifting landscape, spotlights in St. Gabriel's Square beamed life to a winged statue of an angel in flight.

Aunt Claire sat across the corner of the dining table facing Phil with her back to the living room and its keenly interested parties. All eyes switched between the television and the dining room table as Aunt Claire took Phil's hands separately, holding each between her own frail fingers. She spoke in whispers.

Phil's head nodded on occasion and at times, he closed his eyes in concentration. In the living room, heads swiveled back and forth, attempting to follow Aunt Claire's séance and the story line of Dickens' tale. Consequently, neither of the two narratives advanced coherently.

As the living room grew dark, Dell switched on the living room lamps. A hushed dialogue filtered in and except for the television, they remained the only words spoken. Forty minutes in, with the ghost of Christmas present lending his insights to a startled Ebenezer Scrooge, the sound of a chair's legs scraped against the kitchen floor. Now unlatched from her subject, Aunt Claire pulled herself away from the table. She stood visibly shaken. In a pose reminiscent of a church service, her guests stood reverently and stared. No one spoke for several seconds.

Concerned, Dell hissed, "Aunt Claire..."

Her one hand waved him away.

"I'm alright," she said. Neville made his way across the room and met both Aunt Claire and Dell. Finally standing erect, Aunt Claire wiped her eyes with a sleeve and peered back at Phil. In their short interaction, they had established a very personal connection.

"He's one amazing being this friend of yours," Aunt Claire started. "Let's talk in the bedroom."

Neville flagged Phil's attention. "Sit here," he said, pointing to the seat next to Dewey. "Watch the movie. We'll only be a few minutes."

Aunt Claire led down the hall to Dell's former bedroom. She flipped on the light, walked to the bed and sat.

Dell was direct. "Well, is he, you know... an angel?"

Worn as if forced to climb several flights of stairs, Aunt Claire started. "He showed me things... things I can't easily explain."

"Like what Aunt Claire?" Neville asked.

Her eyes searched the room as if spotting images in every corner. Suddenly aware and engaged with new vigor her attention switched back to her two eager young men.

"He spoke of my Ernest and a trip we took, a trip no one else could possibly know..." As she spoke the scene replayed; the streets, the rolling trolley cars, those hopeful dreams found only with young love. "San Francisco before we married, a time when I was young and happy and so in love. I saw Ernest as he was... strong, handsome. Your friend, he showed me that and so much more."

Still doubtful Dell asked, "You're sure it wasn't your own recollection, an old memory coming back Aunt Claire?"

Aunt Claire laughed. "It's not the same, dear nephew. There's a difference. This was a projection like a movie playing in your head. The view an observer might see from a distance. It was a very special time in my life. And he could see it. I thought I had a gift, but this Phil, he... he's one very special individual."

The vision Phil provided rekindled a love she once lived but with it came the pain, the pain of loss. The bitter with the sweet. She sat starry eyed on the bed lost in the scene Phil had projected, a reminder of happier days. Neville sank to a squat while Dell placed a hand on his aunt's shoulder.

"Is he this angel you said he was, a seraphim Aunt Claire?" Neville asked.

Her eyes shifted to meet Neville's gaze. "I asked him of his past and a vision appeared... a child swimming in a pool with an older woman, his mother. You were there too Woody. For most clients what I see are muddled pictures, snippets of the past or the future. But his were so clear, so real, not like anything I've ever encountered. No he's genuine, I'm sure of it."

"That dream he spoke of last week," Dell whispered. "But he didn't mention you in the pool did he?"

"No, I'd remember that," Neville said.

"Everything I asked he tried answering, so I asked his purpose here...a reason for his arrival in Solomon. It seemed blocked. He said it felt like a curtain had dropped down concealing the details. The memory exists but it seems blocked from the accident."

"Great, but if he *is* an angel, how does he even get amnesia?" Dell lamented.

Neville pushed himself up from the carpet. "Dell's right. Angels are, well... angels."

"Well aren't you two the dullest. What are we celebrating this week? Have you never heard of Jesus Christ? The son of God? He was definitely divine and look– look at his human suffering. He died on a cross," Aunt Claire said in a venomous tone.

Dell and Neville exchanged incredulous glances embarrassed by Aunt Claire's quick rebuttal. Of course, they knew of Christ's suffering and death on earth yet they had failed to see the parallels with Phil. Although human in every aspect, his powers seemed all too obvious. As Aunt Claire wisely pointed out, divinity did not necessarily mean immunity. Our inherent human foibles could be an acceptable consequence for an angel, or a god. Whatever the reason for his visitation her assessment appeared credible.

"Now what? He can't remember and you can't penetrate his amnesia," Dell said defeated.

Aunt Claire met their disappointment with a knowing response. "A blow to the head gave him amnesia. A similar blow may remedy it." Her simple statement set both their brains whirring. "That might work," Neville said.

Dell nodded. "I saw it on an episode of Columbo years ago."

Dell's aunt provided a plan of attack figuratively and literally. One bop on the head could be the blow to set things right again and determine Phil's true intentions. After several minutes of discussion, they established that Phil actions demonstrated more the signs of an angel than the evil doppelganger they had once considered. Moreover, with Neville's obvious turn of good fortune all agreed that he appeared to be Phil's intended focus.

With the day a decided success and now agreed on a strategy, they left Aunt Claire's buoyed with confidence. In their anticipation, one rather disturbing question arose: *Who would strike the decisive blow?*

After a magnificent homemade meal, the drive to Rita's remained quiet. With her dental practice closed until the New Year, Rita was expecting Dewey for a prolonged stay. Dell drove the snowbound streets while the question of who would strike the decisive blow popped in and out of both their heads. Of course, each thought the other more capable and each formulated reasons for the other to deliver the fated whack.

Dell's car pulled into Rita's driveway and Neville walked Dewey to the front door. Rita stood posed in the doorway beneath the foyer's bright light, her hair a shimmer of vivid red strands. It had taken time to perfect her demure all too alluring look, Dell mused. For Neville, she projected a delicate halo, a divine radiance. Leaning leisurely against the jamb, she opened the door her eyes riveted on Neville. As Dewey swept inside, her one hand skimmed his wool cap from his head, tousling the blond locks beneath.

From his driveway seat, Dell observed their casual conversation beneath the glow of porch light. With no wind and the night clear, his view remained flawless. Rita's hips shifted seductively, her hand landing softly on the curve below a slim waist, her eyes never leaving his; Neville's clumsy shuffle of feet, his head as it dropped to his chest and then, a sudden pantomime laugh from Rita. The signs were there. Dell snickered to himself watching the antics of two former lovers amid anxious slouching and shifting. Engaged like timid teenagers, they were in the midst of rediscovering what everyone else could plainly see– they belonged together.

As Neville returned, Dell slipped the Taurus into gear. Phil and Arthur sat in the back seat oblivious to the right of passage enacted on the front porch. He stared across at Neville, wearing the same satisfied grin his friend wore.

"That was cozy," Dell said.

Neville again turned his attention back to the house and Rita waving from inside the storm door. "It was… very."

Heading home, the discussion switched to Phil and who would strike the blow. Phil heard his name whispered and leaned in. "What are you talking about?"

The question ended the conversation. In their enthusiasm to find a remedy, they had all but forgotten how they would approach Phil on the subject. Would they enter into a surprise attack, without forewarning? Or would they include Phil and explain the benefits to regaining his memory? After several seconds of silent deliberation, Neville opted for the latter.

Dell pulled into the driveway; the car stopped. Arthur pulled his door open, hurried up the walk and waited impatiently on the front porch.

Unsettled, Neville formed his words carefully. "Ummm... Aunt Claire told us she really connected with you today."

"Yes, she's a very smart lady Aunt Claire," Phil said.

"Yes..." Neville continued to struggle spitting out the words. "She told us something that could be very important Phil. She said if we, if someone gave you a..."

While Neville wrestled with the words, Dell interjected, "She said to bop you on the beaner again and you'll probably get your memory back."

"Yes..." said a breathless Neville.

"Hey, let's go," Arthur bellowed from the porch shivering from the cold. "I've got to see if your mother's home yet." Once again, the past dominated Arthur's limited attention.

Without hesitation, Phil replied, "Okay." He exited the car and joined Arthur on the porch leaving both his caregivers stunned. Inside Dell's Taurus, they sat resigned to the business at hand.

"Okay then," Dell jibed and all four made their way inside. Their night was about to become very interesting.

CHAPTER 30

THE DETECTIVE TWIDDLED a pencil between two fingers while his eyes struggled to focus on the monitor in front of him. Tired from chasing an irrational puzzle, Rob Hoyer's day was ending on a low note. Willis Ogland's disappearance presented a major problem. His initial investigation had led him to a suspect but in the week since, few physical clues had surfaced. Without a direction, he felt stymied on how to proceed.

His interview of Roland DeWitt spiked immediate suspicion. The young man's manner, his impudent replies, his overall demeanor seemed to scream guilt yet he had no real evidence. Viewing Roland's condominium security tape had shown a somewhat happy Willis Ogland entering the building, but with no video of the back entrance Roland's account of his departure remained untouchable. The visitor lot was there solidifying an alibi and his version of events. Even just cause for a subpoena evaded him at this point. Now with two other cases on the go, Hoyer turned to their information-sharing database to garner a lead in the Ogland case.

Minn-Scan was a law enforcement database used by police agencies across six northern states. Over one thousand forces input data related to crimes in each of their jurisdictions hoping to not only update the status of their investigations but also gather new leads in any open cases. Records posted were there for all agencies, much like the FBI's nationwide database. Having already searched the FBI registry, Hoyer had come up empty. He was now ready to proceed in sharing case specifics in hopes of getting a lead.

Before leaving for the day he input the vital information pertaining to the disappearance of Willis Ogland; his name, his place of employment, the date last seen, his 2001 Volvo, its license plate and of course the primary suspect in the case, Roland DeWitt. All the pertinent information and a short blurb on the facts as best he could ascertain.

Hoyer hit the enter key and watched the screen fade to grey and while he waited for confirmation, he lifted his overcoat from the pole beside his desk. A bar graph in the center of the grey filled with green, the numbers climbed and in seconds, he had validation. Download complete.

Leaving work that day, Rob Hoyer could feel his fingers curl in frustration. A sense of defeat crept in as he passed the desks of his colleagues, and reaching the stairs the tension rose in his back. There was nothing more demoralizing than knowing a suspect's involvement in a crime and not being able to find the evidence to prove it.

His detective gut growled knowing he had the right suspect yet without proof, he had little recourse. Infuriating as they were, Hoyer numbered these days less than the ones where he actually accomplished his goals: found evidence, made arrests and compiled a workable case against the suspects he encountered. He left work thinking more of that possibility even in the Willis Ogland case. For any detective, patience was indeed a virtue. With his attitude realigned and his hope now centered on this latest avenue, his tension levels subsided. Another day meant another hope of success.

"I can't do it, it's against my religion," Dell argued.

"Dell you don't have a religion," Neville returned.

"So. It's my new mantra then. No violence."

They stood on either side of Phil trying to decide who was going to implement the plan and whack their houseguest in the head. Neville retrieved a hockey stick from the basement, one of Dewey's Christmas gifts. As he held the weapon, they argued as to who would play executioner. Phil stood in front of the coffee table. His hands covered his face and eyes while Arthur watched intently from his seat on the sofa well away from the action.

"I'm ready," Phil said.

"I brought him here so you have to do it Dell."

"I'm not, and that doesn't even make sense. *You* should do it because you live here."

Neville quickly countered. "You live here, too!"

"I'm ready," Phil offered once more. With his back to both his caregivers, he stood near the outer edge of the coffee table waiting for someone to bop him. The scene held more than a dash of the surreal. Phil had willingly put himself in harms' way to accommodate what Aunt Claire had suggested as a solution to his amnesia. Fifteen minutes in, he continued to wait for the blow.

"Let's cut cards," Dell proposed. "Low man does the deed."

"If you lose you won't do it. I know you won't do it," Neville said.

"Yes I will," Dell countered. Arthur, alone on the sofa, watched the argument continue back and forth, keenly following each as they pleaded their case.

"You're sure?"

"I'm ready... hit me," Phil said again, his voice muffled from the placement of his hands.

"Yes, I'll do it if I lose," Dell assured Neville. He seemed sincere and although Neville had his doubts, he agreed. He placed the hockey stick on the coffee table and hurried into the kitchen. He pulled out a fresh deck of cards from the junk drawer and raced back into the living room. Dell waited while Neville slipped the cards from the box and then intervened.

"I'll shuffle," he said.

"No cheating," Neville returned as he watched his friend riffle the cards. Dell placed the shuffled deck on the computer desk.

"I won't... you go first."

"Hit me... I'm ready," Phil called again in a muzzled voice.

Arthur continued to follow Neville and Dell as they huddled next to the desk, staring each other down. Finally, Neville reached across and cut the deck twenty cards in. Lifting his draw, he showed Dell the result.

Dell laughed. "The six of clubs, I can beat that."

He forced his friend aside, reveling in Neville's disappointment. Dell lifted his sleeve as if to perform a magic trick, reached down and stabbed the deck another twenty cards deeper. Neville slipped closer, watching cautiously and as Dell turned his hand. The card flashed before their eyes. The four of spades reared its ugly face.

Dropping the cards on the desktop, Dell backed up. "I'm not doin' it," he announced.

"You said you would!"

As they squabbled by the desk, a dull thwack sounded. Both men turned in time to see Phil fall face first onto the coffee table. A subdued Arthur held the hockey stick with two hands, wielding it like a pickaxe. He had dealt the decisive blow.

Frozen in dread, Neville gaped at the horrid scene. Their angel had fallen and laid motionless on the table's wood top, a trickle of blood oozing from his lips. He rushed over and relieved Arthur of the stick while Dell hurried to help Phil. Placing Arthur back on the sofa, Neville helped Dell attend to Phil.

He was unconscious– again.

With Phil propped up, Dell turned him sideways seating him slouched on the table. It took both men to support his limp frame. His body drooped and with one hand bracing him, Neville took his free hand and pulled a shirttail from inside his pants. Leaning in, holding Phil's wobbly body steady, Neville wiped the blood from the corner of his mouth. Dell tried prying open his shut eyes to no avail. He felt for signs of life. "He's still breathing."

"Thank God!"

Beneath the slow circuit of small planets, as one tiny moon wriggled its way around a green and blue orb, Jennifer Gilchrist carefully applied a cold cloth to Phil's forehead while his two caregivers waited anxiously for a prognosis. Attractive and certainly intelligent, Jennifer looked to be one of Dell's more astute decisions. Although impressed by her decisive manner, Neville wondered if her short-cropped black hair, mirroring Dell's own pin-straight locks, had any influence on his friend's attraction. With Dell, there was always that possibility.

Neville's father stood in the doorway quietly observing the proceedings all a result of his intrepid intervention. What went through Arthur's mind and just how those meandering thoughts turned to action no one really knew except to say he had expedited the situation.

A soft near imperceptible whirr from the mobile's motor hummed in the background. "I don't think it's a coma, just a slight concussion. The blood's from a split lip. The broken finger'll mend in a month or so." Jennifer pointed to the makeshift splint she had attached to his left hand. After removing the cloth, she grazed an affectionate hand through his damp hair and placed an open palm across his forehead. "No fever," she announced.

Before her current job as a medical secretary in Minneapolis, Jennifer had worked as a nurse's aide for two years. She was the first call they made.

"It must've been a terrible fall... he's got this big lump on the back of his head."

Dell shot Neville an awkward glance. "Yeah... I guess when he fell down the basement stairs he must've bounced around some," he said.

Her hand carefully caressed his matted hair again and staring into Phil's innocent face, his lips curled in a brooding half-smile, she whispered, "Poor soul, he does look angelic laying here."

"I didn't think it was that obvious," Neville murmured, again meeting Dell's narrow-eyed gaze.

"What?"

"Never mind."

"You were right about one thing Dell— he does look a lot like Barney Fife," she said staring at her silent patient. For Neville, he saw the same sense of recognition just in a different way. With his lower lip bruised and an ugly blue forming below his eyes, Phil manifested the appearance of a TV zombie.

Jennifer let out a giggly laugh. "You sure he's not some evil doppelganger?" she asked. Neville and Dell stood dazed somehow transfixed by Jennifer's attempt at comic relief.

"Lighten up," she cajoled. "He'll be right as rain by morning."

Jennifer patted Phil's limp hand, adjusted Dewey's Iron Man blankets tight along his sides and left him to rest. All three slipped by Arthur standing his post by the open door. Neville switched off the light. As they made their way into the living room, Arthur took up where Jennifer had left, sitting bedside with his constant companion these last two weeks. He sat quietly in the dark watching his friend Phil, his eyebrows knitted with apprehension.

Noticing his concern, Jennifer asked, "Were they close?"

"Thick as thieves those two," Dell said taking a place on the loveseat.

"My father has Alzheimer's and Phil... he's had his own issues." Neville left the remainder of what they had discovered unsaid.

"Awww... that's so sweet." Jennifer seemed captivated by the bizarre circumstances. She took a seat next to Dell. Being Neville's first meeting with Dell's love interest, he took the opportunity to get to know her.

They sat in the living room for over an hour telling each other stories of their childhood, their upbringing, noteworthy accomplishments and of course likes and dislikes. As Jennifer cuddled up near Dell, Neville could see their fingers intertwine, a shoulder nuzzle, her wide-eyed gaze veering between him and his best friend, adding comments and laughing comfortably in their company. Yes, Jennifer Gilchrist seemed the perfect fit for Dell.

A clear night sky greeted Neville on the front porch and after thanking Jennifer for her much-needed medical intervention, he watched them disappear around the corner up to Dell's second floor apartment.

He walked back in past the living room and leaned into the

bedroom. There, with his hands folded across his lap, Arthur sat alongside the bed surveying his sleeping friend.

These last weeks afforded Neville's father a partner, a young man with a similar affliction but living out a decidedly different set of circumstances. With his past hidden behind a dark and ever-present veil, Phil remained trapped, shunted aside by time and an inability to interpret the world around him. Their kinship formed from sharing this same outsider view.

Shadows, spawned from Dewey's night light arced across the room against the far wall projecting a larger-than-life image of Arthur patiently sitting guard over a childlike figure, asleep and unaware. A ring of dark replica worlds hung limply above the bed. Neville approached and with a gentle hand tried guiding his father from the bed. Arthur refused with a firm, "No" pulling his shoulder back. After a second attempt and a second rebuff, Neville left him to his duty.

Yet he smiled knowing that deep within his father's damaged psyche, beneath the deadly onslaught of this unrelenting disease, compassion continued to survive. Neville left the darkened room. The shadows of these two diverse men, bonded by a strange kinship, projected a still grey mural and stood watch.

Neville's thoughts tumbled through a litany of questions as he made his way to bed. They made his initial efforts at sleep all but impossible. Adding to his glut of issues, Wagner's "Ride of The Valkyrie" droned in through the bedroom ceiling. Dell's romantic preference filtered down from his love nest above. With the aid of earplugs, Neville finally fell asleep.

In the bedroom down the hall, Arthur's vigil continued through the night.

CHAPTER 31

DELL BOUNCED IN shortly after seven a.m. flipped his slippers beneath the small table in the foyer and headed toward the kitchen. Neville sat drinking coffee at the table. He bypassed the doorway and made a direct trek to Dewey's bedroom. Peering in, Dell witnessed Phil still asleep and a slumbering Arthur Wishwood nestled at the foot of the bed. Curled in the fetal position Neville's father remained dressed in the same blue shirt and slacks from the night before. During the night a tired but determined Arthur had crawled across the blankets and joined his stricken housemate.

The sight of Phil and Arthur lying fast asleep warmed even Dell's sated soul. After observing the unspoiled scene for several seconds, Dell joined Neville in the kitchen.

"How long's he been there?" he asked.

With a last gulp of coffee, Neville paused. "All night... he wouldn't leave."

Dell shook his head and proceeded to the coffee pot on the kitchen counter. "Funny how those two just seemed to connect."

Neville lifted from his chair. "It is strange but a lot of things have been strange lately."

Dell agreed, nodding. "True..."

Neville walked to the foyer as Dell followed cup in hand. "By the way, I really like your latest choice in girlfriends. She's a keeper."

"Yeah, she's got game that Jenny, and she loved my bobble-heads."

"Don't we all." Neville added a faint laugh. "Listen, if and when Phil wakes up call me at work. I want to know if he's okay."

"Will do."

That morning Neville partnered with John Winterburn getting updated on stories he would be leaving in Neville's capable hands. The two carjacking accounts took precedent being of greatest local interest. Earlier in the week, he had written a follow-up article after police released the name of the second victim, Davis Jefferson. John transferred his notes, his prior columns and any sources he had found in the investigation.

John also wrote a short story on Willis Ogland's disappearance, but few actual leads had surfaced. He passed on the name and phone number of the detective in charge, the man who interviewed all the Sentinel employees, Robert Hoyer.

Across from Neville, Sam worked on his political entries for The Sentinel. In this election year, his political views and insights had become a major talking point within the community furnishing endless debate between the Democratic and Republican factions inside the state.

Two hours into his day as he sorted through files, Neville's cell phone rang. Dell's face appeared in his smart phone window.

"Hello?"

"He's awake," came Dell's reply.

"Is he okay?"

"Oh, I'd say he's okay." Dell's voice inferred a rather cryptic allusion.

"So, he's up and back to himself. No after effects?" Neville asked.

"Not quite." Dell hesitated. "Let's just say he's...different."

"Different?" Neville thought for a few seconds and swung his chair away from his computer screen. "Okay, different's alright if he's awake. What about dad... is he alright?"

"He's good, Woody. Phil sent him to bed so he'll probably sleep for a while."

"What about Phil's amnesia?"

"I think Aunt Claire's solution worked, but..."

"But what?" Neville quizzed.

"Phil says he feels great, but what he has to say he can only say to you," Dell said.

"Alright… I'll see him when I get home."

His answer failed at settling Dell. "You sure you wanna wait?"

"I've got too much to catch up on here. I can't leave, not right now anyway," Neville said. But after hanging up Neville could feel the pull; a changed man, different. Yet according to Aunt Claire, not a man at all, an angel, and not just any angel– a seraphim.

Sorting through John's files, his thoughts continued to swing back to Phil who could now surrender the secrets that had inadvertently been locked inside his head, to his father and of course Dell waiting anxiously to hear those same secrets. Neville watched his nemesis Roland saunter by. Thin and pale, he tugged his coat on in a trek outside for another smoke and yet he passed Neville as if invisible. Neville's brain, so over-employed by the workings of what was to come had degenerated into a jumble of questions and projected answers.

By noon, the toll had confused him to the point of misfiling the active files into out dated folders. He was making mistakes he never made, imposing more harm than good. And so compelled, Neville could no longer quell the questions running rampant inside his head. After offering Sam a shorter and somewhat contrived version of events, he left the office and hurried home.

Before Neville could open the door, it swung open. Dell's wide grin greeted him. "Took you long enough," he said.

"I wanted to stay at work, but…" His voice trailed off. Dell closed the door while Neville quickly discarded his winter gear. "Where's Phil?"

"In Dewey's room."

Neville made his approach slowly brushing a hand through his hair in an effort to stay calm. Dell followed close behind and as Neville looked inside the bedroom, Phil caught sight of him and smiled. The ugly bruising around his eyes had disappeared and as Phil sat sideways on the bed, Neville could see the makeshift splint Jennifer Gilchrist had attached the night before lying on the blankets. Phil went back to staring up at the orbiting mobile.

"Dell did a nice job attaching that little moon," Phil said.

"Dell's pretty handy." Neville stepped in. "You're... better."

"Yes, I heal quickly," Phil said, flipping his hand back and forth. "And thanks to you, Aunt Claire and Arthur of course, I have my memory back. Come closer, we have things to discuss."

Neville joined Phil on the bed. Phil appeared much the same as he always did yet today he carried himself differently. He seemed at ease, very much in charge of the situation. Superficially, nothing had changed, yet Neville recognized something unique: an indefinable force seemed to emanate from Phil, a sense of poise and confidence. In one night everything had changed.

Dell took up a post by the bedroom door eager to witness the proceedings. Neville plunged ahead. "Dell said you can only speak to me."

"What Dell told you is true so..." He lifted up above Neville and met Dell's prying eyes. "Can you leave us alone for a few minutes?"

Reluctantly, Dell reached in and grabbed the door handle. "I get it. Yell if it gets out of hand." He yanked the door shut.

"He'll be outside listening, you know that," Neville said flashing a grin.

"It doesn't matter. He'll only hear what I want him to hear."

Sitting alone, both young men continued to stare into an invisible cloud of uncertainty hanging between them. Neville's hands twitched seeking a relaxed position. Phil began the conversation. "Understand first Woody, anything we speak about you are free to share with whomever you like. It's only my mandate that excludes others from becoming involved."

"I understand. My ears only."

"Exactly... To begin with, I didn't plan on the amnesia. That being said, the only real wrinkle is this process, my intervention here, has taken more time than expected. But time is something I have plenty of."

Eyes locked, Neville searched Phil's face. "Are you really an angel?"

A chuckle squeaked out from this man Neville knew as his houseguest these last weeks. "Something like that I guess. And despite what Aunt Claire believes I'm not so sure we have a rank where I come from."

Phil reset himself on the bed. "I've been sent to offer you a gift."

"What kind of gift?"

"Two wishes."

"Two wishes... like in, I wish for a million dollars?"

Phil shook his head. "No, money can't be any part of your requests."

Neville turned away; his empty eyes searched the bed, the shelves of toys, Dewey's bright wall posters, the grey light seeping in through the bedroom window. Was this offer real? And if it was, what wish could he make to better his life, the lives of those he loved? *Those he loved* echoed inside his brain jolting his sterile stare to life. "What about love? Can you make someone fall in love?"

"Rita?"

Neville nodded. "I still love her. I'm just not sure if she'll ever feel the same for me."

Again, Phil's head wagged side to side. "Love, along with all human emotions, can only be determined by the human heart. It's part of free will, a dictate I cannot interfere with. As powerful as wishes are they can't manufacture love. Ironically, it's quite the opposite; love is the engine that drives miracles.

"If it's any consolation, I think Rita was lost for a while Woody. I see signs she's coming around. My best advice; continue to be the man you are, the man you were born to be. Follow your heart."

"Now you sound like Aunt Claire," Neville quipped. He searched his thoughts to find a wish to fulfill a dream, to change a life, a wish that mattered in his world. His sight settled back on Phil eyes. Bulbous eyes newly intense, probing Neville with every glance, every glimmer. What had those eyes seen? Had they witnessed such miracles as he offered Neville here today?

"It can be anything else. A past indiscretion set right, a desired outcome to a current course of events. All can be realized," Phil said.

Neville remained blocked.

In the minutes that followed one prospect emerged. One wish Neville knew he needed to make but other than that one, nothing else. As Phil waited, Neville came up blank on his second wish. Some strange insight arose, compelling Neville to recognize the importance of his one last wish. With his own life seemingly beset by good fortune he struggled to find an heir, someone deserving of this life-altering opportunity, someone whose fate needed reinvention– but who?

Returning to his benefactor, he asked, "Can I think about my wishes?"

"Of course, you should be judicious."

"Thank you. Just give me a day or two. I'm sure by then I'll know what to do," Neville said, relieved. As he stood, curiosity took hold. "How did I get these wishes?"

Phil stood and for some reason he appeared taller. "Miracles are a product of love. Before leaving I'll tell you all I know about the circumstances involved in this gift."

"By the way, what's your real name?" Neville asked.

"It's not important who I am. Let's leave it as Phil for now."

Reaching the door, he yanked it open and found Dell stooped and suddenly embarrassed. Feigning an excuse Dell bent lower and picked lint from the carpet.

"I was just cleaning up… haven't vacuumed in a few days," he said.

Dell's comfort level diminished in the face of glaring eyes and silent smirks. "What, you don't think I was spying do you? Me, spying? I happen to be the embodiment of discretion."

"Dell do we have any tea? I prefer tea to coffee," Phil asked, changing the subject.

"In the kitchen, top cupboard right next to the refrigerator," Dell said.

Phil carried on down the hall disappearing at its end. Dell watched as he made the turn. "That's a change, he knows what he likes." Unable to contain himself, Dell pulled Neville toward the living room. "What'd he say? Is he, you know, an angel like Aunt Claire said?"

"I guess," he said, shaken by Phil's revelation.

"You guess? Is he or isn't he, that *is* the question."

Neville took his friend by the arm. "Dell he offered me a gift… two wishes."

"Two wishes? Like, you can ask for anything…twice?"

"Yes, but no money. Pretty much anything but money or love."

"Why not three wishes? Every story I've ever read had three wishes," Dell said.

"According to Phil, I have two."

Agitated, Dell asked, "What'd you wish for?"

"Nothing yet, but I'll come up with something."

Neville's thoughts wandered back to Phil's words and the gift and no less a gift than any impossible deed beneath the sun times two. How could he have earned such a prize? Who was Neville to be set before so many truly in need in this world? It was all humbling.

In these bouts of skepticism, Dell reminded him of Audrey, of Camillus De Lellis, the hockey game and its unpredictable result, his dead dog, Willard and of course, Phil's magical foretelling of every card in a deck of playing cards. He had witnessed the impossible become possible repeatedly.

Awestruck by his friend's unbelievable predicament, Dell said his goodbyes but not before he agreed to oversee Dewey and Arthur Friday night. A fully alert Phil would also be there. Dell's only caveat was that Jennifer join him. Neville had no issue with the arrangement. Quite happily, he would be in Rita's company.

Arthur woke up in time for dinner, and after all three watched the Bruins play the Islanders on television. A quiet night, Phil took a place on the sofa next to Arthur while Neville half-watched hockey and half-watched the interaction between the two. With Phil awake and well, his father's actions came much more naturally. Contented, he asked for a beer in celebration of Phil's return to life. Neville joined in with a cold bottle of beer, even uncapping one for the former amnesiac.

They sipped beers, watched hockey and with the game in the

second period, the Bruins down three to one, Arthur abruptly injected, "Shoulda never traded Bobby Orr."

Phil leaned across, whispered words into Arthur's ear and for the first time in months, he let out a short guttural laugh. Neville watched his father and Phil content in each other's company. For Neville, his thoughts were elsewhere.

Where had this 'gift' come from?

Yet even as he wondered Phil's words returned; he would tell all he knew before he left. *And when was that?* Neville asked himself. And what of Dell's question? Where did these wishes originate? Three wishes were set in children's fables, stories of witches and goblins. One wish was easy; a shooting star, a wishing well and four-leafed clovers and of course the wishbone of a turkey– superstitions passed on for generations.

Here, the offer came in twos, two chances at redemption– why?

Neville spent the evening watching hockey and anticipating a way through this labyrinth their houseguest posed. Neville faced an issue rarely dreamt let alone lived by men, an angel's perfect offering.

Turning in for the night, he suffered the fate of knowing a partial truth like trying to solve a puzzle absent several key pieces. His brain deliberated over words spoken, the abstract details and of course, those mysterious ever-so magical outcomes. It cluttered the picture, inflating the mystery and like picking at a scab, new blood flowed to form an even larger wound, further muddling the possibilities pouring into his head.

Neville surrendered and sleep came.

The clock's digital display blinked 2:06 a.m.

He heard the gulls cawing. The beach appeared. Beneath the sheets, Neville's legs churned. The sun at noon, a sand pyre climbing near the shore settled into view. The fat man with his passenger, a dark haired, comely young woman laughed as the engine roared, intrigued by the steady rise of an innocent girl into a dulling summer sky.

The blankets tangled in his flailing limbs. Neville moaned a low, *No.* The sky darkened. The gold beach grew dusky grey. Cries wailed from an ever-growing crowd and a new star materialized, brightest in the twilight sky.

Neville called out, *No.* He shot up, a cold sweat draining his face; his legs, his arms snarled in winter covers. He stared into the dark corners of the room, and his heart. His answer came from a dream. Neville threw back his sheets and seconds later, he knocked franticly at Dewey's bedroom door.

"Come in," came the call.

Dewey's room was dark, the nightlight illuminating half Phil, half shadow. Phil saw the strange look on his face and asked, "Are you alright Woody?"

Neville's reply came next. "I know what my two wishes are."

CHAPTER 32

A WARM FRONT ROLLED into southern Minnesota that night providing a reprieve from the blistering winter cold. Temperatures ran above freezing for the first time in two months and with a clear sky, the glaring sun thawed inches of snow. Overlaid with a sloshy ice mix, roads throughout Solomon became a driving maelstrom. Relief would be short lived as a wave of cold air chased in behind the front.

Late Friday morning with Neville at work, Dell debated what show to watch with his two charges when he heard a knock at the front door. Climbing from the recliner, Dell listened to Arthur argue for a replay of last night's Bruins game. Phil, enabled by his newfound linguistic skills, sided with his partner these last weeks.

Taking time from the negotiations, Dell opened the front door to a brown uniformed UPS deliveryman. He held a small parcel in his hands along with a clipboard.

"Package for Arthur Wishwood," he announced. The UPS truck idled in the driveway.

Distracted, Dell yelled back to the living room. "No game… you already saw it."

Dell took the shoebox size parcel. "Sorry."

"Sign here," the UPS man said, shoving the clipboard on top of the box.

Dell signed the name "Arthur Wishwood" and gave back the

clipboard. Staring at the package, he thanked the man and wished him a Merry Christmas.

"Enjoy the holidays," he said and quickly disappeared inside his truck. After a cursory inspection, Dell placed the box on the small table across from the hallway bench along with the rest of the Wishwood mail.

"Well what would you like to watch then Dell?" Phil asked.

"A movie or something else, just not a replay of last night's game. We know they lost four to one," Dell pleaded.

Arthur backed down from his demands and sat, hands folded, on the sofa. Time had once again stymied his train of thought.

"What movie?" Phil asked.

Dell began channel surfing on the cable menu. He came to a list of movies currently available. The Green Mile, a movie based on a Stephen King story, was playing and he switched it on, sat back and tried absorbing the storyline.

His short conversation with Neville had spawned several questions for Phil, yet he was reluctant to engage. He saw Phil in a completely different light as opposed to the ease he felt before with the amnesia riddled Barney Fife replica. Normally a man of few inhibitions, Dell remained wary of this new improved version, a man who by all accounts had performed miracles. Unable to concentrate, he announced the lunch menu as he led out toward the kitchen.

"I'm makin' egg salad sandwiches for lunch. Anyone want more than one."

Arthur turned in Dell's direction. "Egg salad causes cancer," he said in a grim voice.

Phil laughed. "I'll have one Dell, thanks."

"One or two, Artie?" Dell asked, disregarding the complaint.

"Two."

While eating lunch Dell's curiosity overpowered his apprehension and he finally asked, "These wishes, how do they work?"

Arthur listened in, seeming interested but who could know. Phil looked up at Dell seated in the recliner. "Well. Woody made his wishes and I executed them. Simple."

"But how?"

Phil leaned in, closing the space between them. "I manipulate time and circumstance. As much time and as many circumstances as necessary. At midnight tonight, when the end of today converges with tomorrow's beginning, a door between the hours opens and all is possible. In that cusp, Woody's wishes will be realized."

"Diet Pepsi," Arthur bellowed as he finished his first sandwich.

"The witching hour," said Dell spellbound.

"A somewhat crude allusion, but yes," Phil said.

Dell disappeared into the kitchen and returned with Arthur's Diet Pepsi. All the while his brain spun. What were the possibilities within reach? What good could he muster? After a tenuous silence, Dell gave voice to his thoughts. "If I had those wishes I know what I'd want."

"And what would that be, Dell?" Phil asked.

Arthur slurped back pop while Dell continued. "Well, first I'd want a new car for Aunt Claire."

Phil appeared amused by Dell's exuberance. "Yes…"

Dell's keen eyes ballooned as he posed a second request. "And I'd want Glinda, the Good Witch bobble head… to complete my Wizard of Oz collection."

"Nothing too extravagant," Phil noted.

"No, I guess I'm just not the extravagant type," Dell said holding out hope that as Phil's former guardian he might fulfill his wishes. Phil leaned back and began watching The Green Mile in earnest, never indicating either way.

On the sofa next to him, Arthur finished the last of his egg salad sandwiches, took a swallow of Diet Pepsi and followed with a loud belch. That ended the discussion on wishes. All three watched the movie realizing half way through, it was a story based on miracles and lives saved and lives lost.

Early Friday morning Billy Tofflemire received Roland DeWitt's subpoenaed phone records from his service provider. The e-mail attachment numbered eleven pages of calls and twenty-two pages of text messages sent to and by his suspect in the last six months. It took well into that afternoon for the detective to compile a list of numbers Roland called more than once. He cross-referenced the numbers with callers to Roland's cell. From there the detective generated a list of possible accomplices.

He also traced the text messages from Davis Jefferson's laptop, matching them to Roland's record. They were identical to the victim's texts. A long afternoon of diligent police work and Tofflemire had names to match the numbers. It was here he discovered who Roland DeWitt was: the younger son of long-serving Congressional Representative, Gregory DeWitt. And one more prominent name and number, Willis Ogland. Several other names came to light– one David Evers, a Samuel Bennett and of course, Walter Hendry.

Billy checked all the names for possible criminal records and came up empty. He turned to Minn-Scan, the police database, and input a short version of events and the names he had gleaned from Roland's phone records. He hit enter. Nearing five o'clock and quitting time Billy Tofflemire received a hit on the shared network. The name of detective Robert Hoyer, Minnesota State Police appeared at the top of the report.

After reading Hoyer's short but revealing description he gave him a call.

Three o'clock Friday afternoon Sam Charters stood in Hendry's office doorway waving in the staff for their final meeting before the Christmas holidays. Holding several white envelopes in his hand, he smiled and shifted sideways allowing all of the employees into the inner sanctum.

Suzanne sat while the remaining office staff stood behind her chair, hands folded, excited to know their holiday bonus. Neville was especially interested seeing that he was two car payments behind on a vehicle whose best prospects entailed a date with a crusher.

With everyone assembled, Sam took a green hued bottle in hand and poured a favorite cognac into five paper cups lined across the front of his desk. Lifting one cup to each of his staff, he raised his drink. "To absent friends and loved ones."

All eyes shifted to Roland. Unable to maintain eye contact Roland averted the stares. They drank their ration of cognac. Earlier that day he had distributed holiday bonuses to the first floor pressmen. Now Sam slipped behind the desk and leafing through the envelopes read each name, handing out an envelope to each employee and setting two aside, one for Walter and one for Willis. Roland stood, his eyes riveted to the packets on the desk.

"We've had a good year. God willing, next year will be even better," he announced as each ripped open the pay envelope. Hoping for five hundred dollars, Neville peered at the numbers on the check—eighteen hundred dollars, a virtual windfall.

The bonus was the highest ever paid at The Sentinel. Roland stared at the numbers inside his pay packet and felt an awkward sense of disloyalty. He forced a smile knowing the depth of his deceit and the betrayal now set in motion. Conscience slowed his reaction but inside a wave of denial washed over him and as always, he fought the urge to look too closely. He had his reasons. Tomorrow night he would be a rich man. In those few short seconds, he convinced himself that all this was necessary. The end justified the means and the end meant a better life, a life of ease. A life unfettered by his many persecutors.

Sam snapped him out of the haze. "I'll see everyone tonight at La Scala, and bring your appetite." They left the office in a flutter of happy chatter. Neville felt an even deeper sense of gratitude. Since his fated encounter with his nameless houseguest, Neville's entire life had transformed.

In his bedroom, Dewey packed the essentials for a night at his father's while his mother anxiously engaged her sister on the telephone.

"What do I say Megs? It was all a mistake, a… a miscalculation?"

"Rita, tell him the truth," Megan insisted.

"About Spikes?"

"No, of course not. Tell him how you feel now. How you lost

your way for a while. Woody loves you. You owe him the truth." Megan's voice acquired a kinder tone. "Tell him what your heart tells you, that's all."

"Alright, I can do this," a determined Rita said as she brushed a hand down the side of her suede skirt. "The truth…"

"Go have fun. And whatever happens call me tomorrow."

"I will and Megs, thanks for everything."

Rita helped Dewey on with his coat, his knit cap and pulled on her own black overcoat. She had spent most of the day preparing and looked the picture of elegance.

Tonight they would take Rita's four-wheel drive SUV for safety's sake. The break in the weather had lasted into the early afternoon. A severe cold front had moved in and a treacherous ice crust had formed on the roads. With traffic slow, she arrived at Neville's just as Dell's girlfriend traipsed up the snowbound sidewalk. Dewey raced by both women, dragging his backpack.

"You must be Rita," Jennifer said as they stepped onto the porch. Dewey had already disappeared inside.

"And you're Jennifer." They shook hands and exchanged greetings following Dewey's lead into the Wishwood foyer. Neville greeted the two especially happy to see how beautiful his ex-wife looked. As he stared, Jennifer dropped her winter coat on the bench. Brandishing his usual playful smirk, Dell came in from the living room.

"There they are, my two best girls," Dell quipped.

"What about Aunt Claire?" Rita asked.

"Her too."

In the living room, Phil stood while Arthur grinned from his sofa seat as Christmas greetings passed into a crowded front hallway. Dewey held the TV remote in his hands and began negotiations for his choice of programing. No one seemed interested in negotiating so he changed the channel.

Jennifer saw the fully recovered Phil and yanked Dell aside. "He's okay," she said staring. "Last night he had a broken finger– his face was a mess."

"Yeah, Phil has tremendous recuperative powers. I'll tell you about it later."

Neville stood dressed in his finest suit– a dark blue pin striped. After pulling on his overcoat, he guided Rita toward the front door and took the SUV's keys. A growing cold leaked in through the door. As they said their goodnights, Dell pulled him back.

"Now don't do anything I wouldn't do," he warned.

"That still leaves quite a wide birth," Neville said.

Dell let go. "Have fun, and don't worry," he added with a wink.

"I will, Dad."

Rita and Neville left for the Sentinel Christmas party. A quiet ride ensued with both feeling their way through this first date in two years. Small talk involved a common interest: Dewey. Arriving at La Scala, they checked their coats and headed into the main dining area. The newspaper's owner, Carter Ellison stood near the entrance. "So how's our newest feature reporter tonight?" he asked.

Carter knew vaguely who Neville was. Rita's blue eyes proudly peered up.

Neville pulled Rita closer. "It doesn't get any better than this, Mr. Ellison."

They quickly made the trek into the restaurant. The main room itself was scattered with dozens of dining tables clad in festive red linen with each round table centering a poinsettia sprouting from a sculpted white vase. With the room quickly filling up, Neville spotted Sam and John across the hall. Rita drew Neville closer. "The promotion, you didn't tell me... congratulations."

Neville grinned. "Things just seem to be going my way lately."

At the table, Neville introduced his ex-wife to Sam, Sam's wife Paulette and John Winterburn. Although they had met Rita years ago, both his coworkers knew of their recent struggles and warmly greeted Rita as part of the Sentinel family. Neville surveyed the room. Roland sat along the wall two tables away drinking, engaging one of the Sentinel's primary advertisers in animated conversation.

"So how's the world's newest novelist on this night of nights,"

Sam started as they seated themselves. Neville refocused his attention on his table and once again, Rita gave him a vacant but interested stare.

"We couldn't be better," he said absorbed in Rita's blue eyes.

"Novelist you say," Rita returned.

In the dimly lit corner of the room Sam leaned in and recounted Neville's first novel and how it found a place in an editor's hands. With every word, her interest grew and swelled with newfound pride for her former husband.

The room buzzed with holiday energy. The tables continued to fill with honored guests, advertisers, employees and the political realm of southern Minnesota. Neville took leave and headed for the bar. There he encountered Roland waiting in line for a drink. Roland glanced behind Neville toward the table and Rita. "Coming up in the world aren't we Wishy."

"What?"

Having forgotten meeting Rita years ago, Roland pointed. "The girl, she's a beauty."

Neville flashed a grin. "She is, isn't she."

"Where's your friend? What *was* his name, Dill… Dull? The shrimp boat captain there," Roland quipped. His words came out slurred.

"He's gainfully employed at the moment."

Roland picked up his drink from the bar, returned a smirk and proceeded back to his table. Neville took his drinks and on his return stopped at a table nearby and spoke with the first floor press operators, all seated together with their wives. Moving on he ran into Suzanne and her husband Allan, who promptly picked up to join Neville at their table. Next to them, he said his hellos to three Minnesota hockey alumni, now doing the television play by play for the university.

At the table, he set down Rita's drink and joined in on the conversation. John was standing, taking a call from his wife in Phoenix and the rest were happily engaged in what a Christmas party should be: good food, good fun, good friends and a celebration in the spirit of new beginnings. Except for the birth of their son Dewey, Neville's night and his cherished time with Rita, had become the highlight in his young life.

The pizza truck backed out from the Wishwood driveway while inside Dell placed two boxes on the kitchen table and a crowd gathered. He lifted the lids and like a swarm of feasting vultures, a blur of hands attacked the food as if fearing it might leap away.

"Slow down!" Dell yapped. "Don't you people ever eat? It's like you've been locked in a closet for a month."

"Come on honey it's Christmas... enjoy," Jennifer said laughing.

All went quiet save for the hungry growls and snorts around the kitchen table. Dewey knelt on a chair each hand holding a wedge while Phil and Arthur vied for the same slice. Dell pushed his way past Jenny, grabbed several slices and backed out of the ravenous circle.

In less than twenty minutes, all that remained of their pre-Christmas meal were fragments of crusts, meat scraps and molten cheese wads stuck to the cardboard boxes. Returning to the living room, they arranged themselves in front of the television for a night of entertainment. Jennifer was first to start. "What a beautiful tree, so full and brilliantly decorated, and that angel... I've never seen one so bright, so alive."

The angel atop the Wishwood tree was indeed very different as it mimicked a star lit seraph in flight, much like the one flying above St. Gabriel's Square. All eyes studied Jennifer's observation.

"I helped decorate the tree," Dewey said as Dell clicked on the TV.

"Yes, there's something about the ambience that brings angels to life here at the Wishwood house," Dell added. Phil's knowing glance found Dell.

The conversation meandered to what to watch. Dewey, a big Iron Man fan, wanted the latest installment, while Dell and Jennifer opted for a more romantic choice. Phil and Arthur had no preference, so Dell, wanting to placate his nephew, found a rather agreeable alternative.

Leaning forward from his place on the loveseat, Dell waved Dewey over.

"I think it's close enough to Christmas," he whispered, curling an arm around Dewey.

"Close enough for what?" Dewey asked.

"Close enough for your Christmas present," he announced. Dell promptly stood and guided his nephew through the living room, into the foyer. He reached into his jacket and pulled out a small red and green wrapped box, handing it to Dewey.

Dewey fondled the present. "Can I open it?"

"Of course."

He ripped the wrapping off his uncle's present in front of everyone. All watched a little boy's excitement opening his first Christmas gift of the season. He let out a sudden shriek, "Wow... it's an i-Pod. Thanks Unca Dell."

Dell brushed a hand through Dewey's blonde hair. "You're very welcome, Dews. Merry Christmas."

Within seconds, Dewey had the box apart plugging the ear buds into his ears. Dell gave him a quick tutorial on how it worked. Dewey listened for the first song to play, his hand clutching the i-Pod with covetous pride. The Beatles, "Lucy In The Sky With Diamonds" played as he wriggled to the beat.

As they settled in to watch a movie, Jennifer glared. "What about my present?"

"Yours? Is it your birthday?" Dell held his serious demeanor for a short few seconds, but after Jenny bashed him with a sofa pillow, he relented. "It's upstairs... but not until Christmas dear."

In a sudden start, Arthur blurted out, "Angel's wings are made of cheese."

A silence followed.

Dell broke the impasse. "That's the moon, Artie. The moon's made of green cheese."

"Oh..."

Inside the Wishwood home on a cold Minnesota night, they watched movies into the late hours while Dewey sat occupied with his i-Pod. That night Phil remained especially quiet, listening, laughing at times but mum on all fronts. For him, it seemed a time of reflection.

The Sentinel's gala event continued flawlessly. The meal was magnificent, the after dinner speeches by the mayor of Solomon, Hilary Watkins, the Sentinel owner, Carter Ellison and of course the acting editor, Sam Charters were all short tributes to the coming holidays and to greater success in the coming year. Sam added a touching reference to John Winterburn's departure and Neville's subsequent promotion to which the attending guests gave a rousing ovation.

All was going well but for one omission– any mention of Willis Ogland. On this night of celebration one face remained absent from the Sentinel family portrait, one meal went unserved. With the DJ playing a selection of soft pop songs, Roland sat swilling back a vodka cooler. He sat alone, brazenly checking Davis's i-Phone, the numbered accounts now tracked and targeted by the Yo-Yo. Twenty-one accounts aligned in a column on the phone's screen. Roland clicked off and slipped the phone inside his jacket. His mind wandered back to Willis, not thinking of the man himself, but the pleasure of his body. Enamored by desire, Roland's mind clicked. A week without sex, he thought. An eternity for a sexual being such as himself and musing, he returned to the club he visited with Willis and the prospects available.

With the night's presentations all but done, Roland planted his empty glass on the table and set out for a new adventure. He left the party in an aimless search for the pleasures of the flesh. Yes, Willis was indeed remembered but for all the wrong reasons.

Several tables down, Rita cuddled closer to Neville as she shared the night's high spirits with new friends and rediscovered the man she had senselessly tossed aside. Rita could not have been happier and Neville, laughing by her side, held her hand firmly in his reveling in the way the entire night had played out. They fit– perfectly.

Although eclectic and somewhat mundane, the music made for easy dancing and Rita joined Neville on the floor. They lost themselves in a sinuous sway of couples and yet they found something else, something irresistible– each other. A dull gold light flickered in the sway of bodies. As they danced on the dusky floor, the gilded light set a glow about Rita's goddess white features. To him she *was* that goddess.

Affected by the beat, Rita nuzzled nearer feeling the warmth of his neck, the power in his shoulders as he pulled her closer yet. Intoxicated she whispered, "I missed you."

Overwhelmed by a need to see Rita's blue eyes, Neville inclined his head. The dance floor, the couples shuffling nearby, the room itself disintegrated leaving Neville alone in a world where only Rita existed. "I never stopped loving you…never."

For them the party was over.

There was no talk of Dewey on this drive. Rita's hands flirted, massaging warmth and love into Neville's arm while Neville cautiously drove the icy roads. He swiveled back and forth to watch her eyes, her mouth as she spoke the words he had longed so to hear.

An unmistakable magic entered, bonding both by a love once lost, now rekindled. A magic not created by miracles but by the human spirit. Arriving at Rita's home, she led her ex-husband inside. "Drink, Woody?"

"Sure…" His eyes followed her every move.

With the lights set low, the Christmas tree glistened from an angel's glow above. Starlight leaked its way into the living room. Rita returned with Neville's beer and a glass of wine for herself. Tucking a leg beneath her, she nestled in next to Neville. As he sipped his beer, Rita averted his direct gaze pulling away.

"What's wrong?"

She placed her glass on the coffee table. "I have to say it…" she started.

"Say what?"

"I-I pushed you away Woody…"

Neville's head wagged sideways. "You don't. You don't have to explain anything." He pressed two fingers to her lips, halting her confession.

Neville smiled, his hand reached across lifting her downcast chin, caressing her perfect porcelain cheeks with gentle fingers. "I want to be the hero in your life Rita, the hero in our little Dewey's life. I want to be the husband you deserve… always."

With eyes glistening, Rita took her ex-husband's hand and held it. "You always were. I just wasn't smart enough to see it."

For the first time in years, Neville did what he had ached so mightily to do and lost himself in her arms, her precious lips. Rita was the drug Neville needed and he wanted all of her. Guiding her from the sofa, Neville led Rita down the dark hallway and toward the bedroom. Rita disappeared into shadows. He heard the sound of a zipper and worked quickly to relieve himself of his own clothes.

Their marital bedroom seemed transformed from the days Neville knew it. That night twilight shadows altered the room in some mysterious way. His eyes adjusted, following Rita's silhouette shifting through the darkened space, her shimmering blue eyes his only focus. Naked in the dark, they met at the bed and passion took over.

In darkness, Neville and Rita made love as if for the first time, and found a passion neither considered possible before that day. In their loving, they joined as the couple they once thought they could be, would be. Unafraid, bold in offering they each accepted what the other posed.

Their first round of lovemaking ignited a spark in Rita, indefinable, rapturous. Was it love or mere physical release?

That night after a second passionate coupling, Rita realized the love she had forsaken. And for what? Desire or foolish pride, or was it just an illusory vision of love. Pain seared her heart and she confessed a truth untold until now. Ashamed, Rita cried tears Neville could never comprehend and held him closer than flesh on bone.

Tears slowed and cradled in each other's arms they fell asleep.

While Rita slept, Neville stirred. His eyes fluttered involuntarily beneath shut lids. A hum grew inside his head, his back spasmed. Dizziness overwhelmed Neville.

Across the frozen streets of Solomon, Arthur Wishwood slept soundly in his bed. A buzzing began inside his head and his back flexed violently. Eyes quivered beneath closed lids and suddenly awake a vicious nausea gripped Arthur.

Midnight, the witching hour had arrived.

CHAPTER 33

PHIL'S PROMISE, HIS immutable power takes flight and time begins to spin a miraculous track. Time, the one entity that buries paupers and princes alike. In its wake, time creates dual perspectives, transforming heroes to fops and fops to heroes. Time crushes kings and kingdoms. Time makes great men greater and wise men wiser. Time heals and time erodes; our universal constant to which we comply yet sense it as a living breathing chronometer made and used solely for us in our little lives. It seals the fate of the unjust and administers immortal judgment. Time, more than any other dynamic, directs history to speak eternal truth.

A fluid source, time washes over all that was ever born or built and beyond, unbridled by boundaries. Wielded by one all-knowing power, time is the true master of what has been and what will be. Taking shape between these precious spaces of all-powerful seconds, time enters into the fourth dimension of existence, into bold faith and the unseen realm of one almighty dominion.

Time becomes the leveler.

High above Solomon, a pledge made that day began unfolding in brilliant white. A web of luminal spines arced east, a bridge through time and space. Winds descended, inundating the lands and treasured time stood still.

With our earthly clock paused, passive minutes began a rewind hurtling back. Through hours, months, years, a whirling black-white kaleidoscope of day-night spins a maddening path to a familiar place, and time. So repealed, time stopped. Bishop's Bay, Arthur Wishwood's place of birth came into view before procreation. And as his parents conceived a child one circumstance changed, an enzyme previously missing, a chemical addition within his more than five billion chemical characteristics altered his profile reorienting his physical makeup. Neville's first wish altered Arthur Wishwood's life from its very conception.

Arthur grew unchanged from his first trip through time and as the days spun forward time slowed to a second interval, restarting on a sunny day in August, where Arthur's son, Neville patrolled the beaches of Bishop's Bay. Tourists frolicked in rolling ocean surf. The day remained as it was.

August fifth, eleven years in the past and the day preceding Neville's fateful encounter, it all begins again with one change. Jennifer Capaldi's father, Anthony makes the decision to leave work early that day and travel upstate to retrieve his son, the flu-sick younger brother of Jennifer. Staying at a summer camp, the counselors are afraid of outbreak and Anthony drives the three-hour trip, returning home well before Jennifer's bedtime.

Unlike Anthony's first foray when he waited until after work, he arrives home early with his sick son. Under these new circumstances and home early, Jennifer's brother has time to mingle with his older sister. She teases him for abandoning camp and a sick Tony Jr. wrestled his older sister that night. The result– Jennifer Capaldi becomes infected.

August sixth, the morning after, Jennifer is too sick to join friends at the beach. As Neville's day wears on, he stands atop the lifeguard platform glassing the beaches of Bishop's Bay. Without the distraction of Jennifer Capaldi, he continued to monitor the play of children along the shore, the swimmers out further and the general hubbub of activity by an invading tourist horde.

A radio played an old Bachman Turner Overdrive song and as it rang out across the beach, he spied something, a girl's arm flailing behind a large man holding two oversize inner tubes. Beside the girl, he could see another young girl, miming a silent scream as yet another wave crashed against her frail frame.

Neville dropped the glasses and leapt from the tower. As he raced through the crowd, the noise quelled, the radio stopped and all eyes followed his lithe young body sprint toward the water's edge. He dove in gliding past swimmers near shore and in mere heartbeats swam past the man holding the two inner tubes. The girl was under and he dove down where the water ran well overhead. Air bubbles led him to the spot and a terrified young face. Her fish eyes gleamed like polished black beads, her legs and arms flailed franticly. He reached down, curled an arm around her and as she kicked Neville pushed up, up toward the surface, the surface and safety. Holding her head above the waves, he swam for shore while behind him the fat man took hold of the girl's friend and led her in.

On the beach, Neville spread her limp body across the sand and with trained hands, cleared her mouth and began compressions. Water seeped from her pale lips. Neville pointed into the crowd amassing and ordered, "Call 911."

Little Lily Delysle wasn't breathing so he cocked her head and did the job for her. Her mother sat near the young girl's shoulder clutching her sundress with two terrified hands. Neville returned to compressions and suddenly a sputter sounded. Water eked from bloodless lips, Lily coughed a living cough and her wonky eyes opened. The crowd jabbered and Lily's mother shrieked and suddenly wept. The frightened little girl looked up at strange yet happy faces. Startled, her eyes searched to find her mother and when she did, she cried. Neville leaned back and his heart rate ramped down. The crowded beach exploded in delight and Neville felt hands patting his back, congratulations at a job well done. His eyes met Lily's mother still streaming tears of joy and as she held tightly to her daughter, she mimed a heartfelt *Thank you*.

The beach mob parted as Neville lifted from the sand. Skyward, the ever-present gulls cawed as if following the drama. He trekked back to his post on the tower. In his restructured past, the ghost of little Lily Delysle remained the only casualty that day.

Time spun forward, returning to whence it came. For Neville his eyes adjusted, the bedroom reappeared and next to him laid Rita, a perfect picture of contentment. His memories, this impossible rescue of Lily Delysle had changed his view of that past event, yet one part of his psyche held onto the original tragedy, and his pain. It was like a shadow cast against a missing wall, an echo of words never spoken. The dichotomy left Neville emotionally drained and he curled in next to his love, closed his eyes and he found sleep once again.

Arthur's world realigned his eyes popped open filled with a new overwhelming sensation. The physical changes of rebirth had nullified the white mucus that had clogged his brain. The years lost under the spell focused into view. The missing days collected replacing the jumble of disjointed facts and actions. Arthur Wishwood came alive, a broken man reconstructed. Sacrifices made on his behalf collected within and humbled by his loved ones loyalty, silently vowed to repay their compassion.

Gathering himself inside the unlit room, he slid from his bed and found the house quiet, dark, the only light a reflection from stars gleaming off the tinsel of the Christmas tree. On the sofa, Dell his primary caretaker lay asleep.

"Dell," he called. Dell rolled on his side and squinted against the dull light. A shadowy stooped figure stood alongside him.

"Artie?" Dell pulled himself upright. "Are you alright?"

"What day is it?"

Dell checked his watch. The time read two-fifty a.m. "It's early Christmas Eve."

Arthur surveyed his newly revealed world. "I'm back Dell."

Neville's sluggish eyes opened to the bedroom set in morning light. The clock on Rita's side table read 7:17 a.m. A smile emerged as he spied Rita cuddled next to him. He felt changed, a strong sense of redemption flooded in. Then he remembered: the beach and Lily Delysle, alive as he had wished. A new thought quickly came: his second wish, a cure for his father's condition. What of his father? Neville dressed hurriedly, rousing Rita. Still half-asleep, she turned and asked, "Where you going Woody?"

"I have to check on something. Go back to sleep, I won't be long." With a quick kiss, he grazed a hand across her tussled red hair. Rita turned away, wrapped herself in the blankets and fell back asleep.

The sun rose as a ruddy haze along the eastern sky. From the north, a grey formless mass advanced. A winter storm was heading in. Traffic remained light as he arrived home. Rushing in the front door, Neville ran past the foyer. The living room lights were on and Dell lay stretched across the sofa. He sat up and reached for his coffee mug. "How'd your night go?"

"Great, couldn't be better," Neville said. Something about Dell's manner struck him; his all too easy demeanor, his lack of enthusiasm. "Dad, is he okay? Did it work?"

"Oh, it worked. We've been up all night."

Dell's response seemed odd. "What's wrong, why the long face?"

"He woke me up after two and I could see from his first words the wish had worked. We sat up for hours laughing at all the crazy things he'd done and said. Just catching up on all the news. That's when he found the package."

"The package? What package?"

"It came yesterday by UPS… addressed to him. He opened it and everything changed."

Disturbed by Dell's cryptic retelling, Neville took a seat beside him on the sofa. "Well, what was it?"

Dell swallowed, and pointed toward the hallway. "You'd better see for yourself Woody."

Neville followed Dell's direction and found his father sitting sideways on his bed, an open box next to him. In his hands, he held a letter, a letter that continued to occupy his attention. Neville sat next to him on the bed.

"Dad…"

Arthur turned and gave his son a labored smile. Tears tracked his cheeks.

"Are you okay?" Neville asked.

Arthur handed his son the letter. Neville took it and read:

Dear Mr. Wishwood,

It is our sad duty to inform you that on December 3rd of this year Angela Wishwood passed away at our medical facility here in Clearwater, Florida. She died from complications of lupus, a disease she battled these last nine years. We at the Haimes Institute offer out heartfelt condolences, knowing that her spirit, her steadfast determination and kindness was indeed a blessing to everyone here. She will be missed greatly.

Although she suffered from this terrible disease, Angela went out of her way to incorporate a sense of compassion and perseverance. During periods of remission, she worked tirelessly on behalf of both her fellow patients and our staff. She served selflessly these past several years instilling an unflagging faith and courage into all she encountered. Right up until her death, she maintained that same faith and courage. We here at Haimes considered Angela a Godsend.

In accordance with her wishes, she asked her remains be donated to the Haimes Clinic for further research on the disease of lupus. Attached is a copy of the signed consent form. Her few belongings accompany this letter.

Again, we extend our condolences and hope that in knowing the tremendous good she accomplished you may find a semblance of comfort in your loss.

Respectfully yours,

A.J. McKinnon,

Haimes Institute,

Clearwater, Florida.

Tears came.

Neville knew little of his mother. What he did know was that his father loved her. Now she was gone. Sitting silent, the irony was certainly not lost on Neville. Given Arthur's miraculous recovery, the full weight of this tremendous loss hit him like a hammer blow. That same heavy hammer that broke the chains of bondage crushed a hopeful heart. Arthur Wishwood never stopped loving his wife, never divorced her and always hoped for her return. With Angela's death died a dream.

Neville placed the letter back in his father's hands and embraced the man who until this day kept the promise he made a little boy, that he would shed no tears for the woman who abandoned them. That promise now seemed mute.

Arthur finally spoke. "I-I loved her… always," he stuttered. Neville understood that all too well knowing his own unfaltering love of Rita. As always, Neville remained his father's son.

"I know dad."

He embraced the father he loved, a man saved and now whole. In time, a sense of gratitude would return even with their loss. Neville picked up the small box and found what little remained of a life lived, his mother's past. He pulled out a wallet containing forty-four dollars, receipts and a Florida driver's license with a picture of an older version of his faint memory of her. She looked well in the photo.

Deeper inside he uncovered older pictures and one very special memory; a wrinkled snapshot of his mother standing next to a five-year-old Neville at a backyard barbeque both wearing wide grins pointing toward the picture-taker, Arthur. Neville remembered the day and that contented time in his life.

Next, he found a small black book, the title embossed in gold leaf: Twenty-Four Hours a Day and as he leafed through the pages, notations in his mother's hand scribbled in the margins. He set the book aside. The last discovery was a bronze hued coin, a medallion and on its front face was the number '1' stamped inside a triangle. Engraved on the backside was an adage: *Success is Living Each Day Courageously.* As he stared at the scribed words, a sense of loss overcame him. Neville cupped the medallion and slipped it into his pocket.

This was the extent of his mother possessions. Neville placed the remaining mementos inside the box recalling his conversation with her; the impossible call from his mother made just last week and he realized the miracle. Neville put aside the box. "Are you going to be okay Dad?"

Arthur nodded. "I'll be alright. I just need some sleep son." He wiped tears from his swollen eyes.

"Do you remember being sick?"

Arthur looked to his son. "All of it, and I remember how good you, Dell, even Dewey were during these last few years, but…"

"But what?"

"It's like a dream now, a terrible nightmare."

Neville gave his father one last embrace. "Get some sleep. You'll feel better after a rest."

Arthur pulled back the sheets and did as Neville suggested. He slipped under the covers while his son shut the light off. Closing the door Neville stared off into space and wondered of his mother's life. What had happened?

He made his way into the living room. "Is he okay?" Dell asked.

"He will be… he just needs some sleep. And so do you. Go to bed Dell."

Dell lurched to his feet and limped toward the front door. "It's been… interesting," he said giving his best friend a high-five handgrip.

"Get some sleep and Dell… thanks for everything."

Dell gave a short bow and slipped out the front door. With Phil and Dewey still asleep, the Wishwood home was quiet and he thought of time and its miraculous healing effect. In a space of twenty-four hours, his life had completely changed and he had one man to thank for it all. Still he had questions and as he showered, answers continued to remain elusive.

Rita awoke nearing nine o'clock. She had fallen back asleep after Neville's quick departure and slept a most peaceful sleep. Her arms stretched to the ceiling as if to grasp a piece of heaven and her lips twisted to a sly smirk. Rita had become the temptress in Neville's life once again. She yawned and sat up alive with new energy. In those first waking moments, she felt an overwhelming compulsion to dance. To dance and shout to the world, she was in love again and how wonderful it was.

Christmas Eve and Rita's world was alive with all the possibilities only love could provide. She flipped off the covers and approached the vanity naked. Light spiked in through curtain breaches reshaping the room from ambiguous night. A cloud of red hair draped her freckled shoulders, her skin glistened white and pure, glowing warm from an active night.

She spied Neville's t-shirt. In his hurry, he had left it behind. Rita picked up the shirt and held it. As if compelled, she slipped Neville's shirt over her shoulders, modeling it before the vanity mirror. A thought of Megan, her sister popped in and how right she had been. In that moment, she needed to call her.

Rita slipped on a pair of pajama pants, wrapped a sweater around her and sped off into the living room. As she reached for the phone, it suddenly rang. A phone number appeared on the screen; long distance. She hesitated, checked again. Long distance, no doubt. She picked up the receiver.

"Hello."

"Mrs. Wishwood?" the woman caller asked.

"Yes."

"Mrs. Wishwood, would Neville be there?"

Rita sat confused. How could anyone know Neville had been there last night? "He's out right now… can I take a message?"

"Of course. Tell Neville that Janet Delysle from Random House called. Ask if he could possibly call me back. It's important. My number here is…"

"It's on the phone, Ms. Delysle."

"Great, I'm sure he'll be thrilled to hear from me."

"Ms. Delysle, can I ask how you know Neville?"

A short silence ensued. "Janet Delysle, Lily Delysle's mother… from Boston."

The woman's response further confused Rita. "I'm sorry, I still don't quite understand."

"Bishop's Bay, the swimming incident…"

"Bishop's Bay, yes… where Neville grew up," Rita added.

"Mrs. Wishwood, did Neville ever tell you anything about my daughter Lily?"

The sound of her question worried Rita, as if some new skeleton could emerge from Neville's past. "No, not that I can recall."

Janet Delysle went into the near mythic retelling of Neville's heroic actions on that day in Bishop's Bay eleven years ago. How he saved her daughter Lily from drowning that hot summer day, the sixth of August; how at this moment in time, as an acquisitions editor for a major publishing company, she found herself in a position to repay Neville. That, coupled with the fact she loved his manuscript sent along by another client of hers, Sam Charters.

Having only Neville's old phone number, Sam passed it on to his editor, Janet Delysle and thus the reason for the call. Janet relayed the happy news that her daughter Lily had grown to be a beautiful young woman now in her senior year at Boston College, all made possible by Neville's actions that summer day in Bishops' Bay.

Rita listened, yet struggled to comprehend the cycle of events. Her ex-husband would soon become an author published by a woman, whose daughter he had saved working the beaches of his hometown as a lifeguard. After hearing Janet Delysle gush about Neville's unpretentious nature that life-altering day, she sat stunned. Why had he never mentioned such a courageous act? Rita said her goodbyes and thanked Janet Delysle for her interest in Neville's manuscript.

After Dewey's late night, he slept well into the morning. As for Phil, he made his Christmas Eve appearance shortly after eleven a.m. He met with Neville in the kitchen.

"Tea, I need a cup of tea," he said yawning. Phil was dressed in the beige shirt and slacks purchased by Dell. He filled the kettle and set it on the stove to boil.

As he drank his own cup of coffee, Neville watched him shuffle about the kitchen. "They came true, both my wishes came true Phil. And I had the best night of my life. I have you to thank for that."

"Of course…it's what I promised."

"Yes it all happened yet it feels a little funny… having both versions stuck in my head. It's confusing."

Phil leaned against the counter, dropped a tea bag in the cup and waited for hot water. "Not to worry, that won't last long."

"What's that mean?"

"The effects, they change in time," Phil started. "Two weeks from now you, your father, Dell… you'll still be talking about me and all that happened. But the details will have already begun to fade. Six months from now, everything that transpired, who I am, what I was, will all be purged from your memories. What *will* last is what you wished for Woody and only those outcomes. In your world, you will always have saved little Lily; and Arthur? Arthur will never have been sick. That's how it works, the way it's always worked. It's the very nature of miracles."

Neville listened spellbound. Questions circled inside as he watched Phil pour hot water for his tea. His expression took a dour turn. "You knew about my mother didn't you?"

Stirring his brew, Phil glanced back at Neville. "I did, but not while I was sick. The amnesia I experienced was real."

"If I had known about her…"

Phil raised a hand, halting Neville's speculation. "Your wishes couldn't help her Woody."

His head cocked, uncertain. "Why?"

"Why? Because she already turned down that option."

Phil prepared his tea and sat across from Neville sipping from the cup's edge. Neville waited, arching his back uncomfortably, trying to make sense of Phil's explanation.

"And what's that mean?"

Phil folded his hands atop the table and faced his benefactor. "I said I would tell you all I know before leaving. This is it. Your mother had every opportunity to save herself Woody. She chose not to."

"But why, why would she refuse?"

"She made a choice. You see, Dell's musing about the nature of wishes wasn't that far off. Initially there *were* three wishes... they were your mother's. She made just one. She wished to transfer her last two wishes to her son, the son she abandoned. She knew she was dying, but she chose you Woody...you above life."

CHAPTER 34

NOTHING UNDER THE sun; not the reincarnation of Elvis or a landing by Martians in Solomon's St. Gabriel's Square could have shocked Neville any more than what Phil revealed that Christmas Eve. He steadied himself against the table and stared in stunned silence.

A conflict raged inside pitting Neville's early beliefs against the shocking news just shared by this supposed angel. Like factions in a civil war, the sides were set. On one hand, he had a woman who had left him as a child. On the other, the father who had stayed to raise him, love him.

Phil's revelation added a new dimensions to the mother he had demonized for years. Neville pondered his schizophrenic portrait of Angela Wishwood for several minutes and in the end realized that loving his mother, having compassion for her was never a betrayal of his father. Forgiveness came in recognizing the humanness in the flawed actions of a young mother and wife. Angela Wishwood's death provided the prism through which Neville could see her as human.

"She did that for me?"

"Yes… and that's why I'm here, because of my connection."

"You, what's your connection here?"

Phil took a sip of tea. "Well, we're almost brothers."

Neville's brow furrowed trying to imagine the possibilities. "How's that?"

Smiling, Phil lifted from his chair. "Wait here."

He disappeared down the hall and returned with the Acme camera, his only possession. Standing next to a seated Neville, he showed him that one picture of an older woman on the camera screen. "Remember her?"

Neville studied the frame sensing a recognition of sorts. "She does look familiar."

Phil clicked open the back of the camera, made an adjustment and clicked it closed offering Neville another picture from the past.

"That's Sharon!" he squealed. "Sharon Thurber and her little boy... the one hit by the car. I remember that picture!"

"I'm that little boy, Sharon's son Isaac. See, we *are* almost brothers."

Neville recognized the stranger in the hospital bed weeks before but failed to make the connection. Phil did resemble Barney Fife as Dell suggested, but Neville's memory connected the stranger with the likeness of Isaac from Sharon's old photo.

"But how, how..." Neville started.

Phil sat down as Neville retraced his past and the woman who helped raise him those many years ago. Sharon Thurber, the mother Neville never had.

"She loved you too Woody, she still does."

"And you, your spirit, you're...Isaac?"

"That's the reason I was enlisted to help." Phil placed the camera on the table and continued. "This world, the people in it and every part of life is connected in some way Woody. What keeps it together is a power much grander than the sum of its parts here. We can't see it, we can't touch it but it's there. Always has, always will be."

"Is that... God?"

"I know nothing of God, or angels. What I do know... death isn't what determines our lives. It's what we create here that matters."

Isaac picked up his tea, the camera and stood. "It's my time to go, Woody. There's a bus leaving Solomon early Christmas Day... I'll be on it."

"My mother... how did she get these wishes?"

Phil stopped by the doorway. "That I don't know. My part was to offer you the gift. Her love sent me here, so someone loved her… loved her enough to merit a miracle."

Turning back once again Phil flashed a strange smile. "I might not see Dell… tell him to check his e-mail. And when you see Aunt Claire, tell her she's welcome." He left Neville in the kitchen, pondering this newest puzzle.

Shortly after, Dewey wandered into the kitchen half-asleep. Neville sat, still digesting Phil's disclosures and with it, his entire belief system flipped upside down. He saw his life in a completely different light. The woman long thought to be the villain had gifted him a new chance at happiness. Her love had made whole the lives of a son and a father.

Dewey ate breakfast, dressed and after Neville pulled on his varsity jacket both headed back to join Rita. The winter squall arrived in Solomon with the start of the predicted snowfall. Solomon's two yellow snow ploughs lumbered through the streets while privateers in winter-fitted trucks cleared parking lots and private drives. The roads, now teeming with last minute shoppers, remained a concern and Neville took his time reaching his former home.

Rita greeted her son like a lost kidnap victim, bending, embracing him in both arms and planting a messy kiss on his cheek. Neville followed in, much more accepting of Rita's amorous assault. Dewey discarded his winter gear and pulled the i-Pod from his backpack. "Look mom, Unca Dell gave me an i-Pod for Christmas."

Rita studied the gift. "That Uncle Dell, he sure knows what works for you, doesn't he."

"Yeah…" Dewey said plugging the ear buds in. He wandered off toward his bedroom, backpack in tow. Rita led her ex into the dining room, sat him at the table studying his every move with cagy eyes.

"What?"

"Why didn't you ever tell me about Lily Delysle?"

Neville looked away.

"Woody… why?" she asked again.

"It happened so long ago, I guess I forgot." Lost as to how Rita could know of Lily, he asked, "Who told you about that?"

Rita went on to recount the telephone conversation with Janet Delysle and her retelling of that fortuitous day in Bishop's Bay. Her words helped Neville understand the lives this wish had altered. His motive was initially selfish, yet his actions that day were still his and he did not fail in his duty. Without the distraction of Jennifer Capaldi, Neville acted as he would have, bravely without concern for himself.

As the conversation continued, Neville confided the passing of his mother and the effect it had on Arthur. Rita knew of Neville's long lost mother and how little a part she had played in his life. Yet she was still Neville's mother. Rita wrapped her arms around his shoulders in comfort. Neville kept the actual details to himself, finding many aspects difficult to comprehend.

With Dewey busy adjusting and readjusting his i-Pod Rita sat consoling her ex-husband. In a heartfelt attempt to cheer up Neville, Rita announced, "We're going out and I'm buying your Christmas present. Maybe that'll help."

"Okay, but you have to let me do the same," Neville said.

As they climbed into Rita's SUV for a late shopping expedition, Christmas Eve found the Wishwood family happily intact.

Early Christmas Eve, Hoyer stood behind Billy Tofflemire as he buzzed Roland DeWitt's apartment. After an informative conversation the night before, both men readied for a frontal attack. Their plan involved picking up Roland DeWitt to begin the interrogations on the Davis Jefferson murder and the disappearance of Willis Ogland.

After comparing notes, the detectives realized the similarities and relied on experience, intuition and the evidence. It all led back to only one suspect, Roland DeWitt. The investigation also highlighted one very sticky point. Roland was the son of a seated congressional representative and they needed to use kid gloves at least in these initial stages.

They waited. No answer.

Ten floors up, Roland heard the buzz and still in bed, he rolled to his side. He lifted his legs and swung them over the side. Leaning forward, elbows on knees, Roland held his throbbing head. The intercom buzzed again. From across the bed a voice mumbled, "Who's that?"

Roland had given in to prurient nature and his bed partner, a young man Roland picked up in a bar, turned to his side and stared squinting into the light of a new day. "I'll see..." Roland said.

Naked, Roland staggered to the intercom. "Who is it?"

"Minneapolis Police, we'd like to speak with Roland DeWitt."

The pounding inside Roland's head tripled and he stood paralyzed. One look behind exposed a night of debauchery; empty vodka bottles, an ashtray brimming with butts, clothes strewn across the furniture and his bedroom occupied. "Just a minute!"

Roland ran back to the bedroom, jostled his sleeping bed partner yanking his arm. "You've got to get out... now!"

The young man flopped limply back onto the bed. Roland gathered the man's clothes and tossed them onto his prone form. "What's the rush?" he murmured. "Don't you like me today?"

Roland pulled his pants on, charged back to the bed and grabbed the young man by the shoulders. "The police are here. I don't need them finding you in my bed!"

Roland's newest lover sat up and began dressing. Roland helped him to his feet, rushed him through the living room, opened the door and shoved him into the hallway. He threw his remaining clothes out with him.

His latest lover peered back in disbelief. "What the fuck, Rolly?"

"Take the stairs..." Roland shouted. Dazed, the young man dressed as he headed for the hallway door. Roland slammed the door shut and buzzed up the two detectives. Minutes later, he heard a knock. His shaking hands pressed his hair into place, hurriedly buttoned his shirt, took a deep breath and opened the door.

The two detectives walked in and introduced themselves. As his hands continued to smooth rumpled clothes, Roland recognized Detective Hoyer. Standing in the foyer, the detectives got down to business.

"We'd like to ask you a few questions Mr. DeWitt," Tofflemire said.

"Sure, what about?"

Hoyer followed. "Not here, down at the State Police offices. It's about Willis Ogland."

Roland's eyes darted around the room. His first thoughts centered on Davis's phone, his trophy still in his coat pocket. They can't find that, he told himself. His heart rate skipped to triple digits. He needed to find a way to stall and get rid of the phone.

"Alright, I'll get my keys and meet you there," Roland said.

Tofflemire shook his head. "It's best if you come with us, Mr. DeWitt."

"Am I under arrest?"

"Not yet, but we still need you to come with us," Tofflemire insisted.

"Oh…" Roland's mind spun wildly and as he opened his closet door a new angle emerged. "Have you heard anything about Willis, Detective Hoyer?" he asked.

"Nothing yet but hopefully soon," Hoyer said.

Roland pulled on his coat. "I have text messages from Willis on my phone. Maybe that could help."

"Let's see 'em," Hoyer said.

"My phone, I left it at the office. I can pick it up there and show you the last texts I got from him." That was his plan. Maybe he would find time, a few seconds alone to dump Davis's cell phone when they weren't looking. This distraction might work, and yet Roland had not slept a full night in over a week. Was he thinking in his right mind? Had he completely lost control? For Roland, it all came down to this desperate ploy.

Tofflemire and Hoyer agreed. They led Roland down the elevator and into their waiting car. Hoyer sat in the back seat with Roland while Tofflemire drove. It gave their suspect very little wiggle room. Unfortunately, they disregarded procedure because of Roland's father and his position in the community. Roland rode along without handcuffs.

The snow squall continued unabated as Neville, Rita and Dewey exited a small bookstore set along the south wall of St. Gabriel's Square. A yellow plough rumbled by as they climbed into the SUV. As a Christmas gift, Rita purchased her ex a paperback of Stephen King's *Under The Dome,* after hearing of its relevance to Neville's own manuscript. Buckling Dewey in the back, Neville took the passenger seat next to Rita.

"It's your turn. What would you like for Christmas, Rita?" Neville asked.

She beamed a prideful smile. "Your book Woody. I'd like to read *Seven Days* before it gets published."

"That's it? My book?"

"That's all I want. Have you got a copy?"

With Dewey continuing to tinker with his i-Pod in the back seat, Rita started the SUV. Neville thought back to last week and John who returned the copy he read. It sat wasting space in a desk drawer at the Sentinel just across the square.

"You're in luck my dear. I've got one in my desk at work," he said.

Rita guided the SUV across the square's snowbound road, past a trundling yellow plough and through the causeway into the Sentinel parking lot. The lot sat empty except for one car parked near the rear entrance. Ice crackled under the tires as Rita made a slow circle and stopped by the walkway. Through a haze of falling snow, three men trekked toward the Sentinel's back door. Black shadows set against a shifting white shroud.

Neville hopped from his passenger seat while Rita stepped out to clear the wipers of collected ice.

Roland looked back past his two guards. With Neville approaching and Rita out attending the wipers, his brain clicked. With time growing short, his opportunity had arrived.

Leading the detectives to the back door, Roland fumbled his keys. Finding the right one, he unlocked the one side and held it open allowing the officers inside. Snow continued to fall as Neville neared. This last chance, his only chance and Roland made a disastrous decision.

Roland slammed the door shut, reached across and grabbed the snow shovel. In a frenzy, he drove the shovel's wooden shank into the door's handles, locking in the two bewildered detectives and raced down the walk. Rushing wild eyed, Roland used both hands and pushed a confused Neville aside knocking him on his back and headed to Rita's open driver door.

Shocked by Roland's furious advance, Rita came round the truck to meet the sprinting Roland but with a hefty shove, he knocked her to the ground. Neville lifted from the snow and started toward Rita, the SUV and Dewey. Hoyer, Tofflemire peered through the glass slot banging, jerking at their prison doors, unable to budge the shovel wedged in the handles. To his side, Hoyer spotted a red exit sign through the pressroom double doors. He rushed past the doors. Tofflemire followed both headed toward the exit on the building's corner.

Time slowed, the details evolved as if filmed in stop motion.

Roland's panic sent him jumping into the driver seat. He slammed the door and stomped the gas. The wheels spun hard on the ice, caught traction and leaped forward. Over the song on his i-Pod, Dewey heard the slam, looked up and saw a stranger driving off with him aboard. His eyes watered, he screamed.

Neville ran toward the escaping SUV screaming. Dumbfounded, Rita gave chase. Locked into his plan, Roland headed toward the causeway tires spinning wildly, the rear end dancing side to side. Engine noise echoed off the causeway walls. A hulking yellow form materialized through the windswept snow blocking the roadway and Roland's escape. He swerved, stomped the brakes sliding the truck sideways nearly hitting the plough.

Neville closed the distance. From the corner, Hoyer and Tofflemire busted through the exit. Roland gunned the throttle and headed toward the river road. The truck fishtailed, Roland braked but a foot slipped to the gas. He missed the turn, sending the SUV careening up and over the icy berm. The truck slid through the plastic barricade and dragged the fence uprooting the posts. It skidded off shore, onto river ice and lurched to a sudden halt. The truck sat on an ice shelf several feet from the bank, angled sideways along a precarious water boundary. The stop launched a terrified Roland over the console head first into the passenger leg-well. Dewey screamed and in the panic struggled to free himself from his seatbelt.

The river lured the SUV, its front end testing the flowing Snake with a front wheel half submerged. Water rushed in the cavity where Roland landed. He felt the cold sting of the icy river. Falling snow dissolved in the river's surge as it continued unabated. Through the white screen, Neville rushed to the ice-flow. A cracking sounded, the truck continued to list, tipping toward a rushing Snake River. Neville edged out toward the truck, the crackling grew louder. He heard Dewey's muffled screams; saw his arms flailing from the back seat.

Rita came up behind and nearby, Hoyer and Tofflemire pulled up short of the ice. Neville crept closer as the truck continued its slide, water flushing into the passenger compartment. Roland leapt back to the driver's side as Neville neared the back door and his terrified son. The ice crackled louder, Neville felt it shift and the SUV slipped further into the freezing river. Rita screamed Dewey's name from the bank while both detectives watched helplessly.

Reaching the door, Neville pulled the handle. It creaked open as he leaned to it. In the front, Roland knelt on his seat and opened his driver's side door, pushed it out and scuttled to the exit. The truck lurched harder toward the rushing river. Neville yanked the handle, the back door opened and he saw the freezing water rising to Dewey's feet. As Neville bent toward his son, Roland poised on the doorframe and in a leap sprang from the truck toward shore.

The SUV heaved from the force of Roland's jump. The back door swung shut striking Neville's head and knocking him onto the ice shelf. With a loud crack, the shelf let go and the truck slid sideways toward open water. The Snake's watery jaws swallowed the SUV while an unconscious Neville slipped into its icy teeth. Rita screamed and from the truck came the indescribable shriek of a terrified little boy.

The truck slipped deeper into the river its waters rushing

headlong in from the open doors. Tofflemire ran over to Neville floating near the broken shelf and reached to pull him in. Neville drifted half in river half on ice while nearby Hoyer yanked a frightened Roland from the hostile waters.

The SUV drifted toward the center and sank deeper into the jaws of the Snake. Half mad, Rita's frenzied screams echoed back around the empty lot, her heart, her mind staggered by the sight of her son so close yet... yet alone, alone and so, so afraid. She saw the roof as it made a last gasp. Water flooded over and she dropped to her knees, covered her face, her eyes to the horror, crying inconsolably.

Dewey was gone...

The detective grabbed hold of Neville's arm and dragged him closer. By now, Hoyer had set Roland aside and helped his partner pull Neville from the freezing water. Consumed by madness Rita knelt beside him crying, pulling at his jacket prodding, begging him to get up. *Get up and help, get up, get up and....*

When the ambulance arrived twenty minutes later, Neville was conscious. His only solace that day; he did not witness Dewey's unbearable demise.

CHAPTER 35

NIGHT ARRIVED PULLING an invisible curtain around the town of Solomon. Christmas Eve and the unthinkable had happened. Even in this busy time, the town rallied around the Wishwoods that holiday night. The news spread like a plague filling the square, the Sentinel parking lot, the lots surrounding the area with those who heard the story of a little boy and a horrific accident on Christmas Eve.

Hoyer had shipped Roland off to jail while Tofflemire called in a police diver from Minneapolis. All were determined to rescue the body of an innocent child from its icy grave. Neville and Rita sat huddled speechless inside a police car as spotlights trained along the river's bank. Beneath a blizzard snow and freezing water currents, a police diver lifted up onto the platform of a police river cruiser. The diver's head shook side to side. Still no luck, no Dewey and Neville looked away. Rita nestled close unable to watch.

Leaving Arthur to sleep, Dell joined his friends, driving over in Neville's car with a change of clothes. Jennifer Gilchrist arrived after hearing the terrible news. Perched inside Jenny's car they worried for Neville and Rita.

Huddled by the dozens, townspeople watched the scene on the river, Dewey's parents and gave thanks for their own children that ill-fated night. Minnesota state police officers, firemen lined the banks standing ready on a cold winter night, waiting on their solemn duty. On the river, a police boat sat anchored. On its deck, the diver huddled cold and tired. It was Christmas Eve and he had already dived twice. His own family waited at home yet as he looked back to the car and saw Dewey's parents, he nodded back at Tofflemire. He would try once more.

The diver slipped beneath the river waters. A sad night made sadder if they could not retrieve this innocent young boy. Late Christmas Eve, the diver reappeared by the platform and gave Tofflemire the thumbs up. Tofflemire relayed a grim nod to the team on shore, sending them into action.

Firefighters strung a wench cable across to the diver and he disappeared beneath the black surface. Snow continued to filter down as all eyes watched. Within minutes, the whine of the wench motor sounded as it reeled up the sunken truck. The roof appeared, the motor howled on and soon the back end broke the water. Police officers, emergency personnel guided the SUV through the ice and up onto the bank. The wench whined and soon the truck trundled ashore. The crowd on shore scattered as river water emptied from every crevice. Dewey's red tomb gleamed in the spotlights. Paramedics opened the ambulance doors, pulled an unsullied gurney out from inside and set a solemn pose as they waited.

The lights shut off. In the quiet, Neville and Rita left the car and trudged toward the truck, the awful truck and their son. A murmur went through the crowd as one young firefighter opened the SUV's back door. Water spilled out. Undaunted he reached in unbuckling Dewey's limp form. Lifting him out, he cradled the boy reverently, a rag doll in the arms of a giant.

Pushing forward, Rita's shaking hands clutched at her face, crying. Neville held her arm, Dell and Jenny followed. The firefighter headed toward the gurney and the two attendants. Rita struggled through the police line and ran straight to her son, now lying limp on the gurney bed. Neville chased her, but she was too fast. In tears, she leaned over her son and with a gentle hand dragged the wool cap from his head. Dewey's blonde hair lay matted against his head and his eyes stayed shut. His skin glistened like plastic. Rita brushed aside his hair to see his full face, to understand and make sense of a senseless act.

Neville came up behind and took hold of her, clasping tight his love, his son's mother. He needed all his strength. Although weeping himself, he held her. Rita could not let go of her son. With Neville holding her, one paramedic came forward and touched a soothing hand against hers. "Mrs. Wishwood I'm sorry, but we have to do our job."

In the silence, Rita's eyes veered up and she let go. Neville looked down at his son, his only child and as he led Rita away a thought, a hope, a wish took hold. Rita's tears flooded out and as they embraced, he looked past the hushed crowd, beyond the square and out to something, someone. The only one who might know what to do.

Dell and Jenny followed in behind on their solemn march to Neville's car. Reanimated, Neville spun his ex-wife around. "Rita, can you drive?"

She stared up with empty eyes. "I-I don't know."

Neville shook Rita by the shoulders waking her from her morbid trance. "I need to do something, but can you drive home?"

"I-I can try..." she offered.

He took the keys from Dell and handed them to his ex. "This is important Rita. Drive home and pray. Pray for Dewey. I'll be there later."

"It's too late for prayers Woody. He's gone," she wailed.

Neville gazed into sad blue eyes. "Rita... for Dewey's sake, for my sake, just do it okay."

"Alright..."

He watched his ex-wife drive off. Time was short. Neville, Dell and Jennifer jumped into her car and headed straight for the Wishwood home. Dell understood immediately but Jennifer had no clue what mystery lay ahead. All she saw was two men extremely excited in an impossible situation.

Neville jumped from the open door before the car fully stopped and in four wild strides, he reached the porch. His broken heart pounded, his hands balled in desperate fists he pushed open the front door and raced along the hall, past his father and straight into his son's room; Phil's room these last weeks. Phil was packing the clothes neatly into a small athletic bag. He looked up at Neville startled. "Woody what's wrong?"

"Dewey's dead and I need something only you can provide... a miracle." Tears continued swelling from his crimson eyes. "This is hard, especially after all you've done but I need your help... Rita needs your help. Dewey, he's... he's gone!"

"What happened?" Phil asked, stunned.

Neville went on to explain the accident and Dewey's heart wrenching demise at the hands of a lunatic. Arthur stood by the doorway with Dell and Jennifer, tears welling up in his angry eyes. "Oh my god," he whispered, hearing it all for the first time.

Phil frowned, his eyes lowered. Appalled by the news, his actions slowed to a crawl. "I'm so sorry Woody, but I can't do anything. I'm afraid this is beyond even me."

Neville's hands, his arms stiffened. "But it's Dewey damn it!" With that outburst, he wept again. "I just want Dewey to have his life, to grow up, to struggle, to fall in love. I want him to have his chance to live."

In the hallway, Neville's friends and father wept silently. Phil said nothing for a long while. He too loved little Dewey but in his way he understood Neville's son was now safe.

"I was young when I was taken," he said in consolation. It did no good. Phil tried another explanation. "You understand chess, the game."

"Of course, but what's that got to do with Dewey?" Neville words carried a frenetic, near hysterical tenor. Phil remained calm as he set aside the bag.

"Chess has pawns and kings. I am but a pawn– not a king or a queen, just a pawn. A happy pawn, still only that. What you ask I cannot decide. For me, I'm given a task and the means to complete it. The decisions are left to someone, something far greater than I."

"Who then? Is it this god?" Neville scornfully asked.

"I can't say. All I know is that I am just a tool through which this force flows. What you wished for, those verdicts, have been erased. That was my task here. Outside of that I have little influence on..."

Phil's words stalled as his eyes shifted to meet the light, the sun in Dewey's overhead display. The core flickered, a sudden white brilliance blazed and the room vanished in a blinding glow. The light quickly faded, the planets reappeared orbiting the pseudo-sun. Blinded for that split second, Neville's eyes adjusted and he saw Phil's look had changed. Assigned with a new task, a knowing smile seized Phil's awkward face and he acquiesced. "Unless…"

"Anything, I'll do anything! Just save Dewey!" Neville cried.

Raising a hand their audience in the doorway froze, time-stilled statues unable to witness the upcoming conversation

"Yours ears only," Phil said and they went about bartering a deal. It took only minutes to reach a satisfactory outcome.

"To avoid confusion, all memory of these last eight hours will be erased. I'll implant one thought in your mind Woody… *don't leave Dewey.* Is that enough?" he asked.

"Yes," he said wringing his hands.

"Afraid? It's okay to be afraid."

Neville's eyes steadied. "I'm good."

With a second wave of his hand, Phil restarted the clock. Neville walked out past Dell, Jennifer and Arthur back into the living room. All three followed.

"What's this all about?" Jenny whispered.

"It's pretty complicated… I'll tell you tomorrow," Dell said.

"What now?" Arthur asked.

As he took a seat in the recliner, Neville removed his mother's medallion from his pocket and read the words to himself. He checked the time. His watch read eleven fifty-five.

"We wait."

CHAPTER 36

REELING FROM HER son's tragic end, Rita sat parked in her driveway crying uncontrollably wondering how it all went so wrong. Her son was dead and she failed to comprehend Neville's odd direction yet she did as she was told. Crying, Rita lifted her head from the steering wheel and mumbled the Our Father as she exited the car.

Inside the house, she saw the tree and Dewey's presents spilling out below it. Clutching the wool cap, Dewey's wool cap and overwhelmed by grief, Rita made her way to the kitchen. All the while her heart thumped a wicked beat driving a rant rattling in the brain, *Dewey's dead, Dewey's dead, Dewey's dead.* Standing erect, her muscles tensed and seething, she launched the counter's contents airborne with one angry swing. The shakers smashed and suddenly froze midair. Petrified by time, Rita stood locked between today and tomorrow.

The current of time stopped and the primary agent of change in the universe became Rita's indispensable ally. Solomon's skies sparked in electric brilliance. Hurricane winds sweep through the streets of a frail city and humanity lurches to a sudden halt. And with one glorious wink the day rewinds to find its place in time. Back to early afternoon and the bookstore. As Rita climbed into the driver's seat one detail changed and Neville takes a place beside Dewey in the backseat.

Staring back Rita asked, "Aren't you sitting up here with me?"

Neville checked his position, confused. "I guess not."

Rita laughed and after deciding on Neville's book for her

Christmas present, she drove across the cobbled square toward the Sentinel parking lot. One car sat parked in the empty lot and three hazy figures trudged through the snow toward the back double doors. Circling around, the ice crackling under the weight of the SUV's wheels, Rita stopped at the walkway.

As she exited the truck to clean the wipers, she stared into the back seat. Neville sat stationary, making no effort to leave his seat.

"Aren't you getting the book?" she called in.

"Yes, but I can't move," Neville said astounded. Rita flashed an odd look Neville's way, and again she laughed. Phil's directive had locked Neville in place. Through the snow, Neville spied a figure racing down the walk. Roland pushed Rita to the ground and clamored in.

"Roland! What..?" Neville's scream stalled. Dewey heard the slam, his father's screams and began to cry.

"Shut up…" Roland hit the gas. The wheels spun and the truck suddenly jerked forward.

The yellow plough appeared at the causeway corner and Roland slammed the brakes, swerved sideways missing the plough. Neville reached over at Roland but the jostling kept him at bay. Fueled by fear, Roland stomped on the accelerator and aimed for the river road. The truck leapt forward, the rear end shimmied wildly out of control and as he jammed the brake, his foot slipped onto the accelerator. The engine roared to life launching the SUV sideways over the frozen berm, smashing through the plastic barricade yanking out the posts. Tangled in swatches of orange fencing, the SUV skidded across the frozen bank, out onto river ice and stopped abruptly on the edge of an ice shelf. With its front-end overhanging the ice, the truck sat perilously close to the Snake's icy flow.

The sudden stop threw Roland over the center console into the passenger leg-well bathing his hands and arms in the freezing river water streaming in. Thrown to the floor, Neville picked himself up and tended to Dewey crying hysterically. Unzipping his varsity jacket, he leaned over unbuckled Dewey's seatbelt and held him.

The truck lurched, slipping several inches toward the river. They heard ice chunks ding along the truck's flank. In a panic, Roland scrambled back to find a dry space and jerked the SUV in deeper. The passenger cabin was filling fast and now covered Neville's knees. Frantic, Roland shifted to the driver's door, pushed it open and readied to leap out. On the bank Tofflemire, Hoyer and Rita watched in horror as the truck slipped deeper into the river's flow.

Neville reached over, grabbed Roland and yanked him back. "Don't jump, it'll send the truck into the river," he screamed. He knew the momentum would launch them over the edge.

The freezing river water numbed Neville's feet, his legs were cramping still he pulled Dewey closer to him and the back driver-side door. A loud crack echoed like a gunshot, the ice shelf snapped setting the truck slipping sideways into open water. Adrift in the Snake, freezing water rushed in closing Roland's door. The shift sent him into an ear-piercing fit. Roland's manic limbs flailed while Dewey clutched at his father's arm, climbing higher on the seat and Neville.

Neville could hear Rita's ghastly shriek from shore. Hoyer, Tofflemire stood helpless as the truck leveled out and slowly sank from the front end. Water now reached Neville's chest. Lifting Dewey, he held his head above the water. Roland kicked furiously at the driver door in a desperate attempt to free himself. Neville pulled Dewey close and whispered, "I'm going to open the door and when I do you take a deep breath and hold it."

Wide eyed, Dewey nodded too afraid to speak. Half under water, Roland continued to hammer the door but the pressure prevented an escape. Neville waited, the cabin was near full. He nodded to Dewey, tugged him to his lap. Neville flipped the handle, and with both knees pressed against the door and forced it open a crack. "Deep breath!"

Dewey sucked in a lung full of air.

A wash of grey river water engulfed the red roof and the truck disappeared– swallowed whole. Rita fell to her knees clutching tear-filled eyes. Hoyer cursed and kicked as he scurried along the bank, unable to help, unable to stop the inevitable.

Dewey's cheeks ballooned with precious air. Pressing both knees against the door, Neville pushed against the crush of the river. With every ounce exerted, his legs, his arms throbbed from the icy cold pricks stabbing his muscles. Now under water, he added his shoulder to help force the issue. Nearing his limit, the door finally opened. He pulled Dewey to his lap and with the last of his strength; he launched his son up from the doorway toward the surface. Angling his head from inside the truck, he watched him rise.

Through a veil of tears, Rita spied Dewey's knit cap break the water's surface and leapt to her feet. Magically Dewey bobbed above the water. Rita squealed with joy. Tofflemire turned and raced to help. Hoyer quickly joined in. Sputtering, spitting out mouthfuls of river water, Dewey paddled close enough for Tofflemire to grab onto him. While Hoyer called for help, Tofflemire wrapped Dewey in his coat. Rita cocooned him in her arms and held the boy like a precious jewel whisking him off to the safety of the police car.

Below, Neville saw Roland pounding at the door, the window with both feet. The cold, the quiet was numbing. With air trapped inside, the truck sank in slow motion drawn further downstream by the current. Neville swam out and hammered an elbow into the glass, smashing it. His arms, legs grew ever weaker, numb, still he reached in and pulled Roland free. Near frozen, Roland headed straight to the surface.

Neville tried pulling away from the sinking wreck. His arms his legs were past pain– dead. He tried pushing off but could muster no force. He peered up yet continued his descent, and when he swung around, he saw the inescapable truth. The zipper of his beloved varsity jacket had jammed in the SUV's empty window frame. With his strength sapped, his muscles numb and lungs ready to explode the SUV dragged Neville down into the icy depths. Light faded– his lungs burst. Water filled his empty chest and Neville closed his eyes. In his final vision, he saw Dewey safe with Rita on the bank.

Phil had explained the danger involved and Neville took the chance... for Dewey. In divining his connection to water, Aunt Claire had discovered what she believed was Neville's past. Unfortunately, water played dual purposes in his life.

Running out of air, Roland scuttled to the top. Disoriented, he had targeted a spot along the bank. Once there Roland found himself trapped under six inches of ice. The Snake had swallowed the man responsible for it all. In the seconds that followed, Roland's eyes lost focus. With his back flat against the ice, the last sight his brain processed was a black bag lying on the riverbed.

Darkness settled on the square and the Sentinel lot. The ambulance arrived shortly after Dell. He had driven right over in Neville's car upon getting Rita's frantic call. As they treated Dewey inside the ambulance, Jennifer Gilchrist joined them. Dewey would be all right, the attendant relayed, but he should be admitted to hospital for observation.

Just as before, in this same bleak setting, a crowd formed. Rita made the difficult decision to accompany her son to the hospital. She left the man she loved, her son's father alone in the freezing waters of the Snake. Dell assured her he would stay there for his friend, for his family and with Jennifer by his side both urged Rita to take care of Dewey.

Rita wept that night this time for someone else, someone just as special.

Inside the emergency room of Our Lady of Mercies Hospital, Rita sat by Dewey's bed behind drawn curtains. Beds were at a premium and a cubicle was all that remained for overnight observation. Dell and Jennifer had just left after they dropped off Neville's car and keys. Dell relayed the regrettable news. Emergency crews recovered the body of her ex-husband from the red SUV. Jennifer and Dell held their tears for Rita's sake.

She cried and after looked across the bed to see her son's angelic face alive, still vital this Christmas Eve. *Woody made sure of that,* she thought.

Not long after the doctor came by, an older grey-haired man, fatherly. He pressed Rita to go home, rest up: her son was past danger and would sleep the night. Rita mumbled something, rummaged through her purse but stayed seated never looking at the doctor. *It's all part of a mother's duty this worrying,* she thought. How could he understand? He left soon after and while she sat staring at her sleeping son the night shift nurses arrived in the ward. Dewey's new nurse came in, took his temperature and in an easy voice whispered, "All normal."

The nurse came round to Rita, leaned over and with a gentle squeeze of the shoulder offered, "You should do as the doctor asked, Mrs. Wishwood. Go home, rest up. Tomorrow's Christmas, your son will need you."

For some strange reason Rita heard the explanation more clearly from this pretty nurse and felt comfort in her words.

"Go home...he's in good hands with us I promise," the young nurse said. This new nurse had a benign look in her sharp grey-green eyes and Rita somehow sensed an odd bond, a kinship. Her woman's intuition kicked in. Rita lifted from her seat caressed her sleeping son's matted hair, his cheek and gave him a loving kiss. Leaving, Rita checked the nurse's name on her tag and offered, "Merry Christmas, Audrey."

"Good night Mrs. Wishwood."

Dewey was indeed in very good hands.

Here we return to whence we started.

That night Rita returned home in much the same way she had once before. Her face bloated, tears fell freely and in the shift from Christmas Eve to Christmas Day, that same eternal wind swept through the town of Solomon. Homes, city structures shuddered from its mighty blast, the skies sparked incandescent and yet time continued unabated in its passage to another day.

The miracle had happened and in its wake nothing perceptible changed, only the outcome. As Rita knelt weeping on the kitchen floor, her tears mingled with the salt, the pepper and bits of broken glass her heart still ached, her future still seemed bleak. Unknowingly every aspect of life had changed. What remained true was the pain. On Christmas Eve Neville Wishwood died giving all he had to those he loved. As his mother's medallion declared, Neville lived courageously that day. Rita would continue on knowing she once loved a man who died too young and when he died, he saved that which he loved most in life, her son.

CHAPTER 37

WINDS EBBED; A white shroud layered the landscape of Solomon as the snow continued its surge. The Greyhound terminal at St. Gabriel's Square remained quiet, a refuge amid the unrelenting white of the empty plaza. One bus sat idling and near the rear, a young man stood gazing into the square itself. He wore a Golden Gopher varsity jacket. Awestruck, he viewed the snow massed on the cobbled road, the lamplights spraying an incandescence dancing shadows on glassy walls. High above an ice-encrusted statue of an angel in flight cast its silhouette into a clouded sky.

A shorter man, who looked surprisingly like a young Barney Fife, called from behind, "Woody this way!"

Failing to answer, Woody continued to stare. In some strange way, the square made sense to him. As if a construct from a world he once occupied. The shorter man waited. Finally, he walked to join his charge. In a much softer voice, he called again, "Woody it's time go."

He turned and asked, "Is that my name… Woody?"

"Yes, yes it is. At least it was."

Woody stood staring vacantly at his companion. "And your name, what's your name?"

"Call me Phil," the shorter man said. As a gentle prompt, Phil took his arm and guided Woody toward the front of the bus. The snow continued to rake the skies of Solomon. A slush mix sloshed at their feet as they made a path toward the front of the bus.

The taller man started. "It all looks so familiar, so homey... but I can't remember. Why can't I remember?"

Shepherding his friend to the open bus door, Phil answered, "I was told it's a kindness extended to those who serve. Memories can be tricky... good and bad."

At 12:45 a.m. on Christmas Day, they filed onto a southbound bus. Once on board the bus driver, his balding head adorned by a red Santa toque, greeted his primary passengers with a boisterous, "Merry Christmas!"

"Merry Christmas," Phil returned with his own great smile.

Lost as to the meaning of it all, Woody whispered, "Your name... it's Phil isn't it?"

"Yes"

"What's Christmas, Phil?"

"It's a special holiday– a celebration of Jesus Christ's birthday."

"Oh... Who's Jesus Christ?"

"He was a very great man. Some say the son of God."

Satisfied, Woody walked to the back with his friend. He stopped and turned back once more. "And who am I?"

Phil paused as he checked Woody's futile stare, unsure of how to answer. Finally, he found the right words. "People called you Woody."

"Woody, eh!" They walked down the aisle of the empty bus with Woody inspecting the seats, the windows, the rubber-matted floor lost in a dream. "Where are we going Phil?"

"We're on our way to Des Moines, Iowa."

Woody paused, looking inquisitively at his partner. "Why is it I can't remember anything again?"

"You've passed over to a very different place. It takes time to adjust, understand it all."

"Did I have family, friends here?"

Phil's lips formed a cryptic smile. "You did... a fine loving family. A son, Dewey, a wife Rita. Then there was Dell, your best friend and of course your father. They'll hurt for a while, but they'll remember you... always. The life you strived to create here, your legacy, will continue for many years to come Woody."

Woody had little comprehension of his friend's revelation. All that remained was here, now. The past would take time to unfold.

Reaching their seats near the back, Woody and Phil sat side by side. Phil placed his bag on his lap. They were two of only three passengers leaving on the bus that Christmas morning. The engine revved, the bus crept forward from the terminal and Woody looked over to Phil once more.

"What are we going to do in Des Moines?"

After a patient pause, Phil smiled. "You're going to meet someone there. Someone you once knew. There's an old government warehouse on the outskirts of the city. We use it as a transition area. But we'll get into that later."

"Who am I meeting?"

"All will be revealed... in time."

Minutes later the bus joined highway traffic. Few vehicles drove the early Christmas Day roads. Woody took time to ask one more question.

"Des Moines... where's that?'

Snow continued to fall, redefining the landscape of Solomon and as they watched it drift down, the Barney Fife look-alike pulled his friend Woody closer to the window and pointed to the night sky. From the south, one star shone through a clutter of clouds.

"There. We're going there!"

The bus drove off onto the winding highway road. The distance of time, the weather blurred the Greyhound's red taillights yet one look back and both could see the shimmer of angel's wings and shadows shifting high above the town of Solomon. Both men stared skyward into a white winter night and in their transcendent innocence, they followed the Christmas parable of one very special star.

Perhaps in that dim light, within a moment's silent reflection, Woody began to believe that not all angels fly.

EPILOGUE

THE TRUTH, WHAT we experience, is that all mortal life ends. In that desperate haze of loss, we often forgo another more subtle truth. Beyond this physical world, love provides the eternal spark for the soul of man. As part of the legacy Phil referenced, nine months later Rita gave birth to twin boys. She named her newborn sons Huey and Louie. Two weeks after the twin's birth the publisher released Woody's book posthumously.

And for those who ponder life, love, in this cynical world there truly is magic and miracles and if there exists a God and angels they clearly live among us. So, take heart and know that in your ride by bus or train be sure to gaze across the aisle and marvel, for on the journey you may be traveling in good company.

ACKNOWLEDGEMENTS

AS REFERENCED IN my novel, The Lifeguard, writing is, by nature a solitary effort. By no means does that mean it's accomplished alone. Without the support, the patience and the input of several other talented individuals, I would never have realized the book's completion.

To my wife, Bobbie, my first reader, I love you and thank you for your faith in the book. Your patience and encouragement helped push me to the finish line. To my loyal beta-readers, thank you for your input and honest evaluation. You know who you are.

I also want to extend my thanks to Sandra Chmara, who read the manuscript and offered her advice and direction. Thank you again.

Lastly, but certainly not least in effort, I want to thank Bob Stewart, my editor for The Lifeguard. Unquestionably, Bob's insights and attention to detail made the novel a much more interesting read for me the author, and for those who take time out to enjoy it. Bob, thank you, my readers thank you.

Sincerely,

R. W. Hogan